Caspar turned to her, his dark eyes gleaming

The flames of the fire in her boudoir were reflected in his hot gaze. And Flora knew. For months theirs had been a marriage in name only, and she had been unsure of her charms to her husband's experienced taste. But now....

"You look rather warm," he said, his voice husky. "Why not remove your peignoir?"

Her fingers suddenly clumsy, Flora fumbled with the satin ribbons at her throat. The champagne they had drunk seemed to bubble in her veins. Then Caspar's warm, sensuous mouth was pressed to her wrist, kissing the translucent skin. He pushed the lace-trimmed sleeve higher, inching his way up her arm to the soft inside of her elbow.

Each kiss caused wild thrills of response deep inside her. When finally he claimed her mouth, Flora's lips parted under his like a flower opening to the sun. *At last,* she thought. *At last I shall truly be his wife.*

Anne Weale was born in Liverpool, England. She is married, with one son, and currently lives with her husband on the Mediterranean coast of Spain. Her great-grandfather was the first in the family to be published, and it is to him that Miss Weale attributes her writing "genes." Her first Harlequin novel was *Castle in Corsica*. Since then she has written more than forty romances, which have been translated into eighteen languages and sold in eighty countries. Sales of more than forty million copies have proved Anne Weale's reputation as one of the world's finest authors of romance fiction.

ANNE WEALE

FLORA

W❂RLDWIDE

TORONTO · NEW YORK · LOS ANGELES · LONDON

Published April 1983

ISBN 0-373-97004-8

Based on a story first published in serial form in
Woman & Home and later in
Woman's Weekly Fiction Series Omnibus.

Printed in Canada

PART ONE
CHINA 1903

CHAPTER ONE

FLORA SAT IN THE SUN on the hillside, studying the passage in her Latin book that, before their frugal evening meal, Père d'Espinay would ask her to construe.

"Sed mulier cupido quod dicit amanti, in vento et rapido scribere oportet aqua," she read aloud to the lizard basking on a nearby rock. "Which means, 'But what a woman says to her desirous lover should be written in wind and swift-flowing water.'"

Then, lifting her gaze from the page to think about love, she caught the flash of sunlight on metal and, snatching up the field glasses that had belonged to her father and that she took everywhere with her, she scanned the slopes of the hill to the south of her aerie.

It was some time before she could see in any detail the train of men moving slowly down the road to the mission. Throughout China, and particularly in the remote mountain regions where Flora had spent the seventeen years since her birth, the roads were invariably bad. It was a moot point among travelers whether those unpaved or paved were the worst to negotiate. When any important official took up his duties in a distant part of the Chinese empire, the local officials were obliged to put the road he had to travel into some state of repair. But since the work was done grudgingly by forced labor, it was usually made waste by the next severe rainstorm.

"Nowadays an imperial highway is not one that is kept in order *by* the emperor, but rather one that may have to be put in order *for* the emperor," Père d'Espinay had once told his pupil. But although he sometimes made fun of the race among whom he had lived for thirty of his seventy-six years, she knew that he loved and admired them.

As for the road to the mission, it was merely an unpaved track first trodden by smugglers evading the government monopoly of the salt trade.

When the train came into view clearly, she saw that it consisted of about twenty baggage coolies, a *fu-tou* or headman, and the four bearers of a rattan sedan chair. The chair was an indication that the coolies were in the service of someone of standing, or of a foreigner who knew that in out-of-the-way parts of China the respect accorded to anyone with a sedan was often of greater value than a passport.

Flora's father, Tom Jackson, a plant hunter for a famous firm of nurserymen in England, had always taken a chair on his travels; although more often than not it had been dismantled and carried by one of the coolies while her father went ahead looking for specimens. Similarly, the owner of this chair was not at the present time riding in it. Nor could she see him walking ahead of the train or bringing up the rear. All she could see was a dog; a large, lovely, black-coated beast that disappeared frequently on sorties into the undergrowth, to reappear wagging its tail and dangling its tongue. From the dog's unfamiliar appearance, Flora concluded that the traveler must be a foreigner.

Stuffing her book inside her faded blue tunic and replacing the glasses in their case, she scrambled to her feet and began to race back to the mission. She was anxious to give Père d'Espinay the news that tonight he would have the rare pleasure of entertaining a visitor from the world beyond the high mountains that ringed their quiet valley.

IT WAS AN HOUR OR MORE LATER when the train entered the gates of the mission compound. During the interval Flora had changed her everyday tunic and trousers for a black dress similar to those worn by the two nuns—one French and one Chinese—who were waiting beside Père d'Espinay to welcome the visitor. The heads of the nuns were encased in stiffly starched white linen coifs, but Flora's hair was uncovered and hung down her slim straight back in a single thick glossy braid like the queues worn by Chinese men.

Only that morning she had washed her hair with *p'ing-she Fei-tsao,* a soft soap made in the village by shredding the soaked and swollen pods of the soap tree, grinding them to a paste with sandalwood, cloves, putchuk and musk, and making a paste of them with honey. After Chinese women had washed their hair, usually they oiled it. Flora preferred not to oil hers, but to leave it silky to the touch and with a faint scent not unlike the fragrance of burning joss sticks, in which putchuk was also an ingredient.

As the chair bearers entered the compound she noticed the black dog trotting sedately alongside. When the bearers halted, the dog halted. At a word from the man now occupying the sedan chair, it sat down and rolled adoring eyes at him.

He was well over six feet tall, and dressed as her father had used to dress in riding breeches and pig-

skin puttees, with an American shirt, the soft attached collar unfastened, and a kerchief in place of a
tie. His face was shaded by the brim of a Panama
hat, but as he stepped from the chair he removed the
hat and came forward bareheaded to shake hands
with the white-haired priest, whom he greeted in excellent French with only the slightest of accents.

The face now exposed to the light was unlike any
Flora had seen; not that she had encountered many
Europeans. During her father's lifetime his work had
taken him far away from the treaty ports where there
were communities of foreigners.

It was, had she but known it, a face that had arrested the attention and kindled the curiosity of
women far worldlier than she, for it was one that
combined the natural authority—some would say
arrogance—of many generations of English aristocrats with the tough, rawboned, devil-may-care looks
of a born adventurer.

What Flora saw was a man with cool flint-gray
eyes in a face burned brown by the sun and lined in a
way never seen among the Chinese, who were smooth
skinned until they were old. That the two deep
creases down his cheeks and the wrinkles fanning at
his temples had nothing to do with his age was borne
out by the muscular breadth of his powerful shoulders and the flatness of his midriff. His lean cheeks
and jaw were clean-shaven, but his dark hair was
thick with no sign of gray at the temples.

Père d'Espinay welcomed him warmly before pre-
senting the two sisters, one of whom was a mute.
When he turned to beckon Flora forward, he
switched to English and said in his courtly way,
"Flora, dear child, allow me to present Mr. Lomax

to you. Miss Jackson is a compatriot of yours, Mr. Lomax.''

"Indeed? How do you do, Miss Jackson," the stranger said with a smile, taking her small but firm hand in a strong clasp.

"How do you do," she answered primly, her manner subdued and demure to match her novicelike dress.

"While you were on the hill watching us, I was watching you," he informed her. "At first I took you for a boy. You're by far the most fleet-footed girl I ever saw."

He turned to converse with the priest, and for the first time in her life Flora felt an immodest desire to make him look at her again—not as if she were still in the schoolroom, but as if she were a woman, and beautiful.

"WHAT DO YOU THINK OF HIM, my child?" the priest asked her half an hour later when their guest had been shown to his quarters and was bathing and resting before supper.

He had said he had come fifty *li*—more than sixteen miles—which was not a long march on the plains but a long way in mountainous country.

"I don't know," she answered thoughtfully. "I have never met anyone like him. What's your opinion of him, Father?"

Sometimes they talked in French, sometimes in English, sometimes in the dialect of the province. She had a gift for picking up languages quickly, and as well as French he had taught her some Italian and German.

It was many years since the priest had judged men

on a short acquaintance, but he liked to hear Flora's impressions of their infrequent visitors. Her judgment, like that of most women, was often surprisingly accurate.

Before he could answer, she added, "I think perhaps he is like a *yeh lau-tsze*, which is dangerous only when it's cornered."

Although chiefly interested in butterflies, Père d'Espinay was sufficiently familiar with all the wildlife in China to know that she was referring to what the Chinese called the wild donkey, and zoologists the serow. Although she had been only ten when her father had died in a landslide, quite often she would refer to something learned in her years with him.

"I remember we once met a hunter—I think in the Upper Min Valley—whose dog had been killed and who had been wounded himself," she explained, her dark eyes having the faraway expression that was a sure sign that she was recalling her childhood.

The old man was struck by the fact that, knowing so little of men other than the Chinese peasants among whom they lived, she should have recognized intuitively what he himself also suspected: that the man staying under their roof, although outwardly suave and civilized, had a core of ruthlessness in him, a streak of savagery under the polished good manners.

"But you haven't said what *you* think," she reminded him.

"That I will tell you tomorrow when I have conversed with Mr. Lomax at greater length. For the moment, let us turn our minds to Catullus."

AT THAT INSTANT the man they had been discussing was stepping into a high-backed sitz bath specially made to contain his long limbs, carried by one of the

coolies and, whenever the opportunity offered, filled
with hot water. Beside it his personal servant waited
to hand him a glass of whiskey and soda, and to light
the first of the several thin black cheroots he would
smoke during the evening.

Although the man's visiting card—brought to Père
d'Espinay by a messenger half an hour before his
arrival—had introduced him as Mr. Caspar Lomax,
this was not his correct designation. Nor did the card
show, as was customary, his town address in the left-
hand corner and his country address or the name of
his club on the right. It gave only the name of his
club.

He had with him other visiting cards that introduced him by another name, the Earl of Carlyon,
which sometimes he sent round to the *yamen* of a
town's chief official when applying for a military
escort through country infested by bandits. But on
approaching the mission he had decided to use the
name Lomax and to pass for a sportsman and ama-
teur naturalist, which indeed in a fashion he was.

Guessing that the food at the mission would be
plain and possibly meager fare, he had spent much of
the day hunting for the pot and by the end of it had
shot a mixed bag of the pheasant grouse peculiar to
the Chino-Tibetan borderlands, with a hazel hen and
a Sifan partridge. The pheasant grouse he considered
the finest eating of all the gallinaceous birds in western China.

Although rough-shooting in the mountains was
more tiring sport than waiting for beaters to drive the
game over the guns on some great estate in England,
as he lounged at his ease in the hot bath the man was
not tired. The long expedition from Ichang—mostly
on foot—had hardened his already fit physique and

now, contemplating his dinner, he wished it would also be possible later to enjoy a woman. But since he was not the type for whom, when the need arose, any woman was better than none, he knew it must be some weeks before he could satisfy that appetite.

At Ichang—an inland treaty port opened to foreign trade in 1877, at which date the man in the bath had still been in the charge of a governess and had not yet advanced to a tutor—there was a small foreign community including a British consul, some Imperial Maritime Customs staff, a few businessmen and various missionaries. Dining with the consul, he would have dressed for dinner as he did in England. Here, at one of the smallest and most remote of the Roman Catholic missions, he thought it more suitable to put on a dark blue velvet smoking coat.

Flora, who had never seen a smoking coat, could not repress a faint gasp when he strolled across the compound to where she and Père d'Espinay were watching the sun set.

The priest heard her intake of breath and wondered how much of her astonishment and admiration was for the luxurious garment with its matching silk facings and silk-cord frogging, and how much for the man who wore it with such careless elegance and who, for some reason, looked even more tough and virile in velvet than he had in his serviceable traveling clothes.

It must be an effect of contrast, thought the old man, who in the years of his solitude before Flora's advent had fallen into the habit of analyzing such observations. With some men the softness and richness of the material would have brought out a latent effeteness; with this man one was aware that the solid breadth of his shoulders owed nothing to the skill of his tailor.

He's as strong as the coolies who toil up from Yachow to Tachienlu with ten pao of tea on their backs, but he's been better fed all his life, and he's never been a beast of burden as they are, poor brutes, mused the priest.

Aloud he said, speaking English, "A glass of wine, Mr. Lomax?"

"Thank you, Father."

As their visitor seated himself, Flora rose to pour out the *samshu*.

When she handed it to him he smiled at her, but once again it was the smile of an adult for a well-behaved child, not that of a man for a pretty girl. Perhaps he didn't find her pretty. Perhaps she wasn't, she thought glumly. But although she had no means of telling how her looks compared with those of the women of his world, or if among his own people he would be considered a handsome man, she knew there was something about him that was different from anyone she had met before, and it made her feel oddly tense and excited.

She took little part in the conversation before dinner and during the meal spoke only when addressed. This was partly because the roast game was a rare treat that deserved to be eaten with attention, and partly because she liked listening to the unfamiliar timbre of the Englishman's deep voice. Since Soeur Marie-Josephe spoke no English the conversation was in French, which Mr. Lomax spoke with great fluency but with a somewhat drawling intonation quite different from the quick precise speech of the priest, who also illustrated his words with graphic movements of his hands.

The Englishman was not given to gesture, Flora noticed, nor did he toy with the stem of his glass or fidget in any other way. His economy of movement was particularly noticeable in the company of Père d'Espinay and the French nun, but it would have been striking anywhere. He was as relaxed as a cat, and as alert as a cat. She had the feeling that even when he was sleeping an alien sound would bring him awake in an instant.

When toward the end of the meal the old priest glanced down the table and saw his darling, his treasure, gazing with dreaming dark eyes at the tall young man on his right, he felt a faint pang of loss. Until today she had loved him and him alone. He had taken the place of her father and she had become the child he had sired fifty years before, who had died before birth. He loved her, but for some time he had known it could not be long before she began to yearn for a different affection. Physically she had been ready for love for some time, although most of her clothes disguised the ripening curves of her body. Mentally, too, she had been aching for womanhood, but without knowing why she was restless. It had taken the advent of the Englishman to crystallize her longings.

And he, the priest noticed with relief, regarded her as a child. She might have been a young novice, soon to become a bride of Christ, for all the attention he paid to her.

The old man, who knew that his life could not last much longer, studied the other man's face and wondered if he could trust him. For some time Flora's future had been worrying him. To beguile his loneliness and boredom, he had made her a consort fit for a prince if not a *duc*, for in France the ranks were reversed, the *duc* being the higher. Flora's manners were those of his grandmother, who had been a *princesse* of the *ancien régime* before King Louis XVI, Queen Marie Antoinette and most of the French aristocracy had lost their heads to the guillotine in the slaughter of 1793.

Now he knew that in giving her such manners and educating her far above the level of most women, he had done her not a favor but a disservice.

Late that night, when the nuns had retired and he had sent Flora to bed, d'Espinay said to his guest, "I have a problem on which I should be glad of your advice, Mr. Lomax."

"I doubt if there's any subject on which my advice could be of greater value than your wisdom, *mon père*."

"You're too modest. I fancy you have a much greater worldly wisdom than I possess. I lived in the world myself once, but that was a long time ago, and conditions change."

"From what I have read of the classics, human nature doesn't change a great deal," the younger man said dryly. "But for what my advice is worth, you are very welcome to it. You have no objection to my smoking?"

"Not at all. Indeed I will join you."

His cheroot alight, the priest began, "A little less than seven years ago, Flora Jackson's father was killed in a landslide not far from here. It was probably the result of some peasants placer mining for gold, but whatever the cause it left Flora an orphan,

her mother having died when she was six. At that
time she was ten years of age and of quite exceptional
intelligence. She spoke only English and one or two
Chinese dialects, but she picked up French very
quickly and I found she had a voracious appetite for
reading. To my subsequent regret, I amused myself
by educating her as if she were a boy. You might not
guess it from her conduct this evening, but should
you engage her in polemics you could find yourself
soundly trounced. She has an uncommonly logical
mind."

Beyond noticing that the girl had the promise of
considerable beauty in a few years' time, the Englishman had paid scant attention to her.

He said, "Wasn't it Molière who wrote, 'I am
quite agreeable that a woman shall be informed
about everything, but I cannot allow her the shocking
passion for acquiring learning in order to be learned.
When she is asked questions, I like her often to know
how not to know the thing she does know'?"

"Yes, in his play *The Bluestockings*. You are well-
read, Mr. Lomax."

"On the contrary, I'm sure your acquaintance with
Shakespeare is far closer than mine with your greatest playwright," replied his guest. "As for your
protégée, she appears to be familiar with Molière's
dictum. As you say, she made no attempt to put forward her views this evening."

"Oh, no, she would not," said the priest. "She's
quite unaware that she has a superior intellect. But I
fear it must make her future even more difficult than
it would have been had I not interfered with her
development. No doubt you've heard the Jesuit max-
im: 'Give me a child until he is seven, and I will give

you the man.' I find it interesting that for the first seven years of her life Flora had little or no schooling. Her father had taught her her letters, but she had been obliged to read and reread a handful of books until she knew them almost by heart. When she came to me, her handwriting was as ill-formed as that of a young child attempting its first pothooks. That is not to say she was ignorant. She knew as much on the subject of botany as her father, who worked for the firm of Veitch. Perhaps you know of them?''

"Indeed I do. They're nurserymen at Chelsea in London.''

Although he had given no sign of it, the younger man had been growing bored with the priest's eulogy. Now his interest quickened.

He said, "As a matter of fact it was a Veitch man, Charles Maries, who aroused my interest in China. He was a crony of my grandfather's, and when I was twelve or thirteen he paid us a visit. He'd been plant hunting in Japan, but some years before—about 1879—he'd been to China for Veitch and had come up the Yangtze as far as Ichang. I don't know why, but he found the natives unfriendly, and the only plant he secured was *Primula obconica*. After a week he turned back. He had the idea that his predecessor, Fortune, had exhausted China's floral resources, and that conclusion seems to have been widely accepted. Had he only pressed on a few days...." He ended the sentence with an expressive shrug.

It was Père d'Espinay's practice never to question his visitors, but to wait for them to divulge as much or as little information as they chose to reveal about themselves. Most honest men, he had found, needed no invitation to pour out the stories of their lives,

particularly under the influence of a few glasses of
wine. But although the young man at his side had
drunk more than enough to loosen most tongues, it
was evident that he had a strong head and was either
uncommonly reserved or had something to hide.

"Tomorrow you must speak of Robert Fortune to
Flora. He is her hero, and his book *Wanderings in
China* is one of her dearest possessions. As I understand it, when Fortune was working for the Royal
Horticultural Society in the forties and fifties of the
past century, he did exhaust Chinese garden plants.
But of course he had little opportunity to investigate
the wild flora. No doubt your grandfather's friend
was put off, as other have been, by the intensity of
crop cultivation along the lower Yangtze. But if, as
you say, he'd pressed on into the wild mountain
country, which defeats even Chinese methods of agri-
culture, he would have found riches indeed."

"Yes, by God!" was the vehement agreement, followed by a swift apology for the blasphemy.

In general, the priest was as reticent as the younger
man, but now he chose to smile slightly and say,
"You needn't apologize, Mr. Lomax. At the risk of
shocking you, I will tell you that my beliefs do not ac-
cord with the cloth I wear. I am an atheist."

The younger man was not shocked. His life had
made him unshockable. But he was somewhat startled.

"I entered the Church as a refuge from a world of
which I had wearied," explained the old man. "But
my faith never was strong, and it's many years since I
reached the conclusion that, although most men need
some religious belief to support them through the
trials of life, I myself do not. I believe the only

paradise to be on this earth, and death to be followed by oblivion.''

As he paused to refill their glasses his guest remarked, ''I agree with you.''

The priest nodded. The cynical gray eyes and hard yet sensual mouth of the visitor were not those of a man who put his trust in a higher being, or who disciplined his flesh for the betterment of his soul. Père d'Espinay had already deduced that here was a man who relied on no one but himself, and who gratified all his appetites as lustily as, long ago, the old man had indulged his own.

''However, I mustn't digress. It's late and you've had a long day, and although I need little sleep, I daresay you sleep long and soundly. To return to my problem: it is this. My health is no longer good; I expect before long to die. I must make provision for Flora, but what provision? What is the best I can do for her? Is there a place for her in her father's country? Or will she be as much an alien there as she is here among the illiterate peasantry?''

WHILE THE TWO MEN were talking about her, Flora was in her room preparing for bed and wondering why Père d'Espinay had sent her away when she would have liked to stay quietly in the background, replenishing their glasses and listening to their conversation.

Unplaiting her thick black hair, she wondered how long Mr. Lomax would remain at the mission. Perhaps for only one night. By this time tomorrow he might be gone, never to return.

She found herself wishing that it were possible to go with him; to see for herself the world beyond this quiet valley where nothing ever happened. If only she had been a boy she could have asked him to take her.

Then she felt ashamed of herself for wanting to leave the old man who had been so good to her, and who depended on her to understand his dry jokes and to argue ideas with him in a way that Soeur Marie-Josephe, a practical woman with a kind heart but not much intelligence, could not.

Flora knew it was her duty to remain with Père d'Espinay as long as he lived. But for his care, she would not have survived for long the death of her father. Although the priest was seventy-six, it seemed probably that he would live to a much greater age—perhaps even become a centenarian—and the thought of staying at the mission throughout her twenties and perhaps until she was forty filled her with dread.

Always she had missed the roving, adventurous life she had led with her father, and lately her restlessness seemed to have become more acute.

According to Soeur Marie-Josephe, worldly pleasures never brought lasting happiness, which could be attained only by self-denial and service to others. Flora didn't believe her. But if it was true, she wanted first to test the delight of wearing beautiful dresses, jewels and furs, of dancing and drinking champagne, of flirting with handsome men—everything she had read of with longing in the great world outside her provincial existence. She wanted to sample everything life could offer a woman.

CHAPTER TWO

THE NEXT MORNING the priest said to her, "Mr. Lomax has expressed a wish to see the Garden of Eden, Flora. Are you willing to guide him?"

"Of course, if you wish it, Father," she answered in some surprise.

The Garden of Eden was a plateau on the neighboring mountain that Père d'Espinay had found many years earlier, before age and rheumatism had prevented him from walking far beyond the village. She wondered why he had told their visitor about the place. In the time she had lived at the mission, a number of travelers with an interest in botany had stayed there, but he had never mentioned the Garden of Eden to any of them.

"You had better start without delay if you are to be back before dark," the old man advised.

As he watched them set out, followed by the black gundog, he wondered if during the day the Englishman's interest in Flora would be aroused to the point where he would be willing to help her. She was too young and unversed in coquetry to interest him as a woman, but it was not impossible that her scholarship and botanical knowledge might persuade him it would be worthwhile to give her his escort out of China and help her to reestablish herself in Europe.

The night before, Mr. Lomax had had no helpful suggestions to offer and under a superficial courtesy had seemed disinterested in her dilemma. But Père d'Espinay felt sure that after a day in her company his sympathy would be engaged. Although reserved in the presence of strangers, at times Flora had an animation that was very engaging, and when her dark eyes were sparkling with amusement and her lips were parted in laughter she was irresistible.

For Flora the walk was made more pleasant than usual by Mr. Lomax's insistence on carrying her field glasses as well as his camera and vasculum and the pack containing a flask of wine and some food. But although she enjoyed swinging along unencumbered, for the first few *li* she found his company somewhat uneasy—until he mentioned having read Fortune's *Wanderings in China*.

Long before she had found the book in the French priest's library, she could remember sitting in the crook of her father's arm while he smoked his evening pipe and told her about the daring man who, when Queen Victoria was young, had been sent to China to find plants for English gardens. On one of his journeys he had disguised himself as a beggar to avoid the hostility toward foreigners at that time. With anyone who shared her admiration for Fortune she felt an immediate rapport, and soon she was talking or falling silent as naturally as if it were Père d'Espinay matching his stride to her shorter pace.

Gradually the way became steeper and more arduous, until after an hour's climbing they had to traverse a narrow ledge of rock, in places almost overgrown, along the side of a gorge through which flowed a rushing torrent. It was no place for anyone with a poor head for heights, and had she but known it, it was her surefooted lead along a path that would have caused most girls to blench and refuse so peril-

ous a route that made her companion begin to study
her with less detachment.

The ledge led to what appeared to be the mouth of
a cave. Flora beckoned him into the dark interior,
where she fumbled on a shelf of rock and produced a
small Chinese oil lamp. This alight, she plunged farther into the cave, disturbing a colony of bats.

At the thought of the panic-stricken shrieks that
would be emitted by most females with bats flying
past them, because of their misguided idea that the
little creatures would become entangled in their hair,
the man behind her grinned to himself.

At the rear of the cave there was a cleft in the rock.
She paused to say over her shoulder, "It will be a
tight squeeze for you, I'm afraid, but don't be
alarmed; there's no danger of your becoming stuck.
It's narrow only for quite a short distance." As she
entered the cleft she added, "I think it was very brave
of Père d'Éspinay to explore this place on his own.
He was not to know what might happen to him."

"I should have thought him too frail to have come
up here in recent years, but presumably he has or you
wouldn't know the way."

"No, we've never been here together. I wish we
had. On my fifteenth birthday he wrote down the
way to reach it and then, having been here, I destroyed his instructions. You're honored that he
wants you to see it."

"You mean you came here alone at the age of fifteen? Weren't you afraid?"

"Yes, which was foolish of me because I knew
there was no danger. But it is a little eerie on one's
own."

Hunching behind her in a tunnel too low to allow

him to walk upright, and too narrow for the breadth of his shoulders, so that he was forced to move sideways, it seemed to the Englishman that "eerie" was an understatement. He could think of no other woman, and not many men, who would have the courage to venture here alone.

Suddenly the passage turned, and he saw daylight ahead. A few seconds later they were once more in the open.

"We'll go first to the pool and eat there, and then I'll show you the rest of it," said Flora as she extinguished the lamp and left it near the opening. She had breakfasted soon after sunrise and by now was hungry and thirsty.

Almost at once the Englishman saw why the old priest had called the place the Garden of Eden. Never before had he seen such a profusion of rhododendrons, some of them thirty feet tall, and all of them covered with a mass of blossom that almost hid their foliage. The flowers were of every color from crimson and scarlet to silvery pink, yellow and white. Many of the bushes were growing from the fallen trunks of silver firs; some of them were epiphytic; some were festooned with trails of *Clematis montana*. Beneath them grew a carpet of sphagnum moss.

As soon as they left the tunnel he had heard the sound of a waterfall, and soon it came into view, a cascade of shining water frothing into a large pool from which streams drained in several directions. Even in the crags above the pool, rhododendrons had managed to find several footholds.

As they were standing on some flat rocks on the calm side of the pool, he glanced at the girl and asked, "Do you know how to swim, Flora?"

She nodded. "My father taught me when I was a little girl. Sometimes we had to cross rivers by bridges made of slippery logs, and if I had lost my footing I might have drowned before he could reach me."

"Have you swum here?"

Again she nodded.

He began to unbutton his shirt. "Shall we cool ourselves before we eat?"

She averted her eyes. "I can't. I have no bathing dress."

"This is the Garden of Eden, not the beach at Bournemouth," he said dryly. "I shan't be shocked if you dispense with a bathing dress. I haven't one, either. The pool is large—we needn't look at each other."

"I—I would rather not," she said, flushing. "But please don't let that stop you. I'll wander about and you can call when you've finished."

He shrugged. "As you wish."

As she walked away, she wondered what Soeur Marie-Josephe would have said had she heard his suggestion. The nun no longer followed the practice herself because her years with Père d'Espinay had broadened her mind, but in the convent where she had spent her novitiate they'd had to bath in long gowns. When Flora had asked why this was, the nun had replied that it was to prevent evil thoughts from entering their minds. As far as she was aware, the sight of her own naked body had never given Flora any evil thoughts and she could not think why it should. Nevertheless she felt sure that a good man would not have suggested bathing together unclothed.

For some time she wandered through glades carpeted with anemones and primulas, listening to bird-song and watching the many different butterflies that fluttered in the bright air. Presently she heard a whistle that was not that of any bird; it must be Mr. Lomax's signal that she could go back to the pool, she decided.

Eager for her share of the food, she hastened back but found him nowhere to be seen.

"Where are you?" she called uncertainly.

"Here!" He came up out of the water as unexpectedly as a leaping fish.

He must have been lurking half-submerged beneath the ledge on which she was standing, waiting to startle her. In that he succeeded on two counts: first by catching her by surprise, and second by the sight of his bare glistening torso, which was not white, as she would have expected, but the same deep brown as his face.

He grinned at her, showing irregular but healthy teeth. "Why not change your mind and come in? Life is too short to sacrifice any pleasurable experience on the altar of Mrs. Grundy."

For an instant she felt a mad impulse to fling decorum to the wind by shedding her clothes and plunging into the inviting green depths. Often after swimming there alone she had basked on the rocks like a lizard, enjoying the heat of the sun on her naked body, and sometimes a ripple of breeze like the touch of cool fingers on her warm skin.

Why should people have to wear clothes in circumstances that made them not only unnecessary but superfluous? Why, when she wanted to swim, must she be governed by the rules of a culture to which she belonged by name and partly by parentage, but not by education, and certainly not in spirit?

As these thoughts flashed through her mind, the man standing waist-deep in water gave a shrug of his broad brown shoulders and, turning, plunged forward to cross the width of the pool with half a dozen powerful strokes. At the far edge, he reached up to grasp another overhanging ledge and for a moment she stared with a kind of awe at the play of the splendid muscles that lifted him effortlessly upward. Below his waist his skin paled, and the shape of his rump was different from that of a woman, being higher-set and more compact, with hollowed planes on either side. His long lean legs were lightly furred with dark hair.

On the ledge he straightened, shaking the water from his hair before raking it back with his fingers. For some seconds he stood, fists on hips, looking up at the vegetation on the wall of rock. Then he turned, stooped to pick up his shirt and used it to towel himself dry.

Mesmerized, Flora saw for the first time a man as naked as Adam before the Fall, and as unashamed. He made no attempt to conceal that part of the male body whose form and function had until now been something of a mystery to her.

Not that seeing it was very illuminating. She could not relate its form to the little she knew of its function and was gazing with puzzled eyes when, to her profound embarrassment, she became aware that its owner was watching her, visibly amused by her interest in his private parts.

"Oh!" With an exclamation of confusion and a rush of blood to the face, she turned away and hurried to attend to the unpacking of their luncheon.

She was still flustered when he came to her side of

the pool and spread his damp shirt on a bush to dry
while they ate. However, he seemed to have forgotten
the incident, and throughout their meal he questioned her closely about her travels with her father
and about the flora of the mountains surrounding the
mission.

To some extent their conversation took her mind
off the strangeness of sitting within arm's reach of a
man still naked from the waist up. But it did not distract her entirely, and from time to time, out of the
corner of her eye, she flicked a glance at him: at the
burnished bronze shoulders and sinewy, dark-haired
forearms. There was no hair on his chest; it was
brown and smooth, armored with strong pectoral
muscles.

Unlike hers, which was as straight and fine as sewing silk, the hair on his head was of a much crisper
texture, not curly, and smooth when brushed. But
when, as now, it was unbrushed, it reminded her of
the ruffled feathers of a blackbird.

She watched him light a cheroot and, thinking he
had been unaware of her scrutiny, was startled when
he remarked, "You seem to find me as interesting as
I should find a new species of rhododendron."

"I—I'm sorry," she stammered awkwardly. "I've
met so few Europeans."

"There's no need to apologize. I don't mind being under your microscope," he answered with a
quizzical gleam. "If you were a year or two older, I
might be tempted to make a thorough study of
you."

Flora wasn't sure what he meant. He saw her puzzlement and laughed. Then he sprang to his feet and
offered his hand to pull her up. "Come, show me

your garden, little Eve, and perhaps one day I'll come back and we'll eat the forbidden fruit together. But not today.''

She put her hand into his and felt for the second time the strong clasp of his fingers.

For an hour they explored the plateau, which extended over many acres.

''Do you paint, Flora?'' he asked her while he was setting up his camera to photograph some rhododendrons.

She nodded. ''I do, but I have no great talent for it.''

''Nor have I—which is a pity, because no photograph can do justice to the magnificence of these colors.''

At one point he caused her some unspoken alarm by scaling a fifty-foot precipice to gather some species of *Anaphalis*, but soon she saw that he was an experienced climber.

There was a place on the plateau where strawberries grew, and besides eating them, Flora filled a pouch with berries to take back to Père d'Espinay. Picking them reminded her of her companion's reference to the forbidden fruit. Could he have meant that, if she were older, he would have liked not only to kiss her, but to do whatever it was that poets described as ecstasy and the Church as fornication, unless it was sanctioned by marriage?

Perhaps he had merely been teasing her. Or perhaps, if she had had the courage to swim with him, he would have kissed her and unveiled the mystery for her. But because she had been too shy to enter the water with him, he took her for a timid child unready for life, for womanhood.

EARLY THE FOLLOWING MORNING he and his men resumed their journey. He left the priest with a promise that in due course he would send him prints of the photographs taken in the Garden of Eden.

"But whether I shall come this way on my return journey, I can't say," he said as he shook the priest's hand. "Again my thanks for your hospitality, Father."

Having said goodbye to the nuns, he turned then to the girl. "Thank you for being my guide yesterday. The place is well named, except—" the lines around his eyes crinkled suddenly "—that it lacks a fig tree. Goodbye, Flora."

Knowing to what he alluded, she flushed. "Goodbye, Mr. Lomax." For the third and last time their hands clasped.

Presently, watching the train wending downhill while his protégée disappeared uphill on the pretext of gathering herbs for Soeur Marie-Josephe's dispensary, the old man sighed over the failure of his plan. Clearly their visitor had been amused by Flora's company the day before, but not to the extent of being willing to encumber himself with her.

Half an hour later, hunched against a rock at a point from which she could watch the train until the last possible moment, Flora found her sight blurred by tears. It was most unlike her to weep. She had not cried since her grief for her father had healed, and would have had difficulty in explaining the cause of her present tears.

There were no words to describe the complex emotions she felt as the tall man and his black retriever passed out of the valley and out of her life. Her whole body seemed to ache with her longing to be go-

ing with them, not only to see the world but to be
with him—a stranger who in three days had made
himself more important than people she had known
for years. A stranger to whom she meant nothing,
and whom she would never see again.

As CHANCE WOULD HAVE IT, after many months
without any visitors, a few weeks later two more arrived. One was a middle-aged Russian, the other a
compatriot of the priest, although his French was
very different from Père d'Espinay's cultured speech
or Soeur Marie-Josephe's soft country accent.

Flora was out in the hills when they arrived, and
when she returned the Chinese nun, Soeur Benedicta,
hustled her to her room and indicated by signs that
she must put on her black dress, wind her braid
around her head and cover her hair with a coif.

"It's better that these men should take you for a
religious," explained Soeur Marie-Josephe later. "I
don't like the look of either of them, but particularly
the younger man. Avoid him as much as you can,
child."

Flora needed no second bidding. The Frenchman
had the rank smell of someone who had not washed
himself or his clothes for some time; but even had he
been clean, he would not have been prepossessing.
He had small close-set eyes, a low forehead and loose
lips that revealed unwholesome-looking teeth when
he laughed.

The Russian was a man of education. He had lived
in Hankow, the great tea mart of China, where the
trade was largely in the hands of his compatriots. But
why he had left that city, and whither he was bound,
he did not say and Père d'Espinay did not inquire.

On their second night at the mission, Flora was reading in bed when the door burst open and in lurched the Frenchman. Her room was not far from the visitors' quarters; no doubt in his half-tipsy state he had mistaken her door for that of his own room. Although startled by his intrusion, she did not scream, having learned a long time ago that when danger threatened the right reaction was to freeze.

In summer she went to bed naked, and only her long dark hair covered the tilt of her breasts.

The Frenchman reeled into the room. "I thought all nuns had their heads shaved," he exclaimed in a slurred voice.

He was not too drunk to notice the pale golden curves of her shoulders, or the soft rounded mounds of her bosom under the long silky hair that flowed smoothly over one breast but parted over the other to reveal one soft virginal nipple. Flora snatched up the light cotton covering to hide herself from a gaze that made her flesh crawl.

Fortunately, at that point the Russian appeared and dragged his friend from the room with a muttered apology. "He has drunk too much wine, *mademoiselle*. He means you no harm. There's no need to make a complaint. I'll make sure he does not molest you."

The following day Flora overheard a conversation between them that sent her flying to Père d'Espinay.

"For God's sake, Dimitri," she heard the Frenchman say roughly, "what harm can there be in having the girl? I know boys are more to your taste, but I prefer women. Perhaps we should take her with us: she would fetch a good price in any whorehouse. You could say she was an investment. I can use her for a

few weeks, and then when I've had enough we can
sell her. The priest and the nuns won't defend her;
he's old, and they are afraid."

"But the priest is not," said the Russian. "You
touch her, my friend, and he'll kill you. What use is a
girl of that age? She will scream and cry, and where is
the pleasure in that?"

The Frenchman chuckled unpleasantly. "I like it,
Dimitri—I like it. I like them young and unused. If
they squeal, I soon stop their noise."

Flora had thought Père d'Espinay incapable of
rage until she reported the gist of this conversation to
him and saw the fury in his eyes.

"What is a whorehouse?" she asked him.

Reluctantly, he explained to her that unless a
young girl had a father, brother or some other man
to guard her, she stood in danger of becoming a vic-
tim of a particularly vile form of slavery.

"I had hoped it would not be necessary to discuss
your future for some time yet, but it seems I must,"
he said heavily. "If I should die, you will have no
choice but to embrace the Roman Catholic faith and
take the veil, *ma chère*. It will be a great waste of
your beauty, but at least you will be safe from brutes
like that one."

"But if I am beautiful, won't someone wish to
marry me?"

"Perhaps...perhaps," he said, sighing. "The
world, however, is a strange and sad place, and it
would be wrong of me to conceal from you that because you are your father's daughter but have your
mother's hair and eyes, there will be people who will
think you—beautiful as you are—an inferior person.
Do not ask me why. I cannot explain such stupidity; I

can only tell you it is so. Any man who does offer
you marriage will be a good man. Although he may
have nothing else in his favor, you would be unwise
to refuse him. You were born to be a wife and
mother, not a religious. But even the veil would be
preferable to the misery of a brothel.''

Flora shivered. ''I wish Mr. Lomax was still here.
He would soon send these men on their way.''

''Yes; I, too, wish we had his assistance in this
situation. But by now he must be far away and, I
think, unlikely to return by the same way he came.
However, don't be afraid, my child. In the night I
thought of a way to discourage those two from pro-
longing their sojourn among us, and my plan is
already in action. Go now and tell the Russian I
should like to speak to him. I want him to see what is
going to happen very shortly.''

On her way to fetch the Russian, Flora encountered the Frenchman. She would have hastened past
him with downcast eyes, but he blocked her way,
grinning broadly when she tried in vain to dodge
him.

''What's your hurry, little virgin? Have you been
told it's a sin to look at any man but a priest? They
do more than look, I shouldn't wonder, if they live
in the back of beyond with a ripe piece such as yourself. The priest here is old and past it. Maybe when he
dies the next one they send will be younger. Meanwhile why not let me teach you a thing or two?''

''Please, *m'sieur*, let me pass. I have a message for
your friend.''

''That—'' He spat out a word that was unknown
to her. ''He's no friend of mine, my pretty. He takes
his pleasure with boys and men like himself, the dirty

bastard. Me, I bed women. In a civilized country I wouldn't travel with him, but here a man on his own is too easy a target for the bandits."

As he spoke he reached out to grab her, and instinctively she turned and ran. He caught a fold of her skirt and pulled her backward against him, clamping one arm around her waist and, with his free hand, exploring the soft curves beneath the stiffly starched bib that was part of the habit of the order to which the two nuns belonged.

Flora clawed at the arm around her waist, but her nails were too short to scratch him, and her frantic kicks at his shins seemed to make no impression. Considering the clumsy-looking thickness of his fingers—which she had noticed because of his filthy bitten nails—it was amazing how swiftly he undid the buttons of her bodice and thrust his rough paw inside to drag down her chemise.

"Ah!" She heard a grunt of satisfaction as his hand closed over her bare flesh.

She gave a moan of revulsion and struggled wildly to escape. But it was the sudden appearance of Soeur Marie-Josephe that caused him to slacken his hold long enough for Flora to break free.

"Mother of God! Would you risk your immortal soul, man?" the French nun exclaimed in horror.

"I sold my soul to the devil a long time ago, old woman," he replied in an angry snarl. Nevertheless he looked uneasy and slouched away in the direction of the main compound.

"The wicked brute—has he hurt you?" asked Soeur Marie-Josephe angrily.

Flora shook her head, but her fingers were shaking as she fastened her bodice. "I was on my way to tell

the Russian that Père d'Espinay wants to speak to
him.''

"Yes, and quickly, too. They are on their way up
from the village,'' the nun answered cryptically. ''I
will fetch him while you compose yourself.''

Flora understood what she had meant when a short
time later a party of men from the village entered the
compound bearing a motionless body on a bamboo
stretcher. This they placed on the ground before
retreating to stand at a nervous distance from it.

Whether or not the Russian and the Frenchman
understood the exchange in dialect between the priest
and the villagers, they could not fail to understand
Soeur Marie-Josephe's cry of alarm.

"Oh, let it not be the plague! Blessed Mother, have
mercy upon us! Let it be anything but that,'' she exclaimed as she crossed herself.

"Calm yourself, Sister. It may be some ordinary
fever that we can treat. You know how these people
excite themselves,'' the priest said quietly in French.
He advanced to examine the patient.

The Russian was standing near Flora. ''There's
plague in this region?'' he asked her.

"There may be. We haven't heard of it. Soeur
Marie-Josephe is frightened because years ago she
saw a whole village wiped out in a matter of days.
The plague is a fearful disease. Nothing will cure it.
One dies...or one recovers. Most people die,'' answered Flora. She, too, made the sign of the cross on
her forehead and breast.

The old priest knelt by the stretcher, making a
careful examination of the figure, which now she
recognized as that of the village drunk. They must
have plied him with wine until he was in the maudlin

state that later gave place to stupor. The Russian and the Frenchman would mistake his drunken mumblings for the incoherent raving of delirium.

"Yes, I'm afraid it is the plague. He has all the classic symptoms," said the priest, rising from his knees. "We must not give way to fear, my children," he went on as Soeur Marie-Josephe gave a muffled cry of dismay. "We have had many untroubled years here. It is time our mettle was tested. Let us thank God for entrusting to us the task of supporting these poor people in their anguish. I fear very few will survive."

He glanced at the Russian. "If I may advise you, it would be wise to put as many miles as possible between yourselves and this place before nightfall. There is no reason why you and your companion should stay to share our fate. Although if you wish to remain we shall be glad of your help. Digging graves is hard work for women and a man of my age."

"Are you mad? I'm not staying! I'm off!" the Frenchman expostulated. He hurried away to his room to collect his belongings.

The Russian stared at the priest and then at the rest of them. After a moment he turned to follow the other man. Ten minutes later the pair of them were distant figures moving rapidly along the track that led to the west.

"But I don't think the Russian was deceived by our ruse," said Père d'Espinay. "Not that it matters, as long as the Frenchman doesn't say something that goads him into revealing the truth of the matter. They're an ill-assorted pair of traveling companions. I hope we have seen the last of them."

Later, when the nun told him that already the

Frenchman had abused Flora's modesty, the old man
was troubled. It had been difficult for him to speak
frankly to the girl on certain subjects, and he knew
she had gained no enlightenment from Soeur Marie-
Josephe, who had never lived in the world and enjoyed its pleasures as he had. By encouraging Flora
to read freely—his library included a number of
works that would have shocked the nun had she
known of them—he had hoped to remedy the defi-
ciency.

But in case Flora had not read the passages that
would have enlarged her understanding of the relationship between men and women who loved each
other, that evening he felt it necessary to say, "My
child, I understand that the Frenchman inflicted certain indignities on you this morning."

A blush gave her golden skin a delicate apricot
tinge. She nodded, her lashes veiling her soft dark
eyes.

"Don't allow an unpleasant experience to weigh
too heavily on you," the priest went on. "What is
loathsome at the hands of a stranger—particularly
that unkempt lout—can inspire very different
reactions when the man is gentle and the woman is
willing. If the processes of procreation were not
extremely enjoyable, mankind would have long been
extinct. Try to put out of your mind what happened
today."

"Yes, Father," she said obediently.

Presently, watching her as she translated a passage
of Greek to him, he sighed again at the thought of
her subtle beauty being wasted if she had to take the
veil. It was a great pity he had no relations in France
to whom he could entrust her.

That night in bed Flora tried not to remember the disgusting intimacy of the Frenchman's rough dirty hand on her naked breast. She had never realized before—having no reason to consider such a thing—how helpless a woman was against the superior strength of a man, even a man in as poor condition as that one. Although more than a match for her, he wouldn't have stood a chance against a man like Mr. Lomax.

Suddenly, remembering what Père d'Espinay had said about things having different effects in different circumstances, she found herself imagining how she would have felt if the arm around her waist had been English, and the hand unfastening her bodice the lean, well-kept hand of their previous visitor. She would have struggled just the same, but she could not pretend that she would have felt any revulsion. Indignation and confusion, yes. But not the sick impotent rage of being held against her will by a man who repelled her.

Indeed as she thought of Mr. Lomax sliding his sun-browned fingers inside her chemise, her heart began to beat with excited thuds, and she felt a strange tingling sensation in the pit of her stomach.

She was thankful that, being a Protestant, she would not have to confess her impure thoughts to a shocked and grieved Père d'Espinay.

CHAPTER THREE

FOR SOME DAYS life at the mission seemed to resume its former tranquillity, although now in the evenings, instead of reading or talking, often both the priest and the girl would sit in preoccupied silence.

Flora was deeply disturbed by her glimpse of the evil side of life, and by the thought that if anything happened to Père d'Espinay her only sure refuge would be in a convent.

The old man was pondering whether he could muster the strength to undertake the journey to Shanghai with her. Apart from his age and fragility, he knew himself to be in the grip of an incurable disease. At present, with a judicious use of opium, the pain was bearable. But he had no idea how soon his condition might worsen, and the thought of the long taxing journey, and of dying far away from the place that had been his home for so many years, made him hesitate to act. If he should be struck down en route, he might leave Flora in a more dangerous position than her present one.

The decision was taken out of his hands when one evening while they were having supper the refectory door was suddenly flung open. All three were horrified to see the man they had thought themselves rid of—the brutish Frenchman.

"Not digging graves, priest?" he growled. "I thought you'd have had half your flock under the sod by this time."

Père d'Espinay reached for his cane, and tense with apprehension as she was, Flora noticed that he transferred it to his left hand before using it to help himself to his feet.

"I regret having to say it, but you are not welcome here, Gérard," he said in the coldest tone she had ever heard him use.

"Am I not?" The man slammed the door behind him and moved toward the table, reeling a little, obviously more than half drunk.

He snatched up a bread cake and stuffed some into his mouth. Then he reached for the wine. "How are you going to make me leave, priest?" he asked through a mouthful of food. "You won't trick me a second time."

His bloodshot gaze turned on Flora, and she flinched from the rabid gleam in his small piggy eyes.

The priest said to her in English, "If you love me, obey me now, child. When I divert him, run. The village people will hide you from him."

"What ruse are you trying now, priest?"

The Frenchman lurched around the table and, grabbing Flora's black braid, gave it a tug that made her draw in her breath. By twining the braid around his wrist and pulling it downward, he forced her to bend back her head.

"Have a swig of wine, my pretty pigeon." He put the mouth of the flask to her lips, tilting it too far so that the wine gushed over her chin and down her long slender neck to stain the collar of her dress.

"Let her go, oaf!" the priest rasped angrily.

"I'll do as I please with her, old man. If you don't like it, don't watch."

The man's guffaw was cut short as Père d'Espinay

shifted his grip on the cane and with his right hand made a sudden snatch at the handle of engraved silver.

The nuns and Flora were as startled as the man who found the point of a sword pressed against his gross belly. But with her braid still twined around his wrist, it was impossible for Flora to take advantage of his momentary astonishment. She seized her table knife, prepared to hack off the plait at the thickest part. Before she could do so, however, he gave a bellow of rage and sprang backward, pulling her off the stool and making her scream at the agony that seared her scalp as she fell to the floor, all her weight on her fettered braid.

Had the priest used the sword to wound rather than to threaten, or had the two nuns not been too numb with shock and terror to make a concerted attack, the outcome might have been different. But the Frenchman was matched by four people to whom violence was as foreign as it was familiar to him. When a few moments later Flora felt her head freed and staggered giddily to her feet, she saw with horrified eyes that the long narrow blade had changed hands and was now in the Frenchman's great fist. As she sprang to restrain him, he brought back his elbow and drove the point of the sword into the old man's frail body.

What followed was a nightmare of pain and panic. Dimly she was conscious of the two nuns crouched over the injured priest while the Frenchman pursued her around the heavy oak table. She might have evaded him indefinitely, for she was more nimble than he, but he caught her by grabbing the Chinese nun and threatening to cut her throat unless Flora came to him. She had no choice but to obey, but she did not cease to resist the inevitable end. She fought him with all her strength, making him curse her for being a stubborn little bitch.

When she was almost exhausted, he struck her in the face with a force that for a time made everything fade into blackness. But the nightmare was not over yet. She came round to find herself hanging head down over his shoulder, and what followed was worse—much worse. Before she fainted again, she prayed she might die. . . .

WHEN SHE RECOVERED CONSCIOUSNESS, Soeur Marie-Josephe was sitting beside her, holding one of her hands. To Flora's puzzlement, the nun's eyes were full of tears.

For some moments she recalled nothing, and it perplexed her that she could not see out of her left eye properly. Then she moved and discovered that every joint in her body felt bruised, as if she had fallen down a steep slope and been battered against many rocks before coming to rest. Her mind cleared and everything came back to her: her frenzied resistance ending in exhausted subjugation...the door bursting open...her shame at her rescuer's seeing her degraded, sprawled on her back beneath the pumping haunches of that brute. . . .

The sight of her squirming limbs, her muffled whimpers of distress, had ignited Caspar Lomax's violent temper. Grasping the Frenchman by the hair and by the loose flesh at his waist, he had hauled him off Flora's body. The man's yelp of surprise had changed to an animal scream of pain and terror as his groin was slashed with a razor-sharp knife. The man had crumpled to his knees and would have collapsed but for the Englishman's grip on his hair. Flora recalled that the cold hooded eyes looking down at her tormentor had been as merciless as those of an eagle watching its prey before swooping. Once more the knife had gleamed in the rushlight as with another swift stroke he severed the rapist's jugular vein. On the bed, Flora had moaned and fainted.

Now, remembering, she felt a convulsive shudder run through her aching body. She would have wept had the nun not tightened her clasp and said in a tone of great urgency, "You must be a brave girl, my child. Père d'Espinay is dying. He needs you. Be strong. Think only of giving him comfort in his last hour. Tomorrow weep for yourself. Tonight show your love by forgetting what you have been through, and caring only for what he has suffered by being unable to defend you."

To Flora, the news that the old man she loved was dying was the final turn of the rack, and it brought her very close to breaking point. Her mind reeled under the shock. The nun saw a strange wild look in her uninjured eye and feared that the terrible rape had destroyed her sanity.

It would be no wonder, after what she had suffered. She had resisted like a wildcat, and the man had seemed to delight in causing her pain. It was a wonder he had not crowned his bestiality by violating her in front of them. But having given her the blow that had caused her swollen left eye and knocked her almost insensible, he had flung her over his shoulder and carried her to the room he had occupied during his stay, locking the door so that no one could interfere while he took his evil pleasure with her.

To the nun's relief, the girl struggled into a sitting position and said in a hoarse but sane voice, "Yes, yes—I'll come. Help me up, Sister. I feel so dizzy."

"First you must change that dress. Wait while I fetch you a tunic and trousers. I shall not be gone long."

The old woman hurried away, leaving Flora to become aware that the top of her one and only dress was hanging from her in rags where the man's greedy hands had ripped it to get at her breasts. The horrible memory of those lascivious hands and his slobbering mouth fastened leechlike on hers almost broke her threadbare control. She felt too soiled and debased ever to be clean again, and a wave of hysteria swept her as she remembered the final moment of torture before the door had burst open and Mr. Lomax had plucked the man from her.

The nun came back with some clothes and helped the trembling girl take off the ruined dress and replace it with the Chinese garments that were her everyday wear.

"Wait while I tidy your hair." Swiftly the French-woman's hands twined the loosened tresses into a semblance of neatness.

"There! It will grieve him beyond expression to see your poor little face, but he need never know the worst. Let him die believing the Englishman reached us in time."

With the old nun's arm supporting her around the waist, Flora stumbled along the wide cloister built by the priest when he was younger. Her head throbbed. Her arms and legs felt as if they had been dislocated, and between her thighs there was a smarting sensation that made walking acutely uncomfortable.

"Père d'Espinay is in his room. The Englishman carried him there," said Soeur Marie-Josephe, gripping Flora more firmly as she swayed and seemed close to fainting.

Outside the door of the priest's room, they paused and the nun felt the girl inhale a deep breath and straighten herself. Her small firm chin lifted. Her voice was composed as she said, "I can manage now, thank you, Sister."

WHEN CASPAR HEARD THE DOOR OPEN he was sitting close to the bed, straining to hear the weak voice of the dying man. In a corner of the room the Chinese nun's lips were moving in soundless prayer.

As the two women entered, the Earl of Carlyon rose to his feet and left the stool free for the girl. Watching her as she moved to the bedside, he found it difficult to believe that less than half an hour earlier she had lain unconscious in his arms after being savagely raped by the man he had killed. Now the only evidence of her ordeal was her puffy left eye, already beginning to discolor. Otherwise she was neat and tidy, and apparently in full command of herself.

By God, she has guts, he thought admiringly.

"Flora...my dearest child." Feebly the priest stretched out his thin white hands to her, but he had not the strength to lift himself from the pillows piled behind him.

She took his old hands in her young ones, and watching them Caspar noticed that although he had been told she was of plebeian stock, her hands were delicately formed with long fingers and short but narrow nails. There must have been good blood somewhere among her antecedents. That long elegant neck and the small ears, the lobes pierced by fine golden rings, were not characteristic of humble origins. Having seen her bared up to the waist, he knew now that her legs, too, were long and slender, not stocky and muscular even though she could run like the wind.

He listened to her telling the priest that she was all right: that no harm had been done to her apart from the incipient black eye, which would heal within a few days.

"But you, Father...." At this her soft voice did falter slightly.

"Don't grieve for me, Flora. I am glad to die in this fashion—quickly and with little suffering. But for Gérard I should have been obliged to endure a long and increasingly painful illness from which at the end even opium might have brought no relief. To have put an end to myself would not have been against my own conscience, but it would have distressed these two good women who are praying for my immortal soul. It is much better this way, especially now that Mr. Lomax has assured me that you will have his protection at least as far as Shanghai."

The effort of speaking had exhausted his failing strength, and he closed his eyes and lay so still, his hands cold and lax in hers, that she thought he had died.

However, after some moments the old man rallied to murmur, "Give my crucifix and my Bible to Soeur Marie-Josephe, and my rosary to Soeur Benedicta. All my other possessions are yours now. Thank you for lighting my last years. I wish you may find as much happiness as you have brought me."

He had been speaking in English, but his last

words were in his own language, and she had to bend close to catch them.

"Nous n'irons plus aux bois; les lauriers sont coupés."

She recognized it as a line from *Les Cariatides*, one of his favorite books of poetry. "We shall go to the woods no more; the laurels are cut down."

PERE D'ESPINAY'S OBSEQUIES took place in a manner that caused Soeur Marie-Josephe to cluck with disapproval and Caspar to mask an amusement that he felt sure the priest would have shared, could he have been a witness to his own funeral.

It was the practice in China for all those attending a wedding or funeral feast to contribute a "share," usually of money but sometimes of food, according to an established scale. Since the priest had earned the love and respect of several generations in his own and various neighboring villages since first he had come among them in the 1870s, there were many contributors to his feast. The committee in charge of the arrangements did not consult the two nuns but followed their own customs, which included engaging the services of both Buddhist and Taoist priests to chant from their sacred books in ornate pavilions set up in the compound at the mission.

To Soeur Marie-Josephe this bordered on sacrilege, but Caspar persuaded her against making a fuss. It was the priest himself who had told him, with rueful amusement, that in view of the uncertainty as to the best way to reach the regions of the blessed, the Chinese often considered it prudent to take passage by both religious routes.

"Say nothing, Sister," he advised. "These people

mean well. To protest will only give offense and perhaps upset Flora. These are her mother's people, and their ways are not as alien to her as they are to you and me.''

"Her mother died when she was six. There's little of the Chinese in her. She has their black hair and their eyes, but her ways are ours,'' said the nun.

"Nevertheless she has lived in China all her life and will find nothing strange in the way in which they honor their dead.''

Flora heard the undernote of authority in his voice and knew that, although he might defer to her out of courtesy, it was he who was in charge at the mission now.

Privately Caspar found the wailing, the fire-crackers set off to frighten away evil spirits and the ear-splitting music that went on from morning to evening enough to strain the strongest nerves, let alone those of someone in Flora's condition. But she seemed not to mind the cacophony, and perhaps the activities taking place in the compound took her mind off the events of the night before.

She sat in a chair in the cloister with her legs on a cushioned stool and a bandage hiding the ugly bruising around her eye. White being the color of Chinese mourning, she wore one of the Chinese nun's nightgowns, which with its high neck and long sleeves was every whit as modest as her ruined black dress.

The funeral feast took place on the third day after the priest's death, and when it was over a large crowd swarmed in the wake of the thirty-two bearers of the catafalque. As in many country districts, the funeral catafalque, with its multitude of lacquered poles, was owned by a group of local farmers, who on this occasion had waived the fee usually charged for the use of it. Since only a few of the bearers could see where they were going, they were led by the funeral director, who gave his orders in a shrill falsetto punctuated by piercing screams. To each of his orders the whole chorus of bearers responded with shouts like those of sailors heaving anchor, while at the rear of the catafalque the mourners redoubled their wails.

It was as different from the subdued conduct of a European funeral as could be imagined. But for the recollection of his grandfather's death, which gave him some insight into the profound sense of loss the girl must be feeling, Caspar would have observed the ceremony with unalloyed inward amusement.

At the priest's expressed wish the large round grave had been dug on a piece of uncultivated hillside, where for once there would be none of the usual recriminations about the trampling of the crops surrounding most Chinese family graves. The greatest honor was the coffin made of *yin-chên mu*, or long-buried wood. Flora, who since the night of her rape and the murder of the priest had worried Soeur Marie-Josephe by not shedding a tear and remaining unnaturally calm, had explained the significance of this to Caspar.

"Poor people's coffins are made from many pieces of wood joined together, and everyone who can afford it has the coffin painted with black lacquer. With the better coffins each side is cut from a single plank, preferably from *hsiang mu*, which means fragrant wood. The fragrance is a preservative. The coffin they've given Père d'Espinay—'' she spoke his name without any sign of being upset ''—was made for a rich man who was ill, but who has recovered. It must have cost at least four hundred ounces of silver and possibly a thousand, because *yin-chên mu* is scarce and very expensive. They believe it could have been buried as long as three hundred years. Is that possible, do you think?''

"It may be. I shouldn't have thought so."

"Anyway, I'm sure Père d'Espinay would have preferred them to spend the money on something useful to the living, but it does show how much they admired him."

The priest's remains were lowered into the grave to an accompaniment of wilder shrieks from the director, shouts from the bearers and grave diggers, redoubled wails from the mourners and a final crescendo of firecrackers. In the foreground the two nuns wept as they prayed for his soul. From the background came a buzz of chatter from Caspar's coolies and other spectators.

Only two people remained impassive: Flora and the tall Englishman who watched her expressionless face throughout the interment and wondered, with some impatience, how long it would be before she was fit enough to travel, and if he had been a fool to agree to take her with him.

LATE THAT NIGHT he was in his quarters consulting the 1902 edition of the *Kew Hand-List of Trees and Shrubs*, which enumerated three hundred genera of shrubs, fully half to be found in China, when there was an urgent tap on the door.

With a frown of irritation at having his peace disturbed, Carlyon called to whoever it was to enter.

It was the elder of the nuns, in a state of great agitation.

"Monsieur Lomax, the child is not in her room. I went to see if she needed a sleeping draft and found her bed empty. Where can she have gone? Oh, Blessed Mary, can her shame and her grief have turned her mind after all? Ever since these terrible things befell us, she has behaved very strangely."

"On the contrary, Sister, she has behaved in precisely the manner one would expect of a well-bred Englishwoman. Such women do not display their emotions," he replied dryly. "As for shame, that lies not with Flora but with the man who abused her."

"So it may, *monsieur*. But not everyone holds such charitable views," the nun retorted somewhat acidly. "In the eyes of many the poor child has been degraded. That it was no fault of hers won't alter their opinion. I know her better than you do. She's a proud and sensitive girl who will feel her disgrace very deeply."

"Nevertheless I'm sure your alarm is unnecessary. Very likely she's gone to the graveside to give vent to her feelings in privacy."

"But she shouldn't be there on her own at this time of night."

"I agree, and I'll bring her back," said Caspar, resigning himself to the fact that he would have no more peace that night until the girl had been found.

A clear sky and a full moon made a lantern unnecessary. He could see his way up the hill almost as easily as by day, and some time before he reached the grave he knew that his assumption had been correct. He could hear, on the still night air, the sound of inconsolable sobbing. Presently, rounding the last bend of the track and pausing in the black shadow cast by a massive pistachio tree, he saw her crouched by the circle of freshly turned earth, her arms locked around her legs, her head bent close to her knees while she rocked back and forth in a paroxysm of distress.

In the ordinary way, Caspar had little patience with weeping women. Genuine tears embarrassed him; crocodile tears were wasted on him. But as he regarded Flora, a half-fledged girl closer to childhood than womanhood in spite of her recent experience, her misery touched a well-spring of compassion in him.

He stepped forward into the moonlight and, not wishing to startle her by approaching too closely, said quietly, "You shouldn't be up here alone, you know."

At first she seemed not to have heard him, and then her sobbing subsided and she said in a voice made ragged with crying, "Go away. Leave me alone."

"The nuns are anxious about you. I promised them I would find you."

"You have found me. Now go away."

Caspar's patience—always on the short side—had already been stretched to its limit by the unusual events of the day.

"Don't be foolish," he said rather brusquely. "You can't stay here on your own."

"Why not? What more could happen to me?" She began to weep even more bitterly than before.

He was a man who for many years had been able to put his own comfort and convenience above all other considerations. Now it was after midnight and he wanted to be in his room, with a whiskey and soda at his elbow, not hanging about on a hillside where he had spent more than enough time earlier in the day.

Such sympathy as he had felt for her was replaced by a thrust of irritation directed partly at her and partly at himself for becoming involved in her predicament.

"Come now: be sensible, Flora." In three strides he was beside her, pulling her upright. "The nuns are grieving, too, you know. You should consider their feelings as well as your own."

His touch, although not ungentle, had enough force in it to remind her of the brutal hands that had overpowered all her struggles. Suddenly she had a vivid recollection of how the man who was holding her had without hesitation wreaked the most hideous mutilation upon her attacker. In a different way he was as cruel as the Frenchman, and instinctively she tried to wrench free of the hands that held her; the hands that a few nights earlier had castrated and killed.

Caspar's reaction to her struggles was equally instinctive. Sensing her terror and aware that if he released her she might not be easy to recapture, he clamped one arm firmly around her. With his free hand he stroked her hair and began to speak softly to her, as if she were a nervous filly alarmed at being bridled.

After a time his soothing overcame her fear. She discovered that a pair of strong arms could be a refuge as well as a trap. No longer resistant, she relaxed against his tall frame, her head on his shoulder, her weeping gradually quieting until it subsided altogether.

As Flora's grief passed, Caspar's body suddenly reminded him that it was many weeks since he'd had a woman, and here in his arms was a girl with sweet-scented hair and, under her concealing garments, firm breasts and a supple waist. He knew he should pull her away from him at once—but he delayed a little too long, so that his body responded involuntarily to the warmth of her soft flesh and his own natural need.

Thus it was that Flora, lulled by his gentling into the first peace of mind she had known since the Frenchman's reappearance, was made aware, by a sudden stirring between them, that this man must be capable of the same frightening transformation as the man who had been the inflicter of a pain she could never forget as long as she lived. With a moan of remembered revulsion she pulled free and fled down the hill.

FOR TWO DAYS Caspar kept out of her way and contained his impatience as best he could.

On the third day he said to Soeur Marie-Josephe, "I'm anxious to be on my way, Sister. Do you think the girl is sufficiently recovered for us to begin our journey? She won't have to walk; she can be carried by chair."

"She's still stiff and bruised, Monsieur Lomax. Can you not wait a few days more?"

"No—no, I can't," he said shortly. "I am behind time as it is. We must start tomorrow. See that she's ready, if you please."

That night he ate with the women instead of alone in his quarters. When Flora, who had glimpsed but not spoken to him since three nights before at the graveside, came into the refectory and found him seated at the table in his blue velvet smoking coat, a deep flush stained her pale face.

He rose and gave a slight bow. "Good evening, Flora."

"G-good evening," she stammered. "I hear we are leaving tomorrow."

"I am leaving," he agreed. "You are under no compulsion to join me if you don't wish to."

"Père d'Espinay wished it, and I can't remain here. Somehow I must earn my living."

"We shall have plenty of time to discuss possibilities on the way to Shanghai. Meanwhile you should make the most of your last night in civilized surroundings. Our lodgings between here and Ichang will be rough places at best, and at worst scarcely habitable."

"You forget I have traveled before, with my father."

"You were a child then. No doubt you've forgotten most of the hardships."

She did not argue the point, for indeed she could not recall any serious privations during her earlier travels, but only a joyous sense of freedom and adventure.

That night, as she lay for the last time in the bed that had been hers for seven years, she could not help remembering the previous occasion when the Englishman and his caravan had set out from the mission, and how she had climbed the hill to watch them out of sight, longing to go with them. Now her wish had been granted—but at what a price! She was no longer the same girl, and neither was Mr. Lomax the *preux chevalier* he had seemed to her after his first visit.

That he had killed to avenge her did not make the act less terrible. Now she was not even sure that, once away from the mission, he might not try to repeat what the Frenchman had done to her. He had wanted to do it the other night on the hill. She had felt him changing from the way he had been at the pool in the Garden of Eden to the way the Frenchman had been when he had flung her on the bed and let fall his trousers.

She did not think Mr. Lomax would ever force himself on her, like that man Gérard. But now that she had lost her virginity, he would not have the same respect for her as before and might regard her compliance as a fair return for the extra expense of taking her with him. She had no money to pay for her keep on the journey.

Everything she possessed was packed in a bamboo box, and although Père d'Espinay had bequeathed to her his watch and portraits of his family painted on small pieces of ivory framed in gold set with pearls and in one case rose diamonds, their value to her was far greater than their intrinsic worth. She knew she could never bear to sell them, no matter how desperate her straits.

She was sad to part from the nuns, and especially sorry for Soeur Marie-Josephe, who would have no one to talk to in her own language until a new priest arrived, which might not be for many months.

"Come: we must be on our way. We have a long march before us," said Caspar peremptorily, considering the women's farewells too prolonged already and in danger of becoming hysterical. The baggage porters had set out some time earlier, and only the four sedan bearers remained, waiting for Flora to take her place in the chair.

Not having ridden in one for many years, she had

forgotten that the motion was inclined to make people giddy until they became accustomed to it.

At first the gloom of leave-taking hung over her, and she could not resist turning around to take last looks at the mission and the place on the hillside near the pistachio tree. But once the valley was out of sight and the country became unfamiliar, her spirits began to lighten.

Her escort did not walk with them but strode ahead, the black gundog, Thor, at his heels. He had allowed Flora to choose a dozen of her favorite books from Père d'Espinay's library and advised her to carry one or two in the chair in case she should become bored with looking at the scenery and listening to the chatter of her bearers. The rest of the library, she supposed, would remain at the mission for the benefit of the next priest.

By the end of that first long day she was so weary that she fell asleep while the supper was being prepared, and was vexed at being woken up and ordered to eat a meal for which she had no appetite.

"But I'm not hungry, and a heavy meal will keep me awake, Mr. Lomax," she protested after he had roused her.

"To go without food will make you feel weak tomorrow. Afterward we'll take a short stroll, and then you can give me a game of bezique," he answered, adding as an afterthought, "I think from now on you had better use my first name—Caspar."

They were passing the night in rooms in a large clean house that, during their stroll after supper, he warned her was a much better lodging than they could expect in future.

She had to admit, to herself if not to him, that she

did feel less exhausted after the supper he had forced on her. With the meal she had drunk only water, but while they were playing the card game taught her by Père d'Espinay, Caspar poured *samshu* for her. Although she was accustomed to a glass of wine with her evening meal, she had rarely had more than one, and it was not until he refilled his glass without replenishing hers that she realized her head was swimming slightly.

Meeting her glance, he said with a gleam of amusement, "I think three glasses is your limit, my girl. One more and you'll be tipsy."

"Have I had three?" she asked, astonished.

"You have, and tossed them back like a hardened toper," he told her dryly. "If you're wise, when you're on your own you'll remember always to keep an eye on what is being put in your glass. To give a girl too much champagne is one of the easiest ways to seduce her."

Her cheeks, already warmed by the wine, became even hotter. "Have you forgotten? I've been seduced already," she said bitterly, looking fixedly at her cards.

To her surprise, Caspar reached across the folding table on which they were playing and put his hand under her chin.

When reluctantly she met his eyes, he said, "You were taken against your will, which is a very different thing from allowing your will to be fuddled by wine or by passion. You haven't experienced that yet, but you will when you're a little older. Meanwhile you can take my word for it that passion can be as potent as wine, and a greater threat to self-control. Wine can be refused. Passion is a fever in the blood—

except that, unlike other fevers, it can't be calmed by quinine," he added sardonically.

He leaned back in his chair and tossed aside his hand of cards. "We've played enough for tonight. You should go to bed. Good night, Flora."

In spite of the wine and although she had been weary earlier, it was some time before she slept. The words "when you're on your own" echoed in her mind with an ominous ring. She had never been on her own, having first her father, then Père d'Espinay and now Mr. Lomax—Caspar—to look after her. How would she fare when she had no one but herself to depend on?

A few weeks earlier the prospect would not have frightened her, because then everyone she knew had been kind and gentle and the only dangers in life were landslides, floods and disease. Since then she had learned that people could be as dangerous as nature. There were evil men like Gérard to beware of, and evil places like whorehouses where girls became trapped and had to endure repeatedly the loathsome assault on their bodies that he had inflicted on her.

Although Père d'Espinay had said, "If the processes of procreation were not extremely enjoyable, mankind would have long been extinct," she found it impossible to imagine how *that* could ever be a pleasure. Still, a week later, there was a soreness between her thighs, and all over her body were bruises made by Gérard's fingers and the plum-dark imprints of his teeth. She shuddered, wondering if she would ever be rid of the sense of defilement or of the sickeningly vivid memory of being held down, raging but helpless, while he lunged at her, wounding her spirit even more than her body.

IN THE DAYS THAT FOLLOWED, the magnificence of the country through which they were traveling did much to restore Flora's serenity, and each day she was able to spend longer on foot and less time in the chair. The skin surrounding her eye was still discolored, but the swelling had gone down and she was able to see normally, and to dispense with the bandage.

One night, after Caspar had been hunting for the pot most of the day and she had spent too long on foot and overtaxed herself, they were playing chess when he said, "You're unusually silent this evening, Flora. Is there something on your mind?"

Unwilling to admit she had walked too far and longing to lie down, she hesitated.

He said, "I think I know what's troubling you, but I'm sure you're worrying unnecessarily. In fact I'm certain of it."

"What do you mean?" she asked, mystified.

"You're concerned that you may have a child—yes?"

The idea had not occurred to her, but now that he had put it into her head she was stricken with a new revulsion. To give birth to a child by that beast—the thought was unbearable.

Carlyon saw the horror in her eyes and said briskly, "Obviously you are not well versed in such matters, and no doubt you find it embarrassing to discuss them with me. But better a little embarrassment than a needless weight on your mind. You will not have a child for the simple reason that although he ruptured your hymen...." He paused. "Do you know what that is?"

She felt her whole body becoming suffused with

hot color. "I—I know Hymen was the son of Apollo, and the—the god of marriage," she stammered.

"The hymen is the membrane that in virgins protects the passage by which children are conceived and through which they are born," said Carlyon matter-of-factly. "The stretching of the hymen is the reason why women rarely enjoy their first experience of the sexual act—although it isn't necessary for them to suffer the pain you felt. A normal man doesn't inflict pain on a woman. His object is to give her as much pleasure as she gives to him. Don't allow what that blackguard did to you to color your expectations of what you are likely to feel the first time you lie in the arms of a lover. You'll find they bear as little resemblance as—" he searched for a simile that would have particular relevance for her "—as the Indian strawberries by the roadside, which have no taste and which my porters think are poisonous, and the fruit of the *Fragaria filipendula*, which we ate and enjoyed the day we spent in d'Espinay's Garden of Eden."

Perhaps because he showed none, she found her embarrassment abating. "I should like to believe you," she murmured.

"You can believe me," he assured her.

"You said I should not have a child . . . ?"

"Although he had torn your hymen he had not, at the time I removed him, completed the act. To put it bluntly, he hadn't emitted his seed."

She shivered, remembering the flash of the knife, and the blood.

"Do you feel no remorse for killing him?" she asked huskily.

"Should I feel remorse if I killed a rat? Or a pig

that was ravaging crops? No, I feel no remorse," he said coldly. "Would you rather I had let him live, perhaps to do the same thing to some other woman?"

"No...oh, no, I'm glad he's dead. If I'd had a knife I could have killed him myself. But it would have troubled me afterward."

"The death of that swine is the least of the things on my conscience. Your move," he said suddenly, to remind her of their suspended game.

A FEW DAYS LATER they came to a town where, because now he had the girl with him, Caspar decided to apply for a military escort through a stretch of country with a particularly bad reputation.

On the outward journey he had avoided being escorted as often as possible, or contrived to have a guard of six soldiers reduced to two. Not that he grudged the expense of paying the men a hundred *cash* a day for their services, but he had found that, given a chance, any number of authorized and un-authorized ragamuffins would attach themselves to the caravan and could become a nuisance. However, it was a treaty agreement that the provision of an escort made local officials responsible for travelers' safety, the soldiers being supplied with a letter stating their number and destination. At the end of their stretch of the journey the traveler gave them a card signifying that their duties had been carried out to his satisfaction, and their letter was stamped by the district magistrate, who supplied the soldiers for the next stage.

On this occasion, some time after he had sent one of the cards that gave his correct style to the *yamen*,

he received a message that because of trouble elsewhere no soldiers could be supplied. It was a turn of
events that perturbed the porters more than it troubled him, and he was annoyed when he found that
gruesome tales of past ambushes had come to Flora's
ears.

"Don't allow their stories to alarm you. It's highly
unlikely that bandits will attack our large train. They
prefer the odds to be in their favor," he told her.

Flora had not been greatly alarmed. All the men's
tales had been hearsay and no doubt greatly embroidered since their first telling.

Nevertheless she was surprised when, after they
had set out the following day, Caspar went hunting
instead of staying with the train. He came back in the
evening empty-handed, saying there seemed to be little or no game in the wild uninhabited region through
which they were passing.

This being so, the next day she expected him to remain with or near the train, but once again he disappeared. She could not help wondering if, being the
only man with firearms and therefore the one most
likely to be harmed if they should be attacked, he
considered it prudent to absent himself.

It was not that she thought him a coward, but she
did think him strongly self-interested. If game were
plentiful he would shoot enough for them all, but if
his bag were small he would not, as the priest would
have done, have it put in the pot so that all might enjoy the flavor of the meat. He would have it cooked
for himself, his appetite unimpaired by the fact that
the coolies had only maize cakes for supper. Probably he reasoned that they were used to a poor diet,
and he was not. But to Flora, her views influenced by

a man of surpassing altruism, Caspar's attitude seemed a selfish one.

She spent much of the morning in conversation with the *fu-tou*, but later in the day she walked by herself. The journey was reviving many half-forgotten recollections of her earlier travels with her father; of nights spent in charcoal burners' huts, warmed by the heat from the charcoal pit; of the wonderful sight, in December, of the tangerine orchards in the Red Basin of Szechwan, and of gorging herself on the fruit that was so plentiful and cheap that for a penny she could have bought fifty or more.

Their travels through the Red Basin led her thoughts to the man who had called it that, the great German explorer Baron Ferdinand von Richthofen, who had come to China shortly before Père d'Espinay and whose atlas of the country was in her book box.

She sighed, wishing it had been possible to crate all the books instead of only a dozen. Then her reverie was interrupted by a sound she had never heard before and did not recognize as the drumming of hooves. Turning her head, she was dismayed to see nine or ten ponies galloping full tilt down the hill, ridden by men whose wild yells and ruffianly appearance caused the coolies to chitter with alarm.

The crags surrounding the pass offered plenty of ambuscades, and within minutes of breaking cover the horsemen had reined in their shaggy, short-legged mounts and were starting to ransack the baggage. All were armed with swords, knives and long guns slung over their backs, and wisely the coolies did not attempt to resist them.

Nor would Flora have interfered, but when one of

the bandits opened her box of books and began to
fling aside the contents in the hope that they might be
concealing something of value, she could not bear to
see her treasured volumes damaged. Without considering the consequences, she darted forward to
retrieve them.

Although on Caspar's instructions she had removed her earrings and her hair was concealed by a
turban, making her look as much like a boy as possible, her movements and small-boned hands must
have betrayed her. Forgetting the box, the bandit
grasped her roughly by the arm and thrust his face
close to hers.

"They've a woman among them," he shouted to
the others.

With a surge of terror she saw in his eyes the same
greedy gleam of excitement with which the Frenchman had looked at her.

Knowing she could not expect any protection from
the porters, she broke free and ran for the rocks.
Escape was impossible. He would ride her down, and
then he would rape her. Possibly they all would. The
thought of their filthy bodies repeating the horrible
torture from which she had not yet recovered made
her run as she had never run before. Had there been a
precipice near she would have flung herself from it
rather than die at their hands, as she knew she would
if all of them wreaked their lust on her.

ALTHOUGH MOST SPORTSMEN would have carried a different rifle, Caspar favored a Krag-Jörgensen, an
American military weapon first issued in 1892. It was
the fastest rifle in the world; with it an expert could
fire more than forty rounds a minute.

As Flora began to run, he was lying in the classic position of the marksman, his left leg thrown out to one side and his right leg roughly in line with his body. He drew in and held his breath as a gentle contraction of his hand sent a steel-cored bullet slicing through one of the bandits and into the body of another standing behind him.

"Ah, capital," Caspar murmured as the two bodies fell.

He quickly turned his attention to the horseman pursuing the girl and fired three more shots in rapid succession. Whether one or all hit their target, he could not tell. That the rider toppled was all that mattered.

The bandits, unused to battle and thinking themselves under fire from a military escort, panicked and scattered. He picked them off one by one, and when all were down he emerged from his place of concealment and strolled down the hill to join the excited porters, who by the time he reached them had spared him the necessity of finishing off the wounded and were busy looting the bodies.

Flora, who had heard the first shots without realizing that she was saved and had stopped running only as the echo of the last shot died away, leaned, panting and trembling, against a rock. Although she knew that but for Caspar's intervention the bandits would have dealt with her equally callously, the sight of their corpses being stripped, kicked and spat on made her shrink from rejoining the train.

She expected Caspar to call the men to order and put them to work digging graves. Instead, after receiving their vociferous plaudits he and the headman set about rounding up the ponies. She knew the *fu-tou* had in his youth been a groom and was not surprised to see him leap astride one of the animals.

But when Caspar followed suit she was amazed; not that he could ride, for she knew it was a commonplace accomplishment among European men of good-birth, but that he could ride without stirrups or a proper saddle. The pony that he had mounted had only a blanket flung over its own bearlike coat. He road up the slope toward her, his long legs dangling almost to the ground.

"Are you all right?" he asked her as he dismounted.

She nodded. "It was lucky for us you were close by. If you had been farther away...." A slight quirk at the corner of his mouth made her pause. "You were not there by chance. You were guarding us. That's why you shot nothing yesterday."

He nodded. "You had nothing to fear. One man with a good modern rifle is more than a match for any number of those ruffians."

"I wish I had known that at the time."

"If you hadn't been so foolish as to draw attention to yourself, you wouldn't have been in any more danger than the others," he told her crushingly. "Come: we've wasted too much time already." Before she knew what he was about, he had lifted her onto the pony and was leading it downhill.

Flora clung to the animal's mane. She would have felt safer sitting astride but dared not change her position while the pony was moving. She knew that women rode sidesaddle and wondered how they managed not to fall off. Presumably their saddles were designed to make them more secure than she felt at that moment.

When they rejoined the train, her first concern was to gather up her scattered books and carefully replace them in the box. Only one had its spine broken.

"Surely you aren't going to *leave* them?" she exclaimed when it dawned on her that Caspar did not intend to bury the bodies.

He glanced at the nearest of the corpses. "Those men were born to be carrion meat. Far be it from me to deny them their destiny, and the carrion their banquet," he answered indifferently.

SEVERAL NIGHTS LATER they stayed in a large, newly built hostel at an altitude of more than seven thousand feet. One side of the building was fitted with bunks and the other with benches on which porters could deposit their loads. The walls were of wood and the roof of shingles, badly laid. The mud floor was damp, with vegetation springing up in the corners and beneath the bunks. Skins of serow and wild cattle served as mattresses on the bunks.

Among the men spending the night there was a mysterious traveler who looked Tibetan but spoke good English. He invited Caspar to play cards with him.

They played a game unknown to Flora, who sat, a silent observer, comparing the Englishman's clean well-shaped hands with the thin yellow fingers and long clawlike nails of the other man. She was aware that from time to time the traveler cast a curious glance at her, but she thought nothing of it until he said to Caspar, "This girl—she is your concubine?"

If Caspar was as startled as Flora, he did not show it but answered calmly, "We're traveling as far as Shanghai together."

"Where you'll sell her, no doubt?"

"Possibly."

"I should like to rent her for the night. You may name your price."

Caspar studied his cards, and for a hideous moment Flora thought he was considering the offer. Then he said, "Unfortunately I shall need her myself tonight."

The other shrugged philosophically. "No matter. There's a woman of pleasure in a town on my way to-morrow, but she doesn't compare with your girl. Strange, how the mingling of races produces these ex-quisite creatures. I've seen it in many countries. When half-breed women are young, they're as luscious as sugared kumquats. Their looks don't last; it doesn't pay to keep them long.. But while they're still young and fresh...."

He reached out to touch her cheek, but Flora re-coiled, her dark eyes sparkling with anger.

"Aha—not as meek as she seems," said the traveler with a laugh. Clearly he had no idea that she had understood his remarks about her. "I notice you've had occasion to beat her. She's not always as docile as she's been tonight, eh? I like a girl with some spirit. Too tame and they quickly pall."

Caspar made no response to this but turned his head to signal to his headman, who not far away was smoking *so-yen*, cord tobacco rolled into a rough cigar and inserted in the bowl of a long-stemmed pipe.

Because his Chinese was not fluent, Caspar had taken to using Flora as his interpreter. But his com-mand of the language was good enough for him to in-struct the man to make his bunk private by nailing some skins to the uprights.

When this had been done, he said to Flora in dialect, "Go to my bed, *ya-t'ou*, but don't sleep yet. I shall not be long."

At first she was tempted to protest, but he gave her a long steady look that after a moment made her say quietly, "Yes, master." Her submissive manner hiding her inner consternation, she rose from her place to obey him.

The screens put up by the headman did not exclude all the light from the interior of the bunk. Having removed her footwear and climbed inside, she sat for some moments wondering what Caspar had in mind. Through a peephole made by a small rent in one of the skins she could see him continuing his game of cards with the other man.

Was it his intention to share the bunk with her only until the other traveler was asleep, and then to move elsewhere? Or did he intend them to spend the whole of the night together? And if they lay side by side in this confined space all night long, might he not be tempted to use her as the other traveler had wanted to? How far could she trust him? Père d'Espinay had liked him and seemed to feel she would be safe with him. But she could not forget that night he had found her weeping by the priest's grave, when the comfort she had sought in his arms had been swiftly dispelled by her realization that, although he might have more control, he felt the same lust for her body as the man who had raped her.

Was it true, as the traveler had suggested, that from a man's point of view she was as tempting a delicacy as a kumquat preserved in sugar? At the thought of how helpless she would have been had Caspar chosen to rent her to the other man, a surge of umbrage rose in her. When she had called him "master" she had spoken ironically, but in fact she had hit on the truth. Because she was weaker than he and without money, family or influence, Caspar Lomax was her master; and she was his slave, dependent on his goodwill for her safety and well-being, and without any means of defense if he chose to abuse his power over her.

In this mood of angry resentment she saw him finish the game, rise from his chair and bid goodnight to his companion. Then he turned and came toward the bunk, and Flora drew back from her peephole and lay down. With a heart that had started to thud she waited for the screen of skins to be pulled aside, and for Caspar to climb in beside her.

CHAPTER FOUR

ALTHOUGH AT LOW ALTITUDES often the nights were too hot for comfort, high up near the mountain passes the temperature dropped to the other extreme. Earlier Flora had put on a quilted jerkin, which she was still wearing when Caspar joined her in the bunk.

He began to unbutton his shirt, saying as he did so, "You won't need that padded garment tonight. We shall have each other to keep us warm." He stripped off his shirt and began to fold it.

He did not smell rank like the Frenchman. He washed himself every morning and again every evening while their meal was being prepared. Sometimes he washed in a stream, sometimes in a bucket and whenever possible in his hip bath. She had heard one of the coolies remark that Caspar was rare among "foreign devils" in not having the vile smell peculiar to the "big noses." But that, she knew from Père d'Espinay, was not only because of his cleanliness. According to the priest, the reason the Chinese disliked the odor of Europeans, and Europeans complained of unpleasant smells in Africa and the Orient, was as much a matter of diet as of hygiene.

She took off the jerkin, but she did not remove her cotton tunic, merely loosening the collar by unlooping several of the buttons of knotted cord.

Caspar seemed to sense her nervousness. "You needn't be afraid. I shan't touch you. Good night, Flora."

He lay down with his broad brown back to her and seemed to fall asleep almost immediately.

But during the night he did touch her, although he was not at first aware of it.

She had woken up in the small hours and was kept awake by the rumbling snores coming from one of the other bunks. Suddenly Caspar turned over and folded himself around her, his thighs under hers, his chest warm against her shoulder blades. He resettled himself without rousing, one arm sliding around her and coming to rest with his hand on her breast. She was certain he was not awake; she could tell by his breathing. She lay very still, kept awake now not by the snores but by the disturbingly close contact with the alien-feeling masculine body behind her, and by the pressure of his hand. It seemed to burn through her tunic, inducing the same sensations she remembered from many weeks earlier when something the priest had said to her had made her imagine how it would feel if Caspar touched her like this.

Since then her experience of the things that men did to women had convinced her that, although others might be able to submit without disgust to the actions the priest and Caspar had assured her were not always loathsome, she herself would never be able to feel a man's hands upon her without shrinking with revulsion.

Yet now, although she had felt nervous earlier, she could not pretend that his closeness was disagreeable, or that her heart was beating faster from fear. Her absorption in her reactions was interrupted by two or three violent snorts from the man who was snoring, causing exclamations of complaint from other bunks and waking up Caspar.

Flora felt him tense for a moment and then relax. She held her breath, wondering if he could feel her quickened heartbeat or if he was only half-awake and would relapse into unconsciousness without being aware of her body pressed close to his. Then his hand began gently to fondle her, and at the same time she felt the involuntary movement that had frightened her when he held her in his arms on the night of Père d'Espinay's burial.

This time it was not she who pulled away but Caspar. With a sudden violent movement he rolled onto his other side, turning his back to her and leaving a space between them as he had when first he came to bed.

Although the snoring had stopped, it was a long time before she slept, and she sensed that he, too, was awake. Whether he knew she had felt him starting to caress her, she could not tell. Certainly the force of his turning away would have roused her had she been sleeping.

If he wanted to make use of her in the same way as the man who had offered him money for her, why didn't he, she wondered. He was a man who would kill without compunction. Why did he scruple to take her? It was not as if she were a virgin protected among decent men by her own innocence, she thought bleakly.

WHEN SHE AWOKE THE NEXT MORNING Caspar was already up, and when she joined him for breakfast it was impossible to tell if he had any recollection of what had occurred during the night. His manner toward her was unchanged.

As the days passed and her physical injuries mended, Flora was able to spend more and more time plant hunting, and this had the effect of healing the spiritual scars left by her ordeal. With each day's journey her years at the mission came to seem merely an interlude in the life begun with her father and resumed with Caspar. The mission had been a backwater. Now once again she was out in the mainstream, too active during the day, and too healthily tired at the end of it, to have any time for introspection.

One more serious mishap occurred, the first she knew of it being a human howl of agony.

They were crossing some difficult high country, a region of dense rhododendron and bamboo thickets, and the home of the wild cattle known since the time of Marco Polo, who had called them Beyamini. The Chinese knew them as *yeh niu*, and Caspar, who hoped to shoot one, referred to the creatures as takin, having learned of them from the writings of l'Abbé David, the French missionary and naturalist.

Flora ran in the direction from which the cry had seemed to come and arrived at the scene of the accident a few moments after Caspar. One of the coolies employed by him as a collector had accidentally released the trip rope of a deadfall trap set by local hunters. An eight-inch iron spearhead, intended to wound a takin, had pierced the thick of his thigh.

Before long the *fu-tou* and other coolies arrived, some of them breaking into sniggers that anyone unfamiliar with the Chinese would have thought callous. Flora knew they were not really amused by their comrade's injury; it was a misleading nervous reaction. Caspar was too busy dealing with the situation to notice their smiles and giggles.

Since the spearhead had a large barb, it was necessary to cut off the shaft at the point of entry and pull the head out from the other side. Fortunately it had missed the man's bones and arteries, but it had inflicted an ugly wound with considerable loss of blood.

"He won't walk on that leg for some time. He'll have to ride in the chair," said Caspar when, with Flora's assistance, he had given first aid. "You did well, *ya-t'ou*. I'm glad to find you don't lose your head in an emergency. Most women wring their hands and go to pieces."

His praise made her glow. "Do they? That isn't much help. I'm used to such things. The villagers often came to us when they hurt themselves."

Caspar examined with interest the construction of the trap. It consisted of a log poised between the forks of the branches of two trees. A bamboo rope connected the beam to a trip rope concealed in the brush of a roughly trampled-out run made by cattle and probably connecting a grazing ground with a salt lick. The vicious spearhead and its shaft had been attached to one end of the beam at such an angle that a takin would have been struck behind the shoulder had it sprung the trap.

A week or two after this incident, by which time they had left the injured man in a village to recover his strength, they came to a place where Flora knew it would not be easy to live up to Caspar's belief that she never lost her head. In the intervening years she had almost forgotten her fear of bamboo suspension bridges.

The bridge at which they had arrived was near a small walled city on the plain of Chengtu. It was fully eighty yards long and supported by cables made of plaited bamboo culms. Eight cables held the wicker-work footway, and two more cables, slung across at a higher level, supported the side ropes and handrails. Being very heavy, the bridge sagged in the middle and would, Flora knew, be extremely unsteady to cross. Once, long ago, she had seen a man in a hurry attempt to cross such a bridge while a high wind was blowing. He had been thrown against the side ropes, which had given way and pitched him screaming into the torrent below. Although the day was not windy, and the bridge hung still while no one was on it, she felt sick with apprehension as she followed Caspar onto the swaying footway.

She thought she had hidden her fear, but that night while playing chess he said, "Why didn't you tell me you were afraid of suspension bridges?"

She lifted her gaze from the board, wondering how she had given herself away. "I'm not proud of being a coward."

He smiled at her. Usually when he smiled his eyes held a gleam of mockery, but this time it seemed to her that his expression held something of the affectionate amusement with which the priest had often regarded her.

"Far from being cowardly, *ya-t'ou*, you are amazingly intrepid."

"What are girls like in England?" she suddenly asked him, warmed by his praise.

He shrugged. "I have no idea. Very few come my way, and those who do are usually tongue-tied. But the women I meet are too much concerned with their comfort and their appearance to undertake expeditions such as this."

"But there have been some women travelers. I remember Père d'Espinay telling me about the niece of a prime minister of England who kept house for him for a time and then went to live among the Arabs. I can't remember her name, but her father was a scientist."

"That was Lady Hester Stanhope. An exceptional woman, and one I should like to have known."

What Flora would like to have known was something more about him, this man who was now her whole world. But he was adept at parrying even the most oblique inquiries about himself. After traveling with him for weeks she knew no more about his home or his family than she had done when they set out. He was not employed by the Royal Horticultural Society or by a commercial organization, because that she had asked him point-blank. But who else might be financing his explorations, or if he had some private means, she had no idea.

Though he told her nothing about himself, she learned much of interest from him.

"The real affinity of Chinese flora—which is the richest temperate flora in the world—isn't with Europe but with the Atlantic side of America," he told her one day when they were walking together.

"How can that be?"

"It's because of the glaciation of the northern hemisphere in prehistoric times. Then the land connection between Asia and North America was more complete, and plant life went farther north. Gradually the ice cap forced it back toward the equator. When the great cold was over, the ice cap receded again and the plants crept back. But not as far as before, and a lot of the land that had previously been covered by forests was too cold to support vegetation. It's this rearrangement after the Ice Age that, with various other factors, explains why similar flora have become widely separated.''

Carlyon broke off and glanced down at her, half expecting to see the glazed expression that came into most women's eyes when he talked on the subject he found fascinating and they boring. But clearly Flora was not bored. He had all her attention—too much of it. As he glanced at her, she tripped on an exposed root and would have fallen had he not caught her by the arm.

''I'm sorry. I wasn't looking where I was going. Which are the plants that prove your theory?''

''Not my theory. It was first demonstrated by Dr. Asa Gray, the American botanist. For instance, the magnolia isn't native to Europe and western North America, but the eastern side of the country has seven species compared with the nineteen species found here and in Japan. Other examples are the tulip tree, the Kentucky coffee tree, the sassafras and the lotus lily.''

''Have you been to America?''

''Yes, to see the herbarium at Harvard among other things. They have two hundred thousand plants there. I hope to see more of America one of these days, but there isn't time in one lifespan to see more than a fraction of the interesting places in the world.''

''I should like to see Florence and Paris. Have you been there?''

''To Paris, often. Never to Florence,'' he answered.

Sometimes it was she who was able to enlighten

him by speaking to coolies going in a different direction. The most common loads they encountered were lye, shingles and oil cake, but sometimes the men carried bales of crab-apple leaves, or came from the far west of Szechwan and were laden with deer horns.

"When the horns are in velvet the Chinese believe them to be a valuable medicine. You can buy *lu-jung* at every medicine shop, but it's very expensive," Flora explained.

Carlyon had heard of deer horns before and knew they were considered a powerful aphrodisiac. He thought it unlikely that she was aware of this property, if indeed she knew the meaning of the word. For in spite of her surprising sophisticated European-style education, her quick mind and her unusual upbringing, he was actually aware that in many respects she was still an innocent and lacking in experience of the world.

His own medicine chest was equipped to deal with accidents rather than ailments, but included Epsom salts, permanganate of potash and iodoform dressings for treating coolies with stomach disorders or sores, and a plentiful supply of quinine. This, as he had discovered, was one of the few foreign medicines in which the Chinese had confidence. At one night's lodging a man had been down with a fever, and after Carlyon had dosed him with quinine and supplied him with enough to last several days, the word had spread and he had been besieged by requests for it.

One night they slept in a temple. No priests lived there. The place was in the charge of a novice who had lived by himself for three years, without even a dog for companionship, in return for a daily ration of one and a half *catties* of rice, and an annual salary

of two thousand *cash*, which Carlyon calculated to
be the equivalent of half a crown.

In spite of his isolated existence, the novice was
cheerful and helpful and quickly made a fire for
Caspar and Flora to dry their wet clothing. It had
been raining since dawn, and foreseeing that they
would arrive drenched, Carlyon had brought a ruck-
sack containing, wrapped in oilcloth, a change of
clothes for himself and for the girl.

When they set out on the ponies she had insisted on
carrying it, saying that he would lose face if he did
so. Flora had become so vehement and distressed
that finally he had allowed her to bear the light
burden until they were well ahead of the baggage
train.

"There's no point in changing your clothes while
your hair is dripping," he said now, and taking a dry
towel from the pack he threw it over her head and
began to rub with painful vigor.

By the time they had changed and were exploring
the many rooms in the temple, her resentment had
evaporated. While they waited for the porters to arrive, the novice offered them tea, and he and Flora
chatted. From time to time she would translate his
remarks for the Englishman.

Carlyon smoked a cheroot and drank the tea laced
with whiskey from his silver hip flask. It amused him
to listen to the contrast between the loud singsong intonation of Flora's conversation in dialect and her
quiet perfect English.

Flora slept in a large lofty chamber where three
huge images of the Buddha gazed benignly down on
her. Caspar was in the adjoining hall; when she
passed through it next morning, he was sharpening

his razor on a leather strap preparatory to shaving.

They had breakfast out of doors in the sun. Sighing with contentment, Flora said, "Isn't it strange? The Chinese hate journeys. They call traveling 'eating bitterness.' If I were a man, I should travel constantly. I can't think of anything better than setting out in the morning and not knowing whom one will meet, or what lies over the mountain, or where one may spend the night."

"You must have Gypsy blood in you," Caspar suggested.

"I don't think so. My father told me his father was a gamekeeper on a large estate in Hampshire, and his mother was a cook." She realized that he had been teasing her and flushed, regretting her slow-wittedness.

At the next market town they passed through Flora would have liked to buy pins and try dressing her hair in a different, less youthful way, but she had no money and could not bring herself to ask for some when already she was indebted to Caspar for her food and her lodgings.

All too soon, from her point of view, their overland journey came to an end when they reached the banks of the Ta Kiang or Great River, known to foreigners as the Yangtze. Carlyon wanted to see again the five famous gorges between Kuichou Fu and Ichang, where the river narrowed to a third of its usual width and flowed between towering cliffs of prehistoric limestone sometimes two thousand feet high.

They made the first stage of the river journey in a long, turret-built Chinese houseboat with covered quarters at one end and an open deck, which could be

shaded by an awning of *kaoliang* straw matting, at
the other. In the gorges no awning was necessary,
and Flora spent hours at a stretch sitting cross-legged
on deck, gazing with rapt dark eyes at the glens and
waterfalls where the main river was joined by smaller
streams.

The most commanding peaks and crags usually
were crowned by Taoist temples, often with winter-
green, cypress, ginkgo and pine trees planted around
them. Their apparent inaccessibility made her
wonder how the materials to build them had been
transported to such sites, but often, with some such
inquiry or comment on the tip of her tongue, she
would keep silent for fear of making Caspar weary of
her company.

Sometimes he would volunteer information, as
when he said that in more than one place the river in
the gorges was more than sixty fathoms deep.

"And one fathom is the equivalent of six feet, so
try not to fall overboard, *ya-t'ou*."

"How do you know it's as deep as that?"

"Because a few years ago two British gunboats
took soundings on their way up to Chungking. Eventually, I expect, the whole of the Upper Yangtze will
be opened to steam navigation, but meanwhile not
many foreigners venture west of Ichang."

"How far is Ichang from Shanghai?"

"A thousand miles."

Flora relapsed into silence. To travel a thousand
miles by river would not take as long as five hundred
miles overland. Her time with him was running out,
and when they reached Shanghai—then what?

Deliberately she closed her mind to the uncertainty
of the future, determined to concentrate on the felici-

ty of the present. She had known for some days that
the reason she had been so unhappy the first time he
left the mission was that she had fallen in love with
him. What had happened to her after that had made
her distrustful of all men, including him, and even
now she was conscious of knowing very little about
him. But she felt she knew all that mattered, and
since the night at the hostel high in the mountains,
when for a few moments he had put his arm around
her and held her, she had been convinced that only
with him, and with no other man, could she ever submit to the extraordinary act by which children were
brought into being, and which men enjoyed. Whether women could also enjoy it she could only wait to
find out. How could either Père d'Espinay or Caspar
know what a woman really felt when she lay on her
back while a man had his way with her?

Next time perhaps the pain would not be as agonizing, and each time thereafter more endurable. But
how could it ever be enjoyable, except in the sense of
giving pleasure to the man one loved and wished to
please?

From Ichang to Hankow, four hundred miles down
the river, they traveled on a shallow-draft steamer in
the company of a Protestant missionary and his wife.
At first Mrs. Hunter was coldly civil to Caspar and
behaved as if Flora were invisible. But when he explained the circumstances of their being together, the
woman's frigidity thawed. Before they reached
Hankow she offered to take Flora to a tailor to have
some more suitable clothes made.

Flora disliked Mrs. Hunter, who struck her as a
narrow-minded bore, and the clothes that the

Englishwoman ordered, which were made up that day, were uncomfortable and unbecoming. The most absurd item in her new outfit was a wide-brimmed straw terai hat with a puggaree, which according to Mrs. Hunter must be worn at all times to protect the complexion and to avoid sunstroke.

To Flora's relief, the Hunters were staying at Hankow and not continuing downriver in the larger and more luxuriously fitted steamer that plied between Hankow and Shanghai.

When Caspar saw her in one of the white cambric dresses, with white canvas shoes and white stockings, her hair unplaited and secured by a bow of white silk at the nape of her neck, his first comment was, "Good God!"

"I don't look right in European clothes, do I?" she said unhappily.

"No one would look right in those clothes," he remarked dryly. "White isn't your color, and they don't fit you properly. Never mind: at least they show off a very neat pair of ankles." The dresses were of the length worn by girls who were still in the schoolroom.

Flora was not much comforted by this compliment. As it happened, she was the only woman traveling in the first-class section, and she and Caspar had little intercourse with their fellow passengers. But she could not fail to be aware of the curious glances that were directed at them, and of something indefinably unpleasant in the smiles of some of the men as she passed them on her way about the ship.

Her cabin was next to Caspar's. On the second night of the final phase of their journey, she put on a robe of thin red silk, which her father had kept for her after the death of her mother, and let loose her long black hair. Then she tapped on the door of his cabin.

"Come in."

Still fully dressed, Caspar was seated at the writing table with his back to her. As she entered, he turned around to see who had disturbed him.

"Oh, it's you, Flora. Anything wrong?"

"No, I—I wanted to talk to you. But if you're busy...."

"My letter isn't an urgent one. Sit down." He indicated the armchair. "What's on your mind?" Before she could answer, he added, "Now that color does become you, but I suppose you're too young to wear red in public, and it isn't fashionable at present, or wasn't when I left England."

She sat on the extreme edge of the chair and locked her hands tightly together to still their trembling.

"I—I've come to offer myself as . . . as your concubine," she stammered.

His gray eyes narrowed. "What makes you think I require a concubine?"

"I thought all men did, unless they were priests or were married." This was a possibility that had not occurred to her before. "You are not married, are you?"

He shook his head, looking at her with an enigmatic expression that she could not interpret.

Unable to bear the prolonged pause, she said, "It's the least I can do after you've been good enough to bring me all this way, and to pay for new clothes and for a first-class cabin for me. I'm afraid I've been a great deal of nuisance and expense to you."

He said in an oddly clipped tone, "But you are willing to repay me with the use of your body?"

"Yes."

"Do you think Père d'Espinay would approve of your suggestion?"

"I don't know."

"Don't lie, Flora," he said coldly. "You know very well that he would have disapproved most strongly."

She flushed and lifted her chin. "What he would have thought is not important now. He's dead, and he died without knowing what had happened to me. I must do as *I* think fit in future, and you have been very kind to me. I—I want to repay you in the only way I can."

"Unfortunately it's one of my idiosyncrasies that I've never been able to enjoy making love to a woman whose willingness depended on payment—or misguided gratitude. There is no reason for you to feel yourself in any way indebted to me. Your company hasn't been tedious. Such small extra expenses as your presence has incurred are well within my pocket."

He paused before adding caustically, "Keep your body for the man you love—when you have learned how to please him. At the moment, in spite of your unfortunate experience, you're almost as ignorant as most girls of your age. With luck your husband will teach you the art of making love, and then you'll be very glad I didn't accept your offer. Meanwhile go to bed, and we'll both forget you ever made it."

Their cabins were on deck, and late in the night, when no one else was about, Flora flitted from her door to the rails and stood in the shadow of a stanchion, watching the wide moonlit river and the unfamiliar flatness of the countryside beyond its banks.

She was not sure whether to be glad or sorry that Caspar had rejected her offer. In a way she was glad, because it accorded with her desire to see him as a man of honor, not only as courageous but as good as the Seigneur de Bayard, the *chevalier sans peur et sans reproche* who had long been among her heroes.

At the same time she could not help feeling a pang of regret that he would not teach her the art of which he had spoken. She would never again feel his arms around her, never discover what it would be like to be kissed with that wide well-cut mouth that could set in such a grim line when something displeased him, but which more often than not had a twitch of sardonic amusement lurking at its corners.

ALTHOUGH OF SMALL RANK as a Chinese town, Shanghai, one of the five ports opened to foreign trade by the treaty of Nanking, was the most important center of foreign commerce in China and the great emporium of the trade of the whole Yangtze basin.

The city stood on the left bank of the Hwang Pu, twelve miles upstream from the junction with the Yangtze at Wusung and forty-two miles from the lightship marking the entrance to the river, which, like the mouths of most great rivers in the East, consisted of flat banks of alluvium used by the Chinese as rice fields. Near Wusung, a bar across the river formed an impediment to navigation, making it necessary for ships of heavy draft to lighten before continuing to Shanghai; but otherwise the river was well lighted and buoyed, and there was an efficient pilot service.

When Carlyon had arrived at Shanghai, his first sight of the city had been as the ship turned a bend in the river and brought into view first the long line of wharves and warehouses in front of the Hongkew, the American settlement, and then the splendid offices and houses of the French and English settlements that lay behind the tree-lined Bund, the city's famous riverside promenade. Beyond this was another line of warehouses and then a huge fleet of junks lying off the native city.

One vista had merged with another without any break for several miles, combining to give him a strong impression of the wealth and commercial importance of the port. In addition, moored through the length of the river reaches in front of the foreign settlements lay a fleet of steamers and ships supported by men-of-war of different nationalities.

Caspar had viewed this scene by the side of a pretty Frenchwoman, Madame Colbert, who had joined the ship at Brindisi after traveling overland from Paris, where she had been visiting her parents. Her husband, many years her senior, was an important member of the French legation at Shanghai. Before the ship had reached Aden, Caspar had induced her to embark on a discreet shipboard liaison with him, and although he would have ended the connection when they disembarked, she had pressed him to continue to visit her until his departure for Ichang several weeks later.

He had found that the foreign settlements were entirely separate from the native city in boundaries, government and commerce; the English and Americans being under one municipality, and the French making their own laws. Well supplied with introductions, he had soon been caught up in a lively social whirl, although he had preferred to stay at the hotel in the English settlement rather than to accept the many offers of hospitality that had been pressed on him.

Shanghai, he had discovered, offered plenty of outdoor sports including, according to the season, racing, cross-country riding, yachting, racquets, cricket and lawn tennis. The club in the English settlement compared not unfavorably with similar institutions in London, and there was also a country club that had a theater, a ballroom and extensive grounds, with the advantage of including ladies as members.

Before long Madame Colbert had been supplanted by the bored wife of a British consular official in whose shuttered bedroom he had spent many pleasurable afternoons.

Caspar had decided against taking Flora to the English hotel—they might not welcome her, but they would not refuse to accept anyone under his aegis—because it was bound to cause gossip and she would not feel at ease there. He had felt it would not be difficult to rent some private accommodation where they would attract less attention, and so it proved. Within a short time of their landing they were installed in a house in the French quarter whose owners were on leave in Europe.

His next concern was to slake his desire for a woman, and being in a mood to find a petite olive-skinned body or opulent curves of white flesh equally satisfying, he made the choice by tossing a coin.

"Caspar—when did you get back?" exclaimed Netta Beaumont when he strolled into her boudoir.

She had been lying on the chaise longue, reading a novel, when her number-one boy announced him.

Fortunately she was wearing a new and very becoming tea gown.

"A few hours ago," he drawled slowly.

No sooner had the servant closed the door than Caspar took her in his arms and pressed a long hungry kiss on her willing mouth.

"I've been looking forward to this all the way from Ichang," he murmured some moments later, picking her up and carrying her into the bedroom.

As she lay naked on the bed and watched him strip off his clothes—as expert with feminine fastenings as any lady's maid, he had taken no time at all to divest her of hers—Netta felt slightly indignant at being undressed with such celerity and not even a short pretense of making conversation. But although he did not disguise the principal reason for his visit, and in spite of his long deprivation, Caspar still took the trouble to ensure that she was as ready for him as he was for her, which was more than her husband ever did. And afterward he did not sag heavily on top of her, sweating and panting like Jack, but lay with his weight on his elbows, gently kissing her neck and shoulders.

"How long will you be here?" she murmured presently.

"Until the next P. & O. sailing."

Later, while they rested and drank a bottle of champagne, she made perfunctory inquiries about his expedition.

Carlyon knew she was not greatly interested and gave the subject short shrift before asking, "And what's been happening in Shanghai during my absence?"

She cast her mind back over the months since she

had seen him and said with a giggle, "Sir George Frost died of a heart attack brought on by overexcitement in Madam Lermontov's establishment."

"The deuce he did! How do you know?" Caspar asked, grinning.

"I was told by someone who was present. They were watching one of the *tableaux vivants* with which Madam Lermontov stimulates her customers' appetites, and Sir George went purple in the face and fell to the floor. Of course it was all hushed up. Did you never go there?"

Caspar shook his head. He had never found it necessary to patronize brothels, although he had heard of the one to which Netta referred. It was run by a woman of Russian extraction who catered not only to normal tastes but, so he had heard, to every form of perversion.

Before he left her he brought Netta twice to a shuddering summit of enjoyment and then, his own vigor restored, mounted her soft white body and rode her with renewed passion.

He left her exhausted with pleasure, and with his lust quenched for the time being. As a rickshaw took him back to the French quarter he marveled at the number of husbands who, through their own fault, made their wives easy prey for a man like himself. Were it not for *noblesse oblige*, he would have neither reason nor wish to encumber himself with a wife.

Jack Beaumont, whom he had met and categorized as a blustering bore, was only about ten years older than Netta, but obviously he subscribed to the old-fashioned idea that the women men married were too pure to enjoy sexual relations, and that only with women of the other kind could a man give rein to his more libidinous impulses.

It was more than likely, thought Caspar sardonically, that Beaumont was one of the patrons of Madam Lermontov's house. No doubt he little dreamed that his seemingly frigid wife could, if he took more trouble with her, supply all the services provided by the Russian woman's girls, with the additional fillip that while their enjoyment was simulated, Netta's gasps and purrs were the spontaneous response of an intensely sensual nature.

But by this reflection Caspar did himself an injustice. For the same moment Netta was thinking that even if Jack knew how to make love, there could never be the same pleasure in lying beneath his flaccid body, which was as white as her own, that she felt when she opened her thighs to accommodate Caspar's lean hips and clung to his powerful brown shoulders.

He was not her first lover, but he was by far the most accomplished in bed of the several men with whom she had found some relief from the boredom and dissatisfaction of her marital relationship. The thought passed through her mind that if Caspar should offer to take her to England with him as his mistress and to set her up in a house in St. John's Wood, notorious for its love nests, she would be very much tempted to cast off her respectability. But sooner or later he would tire of her, and there was no guarantee she could find another, equally attractive protector.

She sighed, envying men their freedom to have the best of both worlds—society and the demimonde. A woman, unless she was mistress to royalty, had to choose to be good or bad; and such discreet love affairs as were open to her always were overshadowed by the risk of being found out, the dread of scandal.

THAT EVENING for the first time Flora saw Caspar dressed—as he dressed for dinner every night in England—in a white tie and a white waistcoat. During the afternoon one of the servants had brushed and pressed the perfectly tailored black tailcoat and trousers and laundered the immaculate dress shirt that made his deeply tanned face seem even darker by comparison.

Flora, unaware that Englishmen were admired the world over for the ineffable distinction with which they wore the colorful uniforms of their regiments, or the stark black-and-white formality of evening dress, thought Caspar looked even more dashing than he had in the blue velvet smoking coat.

"I'm going to dine at the club," he told her. "Don't wait up for me. I shan't come back before midnight."

She watched him bowl away in a rickshaw, wishing she could accompany him, beautifully dressed, with her hair piled high on her head and her ears and neck sparkling with jewels like the ladies from the neighboring houses whom she saw as they passed, some in rickshaws and some in carriages.

It was clear that the foreign community in Shanghai enjoyed a very gay nightlife, and she could not help feeling a little forlorn at being left to a solitary supper and an early night. At least she had plenty to read, for the house was full of books and periodicals, and the fact that all were in French presented no difficulty.

One of Carlyon's objects in going to the club was the hope of finding there a man from whom he wanted advice. As luck would have it, almost the first person he saw was Lord Richard Creed, youngest son of the Duke of Tasburgh.

The two men had been at Eton together. According to rumor, several years earlier Lord Richard had blotted his copybook in a way that had caused his noble parent to order him not to set foot in England again. After spending some time in India he had come to Shanghai, where his birth, looks and charming manners made him acceptable to hostesses who in England would not have received him.

Caspar had never made a close friend of him, and the rumor of Lord Richard's offense had caused him to raise his dark eyebrows in scornful astonishment. But although cheating at cards was disgraceful, he did not regard it as one of human nature's blackest crimes and saw no reason to cut him.

While they were having a drink together he asked casually, "Is there a doctor in Shanghai on whose discretion one may rely?"

The other man pricked up his ears, wondering what lay behind the inquiry. "That depends on the nature of the complaint."

"Syphilis," Caspar said succinctly.

"In that case you need Dr. Brewer. He's Madam Lermontov's consultant on matters venereal. You've been to her place, I presume?"

Caspar shook his head. "But I've heard of it. It's the house where the entertainment proved too much for Sir George Frost, I hear."

Lord Richard gave a guffaw. "So they say. I wasn't there on that occasion, but I believe it.

Madam is amazingly...inventive. Her *tableaux vivants* are designed to revive the most jaded palates. Even you might learn something, my friend.''

"My taste inclines to the conventional," Caspar said dryly. "Where is this Dr. Brewer to be found?"

"In the Chinese quarter. They say he used to have a practice in Harley Street but was struck off the medical register. I don't know whether it's true, but I do know that he's a good man in the field we're discussing. If your mistress needs an operation, Brewer's your man—at a price! If you think you've contracted a disease, he can cure you if anyone can. I'll jot down his address."

The next day Carlyon told Flora that he was taking her to see the Chinese part of the city. Before they set out in two rickshaws, he said, "You remember I told you you need not fear becoming pregnant as a result of what happened to you at the mission? I neglected to mention, however, another possible hazard."

"Another?" she echoed, mystified and alarmed.

He said, "There are certain diseases that are transmitted during sexual relations. I doubt if you have contracted one, but it's as well to make sure. We're going to see a doctor who specializes in these matters. He will want to examine you intimately, and however much you may dislike it, I hope you'll make no objection. It's in your own interest, Flora. To neglect an infection of that nature is to invite a great deal of suffering in later life. Be a sensible girl and put up with whatever is necessary. It's more than likely he'll give you a clean bill of health."

At the doctor's house, in the native quarter, Flora found herself left in a waiting room while Caspar talked to the doctor. She began to shiver with apprehension, and her nervousness was not unjustified. The tests the doctor performed on her were only slightly less objectionable than the circumstances that had made them necessary. She did not like Dr. Brewer and detested submitting to his examination and answering his questions as to whether she had noticed certain symptoms during the weeks since her rape.

At last, to her relief, he allowed her to dress and dismissed her. Again she was left in suspense in the waiting room while he told the results of his findings to Caspar.

"The girl is clean, sir," the doctor reported. "If her answers to my questions were truthful, there is no possibility that she was contaminated by the man who attacked her. There is no sign of the usual symptoms for either syphilis or gonorrhea. She's a strong and healthy young creature with whom you may take your pleasure without any risk to your own health."

"Thank you. That is not my purpose. I wished merely to ensure her well-being," Caspar said in a cold tone. Like Flora, he did not take to Dr. Brewer.

He would have liked him even less had he been privy to a conversation between the doctor and Madam Lermontov later that day.

"I had on my couch this morning a girl who could solve your problem with Count Leczinska," said Brewer, referring to one of the Russian woman's best customers, who of late had taken to complaining that she failed to supply sufficient variety.

"What girl?" she inquired with a sharp glance.

"She was brought to me by an Englishman who told me she had been raped and might have the clap. She is a Eurasian of quite exceptional beauty. Her

skin is like velvet, her figure perfection," said the
doctor. "Moreover, although not technically a
virgin, she is one for all practical purposes. Count
Leczinska would find her exquisite."

"Who was the Englishman who brought her?"

"Not a resident of Shanghai. Her name is Jackson.
He gave his surname as Lomax, but I felt it might not
be his real name. He struck me as being a man of
considerable importance. I was sufficiently curious
to send a servant to follow him. He's renting the
house of a Frenchman. According to the servants
there, it was not a lie when he disclaimed any personal interest in the girl's health. They occupy
separate rooms—although whether they will continue
to do so now that he knows she is free of disease is a
matter for conjecture."

"She is beautiful, you say?" said madam thoughtfully.

"Not only beautiful but educated. But for her
Chinese coloring and the clothes she was wearing, I
should have taken her for an English gentlewoman.
Suitably dressed, she would be ravishing—a connoisseur's piece. She is worth some inquiries, Natalia."

"Certainly. I will have her investigated," agreed
Madam Lermontov.

A year or two earlier, in 1901, the population of
Shanghai had been estimated to exceed six hundred
thousand people, of whom rather more than half
lived in the International Settlement, although less
than seven thousand were foreigners and fewer still
persons of importance. The activities of the elite, and
of the same upper strata in the French concession,
were as well known to the Russian procuress as if she
moved in those circles. The men—not all, but many

of them—formed her clientele. The women she knew by report because it amused her to spy on them and to know those who were unfaithful, those who drank and those addicted to laudanum. Now and then she indulged in blackmail, not because she needed the money but because it pleased her to inflict mental torture as much as it pleased some of her clients to inflict or submit to physical pain.

Thus she knew without further inquiry that the man who had visited the doctor was entitled to use the name Lomax, but that it was not his correct style. She knew, too, that on his previous visit to Shanghai he had cuckolded at least three husbands, two of them his compatriots and the third a Frenchman. How he had come by the Eurasian girl, and what he intended to do with her, would not be difficult to discover. Most servants were willing to gossip about their employers, and those who were more discreet could be bribed to reveal whatever information was wanted.

ON THEIR RETURN from the native city, Carlyon had luncheon at the house with Flora. She was still upset by the examination in the doctor's consulting room, and he was preoccupied with the problem of what was to be done with her. The meal passed with little conversation.

At one time he had thought it possible to find a suitable niche for her in Shanghai, but since their arrival he had realized this was out of the question. He was beginning to think the only solution was to take her with him to England, where there might be a place for her at Kew, or possibly on the clerical staff of the Royal Horticultural Society. It was what the priest had wanted for her. At any rate, her future was not clouded by the possibility that she was tainted with the disease that, while no longer the sentence to a slow death that it had been in his father's day, still was not always curable. That her young life could have been ruined revived some of the murderous rage he had felt on the night of his return to the mission.

Flora, glancing across the table, saw in the narrowed gray eyes fixed upon her a basilisk glitter that made her draw in her breath.

"What is it? Why are you looking at me like that?"

The glitter faded, and he smiled at her, exerting the charm she had felt the first time they had shaken hands.

"My mind was miles away," he said lightly.

But later, pondering that icy scrutiny, she had an uneasy feeling that he would never forget having seen her sprawled on the bed, naked, her thighs apart, like a girl in a whorehouse. Either that, or he had been inwardly cursing the nuisance of being responsible for her.

They were having coffee in the garden at the rear of the house when one of the servants brought a card on a salver. Flora saw Caspar flick a glance at her and deduced, correctly, that he was considering sending her away before the caller was admitted. However, after a slight hesitation he signed to the servant to bring the visitor to them.

A few moments later they were joined by a slim, debonair, fair-haired man with a curly mustache, who began, "I was wondering if you'd care—" and stopped short at the sight of Flora.

Caspar said, "Allow me to present Richard Creed.

Miss Jackson is the daughter of a botanist who had the misfortune to lose his life in the part of the country that I've been exploring.''

Lord Richard was nothing if not quick-witted. It was one of Carlyon's several eccentricities that at times he chose to travel incognito, and the form of his introduction at once made it clear to his former schoolfellow that the beautiful dark-eyed girl in the dowdy white dress was unaware of the taller man's true identity.

''How do you do, Miss Jackson. I called to inquire if Caspar wished to ride with me this afternoon. But I thought him alone in Shanghai and possibly bored with his own company. I had no idea he had such a charming companion.''

''How do you do, Mr. Creed.'' As she gave him her hand she added, ''Will you have coffee with us, or would you prefer a whiskey and soda?''

Her soft but clear voice, lacking any trace of Chinese accent and sounding very much like that of his youngest sister, surprised him. His acquaintance with Chinese women was limited to those of easy virtue, who tended to simper and giggle. There was nothing like that about this girl. Indeed as he looked at her more closely he saw that although she had the flawless skin of a Chinese beauty, black hair and Oriental-dark eyes, her nose and mouth were shaped from the most exquisite European mold, and her chin, rather firm for a woman, had the hint of a cleft.

''I'll join you in coffee if I may,'' he said, both impressed and intrigued.

She made a signal to the servant still hovering in the background, then turned to Caspar and said quietly, ''I've taken up too much of your time already today. Please don't hesitate to accept Mr. Creed's suggestion on my account. I shall be perfectly happy sitting here with my book.''

"What are you reading, Miss Jackson?" Richard inquired.

"The people to whom this house belongs have fourteen volumes of Madame de Sévigné's letters edited by Monmerqué. I've reached volume five, and I'm hoping there will be time to read them all. They're very entertaining.''

Caspar said, "I'll go and change into riding kit," and he left them together, deriving a good deal of amusement from Richard's ill-concealed surprise at Flora's cultured manners and bluestocking taste in literature.

However, he was not amused when later that afternoon, after he had given Richard a censored version of how she had come under his aegis, the other man said, "I know who would be happy to engage her.''

"Oh, really? Who?" inquired Caspar.

"Madam Lermontov. A girl like that could become her star turn.''

"By Jove, you're an unscrupulous blackguard. Would you have an innocent girl consigned to a brothel?'' he said curtly.

"Innocent, Carlyon? After two months in your company? That I find *very* hard to believe,'' Richard replied, grinning. "You're not famous for scruples yourself when it comes to bedding pretty women. You pulled off a hat trick, I hear, the last time you were in Shanghai.''

Caspar ignored this sally. He did not boast of his conquests, nor did he tell bawdy jokes or gloat over erotic books like many men of his acquaintance. If a woman seemed willing, he pursued her, enjoyed her and in a short time forgot her. His turn of mind was too rational to allow him to feel contempt for a woman whose frailty had given him pleasure. Rather he pitied the fair sex for their vulnerability, both to their own physiology and to the whims of the men on whom they were dependent.

He said with an edge in his voice, "I make no claims to be a saint, but I'm not yet reduced to seducing virgins."

"No, because, as you are aware, to men of normal inclinations a virgin is about as enjoyable as an unripe apple," retorted the other man dryly.

Caspar smiled slightly. "Very true, and for that reason if no other, Miss Jackson survived her journey with me unscathed. Now all that remains is to see her securely established in some respectable post, after which I may wash my hands of her."

"If I were in your place, I should make her my mistress—virgin or not," said his companion. "After all, her mixed blood will preclude her from making a good marriage, and one wouldn't tire of a girl like that as one does of most pretty creatures. Beauty and brains are a rare combination in a woman. Who were her parents? D'you know?"

Beginning to regret that he had allowed Richard to meet Flora, Caspar shrugged. The fact that her association with him must compromise her in the eyes of respectable people was an aspect of the situation that had not struck him before. It might damage her chances of marriage more severely than her hybridity.

"Her father was a gentleman, obviously," Richard went on. "And if the girl is legitimate, the mother must have been a Manchu."

Caspar saw an opportunity to direct the conversation away from Flora. The night before, at the club, another man had mentioned to him that although the Manchus had been the country's ruling class since their invasion of China in the seventeenth century, he foresaw a change of regime before many more years had passed.

"Oh, yes, there's revolution in the air," agreed Richard when Caspar canvased his opinion on the subject. "And the international settlement is the hotbed. The place is infested with radicals and dissidents because now they can't be arrested by Chinese officials without a preliminary hearing before our mixed court, and the policy of our government is to give asylum to political refugees as long as they don't disturb the peace of the settlement. Purely verbal attacks on the Chinese government are usually regarded as an exercise of the right to free speech."

For the rest of their ride he talked about Chinese politics, and it occurred to Caspar that Richard's position as a remittance man, with a hushed-up disgrace attached to him, would be an excellent cover for certain activities in which a bad reputation could be an advantage. The thought would not have crossed his mind but for the fact that he himself, on two occasions, had combined botanizing in eastern Europe with observations of another nature. It was not impossible that Richard worked for the same unpublicized department of His Majesty's Government that had employed Caspar.

That evening again he left Flora to her own devices while he dined à deux with Madame Colbert, whose husband was on a visit to Peking.

Madame had learned from a friend who lived in

the house next to the one Carlyon was renting that his
ménage included a girl, presumably his mistress. But
such was the Frenchwoman's longing to relive the
delights of his lovemaking that she closed her mind to
the knowledge that he was an unashamed and invet-
erate rake whose attitude toward women was little
different from his attitude toward a bowl of hothouse fruits.

After a delicious but light dinner they went to her
bedroom, where he unhooked her gown and unlaced
her corset before pulling her onto his lap. Sliding his
hand up her leg, he gave her the exquisite frissons she
had never experienced with her husband.

When it was over and he was dressing she wept with
shame at her wantonness. Carlyon fastened his dress
shirt and eyed her reflection in the looking glass with
concealed exasperation. Remorse was a state of mind
of which he had no experience and for which he felt little sympathy. To force oneself on a girl of a lower
order, to bully an inferior, to ignore a beggar—these
acts were against his code of conduct. But to bed
another man's wife when the marriage was unhappy—
as it must be if the woman had to look elsewhere for
fulfillment—did not offend his sense of honor.

"I must go, *chérie*," he said lightly when he was
ready. "Come, cheer up and give me a kiss. Unfortunately I have several engagements that will prevent
me from visiting you again. But who knows? We may
meet in London or Paris. So let's say only *au revoir*,
shall we?"

She wept and clung, and made him glad to escape.
She had beautiful breasts and legs, but so had a great
many women, and it bored him to have to bear with
her guilty conscience.

MUCH AS SHE LOVED TO READ, as the days passed
Flora began to long for a change of occupation.
Caspar was out much of the time, and when she attempted to discuss the question of her future with
him he would say only that he was thinking about it
and tell her not to worry. He had forbidden her to
leave the house, but it didn't seem to occur to him
that she might need more exercise than was afforded
by the small garden, or that it was disappointing to
arrive in Shanghai and see nothing of it except for
one brief excursion to the native district.

One afternoon a servant came to tell her that
Madame Lemaître wished to see her. Thinking the
caller must be someone who was unaware that the
owners of the house were away, but glad of any
diversion, Flora asked him to show *madame* in.

She was a young woman, dressed in pale blue with
a lacy parasol to match her dress and the two blue
birds, wings outspread, that decorated the brim of
her large white straw hat.

To Flora's surprise she said in English, "Good
afternoon, Miss Jackson. I am looking for a companion for my younger sister, who is an invalid, and
your friend Mr. Lomax, whom I met at the country
club this morning, suggested that you might be suitable. No doubt he mentioned me to you."

"No. He was out to luncheon today, *madame*.
Won't you sit down?"

"Thank you, but already I'm late for an appoint-
ment with my *modiste*. If you would be so obliging as
to come with me, we can discuss the matter on the
way and then I can take you to have tea with my
sister and see if you like each other."

Flora was delighted at the opportunity to escape

from the house for an hour or so. She hastened upstairs to fetch the hat and gloves bought for her by
the missionary's wife, and five minutes later they
were bowling along in Madame Lemaître's carriage.

"Mr. Lomax did not make it clear precisely how
you and he came to be traveling companions," said
Madame Lemaître. "It's somewhat irregular for a
girl of your age to be in the charge of a bachelor.
Have you no family, Miss Jackson?"

She continued to question Flora until they arrived
at the *modiste*, where she left her to wait in the carriage while she went inside. Her fitting did not take
long, after which they drove to a large house surrounded by a high wall with stout wooden gates,
which were opened to admit the carriage and closed
immediately afterward.

Inside, the house was very luxuriously appointed.
Madame Lemaître showed Flora into a small salon
and asked her to wait there. Soon afterward a
Chinese servant brought her a glass of wine and a
dish of sweetmeats.

In the room adjoining the salon, Madame Lemaître, more usually known as Didi, reported to
Madam Lermontov the answers that Flora had given
to her questions.

"So—she is alone in the world, and you think
there is nothing between them," said the Russian
thoughtfully.

She rose and, crossing the room, put her eye to a
peephole that enabled her to watch Flora sipping the
wine and sampling a sweetmeat.

"As the doctor said, even in unbecoming clothes
one can see her potential. But her present protector
is, it seems, interested only in women of experience;

unlike the count, who will pay a considerable premium to be first in the field. When the wine has taken effect, we can examine her more closely, but I think she will be worth the risk, which is not very great. You've done well, Didi; and as your reward, when the count has had his way with her you may instruct her in your pleasures, which I'm sure she will find a great deal more agreeable than the count's embraces.''

CHAPTER FIVE

WHEN FLORA OPENED HER EYES she was lying on a
bed with no clothes on, in a strange room, and her
mind felt confused and fuddled.

Presently a woman whom she did not recognize
came to sit beside her and said, "Drink this. It will
make you feel better." She put her arm behind Flora
and raised her, holding a cup of wine to her lips.

Then she let her sink back on the pillows and said
in a soft lisping voice, "Don't be frightened. You
have nothing to fear as long as you are a good girl
and do as you're told. If you make a fuss you will
have to be punished. So lie quietly, my dear, and say
nothing, and when Count Leczinska has finished
with you, you can spend the night in Didi's room,
and that you will enjoy very much."

The next time Flora awoke there were a number of
people with her. She was dimly aware that they were
brushing her hair and stroking oil into her skin, making her arms and legs glisten. Presently they helped
her to rise and walk to a long looking glass, where as
in a dream she watched them circle her waist with a
girdle of flashing white stones, rouge the soft tips of
her breasts and fasten a skirt of silver gossamer that
hung in soft transparent folds from her hips to her
ankles.

When she surfaced again she was lying in a different place, on a dais piled with velvet cushions, in a
pool of bright light, being touched and caressed by

more than one pair of hands. At first she submitted, her mind too clouded to make sense of what was happening, her body equally inert. There was music playing, and the girls kneeling around her wore satin masks and scarlet paint on their lips. Their necks and arms glittered with jewels, but they wore no clothes above the waist. One girl, who seemed to be dancing, had spangles fixed to her skin in a pattern that caught the light as she swayed and undulated. The place seemed to have no walls, only diaphanous curtains that changed their colors and came and went like clouds of mist. Flora watched them with puzzled eyes. Where was this? Who were these girls? Was it a dream, or was it real?

Then they began to do things that made her struggle to free herself.

"If you cry out, she will be angry and have you beaten," a voice whispered close to her ear.

Some of the hands that a moment before had been gentle now became clamps, holding her not cruelly but with enough strength to overpower her feeble resistance. She was forced to lie still and submit, hating what they were inflicting on her but feeling too weak to fight. Gradually she forgot her revulsion, forgot everything but the shudders of a strange sensation like nothing she had ever felt before. As the storm of excitement came to a pulsating climax, she heard an outburst of sound that at first she did not recognize.

Then, as she lay utterly spent by the wild surge of feeling, no longer held down but alone on her mound of soft cushions, she knew what the sound was: applause. The things they had done had been performed not for their pleasure, or hers, but for the enjoyment of whoever had witnessed her ignominy.

As the lights slowly dimmed and the burst of clapping died down, she could hear the buzz of their voices, and her drugged mind cleared sufficiently to realize that they were the voices of men, and the smell that pervaded the place was the scent of many cigars.

MADAM LERMONTOV said to the count, "I'm afraid it may be an hour before the new girl is ready to entertain you, count. She is very shy and nervous, you understand, and it was necessary to give her a sedative draft to induce her to play her part in the performance just now. However, the effect should have worn off by the time you have dined, and I'm sure you will have no difficulty in overcoming her timidity. She shall be brought to your room as soon as possible."

The count's pale eyes gleamed. It was some time since Madam Lermontov had provided an inexperienced girl for him, and most of them had been Chinese with disappointingly undeveloped figures. This one, because of her European strain, had, as he had observed during the so-called *tableau vivant*, a much more voluptuous shape.

The fact, as madam had hinted, that the girl might not accept her seduction with the resigned passivity of the others, but would struggle and fight him, only added to his anticipation of the pleasures to follow the excellent cuisine with which the Russian fortified her clients' strength for a night's sport.

While Count Leczinska was eating roast quail and drinking champagne, Lord Richard was bidding his rickshaw boy to put on speed.

Like Carlyon, he had no need to frequent bordellos when he needed a woman. There were other reasons for his patronizing Madam Lermontov's establishment, where, since they were pretty and closely supervised medically, he made such use of the girls as was necessary to cover the fact that his real interest lay in their other clients, who when in their cups were less discreet than when sober.

Richard had entered Madam Lermontov's private theater toward the end of the performance and had not immediately recognized the girl on whose palpitating body all eyes were focused as the one he had met in the garden of a house in the French concession.

His first reaction had been, *by Jove! The hypocritical bastard! He* has *sold the poor little wretch to the Russian woman.*

But almost at once he had realized that although his fellow Etonian had no scruples where married women were concerned and could be brutal in dropping them as soon as their attraction began to wane, Carlyon was not, as he had averred, the kind of unprincipled scoundrel who would consign a young girl to a life of prostitution in order to rid himself of responsibility for her.

As he looked more carefully at the scene in progress on the stage, Richard had felt sure that the girl, although sufficiently conscious to react to what was being done to her, was by no means fully alert. She might be intoxicated, or she might be under the influence of opium. Knowing that he could not rescue her, he had waited until her slim golden hips had arched in the final convulsion; then, while the rest of the audience were indicating their approval of this newest of Madam Lermontov's depraved offerings, he had slipped inconspicuously away.

It was a time of night at which Carlyon might be expected to be dining à deux with one of his mistresses, or entertaining his neighbors at a dinner party with some of his experiences in western China. Although he was incognito, his presence and charm and his gifts as a raconteur were enough to make Shanghai hostesses lionize him almost as eagerly as if they knew his true identity. Therefore Richard was not very hopeful of catching him at home, or that the servants would know where he could be found.

As it happened, Carlyon had intended to spend the evening with the third of the women with whom he had amused himself during his previous sojourn in Shanghai. However, returning late from a day at the country club, he had been displeased to find that Flora had had a visitor and had disobeyed his instruction that she should not leave the house.

In England it was the form for ladies to give their name to the servant who opened the door to them, and the only persons who sent in cards were strangers calling to ask the character of a servant or solicit interest in a charity. But in Shanghai, where sometimes the servants had difficulty in pronouncing foreign names intelligibly, it was not unknown for a card to be sent in, as had been the case when Lord Richard had called.

Flora's visitor, although manifestly a stranger to her, had not given the number-one servant a card. However, the fellow was certain the caller's name had been Madame Lemaître. Since it seemed improbable that, however bored she might be by the limitations of Shanghai society, any respectable Frenchwoman would make friendly overtures to a girl living in a bachelor household, Carlyon was puzzled and somewhat concerned by this turn of events. Could it be that jealousy and curiosity had prompted Hortense Colbert to persuade one of her friends to call on Flora? But if that were the case, and the girl had been invited to the house of a third party in order that Hortense might scrutinize and quiz her, she should have returned by now.

While Carlyon was changing his clothes, and before he had made up his mind what steps to take, Richard arrived.

Without wasting words he said, "I've come posthaste from Madam Lermontov's house. Somehow they've got hold of your little protégée. She's either half-drunk or drugged, and when I left the place she had just been obliged to take part in one of the shows that madam puts on for the voyeurs. This one was entitled 'The Initiation of an Odalisque.' No doubt you can guess the nature of it."

"And you left her there?" Carlyon asked in a voice like a whiplash.

The other man's gaze did not waver. "There are reasons why I can't afford to antagonize the Russian woman. You'll have to rescue her yourself. From what I know of the house and its customers, the first in line for her will be a Pole of high position and base inclinations. But he usually dines before his other pleasures, and he'll want her to put up a struggle, which she wasn't capable of doing at the time I came away."

Carlyon opened a drawer and took from it a pistol. "Will I be admitted without an introduction?"

IN A ROOM AT THE BROTHEL Flora's mind was starting to clear. After the realization that she was lying unclothed and in a posture of the utmost abandonment before an audience of men, everything had faded into blackness.

She had roused to find herself in yet another place, looking at her own supine body, which now was covered by a sheet of red silk. At first she was puzzled by being able to see herself while lying down, but after a time it dawned on her that the looking glass was fixed to the ceiling above the bed. This was such an extraordinary place for a mirror to be that she wondered if she had lost her mind and was suffering from a series of strange and evil delusions.

But the longer she lay there, the more real everything became, and the less she was able to convince herself that what had been done to her was a hallucination conjured by a disordered mind. It had happened, and the terrible thing was that, although at first she had been helpless to prevent it, at the very end her own flesh had conspired against her, and she had not wanted her tormentors to stop inflicting that corrupt but irresistible pleasure on her.

After a time it came to her that she had not been brought to this place for a single act of degradation. It would be repeated. Somehow she had to escape.

Clutching the sheet to her nakedness, she sat up, only to sink back again as a wave of nausea swept over her.

At this point the door was opened by a girl who came in and asked, smiling, "Are you feeling better? I'm Lily. I've come to sit with you for a while."

Was Lily one of the girls who had assisted in her humiliation? A deep flush of mortification swept Flora's face and neck.

"Don't look so upset, dear," the other said kindly. She sat down and crossed her legs, her blue wrapper falling open to show black silk stockings held up by satin garters. "It isn't too bad once you're used to it. I used to be a lady's maid until I was fool enough to fall in love with the master and let him get me in the family way. He wouldn't help me, except to send me to a doctor who would get rid of it for me. Dr. Brewer. You've been to him, too, haven't you?"

"H—how did you know that?" Flora stammered.

"Madam Lermontov knows everything."

From the confusion of the recent past Flora recollected an intermittent awareness of an ominous presence in the background. "Is she the one they said would have me beaten if I wouldn't do as I was told?"

"Yes—and don't you go thinking that's just an idle threat, dear. Madam's a terror when she's angry, and there are several of the clients who'll pay extra to knock a girl about. I don't mind doing a spot of whipping, if that's what they need to excite them, but I take good care they don't get the chance to whip me, and so will you if you're sensible. Anyway, as I was telling you, the master sent me to Dr. Brewer, but the price of the operation was thirty pounds, which I couldn't pay, and the master claimed he couldn't, either. It was the mistress who held the purse strings, you see. She married him for his title, and he married her for her money, as the gentry do as often as not. So the doctor suggested I should come to work for Madam L. to pay for the operation, and after a while I decided I might as well stay with her. It's a living, and although it's not very often you get a nice-looking chap who you'd let have his way with you for nothing, the rest aren't too bad on the whole. Personally I'd rather go to bed with Didi than with any man I've ever known, including the one who put me here in the first place.''

Flora gazed at her in horror, understanding at last that this place must be one of the whorehouses where girls with no one to protect them endured the vile form of slavery of which Père d'Espinay had warned her.

"How long have you been here?" she asked.

"A year and three months. But I'm leaving soon. Madame L. is sending me to a high-class house in Peking that's run by a friend of hers. She's swapping me for a girl there. It makes a change for us and for the clients.''

"And if you decided to go back to being a lady's maid, would she let you?"

Lily said, "I shouldn't want to, but I couldn't anyway. My last mistress sent me packing when she began to suspect the master had his eye on me. He'd had more than his eye on me by then, had she but known it. So I've got no references from her and no way of explaining where I've been since she dismissed me. But if you think being a lady's maid is a bed of roses, you're mistaken, dear. Sitting up till all hours, after you've been on your feet all day, waiting to undress the mistress when she comes back from enjoying herself at a ball—no, thank you. Never again. Perhaps you haven't been in service. I have, and I've had enough of it.''

"No, I've never been in service, and I'm sure it can be very unpleasant if one's employers are inconsiderate. But I know I can't stay here, Lily. Will you help me recover my clothes?"

The other girl shook her head. "I'm sorry. I'd like to help you, but I couldn't risk it. She'd find out and she'd half kill me—or let someone else do it for her. Anyway, even if you could get away, where would you go if the chap who brought you to Shanghai doesn't want you?''

"What makes you say that—that he doesn't want me?''

"It stands to reason," Lily replied with a shrug. "I don't say Madam L. would hesitate to kidnap a girl if she thought she could get away with it. She'd not stop at murder, that one. But I don't think she'd take a girl who'd been living with an Englishman if she felt there was any chance that he'd kick up a rumpus.''

The possibility that Caspar might not be disturbed by her disappearance struck Flora like a blow. Up to that moment she had been clinging to the conviction that sooner or later he would rescue her. Lily had shaken that certainty and sown in her mind the even more horrible notion that Caspar himself might be a party to her abduction. How else would the woman who had called herself Madame Lemaître have known where to find her?

"I—I don't believe it. I may be a nuisance to him, but he wouldn't. . . he would *never* consign me here against my will," she answered vehemently.

Lily looked skeptical. "You know him and I don't, dear. But most gentlemen haven't many scruples when they're dealing with the likes of us. From tales I've heard, they don't always behave as they should toward ladies of their own class, and with a girl who's beneath them. . . .'' She finished the sentence with a grimace of cynical disillusionment.

"Caspar isn't like that. All the time we've been traveling together he's treated me kindly and honorably. I might have been his younger sister.''

"Maybe that was only because he thought you might be infected," said Lily, who had heard the details of Flora's visit to the doctor from Didi. "Has he still not touched you since he found out you were clean?"

Flora shook her head.

"It might be because you're a half-caste," Lily suggested. "No offense intended," she added hastily. Then she shook her head, dismissing that explanation. "No, no—it couldn't be that. You're a peach, if you are part Chinese. It must be that he prefers boys." She saw Flora had not understood this last conjecture and explained it.

"I don't believe it," Flora gasped.

"It came as a shock to me, too," Lily said wryly. "But you won't be shocked by anything when you've been here a few weeks."

She described various other practices that to Flora seemed revolting beyond words, but from which Lily seemed to derive a resigned amusement.

She was interrupted by the entrance of a woman whom Flora knew must be the dreaded Madam Lermontov. She was dressed in black lace, and her black hair was coiffed in the full upswept style worn by the fashionable ladies whom Flora had glimpsed from her window. But even at first glance there was something strange and inhuman about her, and as they looked at each other she saw that the Russian had no lips. Her mouth was as straight as a snake's, and remembering the sibilant voice that had spoken to her earlier while she was only semiconscious, Flora would not have been startled to see a reptilian tongue flicker out from the lipless mouth.

The other strange thing about her was that her eyes

were not the same color. One was gray, the other blue, which had the effect on Flora of making her feel that two people were watching her from behind the slots in one mask. It was an illusion that was heightened by the Russian's thick maquillage. Lily had paint on her face, but mainly on her lips and eyes. Madam Lermontov's face was coated all over with a thick paste of cream and powder, which served to emphasize rather than to conceal the lines of late middle age.

Turning to Lily, she said, "In five minutes from now take her to room eleven."

"Madam Lermontov, you let me go!" Driven by desperation, Flora swung her feet to the floor and stood up, clutching the sheet.

In the act of turning away, the woman paused. "You are here and will do as you're told. If you don't—" she took several paces into the room and dealt Flora a stinging slap on the face that made her cry out and reel backward "—you will be disciplined. Perhaps you had better explain the purpose of these to her, Lily," she added. Touching one of the straps, padded with velvet, that were attached to the brass rails of the bed, she left the room.

It took Flora some moments to recover from the shock of a blow that had made her slender neck feel in danger of snapping.

"The straps are for holding girls down if at first they won't do as they're told," Lily explained. "The count—he's to be your first client—likes a bit of a tussle with a new girl. But once, when a girl fought too hard, he rang the bell and had her strapped. There are two at the top for your wrists, and two at the foot for your ankles. I've only had the straps once, not as a punishment but because the client wanted to make believe he was a Roman general and I was a captive slave, or some silly nonsense. What *I* didn't like was the thought that the house might catch fire before he'd finished, and he might not stop to unstrap me.''

Flora shuddered and sank on the bed in an attitude of despair. The Frenchman had opened her eyes to the brutishness of which some men were capable, and Père d'Espinay had warned her that even the stifling monotony of a convent was preferable to life in a *maison malfamée*. But he had not gone into detail, and never, never had she dreamed that the world was full of seemingly normal, respectable people who secretly, in houses such as this, indulged in the horrible vices described so casually by Lily.

"I shall kill myself," she muttered dully.

Lily said, "I thought that once—but I didn't. It's not so easy when you come down to it. The Chinese take caustic soda, which burns their insides, and I didn't fancy that, or cutting my wrists, or hanging myself. It takes courage to do yourself in, and I'm a coward. While there's life there's hope, as they say, and it isn't too bad here—honest. Now buck up, dear, and I'll take you to room eleven, and if the count gives you two or three glasses of bubbly you won't mind what he does to you.''

On the way along the corridor she allowed Flora to keep the sheet around her. She saw that the girl was in the trancelike state of someone on her way to the scaffold. But it was not impossible that at the last moment she might make a desperate bid to escape, and Lily knew that Madam L. would hold her responsible if Flora were not delivered to the count within minutes of his finishing his supper. Also, although he did not know it, the count would be putting on a show for the occupants of several small stuffy cabinets, and each of these prurient old men, who could no longer perform the act but liked to watch it, would be leaning forward in his chair and applying his eye to the judas hole in readiness for the peep show to begin.

Outside room eleven Lily tapped on the door and would have opened it had it not been opened from within by a stout man with a gray beared.

"Ah!" His eyes glittered lustfully.

Lily pushed Flora over the threshold, at the same time snatching away the sheet and leaving her naked but for the diamante girdle and the skirt of transparent gauze.

It was as the count closed and locked the door that Flora roused from her stupor and experienced a final powerful upsurge of defiance. But before she could dart to the table, grab a knife and threaten to stab him if he touched her, the count seized hold of her wrist and with his other hand tore off the filmy skirt, tossing it aside.

MADAM LERMONTOV was not a woman to lose her head in a difficult situation, but when, a few moments after she had given orders for Flora to be taken to the count, Carlyon's card was brought to her, she felt a thrust of alarm. Almost immediately she realized that it could be only an unfortunate coincidence that had brought him to her house tonight. He must be aware by now that the girl was missing, but there was no way in which he could have traced her so swiftly.

"Have Mr. Lomax shown to my room," she instructed.

She was seated behind a large desk when Carlyon was brought to her, and she saw at once, from his expression, that he had not come in search of pleasure.

Nevertheless she said graciously, "Good evening, Mr. Lomax. Please be seated. May I ask who suggested you should come here?"

Ignoring her gesture toward a chair, he stopped not far from the desk and said in a peremptory tone, "You have abducted a young girl who is in my care, madam. Already you have subjected her to abuses. No doubt you have others in view. Take me to her immediately."

"My dear Mr. Lomax, I think you must be mistaken." Beneath the desk her toe touched a bell.

At once a door concealed in the paneling behind her opened, and a preternaturally tall and massively built Chinese man stepped into the room and moved to one side of the desk, where he stood staring at the Englishman with no flicker of expression on his moon-shaped, badly pockmarked face.

"Now, Mr. Lomax, perhaps you would explain your grounds for making this extraordinary accusation," the Russian said silkily, expecting his arrogance to wilt.

"You're wasting time, madam, and your bully is no match for this." Suddenly Carlyon's right hand, which had been concealed in the folds of the satin-lined opera cloak flung back from his other shoulder, was extended in front of him, holding a Bisley Colt.

"You wouldn't dare!" she said scornfully.

He fired.

Where an instant before a gold drop had hung

from the lobe of her left ear, there was now a rag of
bleeding skin and a bright spreading stain on her
shoulder.

"I will not argue with vermin. I prefer to exter-
minate it. You have five seconds before my next shot
makes a hole between your eyebrows," Carlyon said
calmly.

Almost paralyzed with shock, she saw in his narrowed gray eyes an indifference as absolute as her
own lack of pity for her victims. She was looking at
her executioner, unless she could make herself obey
him.

Carlyon watched her stagger to her feet and move,
shambling like a drunkard, toward the door. He mo-
tioned the man to follow her, and as the giant
Chinese passed him he murmured, "I think we can
dispense with your company, my friend," and struck
him behind the ear with the barrel of the Colt.

Although the sound of the shot that had torn off
her lobe must have been heard in other parts of the
house, none of Madam Lermontov's staff or clientele
came to investigate the noise as Carlyon followed her
stumbling progress up the staircase. However, on the
first floor he had the impression that more than one
door was open by the smallest chink, and that a number of frightened eyes were watching their progress
along the corridor leading to the principal bedrooms.

Beside the door at the end of the passage the
woman slumped against the wall, one hand to her
disfigured ear, from which the blood was still flowing.

Carlyon tried the door and found it locked, but the
latch was not made to withstand the violent impact of
his kick. It burst open, revealing a scene that he had

feared would be a repetition of what he had seen on his return to the mission. Tonight he had come in time. The count, whose lust was less urgent than that of the Frenchman, was still enjoying the preliminary stages of his sadistic pleasures. He and Flora were both on their feet, she with one of her arms behind her back. The count was twisting it higher, making her grimace with pain while his free hand explored the soft curves thrust out by the agonized arch of her spine.

His perverted enjoyment and Flora's suffering was brought to an abrupt end when Carlyon sprang forward and struck him, not with the barrel of the Colt but with a blow from his fist that smashed his nose and sent him reeling.

Released, Flora would have fallen had not Carlyon caught her and held her upright. Before she was fully aware that her ordeal was over, he had wrapped her in the folds of his cloak, swung her into his arms and was striding out of the room with her.

Dazed with relief, she did not notice that shock and loss of blood had caused Madam Lermontov to crumple to the floor unconscious. All the way back to the French concession she lay cradled in Caspar's strong arms, thankful to be safe but already beginning to feel ashamed that, not for the first time, he had been a witness to her degradation.

At the house he carried her to her bedroom, inwardly cursing the lack of a woman to attend to her as the nun had after her rape.

He lowered her onto the bed and sat down beside her. "What happened? How did they induce you to leave the house?"

She told him and asked, "How did you know where to find me?"

"From Creed. He was there, recognized you and lost no time in reporting the fact to me."

"*He* goes to that place?" she exclaimed disgustedly. And then, as she realized the circumstances in which his friend had recognized her, she moaned and rolled over to bury her face in the pillow. "Did. . .did he tell what they. . .what I. . .?"

Her voice was so muffled as to be almost inaudible, but he caught enough words to reply, "He told me you had been drugged and forced to undergo abuses. He didn't go into details. His concern, and mine, was to rescue you. If you find it strange that, being there, Creed himself did not intervene, I'll tell you in the strictest possible confidence that I suspect him of being an intelligence agent for the British government who patronizes that nefarious establishment for purposes other than the usual ones. You needn't fear that he'll broadcast your experience. If my supposition is correct, he is more than ordinarily discreet."

"But there were other men there," she said with her face still hidden.

"But paying less attention to your face than to your figure, I imagine. Come: you've suffered a worse experience with greater fortitude. Don't lose courage now."

Gently he made her turn over onto her back, his gray eyes softer than usual. To her surprise he stroked her cheek with his knuckles, a caress she had seen him give to a small howling Chinese child whom, after a fall, Caspar had set on his feet and comforted.

She said in an unsteady voice, "The worst of it was when I thought that you had arranged for me to go there."

It was the first time she had ever seen him disconcerted. "What in heaven's name made you think that?"

"I didn't want to believe it, but Lily said that Madam Lermontov wouldn't have kidnapped a girl belonging to an Englishman if there was any chance of his making a fuss. When I told her how well you'd treated me during our journey, she said it must be because you were afraid of being infected. She asked if you had behaved differently after taking me to that doctor. When I said no, Lily said it must be because you took your pleasure with boys. She told me such horrible things. . . ."

Her voice broke. She closed her eyes but could not prevent tears from seeping between her eyelids.

"Forget them!" he said abruptly. "Lily lives in an evil world among men with warped minds and strange unnatural desires. They are a vicious minority. Most men aren't like that, I assure you."

"But how can such things be allowed? The man I was with when you came, the one whom you hit, was a count."

"The most notorious of sadists was a marquis," said Caspar. "Now I'm going to leave you for a few minutes, but only to fetch you a draft that will clear your system of the drugs they gave you and prevent you from having a violent headache tomorrow. While I'm gone, take off my cloak and put on a nightgown."

When he had left her, Flora rose unsteadily from the bed and took off the cloak that, being made for his much greater height, enveloped her from neck to foot. She still had around her waist the belt of imitation diamonds. With fingers that shook she unclasped it and flung it, shuddering, into a wastepaper basket beside the *bonheur du jour*. Then she put on one of the two nightgowns bought for her by Mrs. Hunter, climbed into bed and lay waiting for Caspar's return.

DOWNSTAIRS Carlyon had discovered that Lord Richard was still in the house but had kept out of sight when he heard them returning, thinking that Flora might be hysterical.

"What happened? Were you in time?"

"Yes, the count was still engaged in his own peculiar style of love play. Had I not been chiefly concerned to get Flora out of the place, I should have enjoyed giving him a taste of his own tricks."

"He didn't go scot-free by the look of it," said the other man, his eyes on the lacerated knuckles of Carlyon's left hand.

"No, I broke the brute's nose, but a couple of broken arms would have been more appropriate justice."

"How is Miss Jackson? Utterly distraught, I imagine?"

"Distressed, not distraught," answered Carlyon. "She's a girl of remarkable mettle."

"I'm afraid you must think I have played a dastardly part in all this."

"No, I've a shrewd idea why you acted as you did. It was fortunate you were there, but I don't need to tell you that Flora won't welcome another encounter with a witness to her humiliation."

"By Jove, no—I should think not. I shouldn't dream of putting her to that embarrassment."

"Merely as a matter of interest, would you have

acted any differently had the girl in question been, for example, Lady Rose?'' He referred to a pretty and much feted girl who was visiting Shanghai with her grandmother, a dowager duchess.

Lord Richard hesitated. ''I don't know,'' he admitted. ''Damn it all, Carlyon, you can hardly compare your little Eurasian protégée, charming as she is, with Lady Rose.''

''Indeed not! One is a vain little butterfly without a sensible thought in her head, and the other—well, you don't know her as I do, and this isn't the moment to enumerate her qualities. Good night, Creed, and thank you.''

By the time he returned to her room with a pick-me-up that in his salad days had frequently spared him the worst aftereffects of a drinking bout, Flora appeared to be dozing. But as he stood looking down at her, she roused with a violent start and for an instant looked terror-stricken.

Her eyes and lips were still painted with kohl and rouge, and the incongruity between her painted face and the excessive modesty of the high-necked white cotton nightgown made his mouth slant with sudden amusement.

On impulse he said, ''Would you like me to stay with you for a time?''

''Oh, yes—if you would,'' she said gratefully. Then, ''But I don't want to be a nuisance. I'm afraid I've already ruined your evening. You would have dined out, I expect, had you not been obliged to rescue me?''

''Yes, but it doesn't matter.'' He settled his tall frame in a chair by the window and took up a book she had left on the table beside it. It was Voltaire's *A*

Treatise on Toleration, and thinking of the highly
colored novels by Mrs. Baillie-Reynolds and Baron-
ess von Hutten read by most young women, again he
smiled to himself.

Within a short time of finishing the drink he had
brought her, Flora had fallen asleep. Carlyon turned
out the lamp and went downstairs to scrawl a note of
apology to the woman with whom he should have
dined, and to eat a belated and solitary supper.

He had left Flora's bedroom door open, and when
later he passed it on his way to his own room, he
knew by her muffled whimpers that she was having a
nightmare. When he woke her she huddled against
him, trembling with terror. Clearly she had dreamed
herself back in the brothel. He soothed her as he
would a child, holding her close to his shoulder and
patting her back. Presently she grew calmer.

He had not lit the lamp, for the room was bright
now with moonlight. As she lifted her face from his
shoulder, the beautiful curve of her lips stirred a sudden surge of desire in him. He kissed her, and in that
instant all that Flora had suffered at the hands of
Gérard and Count Leczinska was erased from her
mind by the startling pleasure of being kissed by a
man who did not repel or frighten her.

To Caspar, accustomed to the parted lips and
eager tongues of the women with whom he amused
himself, the soft but closed lips beneath his were an
instant reminder that, in spite of the rape, the girl in
his arms was still in spirit a virgin. For a second or
two he was tempted to make her lips soften and open,
and to teach her how to respond.

Instead he laid her on her pillows with a murmured
good-night and left her before he was tempted to

break his resolve never to deflower a virgin other than his eventual bride. As Creed had remarked some days earlier, there was precious little pleasure for a normal man in making love to a shy and inexperienced girl. Although Flora had in the strict sense been deflowered already by the Frenchman, it would still take much patient tuition to make a voluptuary of her, and that was a task for someone else to undertake.

In his own room, preparing for bed, the thought that his choice of a wife could not be delayed for much longer caused a frown to contract his dark eyebrows. And as he considered the inconveniences and irritations that marriage was bound to impose on his previously unfettered life, there came to him an idea at once so astounding and so apt that he was surprised it had not struck him before.

IT WAS LATER THAN USUAL when Flora rose the next morning. When she went downstairs, she found Caspar about to leave the house.

"Oh, must you go out immediately?" she asked anxiously. "I particularly wanted to talk to you. We've been here more than a week, and my future still is unsettled. I—"

"Not anymore," he said briskly. "It came to me early this morning that the solution to your problem has been apparent for some time, had I the wit to realize it."

"What do you mean?"

He studied her puzzled face for a moment or two before he said, "With the exception of the day the train was ambushed, you enjoyed our journey here, didn't you?"

"Yes, very much," she agreed.

"Would you like to continue to travel with me?"

Her dark eyes lit up. "Oh, yes—more than anything, Caspar."

"Good; then the matter is settled. All we need do is to regularize our connection by special license. I'll make the arrangements this morning."

"I don't quite understand. What arrangements? To book a passage for me, do you mean? What is the special license for?"

"It's a license granted by an archbishop permitting a marriage to take place without banns being read out in a church at three Sunday services."

"You...you're suggesting that we should be *married*?" she asked in a faint voice.

"Naturally. Our present relationship may have passed unremarked in the wilds of Szechwan, but it won't in more civilized surroundings. You must have been aware of the construction that Mrs. Hunter put on it before I explained matters to her?"

"Yes, I was. She thought me your concubine."

"Precisely. Being such a godly woman she would naturally jump to the most discreditable conclusion," he said sardonically.

"But, Caspar, you *can't* marry me."

He lifted an eyebrow. "Why not?"

"Well, for one thing because...because I'm a half-caste and you're a gentleman."

"Who called you a half-caste?"

"Lily...the girl in that place. She didn't mean it unkindly. She was simply stating the truth."

"Your logic escapes me. Why is your parentage an impediment to a marriage between us?"

"Because the majority of people despise half-castes. Père d'Espinay warned me about it. He said it was unreasonable, but it was a fact that I must accept.''

"The majority of people are uneducated boors whose opinions are governed by superstition and shibboleth. I see no reason to take their views into account. There is only one possible obstacle to our marriage.''

"What is that?"

"Your aversion to physical contact with me. If that is your real objection, there's no point in sparing my feelings. You had much better be frank.''

"But it isn't. I—I like it when you touch me. I shouldn't have offered to be your concubine if... had it been otherwise.''

"I think you will find it more satisfactory to be my wife. In England when a man has a mistress she is not usually part of his household, as a concubine is here in China.''

"But *why* do you want to marry me?" Flora asked, mystified. "I see the advantages to me, but how will you benefit?''

"By having a wife who shares my principal interest instead of being bored by it, and who will put up with hardships that most of your sex would find insupportable.''

"Your parents—will they approve of me?"

"My parents are dead, and I have no brothers or sisters. My only close relation is my father's elder sister. However, I hope to be more prolific than my father was.''

"But if you have children by me they will be partly Chinese.''

"With the advantage of a well-educated mother instead of a pretty nincompoop whose chief preoccupation is her appearance and whose conversation rests on gossip. It's the extreme triviality of the minds of most women that has kept me a bachelor. It's not their fault, I daresay. Your sex is not lacking in intelligence, merely discouraged from developing it.''

"Have you never fallen in love?"

His gray eyes glinted with amusement. "Frequently, but never to the extent of supposing it would last forever. Marriage is much too serious an undertaking to be founded on something as ephemeral as romantic love. Some communion of interests and a clear-eyed acceptance of one's own and one's partner's imperfections make a much sounder basis for the relationship.''

THEIR MARRIAGE TOOK PLACE on the morning of the day they embarked for England; and since, unlike most young women, Flora had never daydreamed of lace veils and orange blossoms, she was not disappointed by being married in the plain hat and one of the dresses bought in Hankow.

But even during the ceremony she had a vague sense of unease, and within two hours of the service that bound them together, her instinctive dubiety was confirmed by the discovery that when Caspar had dismissed her objections he had been deceiving her.

They had returned to the house in the French concession, and alone in her room she had her first opportunity to study the certificate of marriage that the clergyman had given to Caspar and he to her.

First came the number of the certificate and the date of the ceremony. This was followed by their names and surnames: Caspar George Edward Lomax and Flora Mary Jackson. Then their ages and condition, he a bachelor and she a spinster. In the column headed Rank or Profession there was a dash against her name, but against his was written "The Right Honorable the Earl of Carlyon."

Flora stared at it dumbfounded before her eyes traveled to the next space, in which was written their residence at the time of marriage. In the last two columns were the names of their fathers: Algernon Edward John Lomax, sixth Earl of Carlyon (deceased); Thomas Jackson, botanist (deceased).

The certificate still in her hand, she burst into his bedroom without knocking.

"Caspar, is it true?" she demanded.

"Is what true?"

"That you are a peer. . . an earl?"

"Yes, that is so," he agreed.

"Why didn't you tell me? Why call yourself Mr. Lomax?"

"When I'm abroad I often do. It attracts less attention and spares me much tedious toadying. The possession of a title isn't always an advantage. Lomax is my family name."

"But to keep me in ignorance of it! How could you practice such a wicked deception?"

"I deceived you—yes. But is it such a heinous offense? I should think a bride would be pleased rather than angry at finding herself a countess," he said dryly.

"No doubt most brides would," she retorted. "And so should I, I daresay, if I were a suitable person. But you know my background. My father's parents were servants. My mother was a Chinese peasant."

"Creed took you for the daughter of a Manchu lady. No, listen to me for a moment," he went on as she would have interrupted him. "I expected this reaction from you, Flora, and that's why I didn't enlighten you. I am the best judge of who is a suitable wife for me, and you are much better qualified for that role than some frivolous chit of a girl whose only recommendation is her aristocratic pedigree. You have no cause to be ashamed of your forebears. I've no doubt they were a great deal more respectable than some of the dissolute scoundrels from whom I'm descended."

"I'm not ashamed of my forebears. But I have enough sense to know that I'm not a suitable wife for a man of your rank."

"To blazes with my rank!" he exclaimed impatiently. "More often than not it's a damned nuisance. Were it not for my rank I shouldn't have married at all."

She flinched, and Caspar apologized for letting slip the profanity. But it wasn't that which had distressed her. She had known that he didn't love her, but she hadn't realized until now that their marriage had been forced on him by his obligations to his line.

Since early morning she had been waiting for him to repeat the kiss he had given her after soothing her night fears. But neither before nor after their wedding had he made any gesture of affection. Their only contact had been the touch of his steady brown hands on her nervous ones while they had repeated the vows; when he had slipped on the ring; and when, their hands again joined, the clergyman had said, "Those whom God hath joined together let no man put asunder."

He said bracingly, "Don't look so troubled, *ya-t'ou*. You will do very well, I assure you. Now let's go downstairs and have luncheon. A few glasses of champagne are what you need."

She remembered Lily saying to her, *"And if the count gives you two or three glasses of bubbly you won't mind what he does to you."*

From that echo from the recent past her thoughts went forward some hours to the coming night, when their ship would be gliding downriver and she and her bridegroom would be sharing a cabin.

Would she mind what Caspar did to her?

Since his kiss she had thought she would not; that in his strong arms she would discover the delights that both Père d'Espinay and Caspar himself had assured her were the natural and proper relationship between men and women.

But now suddenly she was afraid again. He was so tall and broad shouldered. If his height and the breadth of his back were greater than those of the Frenchman, surely his other parts must be larger in proportion? Recalling the pain of her previous experience, she repressed a shudder of apprehension.

PART TWO

SHANGHAI TO ENGLAND

CHAPTER ONE

THE AFTERNOON before the mail steamer *Coromandel* embarked on her voyage from Shanghai to Colombo, a well-dressed woman stood on the first-class passenger deck watching the bustling throng on the quayside below her.

The steamer was berthed at Wusung, twelve miles downriver from the city, because lack of water on the bar prevented vessels of deep draft from proceeding farther up the Yangtze without lightening.

A railway brought passengers and their baggage to the docks at Wusung, and blue-clad coolies manhandled the enormous cabin trunks bearing their owners' names and destinations and marked Wanted on Voyage or Not Wanted on Voyage. The cases labeled Cabin they carried on pads on their heads, moving nimbly up and down the baggage gangway as if a heavy leather portmanteau weighed no more than a small sack of meal.

Articles such as hatboxes, bundles of rugs and dressing cases were brought aboard by passengers or their servants; and it was the arrival of her fellow travelers that the woman observed with the keenest interest.

From Colombo, where passengers changed to a different steamer, she was booked to Brindisi in Italy, there to travel by railway to Calais and, after crossing the Channel, to London.

Including the journey by train, the cost of the

voyage was sixty-five pounds, plus an additional charge to secure her exclusive use of a first-class cabin.

Otherwise she might have had to share it with someone joining the ship at one of the intermediate ports. And although she was not averse to sharing her quarters, she preferred to choose her companion—and not from among her own sex.

On the purser's register of passengers she was listed as Mrs. Herbert Roscoe. No one seeing her standing at the rail in a suitably nautical walking costume of white serge braided with navy would have had any reason to suspect she was other than what she appeared to be: a good-looking, respectable matron still on the right side of forty.

In fact she was neither married nor respectable, although for the past four years she had lived as Herbert Roscoe's wife and now professed to be his widow.

He had met her in the notorious Promenade bar at the Empire Theatre in London, at which time everything about her had proclaimed her a lady of easy virtue.

Before coming to England on leave, Herbert had buried a wife who for thirty-five years had given him precious little comfort, in bed or out of it. In Julia he had found the antithesis of the late Maud Roscoe. At supper, in a private room at Romano's restaurant, she ate heartily, drank heartily and laughed heartily. Afterward, on the red plush sofa, she seemed to enjoy herself as much as he did. When he expressed regret that he was too old to repeat the pleasure, she chuckled and bet him five guineas that if he came back to her lodgings—there was no question of her being admitted to his hotel—she would surprise him.

To his astonished gratification, in the early hours of the morning she had won herself five gold sovereigns and five silver shillings. A week before the end of his leave, he invited her to return to China with him.

Julia accepted his offer because, although she had no desire to go to China and expected to be extremely bored there, it was better than staying where she was. Not long before meeting Herbert, she had been put to the expense and risk of an abortion—not her first—and she knew she was lucky so far to have escaped the other hazard of her profession.

Herbert was more than twenty years her senior and could never have been an attractive man. But at least he was sexually normal—more than could be said of some of the clients she picked up at the Empire—and since his powers were on the wane it was unlikely she would have to counterfeit enthusiasm more than once or twice a week. Moreover, he promised her that if after six months together neither of them had any complaints, he would make her his sole legatee.

At the time she had taken this promise with a large pinch of salt. All that mattered was to avoid the decline into sickness and squalor that was the inevitable end of most of the Promenade bar women.

However, not only had Herbert kept his word, but he had left her so comfortably placed that in future when she went to bed with a man it would be for her pleasure, not his.

She was about to turn away from the ship's rail and go to her cabin, there to broach a bottle of champagne and to rest for an hour, when her attention was caught by a couple coming through the crowd. The man was exceptionally tall with an upright commanding bearing that made people move aside to let him pass. With him was a girl whom at first Julia took to be a Chinese in European clothes.

Almost at once she revised the impression. The girl must be a Eurasian. It was only her slanting dark eyes and cascade of raven's-wing hair that had made her appear to be a native. At a second glance, with her eyes now concealed by the brim of her unbecoming hat, she looked much more English than Asian, and very young, still in the schoolroom.

However, it wasn't the girl but the man who caused Julia to linger while they mounted the gangway. Before he had set foot on deck, she was considering ways to make his acquaintance.

A second or two before they passed her, she turned from her place at the rail and would have bumped into him had he not reacted to her movement by immediately checking his stride.

"Oh. . . I beg your pardon!" she exclaimed with an apologetic smile.

The man's hard gray eyes swept over her. For an instant she had the disconcerting feeling that he knew the kind of woman she really was—or had been four years earlier.

Then she realized it was impossible. She had dyed her hair red in those days, painted her face and dressed in flamboyant clothes. Now her hair was its natural shade of brown, her makeup was discreet and her clothes were impeccably ladylike. Even one of her regular clients would be unlikely to recognize her after so long an interval, and in such a different guise.

Certainly this man had not done so. If she had seen him before she would remember him.

Men with his looks had no need to patronize places like the Promenade bar. They could have all the women they wanted: not whores but highborn society ladies who, from some of the tales she had heard, were often no better than tarts, except that they could be had for nothing.

He inclined his tall handsome head, waiting for her to step past him.

Mrs. Roscoe bowed, murmured, "Thank you," and walked away. She had expected to enjoy the voyage home and to find some congenial companionship among the unattached men or those whose wives were not traveling with them. But she had not anticipated feeling the excitement that possessed her as she went to her quarters to relax before changing for dinner.

TO FLORA'S SURPRISE AND PUZZLEMENT, she found that Caspar had reserved the same accommodation they'd had on the river steamer: two single cabins without any private access from one to the other.

"Why aren't we sharing a cabin?" she asked when the steward who had shown them to their quarters had gone away.

"It will be more comfortable to have two; particularly in the Indian Ocean and the Red Sea, where it will be exceedingly hot. You'll find when we get to England that people with the means to live in comfort generally do have separate bedrooms and dressing rooms."

"Really?" she exclaimed in astonishment. "I thought married people always slept with each other."

Then she colored and wished she had held her

tongue. Instinct told her—too late—that it wasn't the sort of remark a well-bred girl made.

"Sometimes they do," he agreed. "But in our case that can be postponed until we reach Longwarden."

"Longwarden?"

"My home."

"Oh. . . I see. How long will the journey take?"

She knew, because he had told her, that from Shanghai to England was more than ten thousand miles, but she had no idea how long the steamer would take to traverse that great distance.

Caspar said, "It depends which way I decide to go. The fastest way is by sea as far as Brindisi, in southern Italy, and from there on to cut across Europe in the P. & O. express train to Calais. From here to Brindisi takes a month. Or one can go to Marseilles and catch a train there. Alternatively, one can go the whole way by sea, landing either at Plymouth on the south coast of England or at Tilbury Docks, which are on the Thames close to London. That would take rather more than five weeks. The choice depends, to some extent, on how congenial or uncongenial we find our traveling companions. As you will already have gathered, I am still incognito. For the time being you are Mrs. Lomax."

A slight frown contracted his brows. "And as such you should have your hair up. You had better ring for the stewardess and ask her to bring you some hairpins. At the moment you look as if you are still in the schoolroom. In Europe when a girl comes out she puts up her hair and never wears it down again, except in the privacy of her bedroom."

Flora said in some consternation, "I'm not sure I can put my hair up. It looks very complicated."

"Ask the stewardess to help you. I'm sure you'll soon learn the knack of it."

The stewardess assigned to her cabin proved to be a motherly woman who, if surprised by the request, had the tact not to show it. Full of praise for its thickness and sheen, she arranged Flora's long silky hair in an upswept style that she said was known as a pompadour.

As she brushed and pinned she spoke of the current hair fashions; of marcel waving and French combing, and of Marteaux curls, Scalpettes and artificial fringes.

Deep waves and a frizz of curls to soften the brow line were the desiderata, Flora gathered. But she did not think they would become her. Her hair was straight and grew in a smooth sweeping line across the top of her broad and rather high forehead. On her, curls would look as absurd as they would on a pony.

When the stewardess had completed her handiwork, Flora said, "Thank you very much. I could never have managed it myself, but now that I've seen how it's done, I think I shall be able to copy it."

"If you have any difficulty you have only to ring for me, madam. I have only one other lady to look after between here and Hong Kong. After that I expect to be busier, but from now until Saturday I'll be glad to dress your hair for you."

"That's very kind of you. Thank you, Mrs. Salter."

Did the pompadour make her look more mature, Flora wondered when she was alone. Perhaps it did; she couldn't tell. She could see that it emphasized her long neck, but was that an improvement? She was inclined to think not. Indeed, the great puffball of hair and the unaccustomed exposure of her nape made her fear that she looked like a mushroom with too thin a stalk.

Nervously she tapped on the door of the neighboring cabin. It was opened by a steward who, until she disturbed him, had been engaged in unpacking Caspar's clothes.

"Oh. . . I wanted to speak to my husband. But I see he isn't here," she said shyly.

"Mr. Lomax is with the ship's butcher, who looks after the passengers' pets, madam," the man explained. "Normally we only carry parrots, cockatoos and a few small animals. It's one of the company's rules that dogs are not allowed on board. However, it seems an exception has been made for Mr. Lomax's dog. Perhaps Mr. Lomax has friends at court, as the saying is. One of the company's directors, perhaps?"

"I don't know," she replied. "He is very attached to his gundog. Which way must I go to find the ship's butcher, please?"

He gave her the necessary directions, but before she reached her destination she was met by Caspar, who said at once, "Yes, that's much better. I may still be accused of cradle snatching, but you can at least pass for eighteen now."

"I feel very strange. . . not myself. I suppose I shall get used to it. I should feel better if I had one of those high-throated blouses to disguise my long neck."

They had met between decks, in a part of the ship removed from the comings and goings of the first-class passengers and their servants.

Caspar put out his hand to touch the side of her

neck, just below her left ear. His fingers slid down to the hollow at the base of her throat.

"A swan's neck is greatly admired in England," he told her. "I'm informed that among the fair sex it's considered even more desirable than a handspan waist."

The slow cool brush of his fingertips against the warmth of her skin sent a queer sort of shiver running through her. She found herself unable to speak for a sudden tightness in her throat.

She wondered with whom he had discussed the physical attributes that women wished for, and how he defined female beauty.

Swallowing to clear the tightness, she asked huskily, "And what does your sex admire most?"

She was wearing one of the blouses procured for her by Mrs. Hunter. The round neckline was finished with a small frill of eyelet embroidery that the missionary's wife had called Madeira work, and a bow of limp ribbon.

Caspar twitched the loops to make them sit better. Then he ran his finger and thumb down the length of one of the loose ends, making her conscious of his knuckles rubbing lightly but with a certain intimacy against her body.

"I can only speak for myself," was his lazy reply. "There are many attributes that please me: rosy lips...pretty shoulders and arms...a shapely bosom; the list is too long to enumerate."

As he spoke, it seemed to her that his hand increased its pressure against her breast while his gaze was fixed on her lips.

Had they been somewhere more private, she felt sure he would have kissed her and perhaps touched her in the way he had once before, during the night they had shared a bunk in the mountain hostel. Suddenly she wanted very much to feel his firm mouth on hers and his lean hand enfolding her breast.

But perhaps because they were in a place where their seclusion could be disturbed at any moment, or because she was only imagining that he felt a desire to caress her, he let go of the ribbon and said, "Come: let me show you the public rooms. You'll find there is usually quite a good library on board."

Masking her inner disturbance, she said, "Your cabin steward thinks you must be a friend of one of the company's directors, or you wouldn't have been allowed to bring Thor aboard."

"His supposition is correct. I'm acquainted with several of the directors. The captain knows who I am, and we shall be dining at his table. I've had a look at the passenger list. For the present there's no one on it whom we might meet again in England. That may not be the case throughout the voyage, but I hope it will."

"I know I must seem very gauche, but I shall try my best not to embarrass you by making too many gaffes," she said earnestly.

"I doubt if you will make any. That was not what I meant," he replied. "I want to spend much of the voyage making extracts from my travel notebooks and writing to fellow naturalists. It's easier to keep strangers at a distance than people from one's own milieu. Not that I have ever had difficulty in discouraging bores," he added sardonically. "It's a technique you will have to learn if you wish to avoid being pestered by gossips and featherbrains."

NOT LONG AFTER DINNER THAT NIGHT he said she looked tired and advised her to go to bed early.

They had been drinking their coffee in a quiet corner of the main saloon, which was comfortably furnished with many groups of chairs and sofas, their flowered chintz covers lending freshness and color to the dark red brown patina of the mahogany paneling.

"It has been a strenuous day for you," he said, rising to his feet. "I shall smoke a cigar on deck and then come below myself."

Not knowing quite what to say—"Good night" was hardly appropriate in the circumstances—Flora gave him an uncertain smile and left the saloon.

Her first act on gaining her cabin was to take the pins from her hair and let it fall to her shoulders. Her head was aching—from either the unaccustomed hairstyle or the strain of being seated next to the ship's genial captain and having to smile at his jokes while being uncomfortably aware that some of the other wives present were watching her every move with critical eyes.

Or perhaps her headache was caused by apprehension at the thought of what lay ahead.

"Your husband will teach you the art of making love," Caspar had said when she offered herself as his concubine. Now he was her husband, and her first lesson was almost upon her.

But in spite of the pleasurable sensations induced by his touch earlier on, she could not rid herself of the fear that the consummation of their union must, in the end, be horribly painful. How could it not be?

ON THE STARBOARD SIDE of the first-class promenade deck, Carlyon stood with one hand on the rail and the other holding a cheroot, which from time to time he raised to his lips.

Never a heavy smoker, he often dispensed with the habit for weeks at a time. He knew that if it became a vice—as it had with his father—it could impair a man's palate for wine and good food and diminish his appreciation of a sweetly perfumed flower or the subtle scents of female flesh.

That evening at dinner, as he sat next to the handsome widow Mrs. Roscoe, his keen sense of smell had detected the unmistakable scent of a sexually excited woman.

In the course of their conversation he had learned that her husband had been many years her senior and that the illness from which he had died had been of several months' duration. Probably it was a long time since she'd had satisfactory relations with a man. Although she hadn't attempted to flirt with him during the meal, he had little doubt that she meant to make up for lost time during the voyage; if not with one of her fellow passengers, then with one of the more personable of the ship's officers.

Whether it was the effect of ozone or the motion of the ship, ocean cruises were known to have an aphrodisiac effect on the female sex. That was if one believed—as he did—that all women were sexual beings. Many men didn't believe it, or only in relation to loose women; not in connection with their own wives and daughters.

The popular delusion that any nice woman was a wholly spiritual creature, immune from the lusts of the flesh, was very convenient for men like himself:

men who preferred impermanent relationships, but not with professional partners from whom there was always a risk of picking up disease.

Thinking briefly about the women he had known—all, with the exception of his father's mistress, other men's wives with passionate natures their husbands had failed to satisfy—reminded him that he was now a husband himself. With a bride who, because of her experience at the hands of the Frenchman and, more recently, in the Russian woman's brothel, was likely to be dreading her wedding night even more than the average virgin.

The task of going gently with her was not one he relished. Although Netta Beaumont and Marie Colbert had taken the edge off the urgent desire for a woman that had built up during his long journey through the hinterland, giving him back the control necessary with any bride and particularly one as severely abused as his young wife, he knew that he would much prefer to be spending the night enjoying the ripe charms of Mrs. Roscoe.

As the thought of her crossed his mind again, a woman's voice said, "Shall I find England greatly changed after four years away, Mr. Lomax?"

He turned. She was standing beside him, a silk shawl thrown over her dress.

"Hardly at all, I should imagine." He tossed the cheroot over the rail. "Have you relations in England?"

"No, no one, but I cannot stay here," she replied. "Perhaps I shall travel in Europe. I may even visit America. Most people have some family ties, but I have none. I am free to go where I please."

They began to walk along the deck, toward two

tarpaulin-covered lifeboats suspended from white-painted davits. Between them was a patch of dense shadow. Just before they drew level with it, Carlyon glanced over his shoulder. The next moment Mrs. Roscoe found herself swept into the dark space.

"And to do as you please," he added before he kissed her.

"You don't waste any time, do you?" she said with a breathless little laugh, when she could speak.

"No," he agreed. "Would you rather I had waited until the voyage was half-over?" He kissed her again before saying, "I'll come to your cabin in an hour. What is your number?"

"Number seventeen, but—"

"In an hour," he repeated, and left her.

ALTHOUGH SHE HAD BEEN EXPECTING IT, the tap on her door made Flora give a nervous start.

"C-come in," she called in a tense voice.

Caspar entered, closing the door behind him. Most of the furniture in the cabin—the washbasin stand, the dressing table and the night table containing a chamber pot—was bolted to the deck as a precaution against rough weather. But there was a light basket-weave chair that could be moved from its place by the door. He lifted it closer to her berth.

"Are you comfortable? Have you everything you need?" he asked as he sat down.

"Yes, very comfortable, thank you."

She had expected him to be in his nightclothes, but he was still fully dressed.

He said, "I've been thinking things over, *ya-t'ou*. As you will not be eighteen until shortly after we reach England, and as there has been little or no in-

terval between my proposal and our wedding, I think
we should treat the voyage as being in the nature of
an engagement. A fuller relationship can wait until
we reach home. In the meantime, we shall have ample opportunity to get to know each other better.
How does that plan strike you?"

Her immediate reaction was one of enormous relief.

"I . . . wh-whatever you think is best, Caspar."

"You agree? Good. Then I'll say good-night."

He rose and replaced the chair, swinging it back
into position with an easy movement of one hand.

He was as strong as the Chinese coolies that hurried about the docks with loads on their heads or on
great wooden yokes, she thought. But he wasn't a
coolie. He was a gentleman. And so far all the other
gentlemen she had seen looked as if without servants
to look after them they would never survive.

He stooped to take one of her hands and lift it to
his lips.

"Good night, Flora. Sleep well."

Unexpectedly, he bent to brush another brief kiss
on her cheek. As he did so her sensitive nostrils
caught a faint whiff of what she took to be his shaving soap, although she had not smelled its aroma
when he kissed her cheek earlier in the day.

She had scarcely answered, "Good night," before
he had gone and she was alone again.

DURING HER YEARS AS A WHORE Julia had learned all
the ways to titillate male desire and give her clients a
good time. But neither the man who had first seduced
her nor any of those who had succeeded him had ever
troubled to ensure an equal pleasure for her.

In Carlyon's arms she experienced for the first time a transport of sensual enjoyment far beyond anything she had known.

Presently they shared a second bottle of champagne and discussed the other passengers who had been at the captain's table—with one exception. Neither of them mentioned Mrs. Lomax.

Later, when he had left her, Julia spent some time drowsily wondering why, married to a lovely young girl, he had chosen to initiate a shipboard liaison with her. Was it possible the beautiful Eurasian with her flawless skin and slanting dark eyes was not really his wife?

There was more to Mr. Lomax than met the eye, she decided. Could it be that the girl was the natural child of a Manchu princess and some important English official who, in a belated fit of conscience, had sent Mr. Lomax to rescue her from the court of the empress dowager?

It would account for the girl's air of anxiety and the troubled glances she cast in his direction from time to time.

In her London years Julia had spent many hours escaping from the problems of reality in the pages of sixpenny novels. She had no difficulty in believing that the man who had just made love to her was only pretending to be a naturalist and was really a professional adventurer who spent his life in a series of dangerous exploits.

The idea excited her. Herbert had been such a dull man. *All* the men she had known had been dull men. To find herself swept off her feet by one who was bold and ruthless in the pursuit of his objectives was more than she had hoped for.

Yawning, she snuggled under the bedclothes, remembering the feel of his broad brown shoulders under her hands, and wishing away the hours until he came to her again.

THE EXPRESS MAIL STEAMER SERVICE run by the Peninsular & Oriental Steam Navigation Company—known throughout the world as the P. & O.—left Shanghai on alternate Tuesday mornings at daylight.

Since this was about 6:00 A.M. most of the passengers were still in their cabins, if not asleep, when *Coromandel* slid away from the quayside, watched by the Chinese stevedores who had released her from her moorings.

Alone on the promenade deck, Flora bade a silent farewell to the land that had been her home, and where the three people she had loved were buried in lonely graves she would never see again. As *Coromandel*'s cables were cast off and winched through the hawseholes, she felt her past life being severed from her uncertain future. It was a heart-wrenching moment, but her pale face remained as impassive as those of the men on the dock who were watching the great ship glide slowly into midstream.

She had come on deck lightly clad, not realizing it would be cold compared with the warmth between decks. As she stood at the rail with the river wind blowing in her face and her mind full of desolate thoughts, a warm coat was placed around her shoulders.

Caspar said, "You shouldn't be here without a wrap. Did the noise of the engines wake you?"

She nodded and thanked him for the coat.

"Oh...I forgot to put my hair up," she exclaimed with dismay.

"And to put on a hat and some gloves," he pointed out, clicking his tongue.

"I'm sorry, Caspar," she said contritely. "I had better go and do it now."

"There's no hurry. I doubt if anyone else will appear on this deck before breakfast." He put his arm around her shoulders.

The comforting gesture, as if he guessed her feelings, almost broke down her tight self-control. She longed to turn to him and hide her face against his chest. But she knew she must not; not in public, where they might be observed by members of the ship's crew.

"I suppose you have sailed from England too many times to feel any pangs when you leave it," she said, knowing he had been on many expeditions before coming to China.

"Yes, to me the moment of departure has always been one of great excitement and high expectations," he agreed. "While some people stand at the stern looking back, I am among those who prefer to be in the bows awaiting the first glimpse of landfall. And a journey never previously undertaken is the most exciting of all."

As he spoke he drew her away from the rail and began to stroll along the deck. "Hong Kong... Singapore, the Lion City...Penang...Colombo... don't the names make you eager to see the places? They did me when I was your age."

"You speak as if I were a child and you an old man," she said with an upward glance at his bronzed face.

"It's a long time since I was seventeen. Before you were out of your cradle, I was at Eton."

The name meant nothing to her. She knew more of France than of England. But having already violated the rules of his world by forgetting to cover her head and protect her hands, she didn't ask him to explain the reference, thereby emphasizing her ignorance.

Instead she asked, "How long shall we spend at each of the places you've mentioned?"

"It varies. Sometimes twenty-four hours, sometimes only a few hours."

They had reached the part of the deck overlooking the bows, and the steamer herself had swung around. Now the berth she had left was astern. Ahead, downstream, lay the mouth of the river and the Tunghai, the Eastern Sea.

Perhaps because Flora was no longer shivering and had Caspar's strong arm still around her, her spirits lifted. She smiled.

"Yes, you're right; it's very exciting. I'm looking forward to it," she told him with resolute cheerfulness.

"I'm sure you won't be disappointed. Now go and make yourself presentable so that we can have breakfast. I'm hungry."

For the rest of that day and for three days more, *Coromandel* steamed down the east coast of China, past the port of Foochow and the coast of Fukien province, where at one time the traders and fishermen had been brutal pirates and wreckers.

Then came the Formosa Channel, a strait a hundred miles wide between China and the mountainous island of Formosa, which some years before, in 1895, had been ceded to the Japanese.

Caspar was interested in the semisavage tribes of Malay descent who were said to inhabit the mountains.

"It's a very bad climate, I've heard: damp, devilish hot and malarious. You couldn't take your wife there, Lomax," said one of the older men at luncheon when Formosa—or Taiwan, as it was sometimes called—was under discussion.

"My wife is accustomed to hazardous journeys and difficult conditions. But no, you are right. I shouldn't wish to expose her to malaria unnecessarily, particularly the malignant form," Caspar agreed.

The conversation turned to the disease that, thanks to Ross of the Indian Medical Service, was now known to be transferred from person to person by the female mosquito, and against which quinine was the only effective remedy.

Although this was a topic on which the gentlemen had more to say than the ladies, Flora had noticed that even when the conversation was on a subject to which all could contribute, one person whose views were never canvased—except by the captain and Caspar—was Mrs. Roscoe.

Sometimes when Flora was sitting on a steamer chair on deck, and had laid down her book to gaze at the distant coastline, ladies who were taking exercise would address some civil remark to her, or even pause beside her chair for a few minutes.

This never happened to Mrs. Roscoe. She received no friendly overtures from her own sex, although Flora had observed that when their wives were not present the gentlemen would sometimes take the opportunity to talk to her.

When she mentioned this curious behavior to

Caspar, his reply was, "She is not a lady in the social sense of the word. The captain and her husband were at school together, and that is why she has a place at the captain's table. He is less of a snob than most of his passengers and continues to treat her with the courtesy due to a friend's wife, even if the marriage was a mésalliance."

"How do people know she is not a lady?" she asked. "She seems to dress and behave in the same way as everyone else."

"Yes, she has a veneer of good breeding, and she dresses well. But her voice sometimes gives her away. There are traces of the industrial North in her vowels, and her manners are genteel rather than well-bred. She drinks tea with her little finger extended—that sort of thing."

"I think it's very ill-bred to ostracize her for those trivial reasons," said Flora indignantly. "If you have no objection, Caspar, I should like to invite her to join us when we go ashore at Hong Kong. I know how cast down I should feel were I on this voyage by myself and treated as she is being treated. Indeed, if Mrs. Roscoe is not acceptable, I don't understand why I am. I suppose people are only polite to me because they can see that you are extremely well-bred, even if they don't know you are an aristocrat. Please—do let her come with us."

For a moment she thought he might refuse. Although he was always courteous to Mrs. Roscoe, he never eyed her fine figure when he thought himself unobserved. Flora's intuition told her that had Mrs. Roscoe been the only woman passenger, most of the men would have enjoyed her society. But she felt sure Caspar's behavior would have been no different from at present. He neither ignored Mrs. Roscoe nor surreptitiously admired her, but treated her as he did every woman.

"Very well, if you wish it," he consented. "Perhaps she can help you to order some clothes. It should have struck me before that your wardrobe is quite inadequate for a voyage of several weeks' duration. You cannot continue to dine in the dress you have worn up to now. You need two or three evening dresses. In Hong Kong, I believe, it is possible to have them made up in a matter of hours."

Mrs. Roscoe seemed taken aback when, that afternoon, Flora approached her and said, "Perhaps you have friends in Hong Kong who will wish you to spend tomorrow with them. But if you have no engagements, my husband and I wondered if you would care to join us when we go ashore?"

After a pause the older woman said, "It's very kind of you, Mrs. Lomax. I should like to join you. Thank you."

WHEN CARLYON CAME TO HER CABIN on Friday night, Julia was reading a novel. She was wearing a loose silk wrapper over a chemise and knickers made of lace-trimmed white nainsook. She had discarded her corset and exchanged Kleinert's hook-on hose supporter for a pair of frilly black garters to hold up her stockings, which were silky black mercerized lisle with lace-patterned ankles.

The novel slipped to the deck as she rose to receive his embrace. He had not come to her the night before, and she had been unable to sleep for wanting him.

She thought it unlikely he had spent the night with

the Eurasian girl—after watching them together for four days, she felt sure they were not on those terms—and as yet there was no one else on board who could have taken his fancy. But after Hong Kong she might have one or more rivals, and already she could not bear the thought of being deprived of the delicious sensations he was so skilled at inducing.

After two or three kisses he sat down and pulled her onto his lap. While he gently nibbled her ear and nuzzled her neck, his right hand fondled her knee, then slowly stroked its way higher, past the garter and under her knicker leg, to find the bare skin of her thigh.

His touch made her quiver with pleasure, but she felt she should hide her impatience for his fingers to seek out their target. Restraining his hand from moving on, she said, "Was it your idea to invite me to join you and Mrs. Lomax tomorrow?"

"It was her suggestion. She thought you might be lonely sightseeing in Hong Kong on your own."

He removed his hand from her leg to open the front of her wrapper and pull the blue satin ribbons that, threaded through lace insertions, drew the top of her chemise into gathers across her full bosom.

"Aren't you afraid she'll suspect there's something between us?"

"She won't suspect it from my behavior, nor—I trust—from yours," was his crisp reply.

"No, no—I'll be very discreet. I like her. I feel sorry for her."

"Why does she inspire your compassion?"

"Well, you aren't a faithful husband, are you? And she's young and still has ideals. Didn't we all at her age?"

She thought, given this cue, he would tell her the truth about the girl. No man liked being taken for a cad when in fact he was a knight-errant.

But he said nothing, instead bending his head to explore her warm powdered flesh with lips and tongue. Within seconds the girl was forgotten.

THE STEAMER ARRIVED at her first port of call while the passengers were having luncheon.

More than ten million tons of shipping a year passed through the magnificent harbor, a huge sheet of water between Hong Kong and the mainland. It was always crowded with vessels of every kind: iron-clad naval torpedo boats, Portuguese lorchas, Chinese junks and sampans.

When the settlement was first established, in the early years of Queen Victoria's reign, it had been considered unhealthy. But improved drainage, better sanitary arrangements and a good water supply had changed it to one of the healthiest spots in the tropics.

Mrs. Roscoe had shopped there before, en route to Shanghai with her husband. While Caspar went off to enjoy the fine public gardens, the two women spent much of the afternoon selecting materials and trimmings to be made up and delivered before the steamer sailed the following evening.

Later they joined him for tea in one of the city's hotels. It seemed he had also been shopping and had bought several bolts of silk for his wife to have in reserve.

This news made Flora regret being persuaded by Mrs. Roscoe that, because Hong Kong was a free port and prices there were much cheaper than they would be in England, she should buy more than she had intended.

"In that case perhaps I should cancel some of the dresses I've ordered," she suggested anxiously.

"Certainly not," Caspar said firmly. "I doubt if you've been any more extravagant than the other ladies from the ship. What excesses, in the name of fashion, have you committed, Mrs. Roscoe?"

"I have been rather reckless, I admit; but after four years in the backwoods my existing wardrobe is sadly dowdy," she answered.

"On the contrary, I should have said you were notably well dressed," he told her.

She was clearly pleased by his gallantry, and so was Flora. After some hours in the widow's company, she felt more than ever drawn toward her, and doubly antipathetic toward those who snubbed her.

Even by day the city of Victoria, with its large handsome houses rising in tiers from the Praya at the water's edge toward the summit of the Peak, was an impressive sight. By night it was breathtaking.

After dinner Flora spent a long time on deck, gazing at the blaze of bright lights from the lower part of the city and the smaller, more distant lights shining from the steep upper slopes.

The lights made by man were golden, but above Victoria Peak hung the stars. Their light was silvery, twinkling from parts of the firmament that were so far away that the distance from Hong Kong to England was a mere step by comparison.

She was leaning on the varnished rail, lost in contemplation of the scene, when two women she did not much like paused beside her. One of them said, "All alone, Mrs. Lomax? Where is Mr. Lomax this evening? And your friend Mrs. Roscoe?''

"My husband has gone ashore. I believe Mrs. Roscoe has retired," she said pleasantly, although she sensed some innuendo behind the seemingly affable questions.

They smiled their thin smiles and walked on, leaving her vaguely uneasy. Presently, thinking it over, she came to the conclusion that it might not be *comme il faut* for her to be on deck alone in her husband's absence.

Why Caspar had gone ashore was something he had not explained; he'd said merely that he had business there and did not expect it to take long. If she wished to retire before he returned, there was no reason for her to wait for him.

She was reading in bed when she heard the light rap on the door that had made her stiffen apprehensively on their first night aboard.

Tonight, feeling no such alarm, she called, "Come in," and laid down her book.

"I knew you were not asleep yet by the light shining through your curtains as I came along the deck," he said.

Unlike the second-class cabins with portholes in the hull of the ship, all first-class accommodation overlooked the deck below the quarterdeck.

This time he did not use the chair but sat on the edge of her berth, which although fixed in position was in the style of an ordinary bed. In the second-class quarters, so her stewardess had told her, the cabins had upper and lower berths.

"You will need some jewels to wear with your new dresses," he said. "I haven't bought you anything elaborate, merely a necklace and earrings. I hope you don't dislike jade?"

Flora shook her head. "But you shouldn't have spent any more money on me, Caspar. My lack of jewels hasn't embarrassed me. But perhaps it has embarrassed you," was her afterthought.

With her half-Chinese looks and her unbecoming clothes, she knew she had not been an ornament to him.

"It has embarrassed me to realize how remiss I have been in not equipping you properly."

As he spoke he took from its box a long rope of carved green beads, which he laid on the sheet. In a second box was a pair of jade-and-gold earrings, the color of the stones matching the beads.

The people in the village near the mission had been too poor to possess a great deal of jade, and certainly they'd had nothing to compare with the quality of these adornments. Overwhelmed by Caspar's generosity, Flora attempted to express her gratitude.

He cut short her thanks, saying, "Pearls are what girls of your age usually wear. But in England you will have my grandmother's pearls, and since in the eyes of the world you are now a married woman, the jade is not inappropriate. Some Englishwomen consider it unlucky to wear green. I trust you don't subscribe to that absurd superstition."

"Oh, no—for in China jade is thought to bring good fortune."

"So I believe. An equally foolish idea. No inanimate object can have any effect on our lives."

"Except that in time of famine jade can be sold to buy food," she pointed out.

"Very true. From that point of view, the possession of it could be lucky. Fortunately we don't have famines in England. What are you reading?"

The book he picked up was a novel pressed upon her by Mrs. Roscoe, who had said she could not fail to enjoy it; although it had been published ten years earlier, it had had a tremendous success.

It was called *Ships That Pass in the Night*, by Beatrice Harraden, and was set in a hospital for consumptives in a German winter resort. The tubercular heroine, Bernadine, who had gone there to get well or die, spent much of the story talking to a fellow patient, the Disagreeable Man.

Some of his more trenchant comments reminded Flora of Caspar, but in general the novel struck her as gloomy and dull, with none of the characters having much chance of recovery.

After a glance at the title, Caspar riffled through the pages, reading a passage here and there.

"This is novelettish stuff. Can you find nothing better to read?"

"It was recommended to me by Mrs. Roscoe. She thought it excellent."

"She may be a useful companion on shopping expeditions, but she has no brains," he said shortly. "Don't let her encroach on you too much. On subjects other than dress you will soon find her conversation a bore."

He bade her good-night, this time without stooping to kiss her.

THE PARCELS CONTAINING HER NEW CLOTHES having been delivered as promised, the next night she was able to appear for dinner in a much more becoming dress of ivory silk trimmed with moiré ribbon of the same shade. It was still a much plainer gown than those worn by most of the ladies, but it fitted her better, was well-cut, and the color suited her skin and the deep clouded green of the jade.

By now she had mastered the knack of putting her hair up and no longer depended on Mrs. Salter. Not that she could attempt the elaborate coiffures of the passengers who had their maids traveling with them; but several small tortoiseshell combs bought during the previous shopping made the task considerably easier. She no longer feared that her hair might fall down in public, putting Caspar to shame.

"Mmm...a marked improvement," was his comment when he saw her in her new finery.

The seating at the captain's table had been rearranged to include a number of newcomers. To her relief, Flora found herself seated next to a Mr. Eliot, an elderly man with whom by the end of the meal she was deep in an absorbing discussion of the kind of literature that Père d'Espinay had taught her to enjoy.

From Hong Kong the mail ship steamed through the South China Sea to Singapore Island, at the southern tip of the Malay Peninsula.

Coromandel berthed at the P. & O. wharf in New Harbour, three miles from Singapore Town, but there was no shortage of transport, including steam trams, gharries drawn by sturdy little Malay ponies, and the small hooded carriages called jinrikishas that had been imported from Japan. They were drawn by muscular Chinese.

Singapore boasted large botanical gardens with every species of tropical vegetation. This time Flora and Mrs. Roscoe accompanied Caspar to see them.

Later he hired a carriage to visit the outskirts of the city, where from good shaded roads could be seen large comfortable bungalows in well-kept compounds.

"I've been told life is very luxurious here," remarked Mrs. Roscoe, twirling her parasol.

She was sharing the front seat with Flora, while Caspar had his back to the driver.

"Very luxurious for Europeans," Flora said dryly. "Have you read what it says in the pocket book?"

This was a small but thick book published by the P. & O. as "a useful companion en route" for its Far Eastern passengers.

The widow shook her head. Unlike Flora, she did not seem interested in the history of their ports of call.

"It describes what it calls the native quarter as not very inviting," said Flora.

"I'm sure it isn't," said Mrs. Roscoe. "I've heard it is full of opium dens and houses of ill repute."

The remark was a painful reminder of Flora's shaming experience at the hands of the Russian procuress. Something of her innermost feelings must have been reflected in her face, for the widow asked, "Are you feeling unwell, my dear? It is very hot today. Would you care for my smelling salts?"

Thinking it simpler to accept the offer than to refuse it, Flora took the small cut-glass bottle from which the other woman had already removed a silver screw tip.

Never having used smelling salts before, she sniffed the contents too vigorously, and the pungent fumes almost choked her. With streaming eyes and feeling exceedingly foolish, she accepted Caspar's proffered handkerchief and buried her face in its folds while she regained her breath.

"How silly of me. I had no idea they were so strong," she said when she had recovered.

"Oh, dear! I'm afraid they have made you feel worse rather than better," Mrs. Roscoe apologized.

"Perhaps we had better return to the ship," said Caspar.

"No, no, please—not on my account. I am not feeling ill, I assure you," Flora protested.

"Nevertheless it is hot, and one can have enough sight-seeing." He gave instructions to the driver.

"Have my parasol," Mrs. Roscoe offered. When Flora demurred, she persisted, "At least let me share it. You should use one, you know, Mrs. Lomax. A hat alone is not sufficient protection from this very strong tropical sun."

She moved closer, holding the sunshade to cover them both.

At first Flora's sense of smell was too numbed by inhaling the fumes of ammonium carbonate for her to be aware of a more pleasant aroma emanating from the woman beside her. But toward the end of the drive, when a slight breeze was blowing off the sea, she noticed a faint scent that seemed to her vaguely familiar.

Then she remembered that during their shopping expedition in Hong Kong Mrs. Roscoe had made discreet use of a little box of beauty powder, which, she had explained, prevented one's nose from shining on a hot day.

When Flora had looked more closely, she had seen that most of the ladies used beauty powder, but it did not always prevent tiny beads of moisture from showing above their upper lips and on their temples. The powder was noticeably pink and therefore of no use to her, unless it was made in other shades, which did not seem likely, since none of the Englishwomen on board had a complexion like hers. Her lips were pink, but her cheeks would never be rosy.

As each gust of breeze wafted the scent of Mrs. Roscoe's powder past her nostrils, she wondered why it seemed familiar when its fragrance was only noticeable at close quarters.

When the carriage reached *Coromandel*'s berth, Caspar stepped down first and helped the women to alight.

"I should go to your cabin and rest for an hour or two, Flora," he said as they walked up the gangway.

"That's what I shall do, too," said Mrs. Roscoe. "It's much hotter here than in Hong Kong. I'm sure none of the people who live here go about at this time of day. Without the breeze from the sea, the temperature would be quite unbearable."

In her cabin, Flora peeled off her gloves and unpinned her hat. Part of the reason the Singapore heat was so enervating was the clothes they had to wear, she thought with a sigh.

Sinking onto the dressing stool, she peered at her reflection. Was her nose shining? No. She looked hot, but without actually glistening.

Suddenly, thinking about beauty powder and the other aids Mrs. Roscoe had mentioned—rouge, lip salve, eyebrow pencil and snow cream for whitening the hands—she remembered Caspar coming to her cabin on their first night on board. As he had kissed her good-night she had smelled the very same scent that had been wafting past her for the previous half hour.

But Caspar didn't use powder. It couldn't have been the same scent, merely one something like it. The only way Caspar could have smelled of Mrs. Roscoe's beauty powder was if he had embraced her and some of the powder on her face had rubbed off on his.

At first the idea seemed so nonsensical that Flora dismissed it from her mind.

However, as she sat in the basket chair reading Boswell's *Life of Johnson*—an important work of English literature lent to her by her new friend Mr. Eliot—it was difficult to concentrate.

Instead she found herself thinking, *but Caspar is the only man on the ship who never ogles Mrs. Roscoe. He paid her a compliment at Hong Kong, but that has no significance. Besides, it was our first night on board. He did sit beside her at dinner, and he did remain on deck for some time after I had come to bed—but he wouldn't have embraced a woman he had only just met. If he had attempted such a thing, she would have been furious with him.*

Would she?

Would any woman truly object to being kissed by him? She remembered her own experience of feeling his lips upon hers and how, for a moment or two, all her mistrust and fear of his sex had been swept away by a wave of delicious sensation.

"All alone, Mrs. Lomax? Where is Mr. Lomax this evening? And your friend Mrs. Roscoe?"

Remembering the tone of voice in which those questions had been asked, she wondered if at the time she had misinterpreted it. Perhaps the exchange of

glances between those two women had not been occa-
sioned by her being on deck by herself, but by a
suspicion that Caspar might be watching the stars
with someone other than his wife.

Could it be that Mrs. Roscoe had not retired to bed
early but had gone ashore with him a second time?

Earlier in the day she had taken a fancy to an
elaborate jade pendant but had hesitated to buy it
because of its high price. Could she have persuaded
Caspar to escort her ashore to look at it again? Had
he bought it for her and then, to appease his conscience, bought the jade beads and earrings for his
bride—who was not really his bride?

*Oh, no—no, I mustn't think such things. There is
no foundation for them; or not much,* Flora told herself.

But the seed of suspicion, once implanted, was not
easy to eradicate. For some time she strove to im-
merse herself in her book, but the narrative, interesting as it was, failed to grip her.

At last she put it aside and decided to go to see
Thor in his quarters in the bowels of the ship. She
had been to visit him before and had been told by the
butcher that the dog was not suffering from his
confinement because Caspar exercised him every
morning very early before the operation known as
"washing decks" began at six o'clock.

It was an admirable aspect of her husband's character that he should make himself personally responsible for the animal's well-being rather than leaving it
to others, she reflected as she followed the somewhat
circuitous route to the butcher's department.

Thor greeted her with a flurry of tail wagging. He
must be very bored by the restrictions of life at sea

compared with the canine delights of journeying through rural China at the heels of his adored master, thought Flora as she fondled his silky black head.

He had never been ashore with them. Caspar felt that since the dog's presence on board was, strictly speaking, against the company's regulations, the fewer people who knew of the concession the better.

The most direct route back to her cabin was by a way that ordinarily she had no reason to go. Suddenly, as she came to a place where the corridor branched in two directions, she saw something that made her stop dead and then hastily retreat several paces.

What she had seen was Caspar stepping out of a cabin and striding briskly away while someone else closed the door behind him.

"I—I want to speak to Mrs. Roscoe. Could you tell me the number of her cabin, please?"

"Certainly, Mrs. Lomax. Mrs. Roscoe is in number seventeen," the purser informed her with a smile.

"Thank you." Flora turned away, her fear confirmed.

She had been clinging to the hope that the cabin she had seen Caspar leaving might have been that of a male passenger. Not that she had been able to think of a reason why he should visit anyone's cabin when everyone in first class forgathered five times a day; not only at the main mealtimes but also at midmorning and at half-past four for tea.

The realization that, from the beginning of the voyage, her husband had been engaged in a liaison with the woman she had tried to befriend made Flora feel physically ill. The hypocrisy of their behavior toward each other in her presence filled her with rage and resentment.

How could they have practiced such a cruel, unscrupulous deception on her? No wonder Caspar had suggested postponing the consummation of their marriage. He had had other, more appetizing fish to fry.

For an hour or more, locked in her cabin, she lay facedown on her berth, not weeping but in great despair. She had known that Caspar should never have married her, but she had never dreamed that within a few hours of their wedding he would carry the scent of another woman's beauty powder on him and had even, it seemed likely, spent that night with her. And all the nights since then, no doubt; not to mention this afternoon's "rest."

At first it was her intention to absent herself from the dinner table on the pretext of having a headache. But then she decided that, little as she felt like eating, she would force herself to behave as if nothing had happened.

As she redressed her disordered hair, she resolved that when the time came for her husband to claim his conjugal rights, she would tell him to look elsewhere. Since he had had no trouble in finding another woman to amuse him on what should have been his honeymoon, he should have no difficulty in continuing his pursuit of light women.

THE STEAMER DEPARTED FROM SINGAPORE at breakfast time the next day, reaching the island of Penang, off the west coast of the Malay Peninsula, at teatime the following afternoon.

Her stay there was only six hours, but this gave the passengers time to go ashore at George Town, the capital, which was on the east coast of the island, overlooking the two-mile-wide channel between Penang and Province Wellesley on the mainland.

By writing ahead, old Mr. Eliot had arranged for a carriage to be waiting to take him to see a waterfall four miles inland, and then to ascend Penang Hill, from which there was a splendid view. He invited Flora and her husband to join him on this expedition. Without consulting Caspar, she accepted.

She wondered if he would have the gall to try to include Mrs. Roscoe in their party. She had no intention of asking Mr. Eliot if the other woman might come with them.

Since her discovery, Flora had managed to be polite to Mrs. Roscoe but had avoided her company, and Caspar's, as much as possible. Her humiliation was still a raw wound.

To her relief, Mrs. Roscoe was left to make her own arrangements. With the erudite Mr. Eliot, now on his way to live with his married daughter in Gloucestershire after a lifetime in the foreign service, she and Caspar admired the waterfall before leaving the steamy heat at sea level for the cooler air at a height of two thousand seven hundred feet.

At the top of the hill, as well as a magnificent panorama of tropical luxuriance they found the Government Bungalow, a signal station and a comfortable hotel where they had some refreshments before returning to George Town.

Throughout the drive Flora sat next to Mr. Eliot and addressed her conversation to him. She was civil to Caspar when necessary but otherwise ignored him.

That night in the first-class dining saloon, and else-where on the ship, there were more than twice as many passengers as had embarked from Shanghai twelve days before.

Next morning, as always on Sunday, the crew were mustered in clean uniforms and inspected by the captain before he conducted divine service.

Afterward the passengers resumed their usual activities: taking constitutionals, playing deck quoits, reclining at ease in deck chairs or standing by the rails and chatting.

Soon the Strait of Malacca was left behind; rounding the northern end of the Dutch East Indies island of Sumatra, the ship had entered the Bay of Bengal and was steaming due west for Ceylon.

In the days before they reached Colombo, Flora made several pleasant acquaintances and was able to avoid spending more than a minimum of time with her husband. At night it was oppressively hot. She found it difficult to sleep and spent hours lying awake in the dark, wondering if he was in his own cabin or in number seventeen.

At Colombo their luggage was transferred to the steamer *Oriental*, a somewhat larger vessel than *Coromandel*.

They were there for twenty-four hours, and had she been less cast down Flora would have liked the city better than any they had seen. The commercial center was known as the Fort because it was built on the site of a Portuguese fortress. Opposite the imposing post office were the Jubilee Gardens, given by Lord Stanmore, a governor of the colony. There was also a long esplanade overlooking the sea; and between the Fort and the private residences among the

Cinnamon Gardens was a large freshwater lake over-hung with tropical vegetation and creepers. She thought it a beautiful place, its hot climate tempered by refreshing sea breezes.

In the *pettah*, the native quarter, lived Sinhalese, Tamils, Moors, Afghans, Brahmins, Eurasians and Malays. There Caspar bought several curios and a number of rubies. He insisted on giving Flora a very fine star sapphire to be set in a ring when they reached England.

She did not want him to buy it for her and did her best to dissuade him. However, he was not to be deflected from buying the stone, which when seen in reflected light seemed to contain a star in its depths.

From Colombo to Aden, across the Arabian Sea, was the longest stretch of the voyage. As the heat intensified and they ended their third week at sea, boredom and discomfort began to fray the passengers' tempers. There were several cases of women fainting.

"It will be hotter than this in the Red Sea," Mrs. Salter told Flora. "Some ladies won't loosen their corsets, which is asking for trouble."

Flora did not wear a corset, for which she was exceedingly thankful. Even when not tightly laced, they must be torture in the heat. She had noticed that Mrs. Roscoe's beauty powder was ineffective when the thermometer showed temperatures in the high eighties.

When they met at the breakfast table, several hours before *Oriental* reached the rocky promontory of Aden, Caspar said, "We shall only be there for three hours, which is not enough time to visit the Tanks."

Flora knew from the pocket book that the Tanks were ancient reservoirs in a remarkable state of preservation.

"I looked round the town on my way out," he went on. "There's nothing much to see, and the heat is extreme—not only from the sun but from radiation produced by the color of the rocks. Unless you particularly wish to go ashore, I recommend staying on board."

"Yes, that will suit me," she agreed in a colorless tone.

He subjected her to a searching scrutiny.

"Are you feeling off color, Flora?"

"No, I am in excellent health, thank you."

"You seem to have lost your appetite. No doubt you find the heat trying. We shall all be more comfortable once we reach the Mediterranean."

It was from Mr. Eliot that she learned that the port of Aden had been fortified by the Ottoman sultan Suleiman the Magnificent. Having first traveled to the Orient as a young man in his twenties, returning to England on leave at regular intervals, Mr. Eliot knew all there was to be known about the places on their route.

"Ivory, pearls and ostrich feathers are exported from Aden," he told her.

"What are ostrich feathers used for?"

"For fans, for feather boas, hats, and also for the headdresses that ladies wear at court," he explained. "I've no doubt that when you reach England you will soon have a number of ostrich feathers in your wardrobe, my dear Mrs. Lomax. They are much in fashion at present. Not that I am an authority on fashions, but I read in *The Times* some weeks ago that last year Cape Colony, which is the southern-most part of Africa, exported feathers worth nearly nine hundred thousand pounds."

"There will soon be no ostriches left!" she exclaimed with a frown of concern.

"At one time they were in danger of extinction," he agreed. "Fortunately before that happened they were successfully domesticated. On ostrich farms it isn't necessary to kill them to obtain their plumes. Nor are the feathers pulled out. They are merely cut off about every eight months. You may wear them with a clear conscience."

For four days and nights the ship steamed through the Red Sea, the nights becoming less torrid as they neared the Suez Canal. Since all the other first-class passengers had been through the canal before, few of them shared her excitement at the prospect of seeing one of the wonders of the modern world.

It was her interest in the canal that to some extent healed the breach between her and Caspar. He, of course, had remained unaware that there was a breach, evidently attributing her subdued manner to the exacting climatic conditions.

Just before they reached the canal, Mr. Eliot was confined to his cabin with a digestive ailment. Deprived of her elderly mentor, Flora turned to her husband for enlightenment.

He told her that although the idea of a waterway linking the Mediterranean with the Red Sea had been Napoleon's brainchild, his engineers' reports had caused the project to be abandoned. It had been left to another Frenchman, Ferdinand de Lesseps, to succeed, against powerful opposition, in building the canal that with ocean telegraphy had revolutionized trade between East and West.

De Lesseps, she discovered, had been one of her husband's boyhood heroes. The indomitable enthusiasm and force of personality that had enabled the French engineer to carry through his world-changing enterprise, even though the khedive of Egypt and the prime minister of England opposed it, and French investors were reluctant to support it, had fired Caspar's imagination.

"Do you realize that the canal reduces this voyage by more than three thousand miles?" he asked her. "If my father as a young man had wanted to go to Shanghai, he would have gone under sail, via the Cape. It would have taken him four months. Today even a cargo steamer that travels at only ten knots can be there in six weeks."

"Were there no steam ships in your father's day?"

"Yes, but it wasn't profitable to use them on the Cape route. There were so few coaling stations that they had to carry fuel to the exclusion of cargo."

They stood side by side at the rail as the ship entered the canal and passed the declining town of Suez, its importance usurped by Port Said at the northern end of the shortcut. On either side of the waterway there was nothing to be seen but a wilderness of yellow stone and sand stretching back to the distant mountains.

At sunset and again after dinner they returned to the deck. It was dark by then; a cold star-lit desert night in which *Oriental* continued her passage by means of electric light reflected in a Mangin mirror that fanned the beam far beyond the ship's bows and across the width of the canal.

"I find it fascinating to think that what this canal represents in terms of scientific achievement and modern commerce has its setting in the most ancient historic land known to us," Caspar remarked as they watched the ship gliding slowly between the red buoys that, because of the brilliant light, could be seen for half a mile ahead.

Wrapped in the warm gray wool cape that was one of the garments Mrs. Roscoe had advised her to have made in Hong Kong, Flora replied, "Yes, it is strange to think of the Romans and the Greeks, and the Persians, sweeping across this great plain. It must have been not far from here that Cleopatra retreated with her treasure after the defeat of Actium."

When he made no comment on this, she glanced up to discover him watching her with a rather strange expression on his face.

"Have I said something foolish?" she asked.

"Not at all. I was merely reflecting on my good fortune in finding a wife whose conversation is not confined to the trivialities that occupy the minds of most of your sex," he said pleasantly.

She was tempted to retort that he didn't seem to mind the triviality of Mrs. Roscoe's conversation. But even as she bit the words back, it struck her that perhaps he was becoming bored with the widow.

"Before his indisposition, your friend Mr. Eliot congratulated me on being married to a young woman of such superior intelligence," he went on. "His admiration for you is such that, were he thirty years younger, I should suspect him of losing his heart to you."

"If Mr. Eliot were thirty years younger, I should lose my heart to him," she returned. "He is by far the most interesting and agreeable man on board."

"Are you including me in that judgment?" he inquired on a note of raillery.

She said in an expressionless voice, "You are my husband. For a wife to admire her husband's qualities above all others goes without saying."

He put his hand under her chin and turned her face up to his.

"Very dutiful!" he said sardonically. "But I am not a Chinese husband requiring that kind of lip service. In what way does your elderly admirer make himself particularly agreeable?"

"He doesn't regard me as a child."

"I see. And you feel that I do?"

"Don't you?" she challenged.

"In some ways—yes," he acknowledged. "Eliot's relationship with you is on an intellectual plane, where to a great extent you meet as equals. Your relations with me are more complex. As well as the difference in our years, there is a great gulf of worldly experience between us. I have not lived the ascetic life of a scholarly bachelor such as Eliot. Any girl of your age would seem young to me. At the outset of their first season, even girls bred in England are almost as innocent of life as novices emerging from a convent. Very often at the end of the season they are engaged to be married, but by then they have grown up a great deal—as you will when we reach England."

He patted her cheek before his hand dropped to his side. "Don't be too impatient to grow up, *ya-t'ou*. You will be a woman soon enough. Then, like the rest of your sex, you'll regret your eagerness to be older."

FOR MOST OF THE PASSENGERS, Port Said marked the
transition from East to West. Those who passed time
keeping a daily note of the ship's speed and her position recorded that only a little more than three thousand miles of the voyage remained.

To Flora, entering the Mediterranean had a deeper
significance. It marked the change in her attitude
toward Caspar's liaison with Mrs. Roscoe. She had
come round to seeing that the pain and chagrin inflicted by his infidelity were a small price to pay for
the good he had done her.

But for his return to the mission she would have
been raped not once but repeatedly. Père d'Espinay
and the two nuns would have suffered further ill
treatment, and the old priest would have died in great
agony of mind. If the Frenchman had not killed her
when he had done with her, she would have been sold
to a brothel even worse than the one from which
Caspar had rescued her a second time.

In between those two horrible ordeals, he not only
had saved her from many other hazards but had
never abused his power over her. Now she had his
name, his protection and a future far more to her liking than the dull narrow life of a religious; the only
safe future that Père d'Espinay had foreseen for an
orphan girl of mixed parentage.

All that being so, what right had she to be ag-
grieved because of his connection with the widow?
No right. She had no rights whatever; only the over-
riding obligation not to be a burden upon him.

This new chastened spirit of acceptance was soon
to be tested when she learned that, instead of
completing her journey by train from Brindisi,
Mrs. Roscoe had changed her plans to conform

with Caspar's intention of going all the way by sea.

The day she discovered this collusion, Flora's anger reanimated—but only briefly. As matters turned out, it was a decision that not only the widow but many other passengers were soon to regret.

At the western end of the Mediterranean, *Oriental* encountered a storm that caused all but one of the first-class female passengers, and several of the men, to withdraw to their cabins, there to remain until the ship berthed at Gibraltar.

"You don't suffer from *mal de mer*, Mrs. Lomax?" remarked the captain when Flora appeared for dinner after some hours of roughening weather.

"Not so far," she answered cautiously.

"It can be a lot worse than this in the bay. But if you haven't felt queasy up to now, you probably have the good fortune to be a good sailor," he told her.

"I hope so."

The groans she had heard as she passed some of the cabins made her hope very much to be spared the miseries being endured by many on board.

Beyond Gibraltar, in the Atlantic, the weather improved for two days. Most of the sufferers reappeared to sit in the sun, wrapped in rugs, and watch the coastline of Portugal.

But long before the notorious Bay of Biscay was reached another gale had blown up. Those who had scarcely recovered from their first bout of seasickness were prostrated by a buffeting such as Flora had never imagined.

To her surprise and relief, she continued to be unaffected, as did Caspar. More than once, as the rolling of the ship made them lurch and stagger on

their way to and from the public saloons, he saved
her from a painful tumble by hooking a strong arm
around her and holding her against him.

Together they continued to eat three substantial
meals a day from a table now fitted with "fiddles" to
prevent dishes and decanters from sliding off the
edges.

Having had some experience of nursing in her
years at the mission, Flora thought she could make
herself useful assisting the hard-pressed stewardesses,
whom she knew to be rushed off their feet attending
to the stricken. When she offered her services to the
captain, however, her husband intervened.

"I think not, my dear," he said decisively. "In a
serious emergency everyone must help. But this is not
like an epidemic in which lives are in danger. Those
who are unwell at present will recover very rapidly
once the weather improves."

"But the storm may continue for some time, and
meanwhile poor Mrs. Salter, who is not feeling well
herself, has scarcely a moment's respite. People ring
for her constantly."

She saw that she had displeased him by arguing
with him.

"I believe I am the best judge of whether your
assistance is necessary, Flora," was his clipped
reply.

"That is so, Mrs. Lomax," the captain assented.
"As you've noticed, members of the crew and the
cabin staff are not immune to the ill effects of rough
weather. But they cannot and do not succumb as
readily as some of our passengers. For the greater
part of each voyage, the stewardesses have ample
leisure. These few days in the bay will not overtax

their capabilities. Your husband is right to dissuade
you from lending your aid.''

But he hadn't dissuaded her, she thought. He had
overruled her; and this was an instance in which she
did not believe that he was the best judge.

To have her suggestion scotched in so magisterial a
manner made her feel as if she were his daughter, not
his wife. It was her resentment of his arbitrary tone
that prompted her to say, ''Very well, if you disapprove, Caspar—although I'm sure Père d'Espinay
would have lent his aid had he been here.''

As she spoke, she gave him a level look in which
she hoped he would read her dislike of being treated
like a child in matters of this nature.

Perhaps the captain mentioned her offer to the
ship's surgeon. A few hours later that officer sought
her out.

''Mrs. Lomax, I wonder if I may trespass on your
good nature? Among the passengers who are ill there
is one whose condition is causing me some concern.
She is traveling alone and needs constant reassurance
that the ship is not about to founder. Unfortunately,
it's impossible for her stewardess to spend much time
with her. If you could sit with her for a while,
perhaps she would sleep and recover from her present
exhaustion. Her name is Mrs. Roscoe. I believe she
embarked from Shanghai, so no doubt you are acquainted with her.''

''Yes, I know Mrs. Roscoe. Have you any objection to my sitting with her, Caspar?''

Her husband, who had been reading in the chair
next to hers until the surgeon approached them, said,
''Naturally not, if her condition is serious.''

Didn't he know, Flora wondered. Were his rela-

tions with the widow so cold-hearted on his side that
when she became unable to entertain him he had
ceased to take any interest in her?

"I will come at once," she said, rising.

"You must not be alarmed by her appearance,"
the surgeon advised her as they made their unsteady
way to cabin seventeen. "Seasickness frequently
makes its victims appear to be *in extremis*—as indeed
they believe themselves to be. Having suffered from
it myself—very few people are such excellent sailors
as you and your husband—I know what it is to feel
that death would be a welcome release. However, to
my knowledge no one has ever expired from it."

In spite of his warning, Flora was shocked when
she saw the dramatic change wrought in Mrs. Roscoe
since her last appearance in public.

She looked at least ten years older. Her skin had a
sickly pallor. There were dark circles under her
sunken eyes. Streaks of damp hair clung to her forehead, the rest being a disheveled mass upon her
pillow.

At the sight of Flora she lifted her arms in a feeble
gesture of entreaty.

"Mrs. Lomax...thank God you have come. I
have been so afraid," she murmured hoarsely, beginning to weep.

"I should have come sooner had I known how very
ill you had been."

Accustomed by now to the violent motion of the
ship as it pitched and tossed in mountainous seas,
Flora braced herself as best she could while bending
over the prostrate widow.

"There's no need to be frightened, I assure you.
The captain says *Oriental* has survived many much

worse batterings. You are perfectly safe, and now that I'm here to keep you company you won't find the noise as alarming as when you were alone.''

Having taken the invalid's pulse and told Flora to encourage her to drink as much as possible, the surgeon left them together.

The cabin smelled strongly of vomit, as indeed did all that part of the ship. But even in the deck cabins it was impossible to open the portholes, which were regularly deluged with spray; although the deck itself was not awash since it was toward the bows.

Probably Mrs. Roscoe was no longer aware of the sour atmosphere, and after some time in the cabin Flora herself ceased to notice it. Meanwhile she did what she could to make the other woman less uncomfortable: sponging the stickiness from her face and hands and finding a clean nightgown to replace the stained and crumpled chemise in which she had lain since being taken ill.

Presently, worn out by what she had been through, Mrs. Roscoe fell into an uneasy doze from which, whenever the vessel shuddered under the impact of an exceptionally large wave, she would rouse with a cry of alarm.

Watching her during the periods when she was sleeping, Flora found it impossible to harbor any animosity toward her. Now, if anything, she felt sorry for her, and shocked by Caspar's callous indifference to her sufferings.

What a hard ruthless man he must be to seduce a woman and then, when she was ill and frightened, to wash his hands of her.

I suppose if he had come to see her since the storm started, he might have been caught here by either her stewardess or the doctor, and that would have caused gossip, thought Flora. *He doesn't scruple to break the commandment—but he does object to being found out.*

Half an hour before dinner she answered a tap at the door to find Caspar's steward standing outside.

"Mr. Lomax's compliments, madam. He's expecting you to join him in the dining saloon and thought you might be unaware of the time."

"Thank you. Please tell my husband that I can't leave my place here at present. The stewardess will bring me a light meal."

"Very good, madam."

A few moments later there was a more commanding rap on the door. This time instead of looking down at the steward, who was a small man, Flora had to look up at her towering husband as she stepped out of the cabin.

"You will join me for dinner in fifteen minutes, please, Flora," he said at his most peremptory.

"Caspar, I cannot. I have given my word to Mrs. Roscoe to stay with her until the storm slackens. She is too weak to move from her berth and is terrified of being forgotten if we have to take to the lifeboats. Yes, yes. . . I know there is no possibility of that. But I can't convince her of it. She is too unwell to think sensibly."

"And you will make yourself unwell if you remain in that fetid atmosphere without rest and proper refreshment. I'll send the stewardess to sit with the silly woman."

"How unkind you are! She cannot help being seasick. I might have been equally ill; would you then have considered me silly?"

"No, because you would have borne your condition with the utmost fortitude and a minimum of inconvenience to everyone else," was his brisk reply. "A well-bred person does not succumb to hysteria, whatever the circumstances."

"Mrs. Lomax? Are you there, Mrs. Lomax?" a voice quavered faintly behind her.

"Yes, I'm here. I'm just coming."

With a reproving shake of her head at Caspar, Flora retreated into the cabin and closed the door on him.

"Was it your husband I heard speaking?" Mrs. Roscoe asked.

"Yes. He was asking how you are. I'm sorry our voices disturbed you. Have another few sips of water and then try to sleep again."

As, with difficulty because of the heaving deck, Flora supported the older woman and held a glass to her lips, there was no doubt in her mind that Caspar would not let the matter rest.

After another brief interval there was a third knock at the door. A stewardess entered.

"I'm to sit with Mrs. Roscoe while you have your dinner, madam," she announced.

When, after hurriedly changing her clothes, Flora joined her husband in the dining saloon, she said, "I hope you don't mean to forbid me to return to Mrs. Roscoe. I couldn't possibly rest knowing that she was alone and in distress, and the stewardess has other people who need her attention. She cannot spare more than an hour."

He said, "I've had a further talk with the surgeon, who tells me that champagne has a medicinal value in cases of prostration. I've arranged for a bottle of

Bollinger to be taken down to her. It should also have a sedative effect. After one or two glasses on an empty stomach, she should sleep as soundly as I shall. If you have any thought of playing night nurse, put it out of your mind. I have no intention of allowing you to exhaust yourself on her behalf.''

"One would think you disliked the poor woman,'' she remarked in an expressionless voice.

"One encounters very few people whose society, in the course of a long voyage, does not become tedious,'' he answered. "Mrs. Roscoe was unwise not to keep to her original intention of disembarking at Brindisi. The bay is always better avoided by passengers who have any doubts about their sea legs. For myself, I find a storm exhilarating.''

"But you didn't know I should,'' she exclaimed. "Don't you think it was rather unfair to assume that I should be equally unaffected by these conditions? I might have suffered agonies of sickness.''

Before he had time to reply they were joined by the captain, who apologized for his lateness. From then on Flora had no opportunity to press the question.

Although by the following morning the storm had abated considerably, for the rest of the voyage the sea was never less than choppy. Conditions in the English Channel were such that a number of first-class passengers remained in their cabins until the ship docked at Plymouth.

Mrs. Roscoe was one of them. For the last two days of the voyage, when Caspar and Flora were able to walk the decks again, filling their lungs with bracing air, she stayed in the chair in her cabin, still with pale cheeks and lackluster eyes.

"I shall stay in Plymouth for a few days. I don't

feel equal to the journey to London at present," she told Flora during their last conversation. "You have been so kind, Mrs. Lomax. I should like you to accept this little gift as a token of my gratitude to you."

"I have done very little," Flora protested, reluctantly accepting the package the widow pressed upon her.

"You have been kindness itself, and this is the merest trifle: a small vial of Oriental perfume. I only wish I had something more lasting to give you. I daresay we shan't meet again, but I shall always remember your sweet face and gentle hands," Mrs. Roscoe told her emotionally.

Flora's instinctive distaste for this sentimental farewell made her see why, his lust for her sated, Caspar had found the widow a tedious companion.

FOR THEIR JOURNEY TO LONDON, via Bristol, in the Great Western Railway's *Cornishman* express, Caspar had reserved a first-class family saloon with an adjoining lavatory.

Their accommodation, labeled Engaged on the windows, was unlocked for them by the stationmaster. Some of their baggage was stowed in their private luggage compartment, but most had to go in the luggage van. The saloon also had an adjoining, less comfortable compartment for the occupants' servants.

The station at Plymouth gave Flora her first experience of seeing Englishmen performing the servile tasks that in the Orient they'd had done for them by "the natives."

"What are those tall metal things?" she asked Caspar as she noticed several porters propelling mysterious objects along the platform by revolving them, at an angle, on their circular bases.

"Those are churns of fresh milk," he explained. "The county of Devon is famous for its milk and cream. We've some time to spare before the train leaves—would you care to have a look at the engine?"

At that moment she was unaware that nearly every schoolboy and many grown men were fascinated by the steam engines that hauled the trains. But some minutes later, when they had made their way along the line of chocolate-and-cream coaches to the immaculate Swindon-green locomotive with its polished copper caps to the chimney tops and the company's motto—*Virtute et Industria*—painted on it, it dawned on her that Caspar's suggestion had been as much for his own pleasure as to interest her.

The engine driver and his fireman, both wearing blue cotton jackets and with heavy mustaches over their upper lips, touched their caps when Caspar said good day to them.

It was clear from his short conversation with them that her husband knew a good deal about the technicalities of their work. Presently, as they strolled back to their compartment while the newsagents' boys with Wymans on their peaked caps carried their wicker trays past the windows of the second- and third-class carriages, shouting "Chocolates...cigarettes...papers," he gave her a surprising insight into his rather inscrutable character.

"There was a time when I aspired to be an engine driver," he told her with the look of amusement that gave his hard forceful features a younger, less formidable cast. "It takes years of hard work first as a cleaner, then as a fireman and finally as a driver of a goods train before qualifying to drive one of the great expresses.''

Later he made her listen to the rhythm of the wheels crossing the rail joints; a different rhythm on the forty-five-foot lengths from that on the stretches of older, thirty-foot lengths. Even the color of the smoke became more interesting when he explained that the plume of white vapor streaming back from the engine changed to dark gray when the fireman had shoveled more coal into the furnace.

For Flora, the two hundred miles between Plymouth and Paddington—speeding along at an exciting sixty miles an hour, faster on the downhill stretches, somewhat slower on the gradients—passed all too swiftly.

Alone in the spacious family saloon, with Caspar discoursing on a subject of particular interest to him, they seemed to recapture something of the relaxed camaraderie they had shared before reaching Shanghai.

Although, he explained, when he was a youth trains had not had the advantage of corridors, and the middle and lower classes had had to travel without access to a lavatory, the *Cornishman* had a high degree of comfort for all its passengers.

There was even a restaurant car where, for those who could afford three shillings and sixpence, a luncheon of soup, poached salmon, roast sirloin, asparagus, Diplomat pudding, cheese and dessert was served at tables for four and tables for two, on either side of a carpeted aisle. Flora thought it the most delightful meal she had ever eaten, with an ever changing view of the English countryside to be seen through the window, and her husband giving all his attention to her.

He had not told her, and she did not ask, whether they would reach Longwarden that day or were to pass the night in London. It was enough to be with him, having various features of the unfamiliar landscape pointed out to her.

"I expected it to be raining," she said.

"No, it doesn't rain all the time," Caspar returned. "Nor is London continually enveloped in a pea-soup fog, although fogs do occur rather too frequently in the winter months. There are times— today is an example—when the English climate is as fine as any in the world. Certainly there is no more varied and beautiful countryside to be found within such a small compass."

"You are glad to be here," she said, watching his keen gray eyes as they scanned the fields and woodlands.

"Yes, I am glad to be back." He turned to meet her gaze. "As I hope you are. As the daughter and now the wife of an Englishman, this is your homeland, too, even if it seems alien at present."

Her first sight of the teeming streets of central London was from the hansom cab that took them from Paddington Station to Charing Cross.

To her eyes it was a most extraordinary vehicle. The part in which the passengers traveled was suspended between two enormous wheels, the tops of their rims on a level with the back of the horse. The driver sat perched very high up behind the cab, with the reins running over the roof of it. He could speak to his passengers through a little trapdoor above their heads.

Climbing into the cab was not easy, especially when hampered by skirts. There was a small iron step about eighteen inches from the ground on which Flora had to place one foot before springing up to the floor of the cab with the other.

In so doing, much to her confusion, she contrived to dislodge her hat on the overhanging reins, and also to brush her skirt against the rim of the wheel. Had it been a wet day, there would have been a smear of mud on the cloth.

To protect the occupants from rain and mire, the front of the cab was enclosed by two half doors, their inner sides padded with leather to match the interior of the hansom. With the doors closed it was very snug and far more private than a rickshaw. There were even, she noticed, blinds to pull down over the side windows.

The seat was just large enough to accommodate two people sitting close together. Because of his uncommon size, instead of sitting shoulder to shoulder with her, Caspar put his arm around her.

"There's more room in a growler," he remarked. "But as you're unlikely to ride in a hansom again, I thought you might like to try it once."

She had taken off her hat when it was knocked askew and had not replaced it but was holding it on her lap. "What is a growler? And why am I unlikely to ride in one of these again?"

"Growlers are the four-wheeled cabs you saw drawn up outside the station. The proper name for one is a clarence. They were named after the Duke of Clarence, who later became King William the Fourth, in the same way that the victoria my mother used to drive was named after Queen Victoria," he explained. "And the reason you won't need to use a hansom in future is that you will have your own carriage. In my opinion the days of the hansom are numbered. Already there are some motorcars on the road, and they are the vehicle of the future, whatever the diehards may say to the contrary."

Perhaps he was right, but for the present the horse was still the supreme means of locomotion. Coming from China, where man was the chief beast of burden, Flora had never seen so many horses. The clatter of hooves and the rumble of wheels combined in a din that she felt must become very wearisome if one had to endure many hours of it; and to her unaccustomed nostrils the air was acrid with the smell of the horse droppings that were everywhere in evidence.

Many weeks later she realized that the most direct route between the two stations would have taken them past Caspar's large town house, and that his instructions to the cabbie had been to take a longer way around. However, at the time such was her ignorance of London that she was not even aware that Charing Cross was another railway station.

She would not have minded had the drive taken twice as long. The fascination of this new and exciting environment, and the different kind of excitement she derived from sitting close to her husband, made the cab journey seem quite a short one.

"Why do most of the horses have leather things over their eyes?" she asked him.

"Those are called blinkers. They're partly to protect horses' eyes from being damaged by the lash of another coachman's whip, and partly to stop them shying when they see something coming from behind.

A horse has a wide range of vision, which it needed to protect it in its wild state," he explained.

It was not until they had boarded another train, this time belonging to the South Eastern and Chatham Railway, that Flora discovered their destination was not Longwarden.

It seemed that Caspar had an aunt—his mother's elder sister—who had been a widow since the age of thirty, when her husband had succumbed to pneumonia, leaving her very badly off. They had had no children and when, after the customary two years, she came out of mourning, Mrs. St. Leger had improved her financial position in one of the few ways open to an impoverished gentlewoman.

Like many another well-bred widow before her, she had become an adviser to members of the *nouveau riche*, who had the means to enter society but lacked her inherited knowledge of its rules and procedures.

From time to time she had presented at court the wife or daughter of some wealthy manufacturer. In the case of the younger debutantes, her assistance had often continued until they made a good marriage. By these means she had been able to support herself in modest comfort, although she had disliked the necessity of living in London and keeping late hours when performing the duties of a chaperone.

Her wish for a quiet country life had been fulfilled by the success of her book, *Manners and Rules of Good Society* (subtitled *Solecisms to be Avoided*), published anonymously "by a Member of the Aristocracy."

It had been very well received, and many revised and enlarged editions had followed the first. The proceeds had enabled Caspar's aunt to retire to a house in Kent, where she employed a small staff and devoted herself to good works.

"She is therefore ideally qualified to help you to learn the ropes quickly," Caspar explained as the train carried them into Kent.

"How long are we going to stay with her?" Flora asked. "If she prefers a quiet life, won't she find having us there a nuisance?"

"I shall not be there," he replied. "I have various things to do in London and shall put up at my club for the next week or two. I should think ten days or a fortnight should suffice for you to pick up the groundwork. Then Aunt Blanche can come to Longwarden until you are ready to make your debut."

"You mean *I* am to be presented at court?" asked Flora, aghast.

"Naturally. Even girls who have come out in the usual way have to be presented again after they marry. It's nothing to be alarmed about."

A brougham was waiting to meet them at the station nearest to the village where his aunt lived. Caspar greeted the coachman by name and inquired after the health of his family.

"He's also my aunt's gardener," he told Flora as they set off. "She has a cook and a parlormaid, and I believe there's also a scullery maid, whom I haven't seen."

"How many servants are there at Longwarden?" she asked.

So far he had said very little about his own house. She had no clear impression of its size, or of the style in which he lived when in England.

"More than my aunt needs. It's a larger house," was his rather vague reply.

None of her questions about Longwarden had elicited detailed answers. She had begun to suspect him of being deliberately evasive, although with what motive she could not imagine.

His aunt's house was a dignified red brick residence on the outskirts of the village. As the brougham passed through the gateway and approached the front door, a formidable-looking personage in her middle sixties came out of the house. She was dressed in a plain gray tweed skirt and striped blouse with a stiff mannish collar and tie. A straw boater with a striped ribbon was set on her upswept gray hair, and a lorgnette on a black cord dangled over the precipice of her bosom.

"Carlyon, my dear boy! How delightful to see you safely returned from your travels," she exclaimed before her nephew stooped to kiss her.

Their greetings concluded, she raised the lorgnette. "And this is your bride. . . ."

Flora had remained in the brougham until Caspar offered his hand to help her alight. Striving to appear composed, she stepped down and, when he had presented her, said with a shy smile, "How do you do."

Whether Mrs. St. Leger was surprised to find that her nephew had married a girl of mixed parentage was impossible to tell. Not by the flicker of an eyelash did she reveal what she was thinking as she looked her guest up and down through the tortoiseshell lorgnette.

A hostess betrays that she is not much accustomed to society when she attempts to amuse her visitor by the production of albums, photographs, books, illustrated newspapers, port-

folios of drawings, the artistic efforts of the
members of the family and the like; conversation being all that is necessary, without having
recourse to pictorial displays. A hostess should
rely solely on her own powers of conversation to
make the short quarter of an hour—which is the
limit of a ceremonious call—pass pleasantly to
her visitor.

Seated in the glass-roofed conservatory at the side
of Mrs. St. Leger's house, studying the chapter of her
book that dealt with the etiquette of the social call,
Flora found herself stifling a yawn.

It was now nine days since Caspar had left her in
Kent, and she could not wait for his return.

Not that living in his aunt's sedate household was
uncomfortable or even dull. She had found a great
deal to interest her, especially glimpses of life among
the lower orders.

At times it worried her that, at heart, she was more
interested in English village ways than in learning
how to behave as the wife of a peer. Perhaps it was
an indication that her plebeian origins were a
stronger force in her character than the veneer of
refinement long and patiently applied by Père
d'Espinay.

Or perhaps it was merely that the French priest had
given her the intelligence to see that most of the complicated formalities that she had to master were
rituals to fill empty lives. Even Mrs. St. Leger, who
considered herself to be busy with charitable activities, actually spent most of her time writing letters, reading or resting.

It was while her preceptress was resting that Flora

was able to explore the neighboring countryside and discover how rural life in England differed from that in China.

One difference she had discovered was that once a week a fisherman came by carrier's cart from the coast, bringing baskets of fresh fish and shellfish. Milk was supplied from a churn brought around to each house on a pony cart and ladled into jugs at the door.

Among the many pedlars passing through was a man who paid two pence for a rabbit's skin and carried the skins, skewered by a stick, on his shoulder. Another pedlar brought sea sand for scouring cooking pans and doorsteps. When the pans needed mending they were given to the scissor grinder, whose barrow had a seat and a pedal that turned the grinding wheel.

There were also the men known as tramps, who slept either under hedges or in places called workhouses, and who would chop wood or dig gardens for a mug of hot tea and a hunk of stale bread and cheese.

Husbands and wives occasionally pay calls together, but oftener they do not. A lady, as a rule, pays a call by herself, unless she has a grown-up daughter, who should then accompany her mother.

As Flora read on, her lashes flickered and the lines of print started to blur. Whenever the sun was shining the conservatory became very warm, especially in the afternoon. The warmth intensified the odor of the palms and ferns, many of them gifts from Caspar.

What was he doing at this moment, she wondered drowsily. Not thinking of her, that was certain. She had a disheartening suspicion that when he had bade her goodbye, without even a kiss on the cheek, he had gone away glad to be rid of her. Even his aunt had thought it strange that he had not stayed with them for one night.

Perhaps the reason he hadn't was that he had known Mrs. St. Leger had only one bedroom for the use of guests and—as he had said on the ship—he meant to defer the consummation of their marriage until they were in their own home.

Flora lifted her hand to hide another deep yawn. She was reclining on a cushioned chaise longue that had a wheel under the backrest and handles projecting from the footrest, so that in summer it could be wheeled into the lawn.

It was tempting to slide down a little, to let the book fall to her lap, to doze for a moment....

She was woken by a touch on her lips and opened her eyes to find her husband leaning over her, supporting himself with a hand on each side of the backrest.

"So this is how you improve the shining hour," he said mockingly.

He had come back. He had kissed her. She felt strangely breathless and trembly.

"Caspar!" she breathed in sleepy confusion.

Something gleamed in his narrowed gray eyes; a light that half frightened, half thrilled her. After more than a week among people whose flesh tones ranged from pallid to purplish, the deep bronze hue of his skin came as a pleasurable shock.

"Well...are you pleased to see me?" His voice

was no longer teasing but deeper and slightly husky.

"Of course." Her insides contracted. Her throat tight, she licked her dry lips.

As she did so, he swooped like a hawk and his mouth pressed warmly on hers. A moment later his strong arms slid under her back, raising her from the cushions and drawing her close to his chest.

Nothing—neither other men's roughness nor his own restrained pecks on the cheek—had prepared her for this kind of kiss, which was neither gentle nor brutal but somewhere between those extremes. She could feel the hard wall of his chest and the muscular strength that held her captive. Yet she did not feel trapped or bound, merely in the grip of a power that was curiously exciting.

To be helpless in *his* arms was...bliss. Her instincts had known that it would be, since their drive across London in the hansom. Now her mind knew it, as well. Not that she was capable of thinking while his mouth moved softly on hers.

The kiss seemed to go on forever, but not to last nearly long enough.

It was ended by the sound of footsteps crossing the polished floor of the drawing room. They had scarcely time to draw apart before Mrs. St. Leger's parlormaid appeared, pushing a trolley.

"I thought you might wish for tea, m'lord."

"That's very thoughtful of you, Mildred."

Unhurriedly he rose to his feet and strolled about, looking at the plants, while the maid spread a lacy white cloth, lit the spirit stove under the copper kettle and arranged the rest of the tea things.

By the time this was done, Flora had partially recovered herself. She was still in a great flutter inwardly, but she did not think that it showed—at least she hoped not. What would Mildred have thought had she seen them?

Manners and Rules of Good Society made no reference to the public behavior of husbands and wives. However, referring to engagements, Mrs. St. Leger had written:

> To dance with each other at a ball, or dance more than three or four times in succession, and when not dancing to sit out in tearooms and conservatories, renders an engaged couple conspicuous, and this is precisely what many mothers are most anxious that their daughters should avoid being, and would rather they were overprudent than that they should run the gauntlet of general criticism.

Leaving the chaise longue, Flora seated herself on the upright chair beside the table and waited for the kettle to boil so that she could fill the silver teapot.

Caspar picked up the book she had left there. "Ah, my aunt's book of rules. Have you mastered it?"

"I have mastered some of it," she answered.

He riffled the pages. "Including the chapter dealing with the pronunciation of surnames?"

"I think so."

"I'll test you. Tell me how you would pronounce the name that is spelled P-o-n-t-e-f-r-a-c-t."

"As if it were Pomfret."

"Very good. And T-r-a-f-a-l-g-a-r?"

"If I were referring to the battle, I should say Tra*fal*gar; and if to the peer, Trafal*gar*."

"Excellent. It appears that you haven't spent all your afternoons playing the Sleeping Beauty."

Caspar's allusion was not lost on her. Among Père d'Espinay's books had been a volume of fairy tales by the French writer Charles Perrault. Before Flora could read French herself, the old priest had often delighted her with the tale of *la belle au bois dormant*: the beautiful princess roused from an enchanted sleep by a kiss from the prince who had penetrated the dense forest that had sprung up around her father's castle in the hundred years since the spell was cast upon her.

"Certainly not!" she said lightly. "It's most unfair that you should have arrived on the one occasion when I have done so. Why didn't you let me know you were coming?"

He tossed the book aside and came to where she was sitting. Taking her chin between his finger and thumb, he tilted her face up.

"If I had, I should have missed the pleasure of waking you up. Was it equally pleasurable for you?"

She tried but failed to hold his gaze. Her long lashes veiled her dark eyes. An apricot flush stained her cheeks.

"I—I think you must know that it was."

"Would you like to repeat the experience?"

"Y—you are teasing me," she said faintly.

His long fingers slid to her throat, caressing the delicate skin. His other hand closed on her wrist and began to draw her to her feet.

"Caspar. . . the kettle," she murmured.

"To the devil with the kettle!"

But as he was bending his head, his aunt swept into the conservatory.

"Carlyon! This is unexpected. You said you would write before you came."

"I am only here for an hour, Aunt Blanche." He let go of Flora to take his aunt's hand and kiss her cheek. "I'm en route to Newhaven. I'm going over to Trouville on Tea Tom's yacht for a few days."

"I see." Mrs. St. Leger looked disapproving. "Your husband is referring to Sir Thomson Lipton, the tea millionaire," she explained to Flora.

"Of whom my aunt disapproves because he started his career as a grocer in Glasgow," he added dryly. "That he is a friend of the king, and the man who healed a serious rift between the English and American yachting fraternities, does not in her eyes outweigh his plebeian origins."

That he should use the very expression that a short time earlier she had applied to herself sent a pang of unease through Flora. She rose from the chair behind the tea table.

"No, no—you may stay there, Flora," said Mrs. St. Leger. To her nephew she went on, "I am aware that you think me old-fashioned, Carlyon, and I acknowledge that at one time my circumstances forced me to know people whom my mother would never have received. But there is no compulsion on you to mix with the *nouveaux riches*."

"I like old Tea Tom," said Caspar. "Later on this year he's going to make another attempt to win back the America's Cup." He turned to his wife. "The cup was originally called the Queen's Cup. It was given by the Royal Yacht Squadron for a race around the Isle of Wight. After if was won by the schooner *America*, her owners presented it to the New York Yacht Club to be held as an international trophy.

British yachtsmen have been trying to recover it for over thirty years, but have never succeeded. In 1893, and again two years later, Lord Dunraven challenged with his yachts *Valkyrie II* and *Valkyrie III*. He blamed his second defeat on the crowded state of the course, and a lot of ill feeling resulted."

He paused to carry a cup of tea to his aunt and to offer her milk and sugar.

"Five years ago, the king asked Sir Thomas to try to patch things up," he went on. "I was one of his guests on board *Erin* when he took his racing yacht *Shamrock* across the Atlantic in 1899. He didn't 'lift the mug,' as he puts it. But he's a first-rate sportsman who doesn't mind losing, and he's determined to bring the cup back to England. We shall probably be invited to watch his next attempt in the autumn."

"Is Sir Thomas aware that you have a wife now?" asked his aunt. "I see you have not announced your return in *The Times*."

He handed her a plate of small sandwiches. "I never do. My friends know that I am in England."

"Such casual habits may have served when you were a bachelor, but they will not do for a married man. To keep your marriage a secret must give rise to gossip."

"I have no intention of keeping it secret. The day I return to Longwarden there will be an announcement in *The Times* announcing that Flora and I were married quietly in Shanghai. The fact that I have been seen in London, and she has not, is easily accounted for. She had needed time to recover from the bad weather in the bay."

"Yes, I daresay that will be accepted," agreed his

aunt. "You have not forgotten, I trust, that next Wednesday is your bride's birthday?"

"Naturally not. I shall return from Trouville on Tuesday."

"Oh, but, Caspar, please don't come back before you wish to," Flora interjected quickly. "My birthday is not of importance, and perhaps Sir Thomas may decide to prolong the visit to Trouville."

I only wish I could come with you, was her wistful thought. But she knew she was not nearly ready to be introduced to his friends. No doubt there would be other opportunities to visit Père d'Espinay's homeland, to see the colorful costumes worn by the country people and admire the many ancient buildings.

"In that case I shall return by the ferry from Dieppe," said Caspar. "What would you like for a birthday present?"

The look that accompanied this question made her wonder if he had decided her birthday should mark the transition of their relationship.

"Père d'Espinay always gave me a book. When he took me into his care he put some aside for that purpose."

"Very well, I will bring you a book, and perhaps some *marrons glacés* or pralines."

"It would be more useful to bring her some French kid gloves and also some embroidered lawn handkerchiefs. The poor child's wardrobe is sadly deficient in everything," remarked Mrs. St. Leger.

"What is your glove size, Flora? I'll make a note of it."

Having done so, he added, "Which reminds me, I have something for you. Something that in ordinary circumstances I should have given you before we were married.''

He took from his pocket a small leather case. It contained a ring, which he slipped on her finger above her wedding ring.

''That is not one of the family jewels, is it?'' asked Mrs. St. leger.

Flora was speechless. She had never dreamed of seeing her hand adorned by not one but a galaxy of diamonds, all flashing blue fire in the sunlight.

''No, this is a ring of my choosing.''

Caspar lifted her hand to his lips and brushed a light kiss on her knuckles.

''Put on your cape and come for a walk in the garden. I must be off very soon. You will excuse us, Aunt Blanche?''

Flora rushed upstairs for her cape, not forgetting her hat and her gloves.

When she joined him in the hall she said, ''I haven't thanked you for the beautiful ring. I feel sure it must be very valuable. I only pray I don't lose it!''

''When it's not on your finger, it will be your maid's responsibility,'' he said as he opened the front door for her.

''My maid?''

''I've told the housekeeper at Longwarden to engage a personal maid. You will need her to look after your clothes. She will also write any notes that need to be sent to your dressmaker, and pack and unpack for you. I seem to remember my mother preferred to have her bedroom dusted by her maid. But that is a matter for you to decide later on.''

They set off along the graveled path that made a

dry walk around the garden even on days when it had rained.

"You spoke of your aunt's disapproval of Sir Thomas Lipton's plebeian origins. May I ask what you told her about me the night we arrived? I presume you must have told her something. She has never inquired into my past life."

"I advised her not to," he answered. "I told her—with perfect truth—that the priest who had brought you up after the death of your parents had been mortally wounded in circumstances that it would distress you to discuss."

"What did you say about my parents?"

"That your father was a plant hunter like myself, and your mother a Chinese lady of gentle birth. Who is to say she was not? You know too little about her to assert that she was of peasant stock. It's equally possible she was a Manchu. Your height and your slender build support that theory."

"Perhaps," she agreed, her tone doubtful.

He glanced down at her. "You don't find my aunt too severe a taskmistress, do you? You are not unhappy staying with her?"

"Oh, no she is being very kind." After a pause she ventured, "But I shall be glad when I can be with you again."

He didn't say, "So shall I." That would have been too much to hope for. But how Flora longed to hear those words.

He said simply, "Yes, I shall be glad to see Longwarden. I've been away almost a year. However, I can't go without my bride. That would inspire gossip. We must go together."

They had reached a part of the garden where the

path was screened from the house by shrubbery. He took out the slim gold hunter that he kept in his waistcoat pocket.

"I must be back at the station by five o'clock. I left my luggage there and walked to enjoy the country-side. It's only three miles, but if I don't leave very soon I shall have to run to catch my train. There's no need to come to the gate with me. We'll say goodbye here—in private."

Before she could guess his intention, he swept off her hat, which she had not had time to pin on, and she was once more in his arms with his mouth upon hers.

Again it was over all too soon. Just as she was beginning to feel that the sensuous movements of his lips called for something more than passive submission on her part, he lifted his head.

Perhaps he misunderstood why her face fell as he released her.

He said abruptly, "At times I forget what a child you are. Don't worry, *ya-t'ou*. Even when we go to Longwarden I shan't force the pace. Say goodbye to my aunt for me, will you?"

And before she could speak he was striding away, out of sight.

THAT NIGHT, as she brushed her long hair and stared at herself in the looking glass, Flora wondered if her mother could have been a woman of the ruling class.

The Manchus had originally been a Tartar people, mentioned in Chinese records of the tenth century. First they had conquered Manchuria, in the northeast of China, and then the rest of the country. From 1644 they had ruled China from Peking. It was they who forced the people to wear the pigtail as a token of loyalty to their regime, the Ching dynasty.

But if Most Rare Flower had been a Manchu, surely Tom Jackson would have known it and would have told his daughter? Besides which, as far as Flora knew, no Manchus were ever as impoverished as her Chinese grandparents had been.

Her mother, whose milk name, Kai Tzu, had meant the Daughter Who Should Have Been a Son, had been born to a family too poor to keep her until she was marriageable, but too scrupulous to kill her or to sell her in infancy. The alternative had been a rearing marriage, which meant her being brought up in the household of her future husband. This had one advantage in that, although not permitted to speak to him, Kai Tzu had at least seen her husband before their wedding and had known something of his temperament. It had also had the disadvantage of putting her, throughout her girlhood, in the power of a more than usually bullying mother-in-law.

Her failure to bear a son—and her suspicion that her baby daughter had not been stillborn, as she was told, but had been murdered by her ruthless mother-in-law—had made her life hardly worth living. When her husband had taken a little wife, the prospect of sipping vinegar—the Chinese term for the disharmony between a wife and a concubine—had been beyond bearing.

Kai Tzu had run away and later had attempted to drown herself.

She had been rescued from the river by Tom Jackson. Although he had seemed very large and hairy and ugly to her, he had been the first person ever to be kind to her. He had renamed her Most Rare

Flower. When she had borne him a girl child he had not despised and reviled her but had been unmistakably delighted.

It had never occurred to Flora to ask her father if he and Most Rare Flower had gone through a form of marriage. Not until after his death had she discovered that the children of unmarried parents were social outcasts, shunned by respectable people. When she had confided to Père d'Espinay that she feared she must be illegitimate, he had said it was not of importance in the life she was likely to lead.

"But if I went to England to find my father's family—would it make them ashamed of me?"

"It might—yes, it might," he admitted. "The degree of disgrace attaching to illegitimacy depends on the standing of the father. The natural child of a king or nobleman may enjoy more respect than the legitimate child of a man of humble birth."

When Caspar had offered her marriage and she had at first refused him, he had forced her to reveal her secret. Like Père d'Espinay, he had seemed to think it unimportant. Since he'd said his only surviving relation was a widowed aunt and had misled her into believing that his social standing was much the same as her father's, he had succeeded in overcoming her doubts.

Now every day produced evidence that, when he was not abroad traveling incognito, he belonged to a world as remote from hers as the moon from the earth.

Although she was inclined to answer her protégée's questions about Longwarden as evasively as her nephew, Mrs. St. Leger had let slip one or two clues to his wealth. Only this afternoon she had referred to his family jewels, and indeed the opulence of the engagement ring he had chosen was proof that he must be a very rich man.

Flora raised her left hand to her throat, watching the diamonds flash and sparkle in the soft flattering light of the candles in the tall china holders standing on either side of the mirror.

She supposed that any other girl would be delighted by the discovery that her husband possessed the wealth to buy new jewels to add to those already accumulated by his forebears. But both her father and Père d'Espinay had brought her up to believe in the Biblical proverb, "Better a dinner of herbs where love is than a stalled ox and hatred therewith."

Even now, with the feel of Caspar's kisses on her lips still a vivid memory, she had little confidence that he would ever come to love her as Tom Jackson had loved the black-haired, almond-eyed mother of his child.

Laying aside the brush, she rested her elbows on the dressing table and cupped her hands under her chin. Examining her face feature by feature, she could find little fault with her nose, mouth, forehead or chin. They were her European features.

But the prominence of her slanting cheekbones and the slightly hollowed planes beneath them were quite different from the full cheeks of English girls; as were her eyes. They were the unmistakable stamp of her mixed blood.

Yet but for one detail they might have been the long-lashed dark eyes of a girl from Italy or Spain. That detail was a small fold of skin hiding the canthus—the inner corner of the eye—which in Europeans was exposed, showing the tear duct.

It was this little fold that gave her eyes the appearance of being uptilted like her cheekbones. This was actually an illusion. If only it were possible to remove the tiny fold of skin she would be left with eyes that in their size and luster would be her best feature.

In China she had not minded inheriting her mother's eyes. Nor did she here, on her own account. It was on her husband's behalf that she felt her Oriental blood to be an embarrassing drawback.

With a sigh she blew out the candles and climbed into the big bed, the room now lit by the oil lamp on the bedside table.

Long after she had turned down the wick, she lay awake in the darkness, remembering the turbulent sensation she had felt while in Caspar's arms...and wondering why he had said he would not "force the pace."

CASPAR DID NOT KEEP HIS PROMISE to return to England for her birthday.

The day before, Mildred came to the drawing room with an orange envelope and a letter opener on a silver salver.

"A telegram for you, m'lady."

The message was brief: "Detained in France—will advise when returning. Carlyon."

Although she herself had urged him not to cut short his cruise with Sir Thomas Lipton on her account, Flora could not help feeling severely disappointed.

Perhaps he was not coming back because of her unsatisfactory reaction to his farewell kiss in the garden. If only there had been time for him to kiss her again, she would have responded much more warmly. Perhaps he had experienced his own first kisses such a long time ago that he had forgotten them; and perhaps even very young men had an instinctive knowledge of how to go about it. But she felt sure that for most girls kissing was like other accomplishments: it required some practice before perfection was achieved.

Since his visit she had been practicing; pressing her parted lips against the back of her hand and emulating the soft pressure that, made by his lips, had sent such strange tremors through her.

When they met for breakfast on her birthday, Mrs. St. Leger presented her with a case containing some visiting cards. On them was engraved in black copperplate, "Countess of Carlyon," with "53 Park Lane" in small letters in the lower left-hand corner and "Longwarden" in the lower right corner.

When Flora had thanked her for the pretty mother-of-pearl case, she said, "You will notice that your title is printed without 'the' in front of it. But you must remember to use 'the' when addressing letters to other peeresses. Strictly speaking, you are still in mourning for your guardian, and your cards should have a narrow black edge. The deep border, gradually diminishing with the period of mourning, is no longer used. However, since he was not your kinsman, and it is advisable for you to make your debut as soon as possible, it is necessary to waive the usual customs."

During the morning a parcel of books came by special delivery from Hatchards, a leading London bookshop. This cheered Flora up considerably. At least Caspar had remembered part of his promise.

Whether he had specified which books he wished to be sent to her or had left the choice to the shop, she had no means of telling.

The volumes, all published by Macmillan & Company, were bound in dark green cloth with elaborate designs in gold stamped on their covers and spines. They included *The Vicar of Wakefield* by Oliver Goldsmith, *Cranford* by Mrs. Gaskell and *Our Village* by Miss Mitford, all with delightful pen-and-ink illustrations by Hugh Thomson. There was also—and this sounded more exciting—*Nightmare Abbey and Headlong Hall* by T. Love Peacock, which had a blue cover and a stylized design of a peacock that made particularly effective use of the gold leaf.

"A very nice selection," said Mrs. St. Leger, when she had examined the titles. "They are all pleasant, well-written tales with which every well-bred girl is familiar. Unfortunately a great many unsuitable novels are being published nowadays. I regret to tell you that you will find some of them circulating at the house parties to which you and Carlyon will be invited after your debut. Do not succumb to the temptation to read meretricious rubbish, Flora. The bad influence of such novels is not to be underestimated. However, the works of Mrs. Gaskell and Miss Mitford are always of excellent moral tone."

Flora, beginning with *Our Village*, found the subject matter dull and the style effusive. She could not believe that Caspar would have read more than half a dozen lines of Miss Mitford's account of a walk through a wood, and she knew Père d'Espinay would have deplored the passage that described the felling of an oak tree.

See how the branches tremble! Hark how the trunk begins to crack! Another stroke of the huge hammer on the wedge, and the tree quivers, as with a mortal agony, shakes, reels and falls. How slow, and solemn, and awful it is! How like death, to human death in its grandest form! Caesar in the Capitol, Seneca in the bath, could not fall more sublimely than that oak.

Her reaction to this exclamatory description was to burst out laughing. Having begun, she couldn't stop. Her slim body shook with laughter until suddenly she found she wasn't laughing but crying.

Fortunately she was alone when this curious reaction overcame her, and she quickly pulled herself together.

WHILE FLORA WAS DRYING HER EYES and telling herself not to be foolish, Carlyon was seated in the salon of Trouville's most elegant milliner, watching as the woman who had been his mistress before he set out for China try on a succession of hats.

They had met by chance the day before he had meant to return to England. There had been no correspondence between them during his absence, but the unexpected encounter on the esplanade at nearby Deauville had been a pleasant surprise.

She was staying at a hotel with her sister, who was recovering from an illness. In spite of a wide acquaintance among the other visitors to the resort, she had not found anyone to flirt with.

Caspar had also been bored by his fellow guests on board *Erin*. The sight of Lady Pansy Travers—she was the daughter of a duke but had married a very rich commoner—strolling toward him under a pink parasol had been a welcome relief from the unusual sense of ennui from which he had been suffering.

Explaining to Sir Thomas that he could not continue the cruise along the French coast but must return to England forthwith, he had moved into her hotel, engaging the suite next to that which she and her sister were occupying.

It was a simple matter to obtain the key to the door that connected the two suites. But in any case her sister was aware of their former relationship and was far too discreet to enter Lady Pansy's bedroom since the earl had appeared on the scene.

"Which do you think is more becoming, Carlyon? This one or the blue?"

Torn between a pink straw tricorne with a matching ostrich feather, which the *modiste* assured her was the latest thing in Paris and several seasons in advance of London fashion, and an equally becoming blue leghorn trimmed with blue and cream ribbon, Lady Pansy turned for his advice.

"I should have them both," he replied.

"What a splendid idea. Yes, I will."

Speaking excellent French, she conveyed her decision to the milliner. Probably the woman spoke some English in order to cater to the middle classes, who were now unfortunately to be found in resorts that had once been exclusive to members of society. However, having made an early acquaintance with the language in the pages of the schoolroom classic *Les Malheurs de Sophie*, Lady Pansy always spoke to the hotel staff and the tradespeople in their own tongue, as did Carlyon and most well-bred people. It was only the parvenus who expected foreigners to understand them, and who raised their voices and made scenes when their orders were met with blank looks and apologetic shrugs.

"That's a pretty hat," said Caspar, indicating a shepherdess style with foliage on the crown, massed flowers on the brim and plissé chiffon beneath it.

"Yes, charming," she agreed, glancing at it. "But I'm not the ingenue type, as you know—" with a provocative glance "—and I never wear yellow, even that very pale shade. It only suits brunettes."

"It was an ingenue brunette I had in mind," he answered before telling the milliner that he would buy it.

"I didn't think you had any youthful relations, and surely none of your goddaughters can be out yet?" she said, looking puzzled.

"I have one young female relation, at present in the care of my aunt, who will need a smart hat before long. Perhaps you would help me to choose some gloves for them. I have a note of their sizes."

"By all means."

Shopping was Lady Pansy's favorite pastime, especially in France, and especially with an attractive man to encourage her to be extravagant.

During his months in the East, Caspar had become even more attractive, she thought, watching him through her lashes. The sun—so ruinous to women's delicate complexions—was flattering to masculine faces. With a turban over his dark hair he would look as lawless and exciting as the wild Afghanistan tribesmen of whom her youngest brother, whose regiment was stationed in the newly established North-West Frontier Province, had sent home some photographs.

Although they were said to commit unspeakable

cruelties, and a white woman who fell into their hands would be better dead, Lady Pansy could not help thinking that, if only they were a little more civilized, it might be rather thrilling to test their prowess in bed.

In fact when Caspar had been making love to her the night before, she had pretended he was one of them, and she his captive. Not that such games were necessary with him, because he was by far the best of her lovers. When—not very often, thank goodness— her husband came to her bedroom, even her vivid imagination could never make his performance anything but a tedious duty.

Having selected the gloves and other presents for his aunt and the girl he had mentioned, they returned to the hotel. There, after she had changed into a tea gown of heliotrope chiffon trimmed with lace and swansdown, she joined Caspar for tea in his suite.

After tea they retired to his bedroom, where she stayed while later he rose and went back to the sitting room to order champagne. He rarely slept afterward. She always felt languid and drowsy.

By the time the champagne had arrived and he returned to the bedroom with it, Pansy had fallen asleep, sprawled in the center of his bed.

She was built like the Rokeby Venus with large, velvet-soft dimpled buttocks and generous thighs. Her waist was small; made smaller, when she was dressed, by tightly laced corsets that left red marks on her flesh. He had always admired her figure and enjoyed her plump arms around his neck and her plump legs gripping his haunches.

But now, as he sat and studied her unconscious

form, she seemed to him somewhat too buxom, and her legs not to be compared. . . .

It surprised him to realize whose legs his mind had conjured: those long slender legs and fine ankles he had seen only once in a dimly lit room at the mission.

The events of that night brought a frown to his level dark eyebrows. He remembered thinking at the time that it would be a difficult if not impossible task to erase Flora's memory of that brutal experience. Now he himself had elected to be the second man to possess her, and he found himself increasingly reluctant to take the step that before long had to be taken.

She was still so absurdly young, with none of the carnality that developed early in women like Pansy, but much later in others. Perhaps, because of what had happened to her, she never would develop those instincts. She hadn't shrunk from him when he had kissed her in the conservatory, but when he had repeated the caress it had been like kissing the closed still lips of a child. Afterward, in her eyes, he had read a wordless appeal to him not to make her grow up.

Among all the women he had known—and there had been many—Caspar had yet to meet one whose initiation on her wedding night had not been an appalling shock. Even Julia Roscoe, who had been in love with her seducer, had confessed to more pain than pleasure.

Flora would not be shocked. She already knew the worst; and he knew enough about women to give her more pleasure than pain. But if before he could gentle her into surrender she fought him off, it would not be for the reason that Pansy had fought him last night.

She had wanted to be overpowered; had relished being pinned down by him, her soft thighs forced apart. But in the case of his bride such treatment was out of the question. It could cause complete mental collapse.

On the bed Pansy stretched voluptuously. "Oh... champagne. Is there some for me?"

She arranged the pillows in a comfortable mound and reclined against them.

"In a minute I must go and change for dinner," she said as he brought her the wine. "Shall I come to you tonight? Or will you come to me?"

"I'll come to you."

His brown hand stroked her white thigh. With Pansy there were no problems.

MORE THAN A WEEK after her birthday, Flora returned from a solitary ramble to find Mrs. St. Leger up in arms after a flying visit from her nephew, who had left her with the instruction that she and Flora must be ready to move to Longwarden the following day.

"Most inconsiderate of him!" she said crossly.

"Why was he in such a hurry?" Flora asked.

"He arrived at Newhaven this morning and was on his way to London in a motorcar with Lady Pansy Travers and her husband. Presumably they were also guests of Sir Thomas. Hubert Travers goes everywhere by motorcar and his wife encourages his obsession. They would only stay for ten minutes. Now that the government has introduced a speed limit of twenty miles an hour—far too fast for safety, in my opinion—Hubert can't drive as fast as he would wish."

"Is Caspar coming to fetch us?"

"No, he will meet us in London. He left several parcels for you. Mildred has put them in your bedroom. Much as I appreciate the gloves he has brought me, I should have preferred to have proper notice of our removal," said Mrs. St. Leger repressively.

Flora hurried upstairs to see what the parcels contained. Among them was a large hatbox. When she opened it, a gasp of delight escaped her.

It was the most beautiful hat she had ever imagined; and by now she had seen many elegant hats illustrated in the columns of *The Lady* and *The Illustrated London News*, two of the periodicals to which her hostess subscribed.

She wore the hat the next morning, making Mildred exclaim, "Oh, Miss Flora, you look a picture!" She realized her slip of the tongue. "Begging your pardon, m'lady."

"Dear Mildred...don't beg my pardon. You've been so kind while I've been here, and so has Cook. I shall never forget my first birthday cake. How I wish I could stay with you longer, for 'Miss Flora' suits me much better than 'Lady Carlyon,' I fear."

The parlormaid, known in the village as "that sour old tartar," said warmly, "If I may be so bold as to give my opinion, m'lady, you'll win hearts wherever you go. Cook was only saying the other day that there's something about you that reminds her of Her Majesty Queen Alexandra...the Princess of Wales, as she was before the coronation last year. 'England's darling,' they used to call her when she was younger. And you've got the same pretty ways, the same kind heart and sweet smile."

At first startled by this encomium and later encouraged by it, Flora set out for London in a well-tailored white serge costume, made in Hong Kong, and the French hat and French kid gloves.

She was eager to see her husband, but she did not mean to let him know it. In spite of his generous gifts, she was hurt by his failure to write to her during his absence, or to send even one picture postcard—although it might be that the latter was among the many things that were "not done" by members of the peerage.

Flora, having seen Cook's scrapbook of postcards sent by nephews and nieces on day trips to Brighton and Southend, thought it an excellent custom. A picture postcard from Trouville, with a few lines in Caspar's own hand, would have soothed the painful disappointment of that brusque telegram.

He was waiting for them on the platform, accompanied by a station official and two porters with large luggage trolleys, when their train reached London.

She had never seen him looking more magnificent. Her resolve to be a little distant toward him was forgotten as she gazed at the gleaming silk top hat that made him seem taller, the black cutaway morning coat with a white Malmaison in the left lapel, and the formal striped trousers, sharply creased down the front, that emphasized his long legs. A wing collar with a silk bow tie, a finely checked double-breasted waistcoat and black patent shoes completed his masculinely elegant attire.

She could not repress a thrill of pride in the outstanding superiority of his person and his tailoring. He was every inch an earl—but would she ever achieve the air and style of a countess? Her hat, she knew, was perfection; but noting the way Caspar's coat sat on his broad shoulders, she became conscious that her walking costume was not as well made as she had thought.

Caspar helped his aunt out of the train. She had a great deal of luggage and was worried some might be mislaid.

"It will all be perfectly safe. Have no fears, my dear aunt," he said soothingly. "Good morning, Flora," he added, raising his hat for the second time.

The wide brim of hers precluded a kiss on the cheek. They shook hands.

Until his parting remark the last time she saw him, she had thought of the move to Longwarden as the real beginning of their marriage. After what he had said, perhaps this would not be the case. Yet surely their so-called engagement could not continue much longer?

"That hat is extremely becoming. I felt sure it would be," he remarked, smiling down at her.

She flushed with pleasure at his praise. "It was very kind of you to buy it for me—and all the other lovely things."

"Lovely girls deserve lovely things," was his smooth reply.

This, she felt, lacked the sincerity of his previous remark. It had too facile a ring. She gave him a polite little smile and moved in the direction of his aunt, who was supervising the arrangement of her baggage on the trolleys.

This was to be taken across London in one of the growlers that Caspar had pointed out to her; and she assumed they would travel in a separate conveyance of the same sort.

Her first intimation of the grandeur of her husband's home life came in the station forecourt. A closed carriage, with the Carlyon coat of arms on the door panel, awaited them. A coachman in a silk hat, white breeches and polished top boots, with many shining gilt livery buttons on his dark coat, sat on the box, controlling a matched pair of grays. With him was a groom to assist the ladies in entering the carriage and alighting from it.

"I don't maintain a stable in London, except in the season," Caspar told her. "This carriage is kept for my use at Thomas Tilling's, the best of the London jobmasters. The coachman and groom are his men. Tilling provides everything but the livery for very little more than it would cost me to keep a brougham in Park Lane, and his harness horses are among the finest in the country."

"Yes, you have never been as recklessly improvident as my brother-in-law," said Mrs. St. Leger approvingly. "To add Turkish baths to his stables was among the least of his extravagances."

"But it was an unselfish extravagance that must have been greatly appreciated by his stablemen," remarked Flora.

Caspar laughed. "The baths were for the horses, not the stable staff."

She gazed at him in astonishment. "Turkish baths for horses!"

"It isn't unusual. A number of large stables have them for horses that are suffering from exhaustion or influenza. It wouldn't have occurred to my father to provide similar facilities for his two-legged dependents. In his day the underservants at Longwarden washed in basins of cold water. They didn't even have a hot bath in front of the fire on Saturday night as the cottagers do."

"You go to the other extreme and are overindulgent with your servants," said Mrs. St. Leger. "It is the greatest mistake to pamper the lower orders. They do not appreciate it. It merely encourages them to take liberties."

"No one takes liberties with me, aunt," Caspar returned somewhat curtly.

To Flora's relief, Mrs. St. Leger said no more on the subject.

Having crossed London for the second time, she found that the next stage of the journey was in Caspar's private railway coach attached to a train to Reading. It would stop at Longwarden Halt, the small station built by the sixth earl for the convenience of guests attending his house parties.

Here the private coach was uncoupled and they were received by the uniformed stationmaster, who escorted them through the station building—part of which was his house—to an open landau.

This was driven by an elderly coachman with whom Caspar shook hands and whom he introduced to her.

"White has lived at Longwarden more than twice as long as I have. He was born on the estate, as his father and grandfather were," he explained to Flora.

Possibly Mrs. St. Leger did not approve of his informality with the coachman, but to Flora it would have seemed unnatural for him not to have some conversation with a man who had known him all his life.

A short distance from the station was a crossroads where the carriage turned left under a festoon of evergreens suspended from the trunks of two large trees on either side of the lane. A little way on, at the boundary of the estate, a mounted cortege of at least twenty of Caspar's tenants was waiting to escort them through the village. Each man was wearing a white rosette on his coat and holding a wand topped with green leaves and fluttering white ribbons. As the carriage came into their view, hats were raised and a loud cheer rang out.

"I didn't expect this," said Caspar. He reached out to give Flora's hand an encouraging squeeze. "There's no need to be nervous. You only have to smile and bow. I will make any speeches that may be necessary."

The village street was thronged with people waiting to welcome the earl home, and to catch a glimpse of the bride he had brought back from foreign parts.

Rosy-cheeked little girls in starched white pinafores and boys with stiff collars waved paper Union Jacks. With their fair hair and light-colored eyes, they were very different from the children she had known in China. As different as she was from the ladies they were accustomed to seeing.

On the green by the village pond was a notice surrounded by flowers: Health and Prosperity to Lord and Lady Carlyon.

But the finest decorations were at the main entrance to the estate, where Welcome in letters of gold had been erected above the great wrought-iron gateway, and the gates and their massive brick piers were almost completely hidden by garlands of white flowers and foliage.

Here the landau came to a halt, the coachman and groom climbed down, and the horses were swiftly unharnessed to be replaced by eight brawny young men.

They pulled it the rest of the way, up a mile-long drive bordered by magnificent elms and lined with cheering, waving spectators.

"They've turned out from miles around," said Caspar, raising his hat again and again to acknowledge the vociferous welcome. "But it's not me they've come to see. You are the attraction, Lady Carlyon." He glanced smilingly at her bemused expression.

Flora was overwhelmed. She had never dreamed they would have this kind of reception, and she was amazed at the warmth of the people's smiles and the spontaneous enthusiasm of their cheers.

Suddenly a youth stepped forward and tossed something onto her lap.

"Those must be some of the first primroses," Caspar observed, looking at the nosegay of pale yellow flowers.

The landau was not moving fast, but already the youth was behind it. Flora sprang to her feet and looked back.

"Thank you! They're lovely," she called to him.

Turning forward to sit down again, she thought she saw censure in Mrs. St. Leger's expression.

"Shouldn't I have done that?" she murmured to Caspar.

"Why not?" he said with a slight shrug.

She had an uneasy feeling that none of the girls qualified by birth and breeding to be his countess would have leaped up as she had just done.

Mortified by her foolish impulse, she went on smiling and bowing until, a few moments later, she had her first sight of the house.

Except that Longwarden was not a house. It was

many times larger than the château that had been
Père d'Espinay's birthplace, which she'd seen in a
drawing.

As her eyes scanned the great central dome behind
the imposing facade of the east front, its portico of
two-story columns flanked by wings each the size of a
mansion, her mind reeled from the shock of realizing
that this tremendous edifice was to be her home, and
she its mistress.

"You d-didn't tell me you lived in a palace," she
exclaimed in a panic-stricken voice.

"Longwarden is half the size of the Marlboroughs'
place. You will soon get use to it," he said carelessly.

The people lining the drive had thinned out, but
ahead of them more were assembled on the lawns surrounding the sweeping circle of carriageway below the
wide steps to the entrance. On their side of the steps
stood a large staff of indoor servants; liveried footmen, maids in black uniform dresses, and others
whose function she could not guess. There were also a
number of women waiting to present large bouquets.

Knowing that in a few minutes she would be expected to receive their offerings with the dignified
composure becoming to her rank as Caspar's wife,
Flora buried her nose in the posy of primroses. For
an instant she closed her eyes, breathing in their faint
sweet scent, redolent of quiet country places where
poor girls could hunt for wild flowers, but not the
Countess of Carlyon.

Then, mustering all her courage, determined not to
let them guess how nervous she was, Flora lifted her
small firm chin and pinned a calm smile on her lips.

PART THREE
LONGWARDEN

CHAPTER ONE

ON THE NIGHT of her first dinner party Flora stood in front of the long looking glass while her maid fastened the bodice of her evening dress.

In defiance of his aunt's pronouncement that nothing but white was suitable for a bride in the first year of her marriage, Caspar had insisted that the dress should be made from the bolt of apricot crepe de Chine he had bought in Hong Kong.

"White is not becoming to Flora. It makes her look sallow," he had said in his most peremptory tone.

He had upset his aunt even more by insisting the dress must be made to be worn without a corset.

"Her waist is slender by nature. I will not have her figure deformed by tight lacing," he had ordered. "I consider it almost as barbarous as the Chinese practice of binding women's feet. Lillie Langtry would never constrict her figure. I remember my father remarking how supple it was compared with the stiff hour-glass shapes of fashionable beauties."

"Mrs. Langtry was an actress," had been his aunt's acid reply before she asked Flora to leave them, since she wished to speak to Caspar in private.

Later Flora had ventured to ask him what had been said during her absence. At first she thought he was not going to tell her. Sometimes when she asked him questions his face would become enigmatic, and when his replies were evasive she thought it wiser not to press the matter.

But on this occasion he had shrugged and said, "According to Aunt Blanche only fast women appear in public without a corset."

"I expect she is right. Perhaps I should wear one. I don't want to shock people—more than is inevitable," she added.

Caspar took her hands. As yet he had not lost the deep tan acquired on his travels. The hands holding hers were as brown as those of the merchant at Colombo who had sold him the rubies. But the merchant's fingers had been pudgy, with long and dirty nails, whereas her husband's fingers were lean, his nails neatly pared. Lately whenever he touched her she felt a kind of inward shiver.

"Do you care what people think?" he asked her.

"Not for myself," she replied truthfully. For herself, she was indifferent to English society's opinion of her. It was only for his sake that she wished to win approval.

Even now, after three weeks at Longwarden, she had not yet accustomed herself to being called "m'lady" by the servants. In her heart she was still Flora Jackson, whose paternal grandparents had been a gamekeeper and a cook; had she grown up in England, she would have been on the same social level as her husband's housemaids.

The staff at Longwarden had been trained to conceal all emotion in the presence of their betters, and however amazed they had been the first time they saw their new mistress, they had not shown their astonishment.

She wondered if the guests at tonight's dinner party would be able to mask their reactions as perfectly. While the servants had no choice but to accept her, the aristocracy and gentry of the county in which Caspar's family had lived since 1598 did have some choice. Because of her husband's rank and wealth they might not be able to shun her; but she guessed there were many subtle ways in which they could make her aware that she was accepted on sufferance.

When she was ready she asked her maid, Burton, to send word to her husband that she would like to speak to him. Since their arrival at Longwarden Caspar had never entered her bedroom, which was separated from his by a small anteroom with a window seat and a splendid view of the park laid out by Humphrey Repton in 1790.

She waited eagerly for the door on her side of the anteroom to open, and for Caspar to see her transformed by the gown and the jewels of his choosing. But presently Burton returned by way of the corridor with the news that his Lordship had gone down some time before.

"Do you wish me to ask his Lordship to come up to you, m'lady?" she inquired.

"No, no—it isn't important. Thank you, Burton. You may leave me."

Flora's tone was tranquil, betraying nothing of her pain that Caspar had not thought it necessary to see her alone for a few moments before her first public appearance.

She gazed at her reflection in the glass, trying to persuade herself that his failure to come could be taken as a mark of his confidence that she would face the evening ahead as calmly as he had once dealt with an ambush by Chinese brigands.

But it was not to soothe her nerves that she had wished to see him; rather the reverse. She had wanted to be alone with him, and on the infrequent occasions when they were alone in a room she would find her nerves in a flutter and her heart beating faster than usual.

She had meant to show off her gown, and to thank him for the three jeweled butterflies that glittered and shimmered in her hair. Then she had planned to move close to him and to stand on tiptoe to kiss his dark, clean-shaven cheek.

She had hoped that when he saw her shoulders and bosom exposed by the fashionably low décolletage, and felt the touch of her lips, he would realize she was a woman, not the child-bride he seemed to think her.

As she was about to leave the room, she remembered the unopened vial of scent given to her by Mrs. Roscoe. At one time she had thought of throwing it away because of its painful associations, but it was still in the casket containing her most personal possessions.

On impulse she unlocked the casket and took the vial from its box. The bottle was sealed with wax, and this had to be scraped away with her nail scissors before she could remove the stopper, which had a glass rod attached to it. She applied the rod to her wrist and rubbed the fluid into her skin for a moment before lifting her wrist to her nose.

The fragrance reminded her a little of the joss sticks the Chinese burned in their temples and shrines. It was also slightly reminiscent of the ferns in Mrs. St. Leger's conservatory. There were other components that she didn't recognize, but which combined to make a fragrance as lovely, in a different way, as the heady gusts of perfume that came from a Chinese hillside covered with wild lilies on a hot afternoon. She knew instinctively that Caspar, with his appreciation of flower scents, could not fail to enjoy this perfume.

Quickly she touched the rod to the sides of her neck, the base of her throat, her shoulders and—after a brief hesitation—the hollow between the creamy curves of her breasts.

Apart from the jeweled butterflies, which Caspar had had specially made for her, her only ornaments were a strand of his grandmother's pearls and her pearl drop earrings.

Although it was ten minutes before the first guests were expected, the servants were already at their stations when Flora went down to the drawing room. Warner, the butler, was standing near the drawing-room door, ready to announce the guests. John, the upper footman, was waiting to open the door when the first carriage drew to a halt under the portico. Edward, the under footman, would take charge of the gentlemen's cloaks and hats, while Kate, one of the housemaids, took charge of the ladies' cloaks.

They had heard the susurrus of her train as Flora crossed the landing and were looking upward when she appeared on the staircase. But for Warner's intimidating presence, the younger servants might so far have forgotten themselves as to watch her descend to the hall, instead of averting their eyes.

"Good evening, m'lady," said Warner, bowing, as she reached the lowest stairs.

"Good evening, Warner. Good evening, John... Edward...Kate."

She smiled at all four; the elderly man who had known her husband from boyhood, and the three young people who would never know that, but for a quirk of fate, she might have been one of them.

Her acknowledgment of their presence gave them the chance to look at her again. In the housemaid's expression Flora read confirmation that her gown and her ornaments were as beautiful as any the girl had seen. But it was the younger footman's reaction that sent a pang of excitement through her. For it seemed to her, just for a second, that she saw in his eyes the message that *she* was beautiful; and if one of her footmen thought that, might not her husband think so, too?

Warner opened the heavy mahogany doors, and with a soft word of thanks she rustled into the drawing room.

She found Caspar standing beneath the full-length portrait of his grandfather that hung above the white marble chimneypiece. Mrs. St. Leger was seated nearby, a majestic figure in steel-gray satin and lace. Instinctively Flora curtsied as she said good evening to her.

The obeisance seemed to please the old lady. She said in her most gracious manner, "Good evening, Flora. Carlyon was quite right: that color is most becoming to you."

"Thank you, Aunt Blanche."

She turned to her husband. But what she saw in his cool gray eyes was not the glint of admiration she thought she had seen in the footman's glance. Caspar's expression was impassive to the point of indifference. "You look charming, m'dear," he said politely.

Inwardly her disappointment was acute. Outwardly she remained unruffled. Since she was unusually tall, in China she had been accustomed to looking down at most men. But even in high-heeled silk slippers she was small compared with her English husband.

Although in his white tie, white waistcoat and tailcoat Caspar had an air of elegant indolence, she knew that his evening clothes concealed a physique of considerable strength and stamina. She had seen him scale formidable cliffs, wade through swift-flowing rivers and perform many other feats.

As yet she had no way of knowing if he was considered good-looking by the women of his own class. Until recently most of the men she had known had been smooth-skinned, unlined Chinese. Caspar had a beard that, shaved in the morning, would begin to shadow his jawline by late afternoon. Although he was not old, already the skin around his eyes bore lines engraved by long journeys in intemperate climates. The two deeper creases down his cheeks were characteristic of all the men in his family, as were the prominent cheekbones and sardonic eyebrows.

To her these features combined to form a face of compellingly attractive masculinity. When he smiled she felt her bones were melting. But now that they were living in England he did not smile at her often. She had a sinking suspicion that, seeing her unalterable incongruity in what was, in spite of his absences, the permanent setting of his life, he regretted the chivalrous impulse that had prompted him to offer her his protection.

"Does my nose deceive me, or do I smell scent?

Surely not?'' Mrs. St. Leger exclaimed in horrified accents.

Flora flushed. "Is. . .is scent improper?"

"Most improper! You may use a little lavender water, and eau de cologne is not objectionable, but *scent* is used only by actresses and women of a certain class," Mrs. St. Leger informed her in a tone of the gravest opprobrium.

"But when I was reading an article about the Queen in one of the illustrated papers recently, it said that as well as Old English lavender water, her favorite perfume was Ess Bouquet," Flora protested in dismay.

Mrs. St. Leger looked disconcerted for an instant. "Is it Her Majesty's perfume that you are wearing?"

"No, but—"

"I thought not. You may be sure what she wears will not be a pungent aroma. Furthermore, she is the Queen and—in spite of her remarkable beauty—no longer a young woman. What is permissible for her is not the prerogative of everyone."

"But what shall I do? I can't remove it," Flora exclaimed, her calm shattered.

"Certainly not," said her husband.

He crossed the short distance between them and bent his tall head toward her until their cheeks were almost touching. He inhaled.

"You smell delicious," he said firmly. "You are too conservative, Aunt Blanche. Flora is using an essence of rare Chinese peonies presented to her by the dowager empress—a signal honor, I may tell you."

"Indeed? The dowager empress? Well, perhaps in that case. . . ."

Mrs. St. Leger stopped short as the door of the drawing room opened and Warner announced the entrance of Sir Vernon and Lady Fitzwilliam.

Radiant with the relief of Caspar's rescue, and the flicker of a wink that he had given her, Flora welcomed their guests as serenely as if she had been a hostess for years. Her amusement at his bland expression as he made up the nonsense about the essence of peonies sustained her until Warner announced dinner.

Caspar led the way with Lady Chiltern, who, being the wife of a Viscount, took precedence over the other ladies, and presently Lord Chiltern gave his arm to Flora.

He was a man in his sixties with a white mustache and somewhat bloodshot blue eyes. As they walked across the hall to the dining room he said, "Your husband tells me you've had a classical education, Lady Carlyon. How did that come about, may I ask?"

Caspar had never warned Flora to be evasive about her parentage; indeed when she had found out who he was, and deplored his folly in marrying her, he had told her not to talk nonsense. But since she knew that Père d'Espinay's life had been, if not ruined, greatly changed by a similar mésalliance, she was profoundly afraid of causing the same kind of odium to befall her husband.

She had decided, therefore, that if anyone asked about her father, she would have to temper the truth by saying that he was killed when she was three instead of, as had actually happened, when she was ten.

It was not a lie but rather a half-truth when she

answered, "I was brought up at a French mission where the priest in charge was a man of great scholarship. Having no pupil worthy of him, he was generous enough to attempt to enrich my poor mind with some of his own erudition. With such a teacher, even a girl must learn something."

Lord Chiltern chuckled. "I happen to be the son of a bluestocking, so you don't have to pretend to be a pretty nincompoop with me, m'dear. If you want my opinion, it's not men who mind clever women—it's other members of the fair sex. You might be wise not to mention to the ladies that you read Latin and Greek. I shan't give you away," he promised with a twinkling glance that made her laugh.

He sat on her right hand at dinner. On her left sat an elderly baronet, Sir Everard Knollys, who was equally affable to her. But she knew it was not on masculine opinion that the success of her debut depended, but on what the wives thought of her. Her real test would come when the ladies withdrew after dinner.

Normally she and Caspar and Mrs. St. Leger dined in a smaller apartment and sat within a few feet of each other. Tonight she was separated from him by the full length of a table seating twenty-four people, and even to catch his eye would be difficult. Between them stood an elaborate silver-gilt table garniture, two pairs of candelabra and a tall ornate centerpiece.

Glancing down the row of faces on Sir Everard's side of the table, she found herself being watched by the only other person present whose age was close to her own. This was a fair-haired young woman, rather plump but exceedingly pretty, whose name, Flora remembered, was Mrs. Hector Layard.

As their eyes met, Mrs. Layard sent her a smile of such sweetness that Flora had the heartening conviction that at least one of the female guests was disposed to like her. For the moment she could not recall which of the men was Mr. Layard. The guests had entered the drawing room in such rapid succession that only a few faces had made a strong impression on her.

The dinner began with oysters, followed by soup with which Warner offered sherry; although not to Flora, who had told him beforehand she would drink only lemonade.

During the first two courses Sir Everard had addressed his conversation to the lady on his left. But when the *turbot Portugaise* was served, he turned to his hostess and asked, "What are your interests, Lady Carlyon? Do you ride? D'you care for lawn tennis?"

He was shy of her, Flora realized. She was not the kind of woman he was used to, and he wanted to have a good look at her, but politeness forbade it. He could only flash brief piercing glances under his eyebrows.

"I'm afraid I do neither," she answered. "I read a great deal, and I like to paint flowers and landscapes. My pursuits have been governed by living in the wilds of western China."

"A dangerous country, by all accounts. No doubt you're relieved to be safely in England." It was a statement rather than a question.

"Yes, indeed," agreed Flora, obediently producing the reply expected of her.

In fact the unrest in China, and the attacks on foreigners and missionaries by members of the Secret

Society of Harmonious Fists—known abroad as the
Boxers—had never greatly disturbed her peace of
mind.

Danger and hardship had been part of her childhood; the price to be paid for adventure and the thrill
of discovery. One of her earliest memories was sitting
in the crook of her father's arm while he smoked his
evening pipe and told her stories of her hero, the
plant hunter Robert Fortune.

However, she felt there was no point in explaining
to Sir Everard that even if she had known about the
Boxer Rebellion in Peking, it would have seemed far
away and much less important than the illness of her
beloved Père d'Espinay. Caspar had already told her
that people who lived in a small country such as
England could not imagine the vastness of China.

"My husband tells me you have a remarkable collection of stamps, Sir Everard," she said, thereby
launching him on a discourse about philately that
lasted until the arrival of the *filets de boeuf*.

She listened with attention, only once allowing her
glance to stray to the other end of the table, where
Caspar was momentarily in view because he was leaning toward a lady in blue with sapphire bracelets on
her wrists. She was evidently an amusing conversa-
tionalist: he was smiling at her chatter in a way that
made Flora long to overhear it.

"Do you share your husband's passion for horti-
culture, Lady Carlyon?" asked Lord Chiltern, turning to talk to her as the meat succeeded the fish and
the hock was succeeded by champagne. "Or shall
you find other occupations for the hours Caspar
spends in his hothouse?"

"I do share his interest, certainly, but I wouldn't

say it was a passion with me," she replied in a thoughtful tone. "No doubt my principal occupation will be the ordering of the household. Mrs. St. Leger has been extraordinarily kind in guiding me through my first weeks here, but we can't expect her to desert her own home indefinitely."

"I find Mrs. St. Leger rather alarming," he confided with a conspiratorial chuckle.

Privately Flora agreed with him. But she had not grown up in China without absorbing some of the profound respect in which Chinese matriarchs were held by their fearful and often cruelly downtrodden daughters-in-law. Caspar's mother being dead, she saw Mrs. St. Leger in that role and would not have thought of criticizing her, even to Caspar.

"Do you? How strange," she said coolly. "I have been impressed by her benevolence."

This was true. She was not unaware that, of all the people who would disapprove of Caspar's marriage to a nobody, his aunt had borne the brunt of the shock. Yet, allowing for her natural severity of manner, she had never been deliberately unkind or tried to make Flora feel her inferiority. Perhaps she was shrewd enough to realize that her nephew's bride was only too conscious of her shortcomings.

"I'm delighted to hear it," said Lord Chiltern.

Something in his expression made her wonder if the remark had been a test of her diplomacy.

For the rest of the course he questioned her about China until, with the serving of the pudding, Sir Everard resumed his pet subject.

As she dipped her spoon and fork into the Dean's Cream, a rich confection of sponge cake, brandy, ratafias and dried fruit that had been a favorite of

Caspar's since he was at Cambridge, Flora wondered
how the other ladies, encased in their corsets, were
able to eat the fifth course with apparently undiminished appetites.

She had noticed at once that their figures were far
more generously curved than her own; their hips
more rounded, their bosoms as full and white as the
breasts of the doves that strutted on the lawn below
the terrace.

The Chinese ate well on such special occasions as
weddings and funerals, and at their New Year cele-
brations. But in between these festivities, even the
families of prosperous farmers lived on a meager
diet, and many poor peasants were half-starved. It
seemed to her that people who feasted every day, as
did the English upper classes, must have palates so
jaded by excess that meals must become a penance
rather than a pleasure.

The pudding was followed by a savory. Fortunately Mrs. St. Leger had explained the menu to Flora, or
she might have been surprised to find that Scotch
woodcock was not a bird but an anchovy sandwiched
between toast and enveloped in hot creamy custard.

It took all her resolution to eat it. When the servants had served the dessert and left the room, she
was thankful to toy with a few grapes, and amazed to
see most of the guests helping themselves to a selection of fruits from the pyramids of hothouse delica-
cies.

Mrs. St. Leger had ordained that not more than an
hour must elapse from the beginning of the meal
until, having allowed the ladies time to drink one
glass of the port that accompanied the dessert, Flora
caught the eye of Lady Chiltern and rose from her

chair. She had dreaded this moment, fearing that some of the ladies might dawdle over their wine, or that it might prove impossible to catch Lady Chiltern's eye. However, neither of these difficulties occurred. In the order in which they had entered it, with the gentlemen standing by their chairs, all the ladies left the room, Flora following last.

As she passed him, Caspar, who was holding the door, gave her a smile that went some way toward fortifying her for the testing time in the drawing room.

The first person to converse with her was Lady Chiltern, who said, "This is your introduction to England, I believe, Lady Carlyon. How I envy you your first English spring. It is quite our loveliest season. Are you fond of poetry? Do you know Mr. Algernon Swinburne's beautiful poem about the spring?"

"I'm very fond of poetry, but I'm afraid I don't know Mr. Swinburne's works."

"Ah, then you have another pleasure in store for you. I feel sure there must be a copy of *Atalanta in Calydon* somewhere in your husband's library. If not, I shall lend you my copy. Now tell me which poets you particularly admire?"

Remembering Lord Chiltern's advice—although perhaps he had not meant his warning to include his wife—Flora thought it wiser not to include Horace among her favorites. There seemed no harm in mentioning Baudelaire.

"How surprising," exclaimed Lady Chiltern. "I shouldn't have thought Baudelaire would have been allowed in the convent where, so Lord Carlyon tells me, you received your education. I remember when I was a child of thirteen or fourteen, my eldest brother went to Paris and brought back *Les Fleurs du Mal*, a book that was later suppressed. Somehow my father found out, and poor Jack was in *very* hot water. However, I believe an expurgated version was published about ten years later."

She paused, becoming aware that the upper footman had approached her with a tray bearing coffee cups, a cream jug and a sugar basin. When she had helped herself, he moved on and Warner presented a small tray bearing the coffeepot. Finally the under footman inquired if she wished for a liqueur.

This Lady Chiltern refused. Turning back to Flora, she continued, "I hope you will come to see me. I am always at home on Wednesday afternoon. But I mustn't monopolize you this evening. Have you talked to young Mrs. Layard? No? Then do let me beckon her to us. She is also a bride, and I'm sure you will like her."

When, after a few minutes' conversation *à trois*, Lady Chiltern drifted away, Flora continued it by saying, "I hear you are also a bride. How long have you been married?"

"Nearly six months."

There was a pause in which it seemed that, unless they were to sit in silence, Flora would have to keep up a flow of questions.

Then the other girl drew an audible breath and said, "Shall you think me impertinent if I tell you how much I admire you for being so wonderfully composed? I was dreadfully nervous at *my* first dinner party. If I had had to converse with Lord Chiltern and Sir Everard, I'm sure I should have died of fright. *You* made Lord Chiltern laugh, I noticed."

"I expect you would have done, too. He is very easy to amuse. As for Sir Everard, he kindly entertained *me* by telling me about his stamp collection."

"Are you interested in stamps?"

"I knew nothing about them until this evening. Sir Everard is an authority, and therefore what he says must interest anyone. What are your hobbies, Mrs. Layard?"

"Oh, nothing out of the ordinary, I'm afraid. I'm not clever enough to be a new woman. Even if I were, papa would never have allowed me to attend a university. He disapproves of education for women. I play the pianoforte and I quite enjoy needlework. My favorite hobby is sketching."

"Which I enjoy, also. Perhaps we might sketch together someday," Flora suggested.

She had never been on close terms with someone of her own age and sex, and she felt that in many ways Mrs. Layard might be a more useful guide to the intricacies of English social life than someone of Mrs. St. Leger's generation.

"Oh, yes—I should like that *very* much," the other girl agreed with enthusiasm.

Flora lowered her voice. "You will think it very remiss of me not to have memorized the plan at the dinner table, but I cannot remember the name of the lady who is coming toward us."

"She is Lady Conroy," murmured Mrs. Layard nervously. "Oh, dear, I find her quite terrifying."

Seen at close quarters, Lady Conroy was even more striking than she had seemed during dinner when Flora had watched her amusing Caspar. Her eyes were as blue as her sapphires, and her hair was a rich chestnut shade. The bodice of her gown was extremely low-cut and seemed in imminent danger of revealing even more of her shape than was already in view. The color of her lips and cheeks owed as much to art as to nature, Flora suspected. She was carrying a fan of blue ostrich feathers.

Smiling at Flora, she said, "I expect your husband has told you what very old friends he and I are. We met at my first ball, and as it was so long ago—he was only a few years my senior—I can tell you that he flirted outrageously. As no doubt he did with you before his intentions became serious."

Returning her smile, Flora responded, "I believe you know Mrs. Layard."

"Yes." As Lady Conroy glanced at Mrs. Layard, the faint smile that touched her lips somehow seemed to be a comment on the other's dress, rather than an acknowledgment of their acquaintance. It made Flora understand perfectly why Mrs. Layard was nervous of her.

"Good evening, Lady Conroy. If you'll excuse me, Lady Carlyon, I must go and speak to Mrs. Duchesne." With an apologetic smile at Flora, Mrs. Layard moved away.

This time it was Lady Conroy who launched the conversation by saying, "You realize, I suppose, that you're going to be dreadfully unpopular?"

This remark, and the appraising look that accompanied it, would have demolished Mrs. Layard. Flora was less easily discomposed, and something Mrs. St. Leger had said to her enabled her to parry the teasing remark.

"I don't expect a warm welcome from the ladies who had hoped to see their daughters in my place," she replied lightly.

"Ah, but it's not only matchmaking mamas whose dislike you must expect," said Lady Conroy. "Caspar has more to recommend him than his position, you know. He is not like that poor little creature's husband—" brandishing the ostrich feathers in the direction of Mrs. Layard "—at whom no one would glance were he not Lord Mordaunt's heir. Caspar is so very good-looking, and so entertaining. His rather wicked reputation makes him doubly attractive. But no doubt that is all in the past. He has changed his ways now. You have reformed him, I expect."

Before Flora could reply, the door of the drawing room opened to admit the gentlemen. Among the first to enter was a gaunt gray-haired man who came across the room to join them and, to Flora's surprise, turned out to be Lady Conroy's husband.

Although she had tried to fix the faces of all the guests in her mind when, with Mrs. St. Leger, she was receiving them, some had made little impression. Women, even if their faces were not memorable, could be remembered by their clothes or jewels: *Mrs. Duchesne. . . diamond aigrette; Lady Gifford. . . ruby velvet*. The men, in their identical evening dress, were less easily distinguished from each other.

Another shock was the discovery that pretty Mrs. Layard was married to a man whose teeth protruded as noticeably as his chin receded, and whose affected drawl and braying guffaw Flora would have found most irritating to live with.

By eleven o'clock all the guests had departed. In England, apparently, it was not the custom for conversation to continue until midnight or later, as had been the case whenever Père d'Espinay had guests.

"You acquitted yourself very well, Flora," pronounced Mrs. St. Leger. "Lady Chiltern was most taken with you, and I was glad to see you talking to Helen Layard, a very nice young woman whose friendship you should encourage."

"I have done so, Aunt Blanche. We are to go sketching together."

Caspar said, "If you'll excuse me, I should like some fresh air. Good night, Aunt Blanche."

He did not say good-night to Flora; nor did he ever. Presumably this was to give the impression that their good-nights were said in the privacy of their apartments.

"I shall retire now," said Mrs. St. Leger soon after her nephew had left them. "All things considered, I think we may count this evening a success."

Flora accompanied her upstairs, and they said good-night at the door of Mrs. St. Leger's bedroom. For some moments Flora debated going down to join Caspar on his stroll in the garden. But if he had wished for her company, surely he would have invited it?

Reluctantly, for she did not feel tired, she went along the corridor to her room. Burton was waiting to help her undress and to unpin and brush her long hair.

"Did you enjoy it, m'lady?" the maid asked, helping Flora to step out of her white taffeta petticoats.

"Yes, thank you, Burton."

But she had not enjoyed it. She had had pleasant but superficial conversations with the Chilterns, and perhaps she had begun a friendship with Helen Layard. Otherwise the evening had been a ritual that she had performed because it was incumbent on her, but which had left her feeling curiously dissatisfied.

Had Père d'Espinay been present, they would have
spent a pleasant hour comparing their opinions of
people and pursuing the loose ends of discussions.
But here there was no one to replace him except her
husband, and since their arrival in England Caspar
seemed to have withdrawn himself. She wondered
what Lady Conroy had meant by her reference to his
wicked reputation.

Some time after Burton had left her, she was gazing into the flames of her bedroom fire when there
was a knock on the door leading to the anteroom.

"Come in," she called in a startled voice.

The door opened and Caspar appeared. "Ah,
you're still up, Flora. I thought you might be. I
wondered if you'd care for a nightcap, as you had no
champagne earlier on?"

"Yes, I should—very much," she said, smiling.

He disappeared for some moments and came back
pulling a trolley on which stood a silver ice bucket
and a covered silver dish. Having steered the trolley
close to the sofa where she was sitting, he returned to
close the connecting door.

It was the first time she had seen him in a dressing
gown, and she thought he looked magnificent. It was
made of very dark green velvet with a great deal of
silk braid frogging on the chest and the cuffs; the
hem swept the floor, showing only the toes of his red
Turkish leather slippers. Beneath the dressing gown
was what looked like a shirt of red silk, open at the
throat, and she took this to be the upper part of his
nightshirt.

At one time it would have surprised her that
Caspar wore such colorful and opulent night attire.
In China he had seemed to be a man who, apart from

being clean and serviceably clad, cared little for the niceties of dress. In England, however, he was always well dressed.

She herself was enveloped in a long-sleeved white cotton nightgown under a matching peignoir procured for her by Mrs. St. Leger. Both garments were exceedingly voluminous with many pintucks and ruffles, and Flora found them most uncomfortable.

She thought it was probably the nightgown that was the cause of her bad dreams. Invariably when she awoke it was ruckled up under her armpits, or twisted into a lump in the small of her back. In China, in summer she had slept in a shift of thin silk, supplemented in winter by a robe of padded cotton, both garments made faded and shabby by much washing.

When Mrs. St. Leger had seen them, she had ordered Mildred to burn them in a tone that could not have been more scandalized had they been verminous. Flora would have liked to object to the arbitrary disposal of two of her few possessions, but after some moments' reflection she had decided to keep silent.

"Did you choose that shroudlike garment, or did my aunt?" inquired Caspar, evidently as much struck by her nightwear as she had been by his.

"Your aunt did."

"So I surmised."

As he spoke, he eased the cork out of the champagne bottle and filled two glasses, one of which he handed to her.

"Are you peckish? D'you care for a sandwich?"

He removed the cover from the dish, revealing a

selection of sandwiches garnished with sprigs of parsley and twists of cucumber.

"Oh, no—I'm not at all hungry. I haven't digested my dinner yet. In China a whole village could have lived for a month on what was eaten in the dining room tonight. I wonder what happens to what isn't eaten? Do the servants finish what we leave?"

"I have no idea. Why not ask Mrs. Foster?" he suggested, referring to the elderly housekeeper who came to Flora's boudoir each morning, but with whom she'd had little direct conversation, since it was Mrs. St. Leger who conducted these daily interviews.

"Yes, I shall," she said, wishing she had not mentioned the matter to him.

According to Mrs. St. Leger, it was to the supervision of her household and to the mastery of English etiquette that she must apply herself most diligently. But tonight Flora had formed the opinion that what she most urgently needed to learn was how to make Caspar laugh as Lady Conroy had made him laugh.

Her husband seated himself in the chair on the far side of the fire. It was a large high-backed chair, too long in the seat for her to sit comfortably in it when Mrs. St. Leger was present, but in which, when she could not sleep, she sometimes curled up to read until the fire died and the room became chilly.

Now, seeing Caspar sitting there, she wondered why she had not realized that it was a man's chair, the only masculine furnishing in an otherwise wholly feminine room. Perhaps it had been placed there for his father, or even for his grandfather.

Caspar crossed his long legs. "Are you still very homesick for China?"

"Homesick? No, not at all. Why should you think that?"

"You've been here only a short time. There are still many things that are strange to you. It would be surprising if you weren't homesick. By the way—" there was a gleam of amusement in his eyes "—where did you get hold of the essence of peonies?"

She had anticipated this question and had her answer ready. It was impossible to avoid an oblique reminder of Mrs. Roscoe, but she could refrain from a direct reference.

"I bought it in Hong Kong."

"I see. Well, although not everyone is as strict in their views as my aunt, and no one of my sex is likely to deplore your use of it, perhaps it would be advisable to use the scent that the Queen likes when you are in public, and reserve the essence of peonies for my delectation," he said in a tone of amusement.

Remembering she had not thanked him for the butterfly ornaments, she hastily repaired the omission.

"I'm glad they pleased you. They looked well— although I have to admit I prefer your hair as it is now."

"So do I," she said with feeling.

She detested the hot horsehair pads that were the foundation of a fashionable coiffure, and which Mrs. St. Leger and Burton insisted were essential, however abundant the natural hair.

"You look rather warm," he remarked. "Why not discard your outer wrappings? I'm sure any night-

gown selected for you by my aunt must be quite as
decorous as a tea gown, probably more so."

She was hot, and when she was reading by the fire
she often did discard the peignoir. But something in
Caspar's manner made her suddenly shy of doing so
now; although, as he had surmised, the nightgown
was fit for a nunnery. She began to undo the ribbons
that fastened the collar and cape.

Caspar sipped his champagne and watched her,
and she found her fingers trembling slightly.

"Would you like to have your bedroom refur-
nished?"

The question surprised her. She glanced at him. "I
don't know. I haven't thought of it."

"Think about it tomorrow. There's no reason why
it must remain as it is now. My mother's great passion was for photography. She took little interest in
household matters."

"Were they happy, she and your father?"

"I don't know. I should think it unlikely."

As she started to take off her peignoir, he rose and
came to assist her.

Had she been removing her motoring coat, or the
bolero jacket of her walking costume, she would
have accepted his help without the least confusion.
But somehow a peignoir was different. As she half
rose from the sofa to free the lower part of the garment, she felt herself starting to blush.

"There, that should be more comfortable," he
said, tossing the peignoir aside and then sitting beside
her on the sofa. He sounded as calm as she was nervous.

Suddenly her intuition told her that he hadn't
come to her room merely to drink champagne with

her. Tonight he was going to regularize their relationship and make her fully his wife.

Her hand shook with apprehension. She drank some more of the pale golden bubbling wine, hoping it would give her Dutch courage and help her to suffer in silence when he thrust that part of himself inside her.

"Was old Knollys a dead bore tonight? I can't believe his conversation was as riveting as your expression suggested. Chiltern's not a bad sort, but most of our neighbors in this part of the country are a dull lot. You'll meet a more interesting set when we move to London for the season."

He began to play with her hair, winding a tress around his fingers.

She tried to think of some intelligent response to his remarks and found herself as tongue-tied as Mrs. Layard had been some hours earlier. As if she were still drinking lemonade, she drained her glass.

"This is delicious. May I have some more?"

"By all means."

He withdrew his hand from her hair and leaned forward to reach for the bottle.

She remembered—how long ago it seemed!—the first night of their journey from the mission, when Caspar had forced her to eat some supper and afterward they had played bezique and drunk *samshu.* *"Three glasses is your limit, my girl. One more and you'll be tipsy.... To give a girl too much champagne is one of the easiest ways to seduce her."*

Probably he didn't remember telling her that. She remembered everything he had ever said to her. Perhaps champagne wasn't as potent as *samshu.* At present she didn't feel in the least intoxicated. She only wished she did.

"Aren't you going to have a sandwich? It seems a p-pity to waste them," she said nervously.

"Not just now...perhaps later on."

Although he was never loud voiced, his reply was quieter than usual; a more intimate tone than any he had used to her before.

When he touched the nape of her neck with the tips of his fingers, she stiffened and swallowed some more champagne. If only it would go to her head, making everything slightly hazy as the *samshu* had.

Caspar took the glass from her and put it aside. He took her hand in his and began to kiss her fingers, and not only to kiss them but to nibble them gently with his teeth.

Eyes downcast, scarcely breathing, she sat motionless while he pressed his lips into her palm. A moment later the frilled cuff of her sleeve was undone and his warm mouth was pressed to her wrist where the blue veins showed through the ivory skin. He pushed the sleeve higher, inching his way up her arm to the soft inside of her elbow, his dark head bent over her arm so that from the corner of her eye she could see how his thick close-cut hair sprang from his temples and grew at the back of his neck.

Such a strong, brown, masculine neck, with the hair tapering into two points as it did on the necks of choirboys. That was because his neck was as lean as the rest of him, not thick like the necks of most men. She found that she wanted very much to raise her free hand and touch him...touch that dark, lustrous, well-brushed hair.

She wasn't quite sure how it happened, but suddenly she was no longer sitting upright. She was leaning back against the cushions and Caspar, still holding her hand, was kissing the curve of her chin with the same little light nibbling kisses he had applied to her wrist.

Her eyes closed, her pulses racing, she felt his warm breath on her neck.

"Mmm...*you* taste delicious," he murmured.

The deep voice, so near to her ear, sent a curious shiver down her spine. An instant later she gasped as his teeth closed on her small lobe, which tonight was bare.

The gasp was not caused by pain. As the first gentle nip was repeated again and again, she was filled with a strange trembling pleasure that increased as he let go her hand to use his long supple fingers to fondle her throat.

She had known how deft he could be in the handling of small fragile plants and in using a pair of fine forceps to dissect them and study their structure. She had not guessed that his fingers would be equally skilled in minutely exploring her body. As his hand slid behind her neck and then upward into her hair to cradle her head, she found herself longing for the moment when his mouth would reach her mouth.

But her husband seemed in no hurry to progress to that kind of kiss. Slowly, slowly, his lips traced a path from her temple, across her forehead and back by way of her eyelids.

She lay without moving against the nest of silk cushions. Although she was outwardly passive and—apart from her quickened breathing—as still as if she had fainted, within was a turmoil of unfamiliar reactions.

He kissed the space between her eyebrows, the straight bridge of her nose, the tip of her nose. Surely the next kiss would be on her mouth? But no, he was kissing her cheeks, returning to the line of her jaw and to all those sensitive places that she had not been aware of, behind her ear, under her chin; places where the warm pressure of his lips caused wild thrills of response deep inside her.

When at last he did kiss her mouth, her lips parted under his like a flower opening to the sun. It was not the practice kisses on her hand that made the difference. It was the arousal of her instincts; the long slow play on her senses that made her forget to be shy.

As their mouths fused, she ceased to be passive. Her hands moved from her lap to his chest and then higher up, to his shoulders. Soon her arms were clasped around his neck.

He kissed her for a long time; until the crash of a log as others supporting it disintegrated made him raise his head and look toward the unguarded fire.

As he rose to replenish the blaze, Flora drew a deep quivering breath. She hadn't known that one kiss could merge with another and go on and on indefinitely.

She saw Caspar turn out the lamps that here at Longwarden were electric, powered by a large private dynamo. With the room lit only by the flickering glow of the flames, he took some cushions from a chair and flung them upon the fur rug made from the skins of Arctic foxes.

Returning to the sofa, he drew her to her feet with one hand and with the other gathered up the cushions that had been behind her. These he added to those on the floor before drawing her down onto the rug to resume their interrupted embrace.

Lying between him and the fire, with plenty of room for them both to stretch at full length, was better than being on the sofa. Soon it was too warm. Caspar sat up and took off his dressing gown, revealing the dark red silk nightshirt with buttons from neck to waist. The top three buttons were undone, showing part of his bare brown chest, not as bronzed as his face and hands but still much darker than her skin.

"Aren't you hot buttoned up in that nightgown?"

He leaned on one elbow beside her, opening the frill around her neck before bending to touch his lips to the hollow at the base of her throat.

Then he kissed her again, a little less gently this time, and she found that she liked the possessive pressure of his mouth. She discovered that kisses could be more intoxicating than wine; dulling the power to think clearly, making her giddy with pleasure even though she wasn't standing up.

The discovery that he had undone several more buttons and was running the tips of his fingers up and down the opening in her nightgown sent a long shiver rippling through her body. She felt the warmth of the flames on her naked breasts as he widened the opening, baring the upper part of her body from her shoulders almost to her navel.

Although he had yet to look at the soft flesh he had exposed, and was continuing to kiss her, she felt a deep blush add its heat to that of the fire. His palm lay lightly on her waist for a moment or two before it slid over her ribs to explore the curves of her bosom.

Once before she had felt his hand there, but
through more than one layer of clothing, not, as
now, on her quivering skin.

She shuddered, but not with revulsion, as she had
when the Frenchman had thrust his rough hand inside her bodice. Caspar's touch was gently caressing;
he might have been stroking a cat. Even his kisses
had softened again.

Suddenly, with the ease of his formidable strength,
he put both arms around her and lifted her into a sitting position, arranging her so that she was facing the
fire and he was seated behind her, his broad chest
making a backrest for her.

For some moments he did nothing more, merely
holding her loosely against him while her breathing
became less shallow and her heartbeats quieted.

Then he gathered all her long hair into two thick
skeins and tossed them forward before half undress-
ing her, pulling the decorous nightgown down from
her shoulders and slipping her arms out of the sleeves
so that it fell around her hips and she had only her
hair to cover her.

His hands fondled the curves of her shoulders and
moved lightly up and down her arms before returning
to her shoulders to make her bend toward the fire. As
her supple body curved forward, she felt his kisses on
her back, his lips roving over her spine.

Her pulses quickened again. When he kissed the
nape of her neck and then gave it several playful
bites, a smothered cry broke from her. She hadn't
known what it would do to her to feel him biting her
there; the primitive feelings it would kindle.

But it seemed that he knew its effect. She heard
him give a low laugh before he drew her upright and

his hands again slid down her arms, this time as far as her wrists. With her hands enclosed in his larger ones, he held her close to him, their arms crossed in front of her so that she was entirely encircled by his strength.

"Put your head back," he commanded softly.

She rested her head against his shoulder, watching the dancing firelight through half-closed eyes, wondering what he would do next, her fears lulled by this slow game of love he was playing with her.

"Your hair shines like falling water... *une cascade noire.*"

Peeping downward, she saw that her breasts were completely hidden by hair, although it did show their outlines. Half-consciously wanting him to continue his fondling, she snuggled against him, rubbing her cheek against his chest.

Releasing her hands, he began to caress her small waist, his fingers fanning out over her slim rounded hips.

Flora gave a voluptuous sigh. "It's nice by the fire." The words were a husky whisper.

"And is this nice?" he murmured, smoothing her belly. "And this?" as he traced slow circles around her navel.

She gave a small nod.

His hands rose higher, beneath the black veil of hair. She closed her eyes, waiting, instinct telling her that each move in the game was a progression, exacting a wilder response.

"Your breasts feel like two ripe nectarines, still warm from the hothouse," he told her, holding them in his palms.

As his thumbs stroked the tender brown tips, she

felt them expanding like buds, sending sweet pangs
of ecstasy through her. Strangely, it was not only in
her breasts that she felt these delightful sensations.
She could also feel them in her thighs; and in that
part of her body that as far as she knew had no name,
but where for long after her rape she had felt both
hurt and defiled.

Now even there she felt pleasure: a lovely, warm,
melting pulsation that she wanted to go on forever.

Caspar took his hand from her left breast, but only
to brush aside the hair that was hiding his soft play-
things from him.

To know he was looking as well as touching made
another deep flush stain her cheeks. The curious
thing was that while part of her was blushing with
shyness, she was conscious of an alter ego that,
far from being shy, was longing to encourage his
caresses.

It was even in her mind to turn around and, rising
to her knees, rub herself sinuously against him, and
to kiss him instead of being kissed. But she dared not
succumb to the impulse. It might be the wrong thing
to do, as so many of her impulses had been.

An instant later she discovered that for once it was
not. Caspar himself turned her around, lifting her to
her knees in front of him as effortlessly as earlier he
had raised her from the thick fur rug.

In this position, tall as he was, it was she who
looked down on him. His eyes gleamed between narrowed lids. He lifted her hands to his shoulders.

"Kiss me, Flora."

She bent, her lips light on his mouth. She felt him
pull open his shirt and then draw her closer, bringing
her breasts into contact with the muscular hardness

of his chest. As she twined her slim arms around his neck, his hands glided down her back to grip the firm rounded cheeks of her small high backside.

Her mind clouded. It was her senses that told her that this kiss was different; that his lips had become more demanding, his hands on her body more urgent.

She could feel the heavy beating of his heart, the violent fluttering in the pit of her belly. Their mouths were juicy with moisture. They were breathing from each other's lungs, lost in a world where sight was not needed—only touch, taste and scent.

When he brought the kiss to an end, she could feel the effort it cost him. She wanted to cry out, "Don't stop! I'm not afraid. Take me...take me...." But she was too breathless, too dazed by that wild surge of passion.

As his hands ceased to press her against him, she would have sunk back on her heels. But before that could happen he gave a sound like a groan and drew her back into his arms. Only this time he didn't kiss her.

His warm mouth closed on her breast. As she felt the heat of his tongue against the sensitive tip, her hands moved convulsively on his shoulders. A spasm of piercing pleasure made her fling back her head and forced a sharp cry from her throat.

It was followed by a muffled clangor from a distant part of the house. Somewhere a large heavy bell had begun a sonorous tolling.

Caspar stopped the sensuous caress. He said something under his breath that she didn't catch: it sounded like an angry expletive.

"What is it? What's happening?" she exclaimed.

For a second or two he didn't answer, remaining seated on the rug with his lean cheek close to her heart. Then he loosened his hold on her.

"It's the stable-yard bell. It means that a fire has broken out somewhere on the estate. We've had a fire engine at Longwarden, and a team trained to man it, since my grandfather's time. I shall have to leave you, I'm afraid. They can manage very well without me, but I always go when I'm at home. It's expected of me."

His mouth twisted ironically. "They are not to know that this is—or would have been—our wedding night."

CHAPTER TWO

"I'LL COME WITH YOU," Flora offered. "Perhaps I can help."

"No, no—there's nothing you can do. It will be no place for a woman."

He strode from the room, leaving her to pull on her nightgown and hurry after him.

By the time she reached his bedroom he had disappeared into his dressing room. She cast a curious glance around the room she had never seen before. Here, the fire had almost burned out for want of fresh fuel. The bed was a massive four-poster of dark English oak. The walls were paneled with the same wood. Instead of the *bonheur du jour* that she had in her room for writing letters, there was a large flat-topped desk piled with stacks of books and periodicals.

Although he attended to matters concerning the estate in his large study on the ground floor, it was evidently here in his bedroom, perhaps late at night, that he worked on his horticultural papers.

She waited for him to reappear, torn between her wish to obey him and her instinct to help in an emergency. Before she had time to resolve this conflict of feelings, Caspar returned, his nightshirt exchanged for a polo-necked jersey, tweed knickerbockers and knitted stockings. He was carrying a pair of stout boots, and as he sat down to pull them on he said to her, "Look out of the window and see if you can see any sign of it."

She hastened to the nearest window and flung back the heavy silk curtains. The night was cloudless, and the parkland surrounding the pleasure gardens looked mysteriously beautiful in the moonlight.

About three *li* to the west—in matters of distance and direction she had not yet broken her Chinese habits of thought—the silvery landscape was tinged with the dull yellow glow of a distant conflagration.

"Yes, I can. It's on the edge of the village, and it looks a big blaze," she told him anxiously.

He tied the laces of his boots and came to look over her head.

"Damnation! That's a thatch on fire. Thank God there's no wind." His hand fell briefly on her shoulder. "Go to bed, *ya-t'ou*. I'll tell you all about it tomorrow."

He gave her a dismissive pat, turned away to snatch up a covert coat brought from his dressing room and was gone before she could reply.

She had been alone only minutes when Caspar's valet appeared.

"Oh. . .I beg your pardon, m'lady," he said on catching sight of his mistress in her nightgown. "I came to see if his Lordship needed assistance."

"He's already gone, Durrell, thank you."

She hurried back to her own room, resolved to ignore Caspar's order and to do what *she* felt to be right.

In China she could have dressed as swiftly as he had. But here, with her clothes in Burton's charge, she had first to search drawers and closets for suitable garments.

A high-necked blouse, the navy serge skirt of a tailor-made walking costume and a boxcloth cape with a collar of Japanese fox were the best combination she could find. Her hair she crammed inside a tam-o'-shanter, and having omitted to put on stockings and petticoats, she concealed her bare ankles with a pair of pale gray felt gaiters.

"You should have rung for me, m'lady," said Burton, arriving, much flustered, as Flora was buttoning these on. "I was that sound asleep I never heard the alarm bell. Mr. Durrell sent Kate to wake me. But I should have heard your bell at once. It rings in my room."

"Never mind, Burton. I've managed. The most helpful thing you can do is make up some beds in the nursery wing. The people whose house is on fire will need somewhere to sleep."

Burton's mouth primmed. "That's work for the housemaids, m'lady," she replied, her dignity offended.

Flora managed to contain her impatience. No one knew better than she the importance of "face"; and clearly, face or the loss of it was as important in England as it had been in China.

"Then please see that they know my wishes. If Mrs. St. Leger should inquire, tell her I've gone to the fire to do what I can."

"But, m'lady, how will you get there? The engine has already left, and his Lordship has saddled a horse, so I heard Kate say. Shall I tell them to send round the carriage?"

"No, certainly not," replied Flora. "That will take at least twenty minutes. By the time they have harnessed the horses, I shall be there. In any case, I expect all the grooms have gone to the fire on the engine."

Presently, hurrying across the park, she found she
was not the only person making a beeline from the
big house to the burning cottage. At varying dis-
tances ahead of her she could see several scurrying
figures. But even had she been on her own, the
English countryside would have held no terrors for
her.

Nearing a group of cattle she began to run, not
from fear but to get there sooner. It was difficult running in a skirt and hampered by the folds of the cape.
Throughout her childhood with her father, and often
during the happy years with Père d'Espinay, she had
known the freedom of wearing trousers, and she
wished she was wearing them now. A pair of knickerbockers like Caspar's would have been by far the
most practical garb for an occasion such as this. But
she could imagine the scandalized stares she would
attract by appearing dressed in that manner.

Arriving at the scene of the fire, she found that not
merely one cottage but a terrace of five was in
danger. One was already past saving, the adjoining
roof was in flames, and the third was in imminent
peril of catching alight. Among the groups of spectators stood the contents of the first three dwellings.
The other two cottages were in the process of being
emptied.

Her arrival passed unnoticed except by one or two
children, whose stares were not an embarrassment.
The attention of all the adults not actively involved in
the fire fighting was focused on the crackling thatch,
or the comings and goings from the cottages being
evacuated.

To Flora, accustomed to the uproar of wails and
yells to which the Chinese gave vent in similar cir-

cumstances, the reaction of these English villagers seemed amazingly phlegmatic. The only sounds of distress came from babies in arms and small children, although one young woman was weeping on the shoulder of another.

The one who was crying was soon to give birth, Flora noticed. In her concern she forgot she was a stranger, unknown to these people and possibly unwelcome among them. Edging her way through the crowd, she approached the two women and said to the one giving comfort, "This poor soul shouldn't be here. Has she no family nearby who can take her in and make her comfortable?"

"No, ma'am, she comes from away and her man is at sea. It's their cottage that is burned down the worst."

"Then she must come to the big house...and so must all these tired children who should be tucked up in bed."

Still warm from her cross-country run, Flora unclipped her cape and draped it around the weeping girl's shoulders, for besides being in tears she was shivering from shock.

An old woman stepped out from a group who had heard this exchange.

"Come now, Sarah Lake," she said briskly. "Stop sniveling and say thank-you to her Ladyship. Giving way to tears won't mend matters, so brace up, there's a good girl." She introduced herself to Flora. "I'm the wife of his Lordship's head gardener, ma'am."

"Then you must be Mrs. Edgefield, of whose gooseberry tartlets my husband speaks of with such relish," said Flora, recalling an anecdote of Caspar's boyhood from the many tales he had told her in the course of their journey down the Yangtze; tales told in such a way that she'd never dreamed the great estate of which he had spoken was his own property.

Mrs. Edgefield beamed her gratification. "His late Lordship had a French chef who didn't take kindly to boys, m'lady. When his present Lordship was hungry for toffee and suchlike, he'd come to my kitchen."

"And was always made welcome, he tells me. Now, Mrs. Edgefield, will you help me? You know everyone and they know you. Would you tell them the nursery wing at the big house is being prepared to accommodate everyone who lives in these five cottages. No doubt other people in the village would give them shelter for the night, but that would mean overcrowding, and we have plenty of room for them."

HOURS LATER as she undressed herself—having sent Burton to bed long before—she wondered if Caspar would be angry when he learned how she had spent the night.

She had seen him at the fire, but he had been too busy to notice her. She had hoped he would have come home by now, but Warner had brought her a message to say that one of the men had burned his hands and his Lordship had taken him to a doctor and might not return before daylight.

Catching sight of the champagne trolley Caspar had brought to her room, which—fortunately, as it happened—Burton had neglected to remove, Flora lifted the lid covering the sandwiches. They were slightly curled at the corners but still perfectly edible. Suddenly she was very hungry.

When she had eaten one sandwich, it struck her

that she would enjoy a second one more in the softness and warmth of her bed. Burton *had* remembered
to refill the stoneware hot-water bottle, buttoned
into a flannel cover to save Flora burning her feet on
it.

She pushed the trolley to the bedside and scrambled onto the high bedstead—only to slither back to
the floor when she thought it would add to her enjoyment if she pulled back the curtains and watched the
dawn breaking over the park.

Strangely, she was not at all tired. With her second
sandwich she sipped a glass of champagne. It was no
longer ice cold and fizzing with tiny golden bubbles,
but it still tasted very nice.

"To you, Baby Lake," she said aloud, raising her
glass in a toast to Sarah Lake's infant daughter, now
about two hours old and lying in an improvised
cradle in one of the rooms in the nursery wing.

Had Mrs. St. Leger had her way, Flora would not
have witnessed the miraculous moment of birth. The
baby, a fortnight premature, had been born very
quickly, before the village midwife could be summoned. Removed from her accustomed surroundings, and not being on intimate terms with those of
her neighbors who were present, young Mrs. Lake
had clung to young Lady Carlyon.

"Don't leave me, m'lady," she had begged.

Flora had not left her, except for the few minutes it
had taken to quash Mrs. St. Leger's objections to her
presence at the confinement.

"I cannot allow such a thing, Flora. It shocks me
that you should consider it. The accouchement of
one of the village women is no place for you. I forbid
you to stay in that room."

"I am not a child to be forbidden, Aunt Blanche. I have promised to stay and I shall stay."

"You don't realize what you are undertaking. Her sufferings can only distress you."

"Then since I shall probably bear a child myself before long, I may as well learn what is in store for me. The known is always less frightening than the unknown," she had answered, quoting Père d'Espinay.

In the event, the delivery had been quick and easy. Instead of receiving the birth of a girl child with gloom and displeasure, as would have been the case in China, everyone present was delighted.

But a son will be important to Caspar, thought Flora, sipping champagne. *As important to him as to a Chinese husband.*

She remembered his last words to her. "Go to bed, *ya-t'ou.*" Translated literally, the Chinese appellation meant something like "slave girl." It was a common form of address to a daughter and one Père d'Espinay had often used in speaking to her.

At first she had not minded Caspar's adoption of the term. Since their marriage it had rankled with her, and when he had used it last night—for by now it was daylight outside the house even though the bedroom was still shadowy—it had goaded her to disobey him.

Deep down she had a great fear that somehow Père d'Espinay had made Caspar feel he must marry her. Although in her more sanguine moods she dismissed this notion as improbable, whenever he called her *ya-t'ou* the fear was revived. Nor could she ever forget his explosive remark on their wedding day: *"Were it not for my rank I shouldn't have married at all."*

Thinking about the long interval between their wedding day and what, but for the fire, would have been their wedding night, she wondered if, had his lovemaking not been interrupted by the alarm bell, he would have slept in her bed or returned to his own. She felt sure that her parents had always slept close to each other; but of course theirs had been a love match, not a marriage of mutual convenience.

She wondered how long it had been, after rescuing her from the river, before her father had taken possession of her mother's body. Perhaps, in spite of her marriage and the child she had borne to her Chinese husband, Most Rare Flower had also been afraid of being hurt by her tall bearded English rescuer.

If so, what relief and joy she must have felt on discovering that the things men did to women were not always painful and degrading.

Although Flora had yet to experience the culminating act, after last night she had more confidence in Père d'Espinay's assurance that the processes of procreation could be extremely enjoyable.

Tonight I shall find out for myself, she thought with a quickening of her pulses.

WHEN SHE AWOKE the room was in darkness and she had no idea what time it was. She stretched. Could she have slept all through the day? Could it be evening?

Becoming more alert, she realized that the heavy interlined curtains, which she had left open, had been drawn across the windows while she was sleeping. It was not really dark. When she opened them she could tell by the direction of the sun that, although she seemed to have been asleep for a long time, it was still morning. She looked at the clock on the pier table between the windows. It was nearly half-past eleven.

When Burton answered the bell, Flora had already begun to draw her bath. The up-to-date plumbing at Longwarden was an innovation made by Caspar. Not only had he modernized the bathrooms adjoining all the principal bedrooms, but the servants had bathrooms, as well; two for the women and two for the men.

These had been shown to Flora on her first tour of inspection. It had been evident from their comments that both Mrs. St. Leger and the housekeeper thought that, even though they were starkly utilitarian compared with the mahogany-paneled, brass-tapped baths put in for the Carlyons and their guests, baths for the staff were an unnecessary extravagance.

"I shan't want breakfast this morning, Burton," she said when the maid appeared. "A cup of tea while you're doing my hair is all I need. I'm impatient to go and see Mrs. Lake and her baby."

"His Lordship said you were not to be disturbed until you rang, but that if you should come down before luncheon he would like to see you in the orangery, m'lady."

"Oh. . . yes, very well," answered Flora, hoping her face had not fallen.

Such a summons from Caspar could only mean that he *was* displeased with her.

Usually while Burton was brushing her hair and pinning on the hated pads, she drank China tea and allowed its subtle flavor and fragrance to waft her into a reverie. This morning, however, the summons from her husband loomed over her, filling her with apprehension.

The clock had struck half-past eleven before she was ready to go down. She could have dressed herself in half the time, and it made her simmer with impatience to have to stand like a child while Burton tied the tapes of her petticoat in a perfect bow and carefully rolled black lisle stockings to just below her mistress's knees, where—in the absence of suspenders caused by Caspar's interdict on corsets—they had to be held up by garters.

"You will never look well dressed without a corset, m'lady," said Burton, as she did almost every morning when at last the ritual was completed.

And, as she did almost every morning, Flora replied, "Perhaps not, but I'm sure I am a great deal more comfortable."

Today, at the maid's suggestion, she was wearing a high-necked blouse of white lawn and lace, with a skirt of dark blue vicuña serge cut in the mermaid style that was close-fitting down to the knees, where it flared at the back.

At the front the hem showed the polished toes of her black calf boots, but at the back it was four inches longer and trailed on the floor. A broad belt of matching velvet, fastened with an ornate silver buckle, completed the outfit.

On her way downstairs she met Kate. This in itself was unusual, for, as she had been told by Mrs. St. Leger, well-trained servants were seldom seen about the house after breakfast.

Her first conversation with Kate had been soon after Flora's arrival at Longwarden. Waking early and having nothing to read, she had slipped downstairs to the library, wearing her nightclothes, and had found the housemaid at work halfway up the grand staircase.

The staircase at Longwarden was the only one of its kind in England. No other great house had a silver balustrade, although there was one in the Petit Trianon, the château built by Louis XV in the park of his palace at Versailles for Madame de Pompadour, and later given by Louis XVI to Marie Antoinette.

The Longwarden balustrade was a copy of the French one. It had been commissioned by Caspar's father when making improvements to the house in honor of a frequent royal visitor, the then Prince of Wales, now in the third year of his reign as King Edward VII.

It was Kate's special task every morning to polish a section of the balustrade so that it never became tarnished. At first, when Flora had paused to talk to her, she had been shy and tongue-tied. Subsequently Flora had made a point of visiting the library at the same early hour on most mornings. Gradually she had succeeded in coaxing Kate to talk more freely to her, until now they were on better terms than Flora enjoyed with her personal maid.

In the afternoons, the female servants wore black with frilly caps and aprons. Before luncheon they wore print dresses with plain caps and aprons, and usually Kate's round cheeks were as rosy as her pink print uniform.

Today, as the housemaid drew aside to wait for her mistress to pass her, Flora noticed how pale she looked.

"Good morning, Kate," she said, pausing. "I am

only just out of bed. If you were up at your usual
time, you must be feeling very tired after the disturbed night we all had.''

"Good morning, m'lady. Yes, m'lady.''

The girl kept her eyes downcast, and her voice
sounded curiously hoarse.

"Is anything the matter?''

"No, m'lady. Excuse me, if you please.'' The maid
bobbed and hurried away, as if on some urgent er-
rand.

Puzzled and slightly uneasy, but preoccupied by
her upcoming interview with Caspar, Flora continued on her way. Perhaps Kate looked wan merely
because she was tired.

The orangery at Longwarden had been built by
Caspar's grandfather, with whom he had enjoyed a
closer relationship than with his father.

"The old lord,'' as he was called, had been an eccentric character who at the age of sixty had abandoned his place in public life to devote the next thirty
years to enthusiastic botanizing.

He had lived in a small suite of rooms adjoining
one end of the great glasshouse, where he had been
attended by his valet and fed by Mrs. Edgefield. He
had disliked his heir, tolerated his equally idiosyn-
cratic daughter-in-law, and doted on his grandson, in
whom he had very early inculcated his passion for
plants.

He had died, still in full command of his faculties,
while Caspar was at Eton, and had scandalized the
local bourgeoisie by leaving instructions that he was
to be buried, without benefit of clergy, not far from
the orangery. His grave, he'd specified, was to be
marked only by a *Morus nigra*, for which his remains

would provide valuable humus and which would
eventually bear mulberries for the enjoyment of his
descendants.

As she left the house by the vestibule known as the
Garden Entrance and followed the wide graveled
walk that curves around the edge of the shrubbery to
the small east door of the glasshouse, Flora wondered if Caspar's grandfather would have approved
of her.

The east door led into the fernery, planted with
tree ferns brought from New Zealand by the old
lord's younger and favorite son, an adventurous
young man who had died of a fever in the East Indies.

The humidity in the fernery made it an uncomfortable place in which to linger, but Flora liked the rain-
forest smell and the sound of water trickling into the
pool where the golden orfe lived. It would not have
surprised her to see the tail of a snake whisk out of
sight as she passed along the narrow path between the
banks of ferns and other tropical plants.

As she stepped through the door leading into the
dryer and more comfortable heat of the orangery,
she heard Mrs. St. Léger's voice saying, "...how-
ever, I didn't come here to talk about that."

"No? What did you wish to talk about?" Caspar's
tone sounded as if he were giving his aunt only part
of his attention. Probably he was bending over the
table of special seedlings.

"Is Flora enceinte?"

The question made Flora pause in the act of closing
the intervening door. Evidently it startled Caspar, as
well. There was a marked pause before she heard him
reply, "Not to my knowledge. Why do you ask?"

"No doubt you are unaware, Carlyon, that your wife spent part of last night at the confinement of one of the village women."

"You are mistaken, aunt. Very little happens at Longwarden of which I am not aware."

"Surely you cannot approve of such a circumstance?"

"No."

"Nor do I, as you may imagine," Mrs. St. Leger continued in a shocked tone. "However, when I remonstrated with Flora, she refused to listen to me. She said—and I quote her very words—'Since I shall probably bear a child myself before long, I may as well learn what is in store for me.' You say very little escapes you, Carlyon, but I think you would have been a good deal surprised had you seen Flora's manner to me last night. It was far from respectful, I must tell you. Indeed she revealed a wild streak that, were I her husband, would cause me considerable disquiet."

"You must not criticized her to me, Aunt Blanche."

Caspar's tone remained quiet, but now there was a steely note in it.

It was at this point that Flora realized she must make her presence known to them. Closing the door more noisily than was her habit, she advanced into the orangery, where marble-paved walks formed a figure of eight around two large raised beds of subtropical trees and shrubs.

"Good morning, Aunt Blanche. Good morning, Caspar," she said as she joined them in the vinery leading out of the orangery.

Before either of them could answer, she went on

quickly, "I owe you an apology, Aunt Blanche. You have been very kind and patient with me, and last night I forgot the deference you have every right to expect from me. I am truly sorry if my behavior offended you."

"I accept your apology, Flora," said Mrs. St. Leger magnanimously. "I have no doubt you soon regretted your unwise disregard for the counsel of age and experience."

"Oh, no—not at all," said Flora honestly. "I feel that seeing the baby born added so greatly to my own experience of life—and made me less afraid of my own confinement."

Mrs. St. Leger drew in her breath, but before she could utter Caspar intervened. "If you will excuse us, Aunt Blanche, I should like to see Flora alone."

Her aunt rose from the cane chair in which she had been seated. "Certainly, Carlyon, certainly."

Evidently expecting him to deliver a reprimand far more severe than any reproof she might bestow, she swept out of the vinery.

He waited until she had gone. "So. . . you chose to disobey me, *ya-t'ou*? What have you to say for yourself?"

He was wearing a lounge suit of light gray herringbone tweed with a matching single-breasted waistcoat and a dark gray four-in-hand tie with a wing collar. His posture was one that in China had seemed characteristic; his heels placed some inches apart, his knees braced, his hands behind his back.

According to a joking remark made by Mrs. Roscoe, speaking of one of the ship's officers, this was a stance adopted by all Englishmen when they were required to castigate an unruly inferior, confront an enemy, assess a hazardous situation or perform any unpleasant duty.

Facing her husband now, she found it hard to believe that not many hours earlier he had sat on the rug in her room in a red silk nightshirt, fondling her naked body. This morning those passionate moments in the firelit shadows of her bedroom seemed like a happy dream that had no relation to reality.

"What I said to your aunt last night," she finally answered his challenge, outwardly calm but inwardly quaking. "I am not a child—nor am I your daughter," she added pointedly.

"But when we were married you did promise to obey me, did you not?"

"Yes—but I don't think the promise in the marriage service means one must always obey *blindly*. Père d'Espinay used to say that the first duty of a Christian is to God, and of an unbeliever to his conscience. My conscience told me I ought to go to the village and see what help I could offer."

"I see." Caspar's tone was dry as he went on, "So I cannot rely on your obedience? You will comply when you see fit, but at other times do as you please—is that it?"

The set of his mouth was so stern that she felt her lips starting to quiver.

"I want to please *you*," she said in a low voice. "But how could I go to bed and sleep when there were people in danger—people needing help? Would Lady Chiltern have done so?"

"Probably not, but Lady Chiltern is not a young woman, nor is she a stranger to this country. You are both, and that is why I told you to go to bed last night. Seeing you as you are now—and last night at dinner—

it's difficult to remember that you are as accustomed
to hardship and all manner of perils as girls brought
up in this country are *un*accustomed to them.''

A faint smile relaxed the hardness of his mouth.
''When the rarest of all my exotics burst into bloom
before dinner last night, our guests would have been
most surprised to learn how hardy she was in the
habitat where I discovered her.''

It took her some moments to grasp that he had
paid her a compliment. ''You're *not* angry with me!''
she exclaimed. A flush of relief and pleasure colored
her cheeks.

''On the contrary, it's I who should be in disgrace
for using language unfit for your ears. I beg your
pardon,'' he said, bowing.

Her delicate eyebrows contracted until she remembered his swearing at the realization that the blaze
was made by burning thatch.

''Oh, that didn't shock me,'' she answered. ''My
father used that word quite often.'' And then her
flush deepened with chagrin as she thought that, had
she been a lady, she *would* have been shocked by bad
language.

If the same thought was in Caspar's mind, he did
not show it, but said, ''I had not expected to see you
up so early. Which reminds me—while I have no serious objection to your drinking champagne while in
bed, even though when you fall asleep with the glass
in your hand there's some risk of it breaking and cutting you, I hope you will never be tempted to smoke
cigarettes in bed. You would find I should be very
angry if Longwarden went up in flames.''

His teasing pleased her. It was like the sun coming
out on a day that had been gray and chilly.

"How did you know I had been drinking champagne in bed? Did Burton tell you?"

"Burton knows nothing of your dissipation. I removed all signs of it long before she was about. I came to your room to discuss the events of the night, but you were already fast asleep."

"Oh, I see. How is the man whose hands were burned? Are his injuries serious?"

"Not serious. Inconvenient merely, since he will be obliged to wear bandages for some time."

He brought his hands from behind his back and she saw they were heavily bandaged, one into a shape like a paw, and the other with the fingers and thumb showing.

"Caspar!" she cried in dismay. "It was *you* who was hurt. Why didn't Warner tell me?"

"Because I instructed him not to; and unlike my unruly wife, my butler obeys me to the letter—even if his conscience pricks him when I ask him to circumvent the truth," he replied sardonically.

"How did it happen? What were you doing to get your hands burned?"

"The fire was hard to control. Although we managed to save the last cottage, we might have spared ourselves the trouble, since the others are not worth rebuilding. I mean to have a new row erected."

"Yes, but how did it happen?" she persisted.

He shrugged. "The fire swept through the third cottage faster than I anticipated."

She saw that he did not intend to reveal any further details. Knowing who would tell her the full story, she let the subject drop and asked, "Are the burns very painful? How often must the dressings be changed?"

"They are somewhat uncomfortable," he admitted. "I'm afraid I shall need your assistance with tasks that require the use of my left hand. My right one is not wholly useless. I can still hold a glass and manage a fork fairly well. As for the dressings, our medical man will attend to them. Ah, here comes Edward with my pick-me-up. Will you have some champagne with me, Flora—some more champagne, that is to say," he teased with a mocking lift of one eyebrow.

She laughed and blushed. "Yes, please."

When the footman had set down the ice bucket, Caspar said, "Thank you, Edward. Fetch another glass for her Ladyship, if you please. Good morning, Edgefield. Come in," he added to the head gardener, who was hovering on the threshold.

"Good morning, m'lord . . . m'lady."

His bowler hat clasped to the bib of his green canvas apron, the old man entered the vinery.

"There's a parcel from foreign parts, m'lord. I thought you'd wish to know immediately."

"Yes, indeed! Have it brought here at once. It must be the lily bulbs from China. They've reached us sooner than I expected. This makes today an occasion. You must drink a toast with us, Edgefield. Catch up with Edward and tell him to bring you a tankard of porter, will you?"

"Thank you kindly, m'lord."

"What is porter?" asked Flora after the gardener had left them.

"It's the strong ale that Edgefield likes best," he explained. "You must help him unpack the bulbs, Flora. I had hoped to plant them myself, but now I must depend on you and Edgefield."

"Of course I will help," she said eagerly. "Caspar, before he comes back, why did you agree with your aunt that I shouldn't have stayed with Mrs. Lake while her baby was born?"

"You overheard that, did you?"

"Yes; I didn't mean to eavesdrop, but I came through the fernery and as I opened the door I heard your aunt mention my name. You see, Mrs. Lake is a newcomer here, as I am, and with her husband at sea she must feel doubly alone. She begged me to stay and I promised. I couldn't break my word, could I? Even if it was undignified."

"I doubt if it was your dignity that caused my aunt's concern. No doubt she thought you would be alarmed and distressed, as she would have been at your age." He looked at her thoughtfully. "How much more enlightened your generation may be, I am not altogether sure."

"It would have been dreadfully distressing had Mrs. Lake died, or had the baby been stillborn," Flora acknowledged. "But when the mother is strong and the baby is healthy, I think it is all too interesting to be in any way upsetting. Unless one is exceptionally squeamish, as people were in your aunt's day. Perhaps they still are in this country."

"I believe girls are generally kept in ignorance of certain aspects of life, and I shouldn't have thought Père d'Espinay would have spoken of such things to you. Did you know what was to take place when you gave your promise to Mrs. Lake?"

"I had never seen a human birth, but I'd seen a cat having kittens. The cat at the mission had kittens every few months, and often she had them in my bedroom."

Edward returned, soon to be followed by Edgefield and two of his underlings carrying a crate. Seeing it again, and the Chinese characters painted on it, gave Flora a vivid recollection of the waterfront at Shanghai and her last days in China. As she remembered the grave on the hillside north of the mission, her eyes filled with tears and she felt an ache in her throat. She blinked, hoping Caspar wouldn't notice.

The bulbs had been encased in clay, packed in charcoal and shipped at silk rates. They emerged in excellent condition, causing Edgefield to murmur approvingly that they could not have been better packed had he done it himself.

IT WAS LATE IN THE AFTERNOON before Flora had time to visit Mrs. Lake and her infant. They already had a visitor with them.

"Good afternoon, m'lady," said Mrs. Edgefield, rising from her chair to bob a curtsy.

Flora had intended to call on her at her cottage and was pleased at this early opportunity to find out how Caspar had hurt himself. But she did not mention the matter until she had chatted to Mrs. Lake and admired the baby.

"She's not the first baby you've handled. I can tell that, m'lady," said Mrs. Edgefield, her blue eyes bright with kindly curiosity.

"Oh, no—by no means," agreed Flora. "I have often cuddled Chinese babies. Have you decided what to call your daughter, Mrs. Lake?"

"If it wouldn't be an impertinence, I should like to call her after you, m'lady."

"I should be most flattered. But do you know what my name is?"

Mrs. Lake shook her head.

"You may not like it when you hear it. My father was a botanist, and he gave me the name of the Roman goddess of flowers and springtime, and also of fruit and vines. Her name was Flora."

"I think it's a beautiful name, ma'am."

"Nevertheless I think you should consult your husband before you decide."

"Yes, and he had better consult his Lordship, for he might not approve of her Ladyship's name being given to every Tom, Dick and Harry," put in Mrs. Edgefield.

Flora stifled a gurgle of laughter. "Oh, I'm sure he will have no objection. I'll ask him myself, Mrs. Lake. By the way, were you there when my husband burned his hands, Mrs. Edgefield?"

"Indeed I was, m'lady, and if you won't mind me speaking plain, for I've known his Lordship since he was no bigger than the mite you're holding in your arms, it was a brave but foolish thing he did for old Mrs. Crane last night. But he always did have a reckless streak in him, and the old lord used to encourage him."

"What happened precisely?" asked Flora.

"It was like this, m'lady," began the gardener's wife, in the tone of a woman who likes nothing better than to do full justice to a story. "Old Mrs. Crane is nearly ninety, and if it were not for his Lordship paying a woman to nurse her, she'd have been in the workhouse long ago. But her husband was head keeper to his late Lordship, and his present Lordship was always very much attached to Crane. He and Nelly only had the one son. I never knew him myself, for I didn't come here till 1859, but I've heard he was a fine strapping fellow and might have been head keeper now had he not lost his life in that terrible war in the Crimea."

She paused to shake her head and sigh. "He was only nineteen when he was killed, poor lad, and his mother was almost demented with grief when the news came. From what I've heard tell, it was she who had made him enlist. She wanted to put a stop to him courting a girl she didn't like. In her eyes none of the local girls were good enough for him. However, that's as may be. She paid for her jealousy, poor woman. When he was killed she was coming to a difficult time of life, and she went off her head and has never been right since that time. Since her husband died, the only person she has talked to has been his Lordship. It's my belief she sometimes mistakes him for her son."

"Does he visit her often?" asked Flora.

"Whenever he comes to the village. Not a long visit, you understand. But he'll call in there for a few minutes to see if there's anything she wants and if she's being looked after proper. If his Lordship gives his word to anyone, you may be sure he will keep it, no matter if it suits his convenience or not. He's like the old lord in that way, not like his father. His late Lordship cared for nothing but hunting and race meetings and suchlike. He was in the Marlborough House set when the King was Prince of Wales. Not that it's my place to criticize him. You'll have to pardon me for speaking my mind to you, m'lady."

"You will not offend me by praising my husband, Mrs. Edgefield. Although I don't need to be told of his kindness to people in trouble. I owe more to his goodness than anyone."

Feeling that this last remark might perhaps be an indiscretion that could fuel a great deal of gossip, she went on quickly, "But you haven't finished your account of what happened. Please go on."

"After they'd brought her out of her cottage, old Nelly Crane became very distressed. It seems she'd had some kind of seizure on account of the shock of her bed being moved, and no one could make head nor tail of the sounds she was making. But his Lordship knew what was troubling her. Although the cottage was ablaze, he rushed inside and fetched out an old tin hatbox that was what all the fuss was about. It was full of her keepsakes, you see; her souvenirs of her son. You'd think she'd have kept it by her bed; but no, she wouldn't do that for fear it was stolen from her. It was kept locked away in a cupboard in the room where her son had slept."

"Thank goodness I was not watching but had left to bring Mrs. Lake here. I should have been horrified," said Flora.

"So were we all, m'lady, for it was touch and go whether his Lordship would come out safely. If you'd seen what a furnace it was, you'd have been surprised it was only his hands that were burned."

Later that day, meeting her husband in the hall after the dressing gong had summoned him from the garden and her from an illicit hour in the library, Flora said, "Mrs. Edgefield has told me what happened last night. Oh, Caspar, you might have been killed!"

"Yes, it was dashed stupid of me."

"Stupid? I call it courageous."

"No, I acted on impulse without any thought of the hazards. True courage is never foolhardy. Had a

life been at stake my rashness might have been justi-
fied. But to risk the future of my family for a few tat-
tered relics of a man who died fifty years ago—that
was folly, not bravery."

As they began to mount the stairs, she told him,
"*You* may not think so, but in the village you are a
hero."

"The opinion of the village is not one I value greatly. They would just as soon make me out a villain.
Like all uneducated people, they thrive on gossip and
myth and have little respect for face," he said
cynically.

"You speak as if you despise them, and yet you
treat some of them—Edgefield, for instance—as if
they were almost your equals."

"In his province Edgefield is my superior, and so is
Prime, my head keeper, and Little, my farrier. I
respect and value any man who is a master of his
craft. But even a cursory study of history shows how,
in every age and every country, the mass of the
populace are incapable of rational thought and are
led, or misled, by their idols, whom they raise up one
day and may pull down the next. No one could have
been a more popular hero than the Duke of Welling-
ton after the defeat of Napoleon, yet not so many
years later the mob was hurling stones at the windows
of Apsley House. However, I expect you are more
conversant with French history than with English."

"Yes, but it is an unbalance I mean to correct now
that I have such a splendid library at my disposal.
Not that I shall indulge my weakness too often," she
added hastily.

"Your weakness? Do you mean your love of reading? Who put that idea in your head? My aunt, I sup-

pose? You need pay no attention to her on that subject," Caspar said decisively. "If I had wanted a wife whose most strenuous intellectual exercise was a study of fashion plates, I should have found one with ease. As far as I am concerned, you may spend all your time in the library if that is where you are happiest."

It was on the tip of her tongue to say, "I am happiest with you," but they had reached the door of her bedroom, and when from force of habit he moved forward to open it for her, she tried to stop him by exclaiming, "Oh, do be careful."

"I can manage it," he said, but she saw that he winced a little as he turned the knob.

"Thank you, but I think you should try to be less punctilious until your hands have healed. Did the doctor give an opinion as to how long that might be?"

"Not less than a month." Frowning, as if her inquiry had annoyed him, he concluded their conversation with a formal inclination of his head before striding off along the corridor.

The afternoon had provided Flora with much food for thought. After pondering Caspar's statement that as far as he was concerned she might spend all her time in the library, and thinking how pleasant it would be if only she could take him at his word, she came to the conclusion that he had no idea how much of her time must be spent performing the complex rituals of English social life.

According to Mrs. St. Leger, even when an invitation had been refused, it would be necessary for Flora to call at the house a few days after the occasion, there to leave not only one of her own engraved visiting cards, but also two of Caspar's slightly smaller and thicker cards, all three cards having had their right-hand corner turned inward to indicate they had been left by Flora in person.

Soon the season would begin, lasting from May until the third week in July, and consisting, so it seemed to her, of a ceaseless whirligig of balls, theater parties, receptions, concerts and nights at the opera interspersed with Saturday-to-Monday sojourns at country houses. During these she would be expected to change her clothes at least sixteen times. When fittings were added to this program, it did not leave much time for reading, she thought with a sigh. But if this was the price she must pay for being Caspar's wife, she would pay it willingly.

She remembered Mrs. Edgefield's remark: *"If his Lordship gives his word to anyone, you may be sure he will keep it, no matter if it suits his convenience or not."*

Had Caspar given his word to Père d'Espinay?

"He always did have a reckless streak in him." Perhaps on the far side of the world to marry a girl with her background had not seemed a mad thing to do, any more than at the scene of the fire it had struck him as folly to risk his life and the succession of his earldom for an old woman's box of mementos.

ALTHOUGH CASPAR HELD NO RELIGIOUS BELIEFS, when he was in residence at Longwarden on Sunday he always attended morning service at the parish church.

He explained this practice to Flora by saying that were it not for their faith in an afterlife, many working-class people would find their present lives insupportable. It was therefore important that people born to good fortune should not undermine the hopes of those born to inescapable hardship, ill health or other miseries.

"I must ask you to support me in this, Flora. It takes only two hours a week. The parson here is not an interminable preacher," he said to her before the first occasion.

"But of course I will go to church with you," she had answered.

Indeed it had become one of her pleasures to sit in the family pew and watch her husband standing behind the lectern, reading the lessons.

During the sermon he would sit with his arms folded over his chest and his eyes fixed on the parson's face. But she suspected that he only appeared to be listening while really his thoughts were elsewhere. Her own thoughts were chiefly of him, but sometimes they drifted into recollections of the time before she had known him.

A reference to the Virgin Mary would remind her of Most Rare Flower, although it was so long ago since her mother had died that most of her memories had faded. Now she had only an impression of callused but gentle hands, smiling dark eyes and a loving voice speaking Chinese to her.

Sometimes the vicar's choice of text would call up memories of the French priest who had encouraged her to read the Bible not for the good of her soul but for the enjoyment of great literature. She would think about Père d'Espinay's early life, when, for love of the girl whose portrait miniature was now among her most treasured possessions, he had sacrificed a great inheritance.

On the Sunday following the fire she sat thinking

about her wedding night, now postponed, it seemed, for at least a further four weeks. She remembered the reason Caspar had put forward for the original postponement: that they had had no engagement in which to become well acquainted.

At the time, because of her underlying fear of him, she had accepted that statement and agreed to his suggestion with relief. Now, from what she had learned from Mrs. St. Leger of English manners and customs, it seemed to her that on their wedding day she and her bridegroom had known each other a great deal better than most couples.

They had frequently been alone together. They had discussed all manner of subjects. They had survived a number of hazards of a kind in which any peculiarities of character that either of them might have been hiding must have been revealed.

"Never marry a man until you have seen his temper," Père d'Espinay had warned her once.

She had been unconscious when rage had driven him to kill her rapist. Clearly he had a violent temper, but only rarely did he unleash it. She had seen him in several situations when a less self-disciplined man would have shouted and cursed, and perhaps used his fist or his whip.

But in spite of his height and his physical strength, her husband's authority did not depend on his power to impose his will by force if he chose. He was like Père d'Espinay: his strength of mind showed in his face. The Frenchman had been old and frail, and Caspar was young and virile; but both men were the type to die in defense of their strongest beliefs: Père d'Espinay for godliness, although he had no longer believed in God, and Caspar, also an atheist, for his somewhat different code of life.

She was lost in this reverie when his touch on her arm roused her from her absorption in the past and recalled her to the present. The sermon had reached its conclusion. The service would soon be at an end.

Mrs. St. Leger had not come with them that morning, being indisposed with a chill. As they took their seats in the carriage drawn up at the lych-gate, Caspar said, "Where were you during the sermon? At the mission?"

She nodded. "I'm sorry. Was my inattention very noticeable?"

"Only to someone equally inattentive." He raised his hat and bowed to members of the congregation who were going home on foot.

Flora wondered where his thoughts had strayed, but she could not guess and hesitated to ask. In many ways, she reflected, her husband was a greater enigma now than when they first met.

CHAPTER THREE

IN THE DAYS THAT FOLLOWED she had two encounters that, although they threw light on Caspar's past, did not encourage her to hope he might become fond of her.

First, she had a visit from Mrs. Layard.

Mrs. St. Leger having left them alone together, Flora suggested, "Shall we stroll in the garden, as it's such a beautiful day?"

"Oh, yes, that would be delightful," Mrs. Layard agreed.

They were in the small yellow drawing room that had French windows leading onto the terrace. Flora would have stepped through them had not Mrs. Layard said, "I gave my parasol to the servant. Do you keep a garden hat close by, or shall you have to ring for your maid?"

The European custom of never going out without a hat was particularly trying to Flora, who liked to feel the sun on her head and had grown up unaware that its rays were considered extremely deleterious to a pretty complexion.

This restriction was all the more irksome because, since her complexion was by nature the color of ivory rather than the apple-blossom skin admired in England, she knew she could never compete with pink-and-white beauties.

She said, "Burton is out this afternoon. I'll go up and fetch it myself. I shan't be a moment."

"You *were* quick," remarked Mrs. Layard, looking quite startled when after a brief interval her hostess reentered the room, wearing a Watteau hat and carrying her own and her guest's parasol. Knowing where Kate would have put it, she had fetched it herself to save time.

"Was I?" Flora responded, crossing the room to a looking glass to make sure she had put her hat on straight.

There being no servants about, she had picked up her skirts and run up the stairs two at a time. She knew Mrs. St. Leger would have been shocked, and she wondered if Mrs. Layard also would have thought her unladylike. Although it was a nuisance to have to wear it, the Watteau hat *was* becoming. It had eighteen cream silk roses stitched on top, and an equal number beneath the brim.

Unfurling their silk parasols, the two women sauntered onto the terrace and began to make friends with each other.

Speaking of the coming season, Mrs. Layard said, "You are having your wedding dress altered for your presentation, I expect?"

"No, my court dress will have to be made. The dress I wore for my wedding was lent to me by a missionary's daughter," Flora explained. "You see, I had spent all my life in a very remote part of China, and the only dress I possessed was a black one made for me by Soeur Marie-Josephe, one of the nuns at the mission."

"How I envy you," said Mrs. Layard. "I have traveled very little, and I'm sure I shall never visit the Orient. It must be so strange and interesting. You speak Chinese fluently, I expect?"

"I understand Cantonese, which is one of the principal dialects. But what interests me is *your* childhood. I wish you would describe it to me, for I know so little about the way girls are usually brought up, and it puts me at a disadvantage."

"There is really not much to tell. We are kept in the schoolroom until we come out, and then, unless one is a wallflower, very often one ends one's first season by becoming engaged and then married," Mrs. Layard explained. "A wallflower is someone with whom no one wishes to dance," she added, in case Flora was puzzled by the expression.

"And were you engaged in your first season?"

"Yes," replied Mrs. Layard.

But she did not go into details, from which Flora deduced that the circumstances of her engagement were not a source of happy reminiscence to her.

"And your former home? Is it far?"

"No, fortunately not a great distance. I should miss my sisters very much if I saw them only infrequently. My eldest sister, Louise, is married and living in India, but my younger sisters are still at home. Margaret is coming out soon, so you will meet her, I hope. Oh, there's Lord Carlyon ahead of us," she observed as they reached the end of the Broad Walk, where the garden ended and the park began.

Caspar was talking to one of his gamekeepers, who like all the keepers at Longwarden was wearing a black hard felt hat, a bottle-green velveteen coat and a red felt waistcoat.

As Flora and her visitor drew near, the man touched the brim of his hat and set off across the park.

Caspar turned to greet them. "Good afternoon, Mrs. Layard," he said, raising his hat.

It seemed to Flora that during their brief conversation before Caspar bowed and walked away, Mrs. Layard was not wholly at ease with him.

When he had gone, she admitted it, saying, "Lord Carlyon is very much changed since the first time I met him, but he still makes me nervous, I'm afraid. I shall never forget my consternation when he asked me to dance at my coming-out ball. I knew he was only being civil because of his acquaintance with papa, but still it was a great ordeal for me."

"Was it? Why?" asked Flora, startled.

"Oh, because he had been the most eligible bachelor in London since the season when Louise came out. Even the prettiest debutantes stood in awe of him. Perhaps he has never thrown *you* into confusion, and I must say he never *tried* to do so with me, or with any shy person. I suppose it was his reputation, rather than his manner, that was so perturbing."

"What was his reputation?"

"Shocking!" confided Mrs. Layard. "I have heard people say he was as fast as his father, and *he* was in the Marlborough House set, you know."

No sooner had she spoken than she realized her indiscretion. A deep blush suffused her face. "Oh, dear, I should not have told you. I forgot—that is—I *beg* your pardon."

Flora was guiltily conscious that she had encouraged the *faux pas* that she could and should have averted.

"It was only gossip, and probably much exaggerated," Mrs. Layard continued awkwardly. "As I say, he is greatly changed now. I noticed it when we dined with you. When Lady Conroy was flirting with him, *his* manner was markedly indifferent."

It had not seemed indifferent to Flora when she had looked down the dining table and seen Lady Conroy sparkling with jewels and witticisms, and Caspar listening with a smile.

"Flirting is Lady Conroy's pastime, and perhaps one can't altogether condemn her. She is such a beautiful creature, and her husband is so old and dreary. They say she was not always heartless. The young man she loved was ineligible and her parents forbade her to see him," went on Mrs. Layard.

"She is very elegant," said Flora, seeing a chance to turn the conversation into a safer channel. "I wonder who is her dressmaker?"

"She goes to Lucile in Hanover Square. All the most fashionable people go there. Lucile is the sister of Mrs. Elinor Glyn, the author of *The Visits of Elizabeth*. Have you read it?"

Flora shook her head, and Mrs. Layard continued, "You must let me lend you my copy. It's most amusing, and as Mrs. Glyn is in society and writes from firsthand knowledge, you might even find it helpful to read it before the season starts."

"Thank you; I shall read it with interest," replied Flora.

AT DINNER THAT NIGHT Caspar said, "That was a most becoming hat you were wearing on your walk with Mrs. Layard this afternoon, Flora."

She flushed with pleasure. "I'm glad you thought so."

"Did you find her company congenial?"

Before she could reply, Mrs. St. Leger intervened. "My dear Carlyon, what a strange question. Why should Flora not find her congenial? I can think of no more suitable friendship. In my opinion, Helen Layard sets an example that many of her generation would do well to emulate. She was always a dutiful daughter, and I have no doubt she will be an equally exemplary wife and mother.''

"You may be right, aunt," said Caspar. "Nevertheless I am not convinced that Flora is well advised to foster the acquaintance."

"Do you dislike her?" Flora asked him.

"No, I don't dislike her, but neither do I like her," he answered. "She has always struck me as a timid, prudish little thing, and I know she has the reputation of being extremely gauche for her years and making embarrassing gaffes."

"If you don't approve, I won't make a friend of her."

To her surprise, he said in a tone of impatience, "Now that is precisely the response I should expect from Mrs. Layard had her husband expressed an unfavorable opinion of you. You will not please me by becoming *too* dutiful, Flora. Your friends should be of your choosing, not mine."

She could see that Mrs. St. Leger was very much put out by his remarks, and her disapproval was exacerbated when he added by way of an afterthought, "I should think you might find Sylvia Conroy a more stimulating companion."

"Lady Conroy!" ejaculated his aunt. "Surely you cannot be serious? Lady Conroy is years older than Flora, and you must know her reputation."

"I know she has many detractors—as does any beautiful woman," he said with a shrug. "No doubt Flora will be similarly abused."

Flora's eyes widened. Was he implying that she

was as beautiful as Lady Conroy? Although Père d'Espinay had called her beautiful, she had thought him prejudiced by affection.

"I am certain Flora will never incur the gossip that surrounds Lady Conroy. Were it not for the general esteem in which her husband is held, there are many hostesses who would not receive her," Mrs. St. Leger announced repressively.

"Were it not for her esteemed husband, she would not be driven to the expedients that make her the subject of gossip—much of which is quite without foundation," Caspar replied equally curtly.

He turned to his wife. "Sylvia Conroy married her elderly husband while believing herself to be brokenhearted over some penniless subaltern of whom her father disapproved," he explained. "She has known a great deal of unhappiness and is regarded outside her particular set with suspicion and jealousy by the majority of her sex. However, she has many admirable qualities, including excellent taste in dress. Which reminds me; I asked her if she would introduce you to her dressmaker and help you to order your court dress. The local dressmaker was competent to make your clothes for this transitional period between our arrival in England and your presentation, but your clothes for the season call for skills of a somewhat higher order."

"If you have finished your peach, Flora, we will withdraw and leave Carlyon to smoke his cigar," said Mrs. St. Leger at her frostiest.

He rose to open the door for them. When his aunt had passed him, he gestured for his wife to wait.

"Flora will join you in a few moments, Aunt Blanche."

He closed the door and stood with his back to it, his dark brows drawn down in a frown of suppressed irritation.

"I'm becoming more than a little tired of my aunt's society. Could you dispense with her guidance from now on? We shall be removing to the London house before long."

"But as she is to present me, don't you think her feelings would be hurt if you suggested she should leave before then?" Flora asked.

He stared down at her for some seconds, his gray eyes oddly intent. "I suppose you are right," he said at length. "But between Aunt Blanche and these deuced bandages, I...I find my temper somewhat strained at times."

He opened the door to let her out. "Before you retire, will you write a note to Sylvia Conroy asking her to suggest a suitable day for your visit to her dressmaker? When you receive her reply, I will arrange for our carriage to be put on a convenient train."

"Yes, I will. Do I take it you won't be joining us later in the drawing room?"

"I think not. Do what you can to soothe Aunt Blanche's ruffled feathers. Good night, Flora."

"Good night."

Disappointed, for she knew she was unlikely to see him again before luncheon the following day, she crossed the hall.

She had scarcely closed the drawing-room door behind her before Mrs. St. Leger began, "Far be it from me—"

"I am sorry to interrupt you, Aunt Blanche, but if what you have to say is in any way critical of Caspar,

please do not say it to me. Instead perhaps you would
explain what is meant by 'the Marlborough House
set.'"

For some moments Mrs. St. Leger's heightened
color and heaving bosom seemed to presage an outburst of wrath. However, when eventually she spoke,
her tone was displeased but controlled.

"Marlborough House was the home of the King
and Queen when they were Prince and Princess of
Wales. Unfortunately the Prince did not follow the
estimable example of his father, the late Prince Consort, but surrounded himself with people whose only
object in life was the pursuit of pleasure. I regret to
say that my brother-in-law, Caspar's father, was an
intimate friend of the Prince, and no doubt it was
with reference to him that you heard the expression
used."

"Yes, it was."

"Then let my poor sister's fate be a lesson to you,
Flora. She bore much but never complained. We will
not speak of it again, but I should be failing in my
duty if I did not warn you that Caspar bears a strong
resemblance to his father, not merely in his appearance but in his nature."

With which admonition she rose and swept out of
the room.

FLORA'S FIRST PROPER VISIT TO LONDON took place on
another warm springlike day and began when Lady
Conroy's carriage arrived to convey her to the station.

When she emerged from the house, she found her
husband standing beside the carriage chatting to its
elegant occupant, who was dressed in a navy blue

costume with a double-breasted bolero jacket fastened by eight silver buttons. A navy blue Breton straw, its brim edged with white silk ribbon and its crown ornamented with an enormous bow of the same ribbon, was perched on her rich red brown hair.

At the sight of his wife, Caspar broke off his conversation to raise his hat and say good morning to her. As Flora climbed into the carriage, she was conscious that Sylvia Conroy's beautiful eyes missed no detail of the strapped and pleated skirt of pale gray hopsack and the blouse of peach-colored silk that Burton had advised Flora to wear.

"I mustn't delay you from your chiffons," said Caspar when the footman had closed the carriage door. He stepped back and bared his dark head again.

Lady Conroy said, "You may drive on, William," to her coachman.

Some way down the drive, Flora glanced over her shoulder and saw Caspar still standing on the graveled sweep in front of the graceful white portico. As she looked back, he turned away and she checked her impulse to raise her gloved hand and wave. Probably it was not done to wave. Resuming her former position, she found Lady Conroy watching her with an expression she could not interpret.

"Are you looking forward to the season, Lady Carlyon?" she inquired.

"Very much," replied Flora, not altogether truthfully.

Had she been free to do as she pleased, she would have chosen to stay at Longwarden throughout the spring and early summer. Her father had often described the beauty of the English countryside in May and June, and it puzzled her that English society should choose to spend those months in London.

"Caspar has suggested that I may be able to enlighten you on points that, being herself retired from the social round, Mrs. St. Leger may have omitted to mention. Has she warned you, I wonder, that your acceptance or refusal of invitations to Saturday-to-Mondays must be governed by your husband's interest, or lack of interest, in your hostess's garden?"

"I think you are teasing me, Lady Conroy," said Flora, smiling.

"On the contrary, I assure you. Ask anyone. It is an acknowledged fact that during the hours of daylight Caspar can never be relied on to play lawn tennis or croquet, or to join in any entertainment that his hostesses have arranged for their guests' amusement."

"If that is true, I'm surprised they continue to invite him."

"Ah, but it is his elusiveness that is part of his charm. Once darkness has fallen the case is altered. When he is unable to botanize, he becomes a most amusing companion...as you know."

Flora could think of a number of words to describe Caspar's company, but "amusing" was not one of them. She wondered if Sylvia Conroy knew a side of his nature that she did not, or if that was merely an impression her companion wished to convey.

The carriage was approaching the gates, which had been opened in readiness by the wife of the keeper who lived in the lodge. Smiling at her, Flora wondered about her life in the neat little house with its pointed windowpanes and spotless curtains. The woman had a young child on her hip, and a shy older child was lurking behind her, thumb in mouth.

"Have you any children, Lady Conroy?" she inquired as the carriage bowled through the gateway and turned onto the highway in the direction of Longwarden Halt.

"Oh, yes, several. The boys are at school, and the girls are still in the nursery."

It seemed to Flora that "several" was a strangely vague way to refer to the number of one's offspring. As if she read the thought, Lady Conroy said in a bored tone, "I am not at all maternal. Shall you be?"

"I don't know. I should think I might be able to remember the number and names of my children."

Flora spoke without thinking and immediately regretted a reply that she knew was unbecoming to her position. To have allowed even a tinge of sarcasm to color her answer to someone who was her hostess and mentor for the day was, she realized, a solecism that would have made Mrs. St. Leger shudder.

To her surprise, Lady Conroy's reaction was to laugh and exclaim, "How refreshing! You are not in awe of me."

"Are many people in awe of you?"

"Oh, yes. Little Mrs. Layard is terrified of me, although I can't imagine why, since there isn't the smallest danger of my flirting with *her* husband."

"From what you tell me, a great many people would be delighted to flirt with my husband, so I must either be worried continually or not worried at all. I think the latter attitude is the more sensible," answered Flora cheerfully.

In the shade of her navy-and-white parasol, Sylvia Conroy's vivid eyes gleamed with not unfriendly amusement.

"I see Lord Carlyon was right and Lady Chiltern

was wrong. She thought you 'a sweet, docile creature'—just what one would expect with your convent and Oriental background, so she told me.''

"And what did my husband say about me?"

"That you had common sense and spirit—two qualities notably lacking in most girls of his acquaintance. Shall we discard formality? May I call you Flora?"

"Please do."

"I expect you know my name is Sylvia. Oh, damnation, here comes a motorcar. Protect yourself with your sunshade."

Flora followed her example and held her own pink-lined parasol so that it offered some protection from the clouds of dust left in the wake of the scarlet-wheeled De Dietrich tonneau that had caused Lady Conroy's coachman to rein in the horses and hold them in check until it had passed.

"I'm sure that abominable automobilist was exceeding the limit," exclaimed Sylvia Conroy crossly as the carriage began to move forward. "Caspar tells me he is intending to take up motoring. Will he persuade you to ride with him? He would never induce me to do so. I will *not* make myself look a fright in one of those hideous mica masks that are the only protection from the clouds of dust."

At Longwarden Halt they were met by the stationmaster, and a few minutes later the train to London steamed in. Once ensconced in the private coach, Sylvia opened a small velvet bag and took from it a jeweled box containing cigarettes.

"You don't smoke, I imagine?" she said to Flora.

"No."

"Try one."

Flora shook her head. "No, thank you. I did try one some years ago, but I didn't enjoy it."

"They always taste vile at first. It takes some time to acquire the habit. How were you able to try a cigarette in a convent?"

"It was a mission, not a convent. A visitor left some cigarettes behind. I asked Père d'Espinay if I might try one and he said yes."

"At a Protestant mission you would have been punished for suggesting such a thing. I much prefer the Roman Catholic view. When my husband dies I may live in France."

"Is Lord Conroy ill?" asked Flora uncertainly.

"No, no—but as he is twenty-four years older than I am, it's not unreasonable to expect him to die before I do." Sylvia puffed at her cigarette, her gaze on the passing countryside. "I should never marry again. No one who had been Edgar's wife would consider a second marriage."

Her tone was so soulful that had Flora not met Lord Conroy, she might have supposed that his wife adored him. Then Sylvia glanced across the compartment, and for an instant her blue eyes were bright with bitter irony before she changed the subject by saying briskly, "Now, let's discuss your court dress."

A brougham from Lord Conroy's town house was awaiting their arrival, and they went first to Maison Lucile at 23 Hanover Square. On the way there Sylvia told Flora that in private life "Lucile" was Lady Duff Gordon, who had married Sir Cosmo in 1900, following the failure of her first marriage and the subsequent poverty that had inspired her to earn her living with her needle.

"When I first went to her she had premises in Old
Burlington Street, and from there she moved to 17
Hanover Square, which she rented from Sir George
Dashwood. Now she and Sir Cosmo live there and
her salon is at number 23. It was she who introduced
living mannequins to London, you know. She borrowed the idea from the French," Sylvia explained.

The salon had gray brocade curtains and a mini-
ature stage draped with olive chiffon on which man-
nequins named Hebe, Gamela, Florence, Phyllis and
Dolores displayed gowns with such fanciful names as
"When Passion's Thrall Is o'er" and "Give Me Your
Heart."

Comparing her own slender limbs with the generous contours of the big beautiful mannequins, Flora
was doubly conscious that her figure did not conform
to the fashionable ideal.

After the gowns had been paraded, the designer
herself came to talk to them. Evidently Sylvia was
one of her favorite customers, and she hoped Sylvia's
protégée might be equally extravagant.

Later Flora was taken to a private room to be
measured.

"I've never heard of anything more absurd," said
Sylvia, arching her eyebrows, when Flora was forced
to explain Caspar's views on tight lacing. "You cannot be guided by your husband in matters of fashion."

Between them she and the fitter wore down Flora's
resistance until eventually she gave way and allowed
herself to be encased in a straight-fronted corset of
white coutil. First the busk was adjusted and then the
silk laces were tightened, starting at the waist and
working upward and downward until her lower ribs

and hips were reshaped into the fashionable swan bend. Finally white satin pads were pinned under her arms and on her hips to accentuate the smallness of her waist.

"Ah, this is altogether better," said Sylvia, appraising the result.

Looking at her reflection, Flora had to agree that the corset, although far from comfortable, did give her an air she had lacked before.

"But if Caspar finds out he may be furious," she confided when the fitter had left them for a moment.

"He won't know, my dear," Lady Conroy promised her. "Men notice only effects, never the means by which we achieve our ends."

"He may not notice, but he has only to touch me to feel them."

"In your boudoir, under a tea gown, you need only wear a ribbon corset. Not even that, if you don't wish it. You're not going to tell me that Caspar is still such an ardent bridegroom that he embraces you anywhere and everywhere, regardless of the servants walking in?"

"Oh, no—of course not!" said Flora, blushing.

"Even in private I should think the state of his hands must be rather a handicap at present," Sylvia continued quizzically. Clearly Flora's confusion amused her. "Or do you make love to him like Théodora to Andreas?" She saw the allusion meant nothing to Flora and explained, "Théodora is one of Madame Sarah Bernhardt's most famous roles. I was taken to see the play in Paris when I was sixteen. I went with a somewhat disreputable uncle, and when my aunt found out she was furious. It wasn't considered a suitable play for a young girl. She would

have been even more annoyed had she known that
my uncle kissed me on the way home.''

"How unpleasant for you."

"Not at all. I liked it. Don't you like your admirers
to kiss you?''

"I—I like Caspar to kiss me." Flora wondered
what Sylvia would think if she knew their marriage
had yet to be consummated.

"Such a dutiful bride!" Sylvia teased her. "Your
husband certainly should be an accomplished lover;
he has had plenty of practice. But even a harmonious
marriage lacks the spice of a love affair. I'm sure
you'll have plenty of chances to compare Caspar's
kisses with other men's during the season.''

Before Flora could reply that she had no wish to
engage in love affairs, the fitter returned and the conversation reverted to matters of fashion.

They had luncheon at the Conroys' house in
Berkeley Square, and while they ate Sylvia told Flora
anecdotes intended to amuse her. She did laugh at the
story of the lady who, during a shooting party at a
country house, was urged by one of her admirers to
leave a rose in her keyhole, but who, greatly to his
discomfiture, left it in the keyhole of a room occupied by a bishop and his wife.

In general, however, she found Sylvia's tales dis-
quieting and distasteful. They conjured a milieu in
which marriage was a convenient arrangement, love
was a pastime, and the only unforgivable misdeed
was to be indiscreet and cause a scandal.

When she said as much, Sylvia agreed. "As some
Frenchman put it, *'La scandale du monde est ce qui
fait l'offense, et ce n'est pas pécher que pécher en
silence.'*''

It is a public scandal that offends; to sin in secret is no sin. Flora remembered the cynical saying and its author—Molière. But the seventeenth-century French dramatist had been referring to his own times. She had not expected to find the aphorism equally applicable in twentieth-century England.

"On the subject of country-house dalliance, Mrs. Keppel has coined an amusing phrase," Sylvia added. *"A chacun sa chacune."* She gave her light trilling laugh.

"Mrs. Keppel?"

"Alice Keppel. She's married to George Keppel, who is Lord Albemarle's brother. She is the King's latest mistress—and his last, I should imagine."

"But the King is an old man," Flora protested. "And the Queen is so beautiful."

"No wife, however beautiful, can prevent a man straying once he is used to her, my dear. They say the King and Queen were very happy at the beginning. But she had six children in seven years, and a week before the birth of her third child she was struck down with rheumatic fever. It was a miracle she lived. I daresay after the sixth child she wouldn't risk having another."

"But to have a mistress at his age, and for everyone to know it...! How it must wound her," Flora exclaimed.

"I don't suppose she minds in the least. Most wives prefer it when that side of marriage is finished and they and their husbands can each go their separate ways. You may not think so at present, if you have a *tendre* for your husband, but you will in a few years' time."

After luncheon they shopped for hats, and Flora

could not resist buying a pale green straw trimmed with matching ostrich feathers. They reminded her of old Mr. Eliot, her friend on board ship.

When they returned to the station she was surprised to see Caspar's tall figure strolling up and down the platform. He was looking particularly distinguished in a gray morning coat with striped cashmere trousers and a silk hat, which he took off as soon as he saw them coming toward him.

"What brings you to London?" Sylvia inquired when they reached him.

"I should have accompanied you this morning. It wasn't until later that I thought it might be as well to have a second opinion about my hands. I saw a man in Harley Street, after which I had luncheon at my club and did some shopping. I needn't ask what those are." He indicated the bandboxes carried by their porter.

"What did the doctor here have to say about your hands?" asked Flora when he had tipped the man.

"I should have gone to him sooner. He disapproves of the ointment prescribed by our local medical man. He says it has retarded the healing. But the burns should soon improve under his treatment. Tell me how you have spent your day."

It was chiefly Sylvia who conversed with him. Her energy seemed undiminished. Flora felt tired, and worried about Caspar's hands. She felt sure he would not have consulted a specialist had he not been enduring great pain. It filled her with remorse to remember how blithely she had set out for London that morning, leaving him with nothing to do but to kick his heels. At present he could neither ride nor drive, and the practical gardening he enjoyed was also impossible.

A FEW DAYS LATER she was in her boudoir when her maid brought a large parcel to her.

"Shall I open it for you, m'lady?"

"If you would, please, Burton. I'm not expecting a parcel. What can it be, I wonder?"

Stripped of its outer wrapping of stiff brown paper, the parcel revealed itself as a pale blue box, the lid embossed with a garland of silver flowers. The contents were swathed in pale blue tissue paper, and before she parted the leaves of tissue Flora opened a small sealed envelope containing a card on which was written, "I hope my taste is more to your taste than my aunt's. C."

The message puzzled her momentarily but was soon made clear when inside the tissue she found an assortment of nightclothes such as she had never dreamed existed.

Burton put on her prim face when Flora held up a nightgown of transparent amber chiffon trimmed with delicate lace dyed to match. However, she did not disapprove of a dozen pairs of the finest black silk stockings.

"I must try them on." Without waiting for the maid to assist her, Flora plumped down on a chair and began to unlace her boots.

"You will wish to wear shoes with silk stockings, m'lady," said Burton, hurrying to fetch a pair.

By the time she returned Flora had peeled off the black lisle stockings that Mrs. St. Leger considered more serviceable for day wear. The silk stockings with their ornamental clocks were far more flattering to her ankles.

She decided to go in search of Caspar immediately,

and she found him talking to one of the under gardeners who was working in the wide herbaceous border that Caspar had had planted before his expedition to China.

Flora smiled at the gardener and said good morning to him. "Might I speak to you privately?" she asked Caspar.

"Certainly."

They began to stroll along the grass path.

"Your sedate demeanor as you approached us would have been more convincing had your cheeks been less flushed and your breathing less noticeable. You've been running, *ya-t'ou*," he said dryly when they were out of the man's hearing.

"Only when no one could see me. Otherwise it would have taken so long to find you. But I'm sorry; I know I shouldn't. I do *try* to be decorous," she said earnestly.

"My dear girl, don't sound so contrite. When my hands have improved I shall teach you to ride. An early-morning gallop in the park will relieve some of that pent-up *joie de vivre*. Now, what is it you wish to tell me?"

She glanced over her shoulder to make sure they were not observed. Then she picked up her skirt and raised it, revealing her ankles.

"I'm wearing the stockings you bought for me." She stood on one foot and extended the other for his inspection.

"An extremely well turned ankle," said Caspar gravely. "But if my aunt should come round the corner she will read you a lecture that will last until luncheon."

Flora laughed and let her skirt fall. "I wanted to

thank you at once. The nightgowns are exquisite. . .
as lovely as butterfly wings.''

"You must show them to me sometime."

"Yes. . .yes, I will." Something in his eyes made
her shy of him, and after repeating her thanks she
made an excuse to escape.

That afternoon, in the library, she was dipping
into a volume of Montaigne's essays when she came
upon a precept attributed to the daughter-in-law of
Pythagoras. It was that a woman who goes to bed
with a man ought to lay aside her modesty with her
skirt and put it on again with her petticoat.

It was reading this advice in Montaigne that gave
her the courage to enter the anteroom that night and
put her ear to Caspar's door to make sure his valet
had left him. Burton had left her some time before,
and although the maid had said only, "It's very
flimsy, m'lady. I do hope you won't take cold in it,"
it had been clear that she thought the amber nightgown a most improper garment for her mistress to
wear.

Flora herself had been somewhat taken aback by
how little of her was concealed by the soft folds of
chiffon. The nightgown had a peignoir to match, and
two layers of chiffon and lace were less revealing
than one, but even so it took all her resolution to tap
on the door of Caspar's room.

"Come in."

She found him seated by the fire with a whiskey
and soda at his elbow, a cigar in his left hand and a
pen in the other despite the bandages. He had been
writing on a pad on his knee, but he put it aside as she
entered and rose to his feet.

"I—I came to show you one of the nightgowns. It

fits me perfectly,'' she said nervously as she walked forward.

Caspar looked at her in silence for some moments. The firelight accentuated the powerful structure of his face; the broad forehead, the commanding nose, the resolute mouth and chin.

At length he said, "So I see. Will you excuse me, Flora? I'm afraid I can't chat to you tonight. I have promised an article to William Robinson, the editor of *The Garden*, and it must be in the post tomorrow morning.''

"Would you like to dictate it to me, since writing is difficult for you?''

"No, thank you. That isn't necessary. Good night.''

Dismissed, and in such a snubbing tone, she murmured good-night and retreated.

Sitting by her fire, watching it die down, her thoughts in renewed uncertainty, she wondered if it had been folly to take the advice of a woman who had lived and died twenty-six centuries ago. Perhaps, in spite of what he had said in the garden that morning, Caspar had disliked her boldness in going to his bedroom. Perhaps it had been unladylike, the kind of conduct that was acceptable from a mistress but not from a wife. Perhaps a wife should be shy and nervous, as indeed she had been at first on the night he had come to her room.

Presently, climbing into bed, she knew that she wouldn't be able to sleep yet. She had left Montaigne's essays in the library. From a pile of books on her night table she chose a volume of verses by Lord Byron, one of England's most famous poets, who according to Mr. Eliot had influenced the whole of

European literature before dying of a fever in Greece at the age of thirty-six.

As she flicked over the pages, her attention was caught by some lines in a poem titled *Don Juan*.

She sits upon his knee, and drinks his sighs,
He hers, until they end in broken gasps;
And thus they form a group that's quite antique,
Half naked, loving, natural and Greek.
And when those deep and burning moments pass'd,
And Juan sunk to sleep within her arms,
She slept not, but all tenderly, though fast,
Sustain'd his head upon her bosom's charms.

Tonight, after his curt dismissal of her, she found it impossible to imagine Caspar sinking to sleep within *her* arms; and although the girl in the poem "spoke not of scruples, ask'd no vows, nor offer'd any," Flora was not at all sure that she could share deep burning moments with a man who never pretended to love her, and who might never love her.

Perhaps I should have taken the veil, she thought disconsolately.

But apart from the fact that she had no vocation, to become a religious had seemed to her a form of imprisonment. Caspar's offer of marriage had come like a gift from the gods.

What she had not foreseen was how painful it would be to develop a *tendre* for him, and never to be loved in return.

PART FOUR
PARK LANE

CHAPTER ONE

ONE THE DAY before the household removed to London, during a week of such glorious spring weather that it seemed a shame not to postpone the departure, Flora and Helen went sketching together.

The scene they had chosen to paint was an old stone bridge over the stream that fed Longwarden Lake. Since it was not far from the house they set out on foot, followed by Edward carrying the hamper containing their luncheon, and by the hall boy carrying their easels and paint boxes.

To Flora, long accustomed to doing her own fetching and carrying, it seemed absurd that two healthy young women should need a man and a boy to be their baggage porters over so short a distance.

It was her first encounter with the hall boy. When she asked him his name and the nature of his duties, he told her he was Alfred; he cleaned the boots, filled the coal scuttles and log baskets and waited on the servants' hall.

"He's Mr. Warner's grandson, m'lady," explained Edward.

"And do you aspire to become a butler one day, Alfred?" she asked.

"Yes, m'lady. I 'ope so, m'lady," he said earnestly.

His voice had the local accent, which made her wonder if on the other side of the green baize door Warner relaxed his stately manner and spoke in less

measured tones than when he was addressing his
master. It was difficult to visualize this boy, whose
water-slicked hair sprang into an unruly tuft on the
crown of his head and whose eyes held a mischievous
sparkle, ever becoming as dignified and grand as
Warner.

*But how incredulous my grandparents would have
been had they been told I should marry a peer and be
presented at court,* she reflected.

Presently, perched on a camp stool, drawing the
outline of the bridge, she found herself pondering the
circumstances that shaped people's lives. Had it been
chance or destiny that had caused her father to be
near the spot where her mother had intended to put
an end to her misery? Perhaps it had been his fate to
survive many hazards only to die in a landslide near a
mission where his daughter would not only be shel-
tered but be given years of concentrated education,
so that by her seventeenth birthday she had acquired
the manners of a French aristocrat and the intellectual resources usually reserved for the male sex and
denied to females.

She wondered what Caspar would have done with
her if she had not had the benefit of Père d'Espinay's
influence. Would her English blood and her defense-
lessness still have outweighed her plebeian origins?

Absorbed in her thoughts, she did not notice that
Helen was being uncharacteristically silent. Suddenly
she was roused from her reverie by a sobbing sound,
quickly suppressed. Turning, she was dismayed to see
Helen hunched on her stool with her handkerchief
pressed to her lips, her eyes tightly closed to prevent
any more tears following those that already left their
traces on her cheeks.

"Helen!" Flora exclaimed, jumping up to go to her. "Are you ill?"

Helen shook her head.

"Then what is it? Tell me!" begged Flora, kneeling beside her and putting an arm around her.

Helen's response was to bury her head on her friend's shoulder and succumb to an outburst of weeping. It must have been pent up for weeks, thought Flora, feeling the violence of the other woman's distress and wondering why she was so upset. Could it be that she was enceinte and terrified by tales of agonizing birth pangs?

It was some time before her sobs began to subside. When at last she showed signs of recovering herself, Flora said, "Come into the shade and I'll pour you a drink of lemonade."

She drew Helen to her feet and steered her toward the willow where Edward had left the picnic basket and spread a rug on the ground for them.

"Y—you m-must think me dreadfully ill-bred. I do apologize, Flora," were Helen's first husky words when, having sipped some lemonade, she was able to command her voice.

"I think you are very unhappy," Flora said gently. "And what are friends for if one cannot share one's troubles with them?"

Helen's eyes brimmed. For a moment it seemed that a second paroxym was imminent, but she managed to control herself sufficiently to say in a low voice, "My trouble is one I cannot share with anyone—not even you, dearest Flora."

"I believe I know what it may be."

Helen looked startled. "You do? Oh, surely you cannot?"

"No one's agony of mind is ever unique," answered Flora, echoing Père d'Espinay. "There are always a great many other people who have endured the same anguish. Indeed I suspect that your worries are shared by the majority of women, and particularly by brides such as ourselves."

"Do you think so?" said Helen forlornly. "Do... do *you* find it equally distressing?" She avoided meeting Flora's eyes, and her face, already flushed from weeping, was suffused by a wave of deeper color.

"No, but I'm not a nervous person."

"I am not as much nervous as... repelled. It is all so... so very unpleasant. My sister did try to warn me in one of her letters, but I didn't understand what she meant. I had no idea—never dreamed...." She started to cry again.

"Perhaps your sister was unfortunate, but that is no reason why you should be," said Flora. "I must take you to visit Mrs. Lake, whose baby was born at Longwarden after her cottage caught fire. She will reassure you better than I can, for I was an onlooker merely. But even I can tell you that it wasn't at all the ordeal Caspar's aunt had said it would be, and which you have heard it made out to be. When is your baby expected?"

Helen looked blankly at her. "I'm not expecting a baby. I only wish I were. Then Hector might not—" She broke off, biting her lip.

Flora watched her in uneasy silence. A glimmer of comprehension was dawning at the back of her mind.

At length, her face averted, Helen said in a voice of desperation, "Flora, what *am* I to do? I ought not to speak of it, I know, but I am so wretchedly unhappy.

If only mama had explained. She did say there were
aspects of marriage that were sometimes rather disagreeable, but I thought she meant Hector might lose
his temper now and then. Papa is inclined to be
somewhat choleric at times.''

Flora sought in vain for a reply that, although not
unsympathetic, would neither encourage further con-
fidences nor reveal her unfitness to receive them.

''Don't you think that, perhaps, after a time it may
become less disagreeable?'' she ventured uncertainly.

''Oh, no—never, never!'' exclaimed Helen vehemently. ''It can only become more intolerable. No
doubt it is different in your case. Although you try to
conceal it, one can see that you feel the deepest affection for your husband. But where there is no such affection, you cannot imagine how abhorrent one's
obligations are.''

''But why did you marry your husband if you
found him displeasing?''

''My parents wished it,'' said Helen simply. ''I
didn't dislike Hector at that time. He isn't handsome
or dashing, but he seemed a kind, pleasant man. I
thought I should like being his wife and having a
home of my own.''

She drew a shuddering breath and blotted her
cheeks with the dry handkerchief Flora had offered
her. ''Now my only comfort is the hope that when I
am expecting a baby, Hector will leave me in peace
and turn to a mistress for. . . all that.''

''Helen, you mustn't say that. I'm sure such an action on his part would cause you even greater distress,'' said Flora, thinking of her mother. ''Have
you told him how unhappy you are?''

Her friend looked aghast. ''No, no—how could I

speak of it? What can't be cured must be endured, as Nanny used to tell us.'' She turned up the small jeweled watch pinned to her blouse. "We must go back to our paintings, or we shall never finish them.''

At one o'clock they had luncheon. Flora ate little, for the day had become extremely hot. But Helen's appetite seemed unaffected and she did full justice to the collation.

Afterward she said, "I think I shall doze for ten minutes,'' and arranged herself comfortably on the rug, with a cushion under her head.

It soon became clear that, exhausted by her emotional outburst and replete with food, she was likely to sleep for at least an hour. All morning the stream had been tempting Flora to wade in it. Now that Helen was unconscious she could no longer resist the enticement of the gently flowing water.

The warm, sheep-nibbled turf of the stream bank felt delightful under her bare feet. When she had bundled up her skirt and stepped into the stream at a spot where the bottom was sandy, she could scarcely repress an exclamation of pleasure.

She had been in the water for some time and was standing very still to admire a particularly handsome green dragonfly when a voice behind her said suddenly, "You'll catch it if your mistress wakes up.''

With a gasp, she swung around to face a young man in soldier's uniform who was standing on the bank grinning at her.

"Who are you?'' she demanded.

"Corporal Jim White,'' he replied with a playful salute. "My old man's his Lordship's coachman. I heard that his Lordship had found himself a wife in China, but they didn't tell me about you. I've an idea

I'm going to enjoy this leave more than usual," he added, eyeing her slim bare legs, which were visible almost to the knee and which she could not conceal without wetting her skirt.

Flora wondered what she should do. She could visualize the scandalized faces in the village if the tale was spread that Jim White had caught the new Lady Carlyon disporting herself in the stream with no hat on her head, and her lower limbs exposed to view.

It might be better to let him continue to think she was the maid and the recumbent figure under the willow was Caspar's new wife.

Before she had made up her mind, the corporal said, "I don't want to frighten you, m'darling, but there's a big old pike in this stream. If he's lurking in those rushes behind you, which is where he usually hides himself, and he should catch sight of your ankles, he's liable to take a snap at 'em. Look out! Here he comes."

With a yelp she leaped for the bank. To help her the corporal sprang forward, put his hands under her arms and swung her up onto the grass. He was a burly young fellow, not tall but very broad shouldered, with a deep powerful chest to set off his bright scarlet tunic and shiny brass buttons. From the ease with which he swung her to safety, he might have been lifting a child. When he set her on her feet he did not release her but took her firmly in his arms and gave her a hearty kiss.

It was not an unpleasant experience. His mustache smelled of beer and prickled her upper lip. But the pressure of his lips on hers was not rough or in any way repulsive.

As soon as he lifted his head, she knew by the merriment in his eyes that the pike had been an invention to throw her into a panic.

"You'll be the one to catch it, Jim White, if I tell his Lordship," she said as she pushed him away and shook out her skirt.

"Oho! So he's interested, is he? I can't say I blame him if he gives you a cuddle when her back's turned. I daresay she's nothing to look at, and you're as pretty as they come."

"Were you told she was nothing to look at?"

"No, she may be a beauty for all I know. But the gentry don't marry like us, where the fancy takes 'em. They marry for money and suchlike."

"For your information, her Ladyship hadn't a penny, and his Lordship is not in the habit of kissing the maids behind her back. I'm sure he would be most annoyed if he knew how you tricked me just now." She gasped and shrank back, her eyes dilating with alarm. "Oh, is that a bull coming toward us?"

As Jim White glanced over his shoulder in the direction where a herd of cows was grazing, Flora lunged at him with all her strength. Had he been less solidly built she might have achieved her intention of pushing him backward into the stream. But although she succeeded in making him stagger, he quickly recovered his balance and grabbed her by the wrists with the obvious intention of repeating his previous embrace.

"No, please—let me go," she appealed, regretting her assault on him.

"You little devil! You'd have had me in the water, wouldn't you?"

"Yes, because you deserved it," she retorted.

"Oh, did I? We'll see about that."

Flora was stronger than she looked, and she would have put up a struggle had not her resistance been obviated by a voice from the bridge saying coldly, "She asked you to let her go, corporal."

The skirmishers separated and stood in uneasy silence while Caspar came down from the bridge and walked toward them.

His face almost as red as his tunic, the soldier said sheepishly, "Good day, m'lord. It was only a bit of a lark, m'lord."

"So I observed," remarked Caspar, eyeing him with an expression that made the young man look even more uncomfortable.

How long had her husband been watching them, Flora wondered. Even if he had not been near enough to prevent her being kissed the first time, he must have witnessed the embrace as he came toward them. But for his still unhealed burns, would he have grabbed the soldier by the collar of his coat, as she had once seen him seize a drunken European seaman who had been molesting two old Chinese? Or was most of his anger directed at her for behaving in a way that exposed her to such familiarities?

"You had better cut along home, where no doubt your mother at least will be pleased to see you," said Caspar at his most sarcastic.

"Yes, m'lord...thank you, m'lord." The corporal shouldered his kit bag and began to walk off. Then he paused. "You won't be too hard on the young person, m'lord? It wasn't her fault. I tricked her."

"I will bear that in mind. And you might bear in mind, corporal, that if it comes to my ears that the young person has been the subject of gossip in the village, this will not be the end of the matter," Caspar said crisply.

"Yes, m'lord...very good, m'lord." With a glance at Flora that held a hint of apology, the soldier marched off across the meadow.

Caspar watched him for some moments before turning to his bride. He subjected her to an appraisal that began where her bare toes showed beneath the hem of her skirt and traveled slowly upward to her face.

His expression told her nothing of his feelings, and although she tried not to let his regard discompose her, in the end she had to surrender by letting her gaze fall to the ground. In an apprehensive voice she said, "I—I thought you would not be back from London until this evening."

"And I thought you and Mrs. Layard were to spend the day sketching," he replied.

"We were sketching this morning, but after luncheon Helen fell asleep, and it was so hot, and the stream looked so cool and refreshing...but I know I should not have succumbed. I'm sorry, Caspar."

"I should be interested to know how White's son induced you to fling yourself into his arms."

"He said there was a pike coming for me."

"This stream is too small to accommodate a large pike, and even an exceptionally large one would be most unlikely to mistake your feet for its normal prey."

"But I was not to know that, was I?"

"I suppose not." In the shadow of his straw hat his eyes were still enigmatic. He was dressed to suit the heat wave in cream flannel trousers and a blazer, with a bow tie in place of his usual four-in-hand tie.

"You didn't seem greatly disturbed by the outcome of the corporal's strategy. I should have thought that would have alarmed you more than being attacked by a fish."

"It might have done in some circumstances. But he wasn't dirty or drunk. I should think anyone would prefer to be kissed than bitten to the bone."

Caspar took from the pocket of his blazer a handkerchief of fine white linen. He held it toward her. "You had better dry your feet and put on your shoes before someone comes along who knows that you are not some 'young person.' "

She accepted the handkerchief. "Thank you."

It was awkward, standing on one foot and attempting to dry the other without either looking ungraceful or displaying an indecorous amount of petticoat.

Suddenly, for the second time in ten minutes, Flora found herself in masculine arms. But Caspar's object was not the same as Corporal White's; his intention was merely to carry her as far as the bridge, where he set her down on the parapet.

"I would offer to dry your feet for you, but for my hands." He leaned on the parapet near her and looked at the stream flowing beneath it, a position that made it possible for Flora to raise her skirt and cross her legs without being unnerved by his surveillance.

"Didn't it hurt your hands to carry me?"

"Not as much as it would have done a week ago. They're improving rapidly now."

She rubbed at a small strand of weed that was stuck to her instep, her fingers made clumsy by the turmoil going on inside her. Being held in her hus-

band's strong arms had disturbed her far more than
being kissed by the son of his coachman.

"Where did you leave your shoes? I'll fetch them
for you," he said.

She told him and he strolled away, leaving her still
unsure whether he was angry or not.

She had rolled her stockings into a ball and put
them inside one of her shoes, with her forget-me-not-
blue garters inside the other.

When Caspar returned, he placed the shoes beside
her on the parapet, but instead of resuming his
former posture he crossed to the other wall of the
bridge and leaned against it, facing her. Clearly he
meant to watch her put on her stockings, and as she
unrolled them she wondered if he thought it would be
a lesson to her never again to remove them in a public
place.

Perhaps for Helen to put on her stockings in front
of Hector would have been an ordeal. But Flora, who
strove for decorum out of a wish to conform and not
from any inborn or inculcated primness, was only
reluctant to do so in case Caspar thought her calves
too slim, her knees not sufficiently rounded. Her
ankles, she knew, were not unpleasing, but judging
by advertisements for stockings, in all other respects
the perfect leg was more generously formed than her
own.

She was on the point of raising her skirt when a
voice from the bank made her turn.

"Flora, why didn't you waken me? I didn't mean
to doze for so long. Good afternoon, Lord Carlyon.
I thought you were in London today," said Helen,
walking toward them.

"Only this morning, Mrs. Layard. May I see how

your painting is progressing?'' Before she could join
them on the bridge, Caspar strolled down to meet her
and to steer her toward her easel.

He did not remain with them long, but returned in
the direction of the house, saying he had some letters
to write, and leaving Helen unaware of what had
transpired during her nap.

CASPAR'S LONDON HOUSE was in Park Lane, and
since all the principal rooms overlooked Hyde Park,
and there was a garden at the rear, Flora found herself less conscious of being ''in city pent'' than she
had feared.

The house was about ninety years old and had
many of the features fashionable in the early part of
the previous century. The windows of the first-floor
drawing room were shaded by a decorative canopy
and opened onto a bow-shaped balcony with a beautiful classical railing that, being painted black,
looked like lace against the white stucco facade.

Since the house was much smaller than Longwarden, Flora had thought it possible that she and
Caspar might share a bedroom in London; but she
found this was not the case. As before, they had
separate bedrooms, and the only differences were
that the rooms were smaller and had no anteroom
between them. At first she thought they were not
connected, but then she discovered the door was a
concealed one, known as a jib door.

Her room was known as the Tent Room. Its ceiling
was draped with green and white silk, and instead of
a cornice there was a border of matching tabs with
large green silk tassels between them. As the room
was circular in shape, the ceiling reminded Flora,

with some amusement, of the underside of a mushroom.

A few days after their arrival she made her debut at one of the evening presentation courts that the King had commanded to replace the afternoon drawing rooms held during the old Queen's reign. Afterward she felt sure she would have spent the day in a fever of nerves had not Caspar provided a most effective distraction.

She was having breakfast in bed—Mrs. St. Leger having advised her to spend the day resting—when Burton answered a tap at the door and came to the bedside to say, "His Lordship intends to walk in the park in one hour's time, m'lady, and he wonders if you would care to accompany him."

Flora's spirits soared. "Tell his Lordship I shall be delighted. I'll get up at once," she replied.

Presently, when her maid inquired what she wished to wear, she asked, "Shall we meet many people during our walk, Burton?"

"I couldn't say, m'lady. A great many ladies and gentlemen *ride* in the Row every morning, but I don't know if many walk there."

"Then I shan't wear one of my new costumes. One of the Longwarden costumes will be more suitable if his Lordship intends a *brisk* walk."

"Yes, m'lady."

Did Burton guess, Flora wondered, that she was nervous of wearing her new Lucile creations in case her husband noticed the difference in her outline and was furious at her disobedience?

Caspar was waiting in the hall when she hurried downstairs.

"Good morning. I hope I haven't kept you?"

"Good morning. No, you're most punctual. We shall have a companion. You have no objection, I hope?"

Flora had every objection. She had hoped to have him to herself, but politeness forced her to say, "Not at all, but I thought Aunt Blanche disliked walking."

"She does." He walked to a bellpull and tugged it.

A few moments later Edward came through the door that led to the servants' quarters. With him, on a leather lead, was a small, sturdy, short-haired black dog with a crumpled-velvet face and tightly curled tail.

"This is Jacopo," said Caspar. "Jacopo, this lady is your mistress. See that you take good care of her."

"He is mine?" she exclaimed delightedly. "You bought him for me?"

The dog on hearing his name had fixed his soft eyes on Caspar. Now, as Flora spoke, he looked at her with such an anxious-to-please expression that she could not resist going down on her knees beside him to stroke his coat and fondle his velvety ears. "Oh, Jacopo, you are *beautiful*! No, I beg your pardon—most handsome," she corrected herself.

"I think he is remarkably hideous," said Caspar sardonically. "However, I daresay I can tolerate him, which would certainly not be the case with one of those yapping Pomeranians that I'm told are more fashionable at present."

"If they are those fluffy little creatures, I don't care for them, either. What kind of dog is Jacopo?"

"He's a pug. Thank you, Edward," he added as the footman, having surrendered the dog's lead to Flora, brought her husband his silk hat and cane.

They left the house, and Caspar offered Flora his

arm to cross Park Lane. A hansom cab was approaching, followed by a smart delivery van from Fortnum & Mason's grocery shop. As they stood on the pavement waiting for those vehicles to jingle past, she looked down at her new pet; but although her attention seemed to be focused on Jacopo, in fact she was conscious of nothing but the strong arm supporting her gloved left hand. However, the fluttering sensation induced by the contact did not last long. When they reached the far pavement she had to remove her hand, knowing it was not done to walk thus except when crossing a road, or when one was old or infirm.

"How old is Jacopo?" she asked as they entered the seemingly endless green vistas of Hyde Park in fresh green leaf.

"One year old, and already well trained, as you see," he remarked with a glance at the pug, who was trotting at her heels with the rolling gait of his breed. Caspar shifted his gaze to Flora's face. "I thought an untrained puppy would be an unnecessary complication in our lives."

Something in his expression made her suspect that this remark had a double meaning, but almost at once he went on, "I chose a pug for three reasons. First, because he is particularly well adapted to a town-and-country life. He can walk several miles without tiring, but when we are living in London it won't ruin his condition to have less exercise—that is, if you can resist the temptation to feed him tidbits. All pugs are inclined to be gluttons, so I've been told, and he'll soon become stout if you spoil him."

"Oh, but I shan't," she assured him. "What were the other two reasons?"

"Being short coated and fairly long legged, pugs

don't require as much grooming as Pomeranians and Pekingese. The third reason was that they are patient with children."

"He certainly looks very good-natured," Flora remarked in what she hoped was an airy tone. Although Caspar's reference had at once made her think of *their* children, perhaps he had been speaking of children generally, and in that case she would rather he did not guess what had sprung into her mind.

"Do you think he is likely to run away if I let him off the lead?" she asked. "No, perhaps it would be wiser to wait until he is more accustomed to me."

"I doubt if he'll give you the slip. Try him."

She bent to unclip the lead from Jacopo's collar, and after some hesitation he trotted toward a nearby tree. Having investigated the bole, he returned to the path from which he soon strayed in another direction, but he never went far and always kept an eye on his companions, as if he feared they might give *him* the slip.

"My grandmother had several apricot pugs. In her day black puppies were thought inferior and drowned," said Caspar.

"Oh, how cruel and stupid," Flora exclaimed. "I should have thought black was a far more suitable color for a dog than apricot."

"It's a misleading term for a deep cream color, and a silver pug has a fawn coat," he explained. "This dog is a scion of Lady Brassey's famous Jacopo. It was she who brought black pugs into fashion by taking the first four prizes at a dog show at Maidstone about sixteen or seventeen years ago. The story is that they were bred from some black pugs she brought back from China after she and her husband completed their voyage round the world. I think it was probably her account of her travels that inspired my interest in China.''

"Did you know her?"

"No, she died of a fever while I was a schoolboy, and she and my parents didn't move in the same circles.''

"I wish you would tell me about your parents. You once said you thought it unlikely that they had been happy, and your aunt has spoken of your father being in the Marlborough House set. But I know very little about your mother.''

"I seldom saw her. My nurse took her place in my affections. I must take you to see Nurse one day. She is very old now and lives in retirement at Brighton.''

After a slight hesitation Flora said, ''Your aunt once referred to 'my poor sister' and spoke as if your father had treated her badly. Did he?''

"He wasn't a faithful husband, but neither was she a devoted wife. As I've told you, photography was her chief interest. The match was arranged by their families, and they suited each other even less than is usually the case. It isn't only in China that marriages are contracted by the parents rather than by the parties most directly involved, you know.''

Without pausing to consider whether it was inadvisable to remind him of the episode by the stream, Flora said, ''No, in Corporal White's words, 'The gentry don't marry like us, where the fancy takes 'em. They marry for money and suchlike.' ''

"Generally speaking; not always," was Caspar's only comment.

She plucked up her courage. ''You were an exception, I gather? No bride was selected for you?"

"No, because my father was killed in the hunting field when I was nineteen, and my mother, being something of a recluse, was not in a position to choose a wife for me."

"Helen says you were the most eligible bachelor in London from the time her elder sister came out."

"Yes, I believe I was," he agreed. "But not on account of my good nature, or surpassing intellect, or charm of manner. It was merely that there happened to be a dearth of peers for several years, and also my mother was known to have been the heiress to a very considerable fortune, which not even my father's excesses had succeeded in dissipating."

She had never seen a more cynical expression on his face, and she wondered if perhaps there had once been some beautiful creature whom he adored but by whom he had been disillusioned.

He went on, "I think I should warn you, Flora, that before the season is over you will have been told a good deal to my discredit."

"I shall not believe it," she said firmly.

"But it will be true," he answered dryly. "For a number of years I followed the pattern set by my father, except that I never neglected Longwarden."

"I have always known you must have had small wives," she said, using the colloquial Chinese expression for concubines.

Caspar frowned, but before he could answer their attention was diverted by a large dog of mixed ancestry that came bounding toward Flora but was intercepted by Jacopo, bristling with outrage.

The large dog was followed by a small boy in a sailor suit and black stockings who retrieved his pet's lead and, addressing Caspar, said admiringly, "I say, sir, your little fellow is full of pluck, isn't he? Considering his size compared with old Bruno's, I mean."

It seemed that the boy was the son of some people Caspar knew, and Flora thought he must be lonely, since he attached himself to them for the rest of their walk. By the time he said goodbye and scampered off, they were too near the house to have much further conversation.

In the hall she repeated her gratitude for Jacopo, after which she began to mount the staircase and Caspar turned toward his study. Before she was halfway up the flight, however, he called her down and said, "As you know, my own dogs are not allowed in the house with the exception of Bluff, and he is confined to the ground floor. Naturally you will want to have the pug with you in your boudoir, and I have no objection to that. Whether you allow him in your bedroom is a matter for your judgment, but I hope you will not permit him to emulate Josephine's pet dog, Fortuné. You've read of his crime, I imagine?"

"No, I haven't."

"Fortuné was allowed to sleep on Josephine's bed and became so spoiled and jealous that on Napoleon's wedding night the dog bit his leg. Napoleon took it very well. I should be less equanimous."

FLORA MADE HER CURTSY to the King and Queen in a gown of primrose velvet, with three white ostrich feathers nodding above her black hair and a veil of fine old French lace drifting down over her train. Pearls gleamed in her ears, around her throat and on the wrist of her long white gloves; and just before they left the house Caspar presented her with a magnificent rivière of diamonds.

"A belated wedding gift," he had said, fastening it for her, his fingers brushing her shoulders.

He came with them to the palace and watched her go through the ordeal of making her curtsies to Their Majesties, and having her train flung over her arm by a page in order for her to walk backward into the supper room.

"Well done," he said when it was over.

Afterward, driving home and listening to Mrs. St. Leger's criticisms of the unmarried debutantes, most of them granddaughters of the debutantes of her own day, Flora had felt a glow of satisfaction at having acquitted herself so that even this captious old lady had found no fault with her performance.

But later, as she lay in bed, the thought uppermost in her mind was that although she had made her entrance into society, she had yet to bridge the infinitely more daunting chasm between girlhood and womanhood. . . .

Within twenty-four hours of her debut she was at her first ball, wearing a gown of pale green satin embroidered with swirls of silver beads. It had angel sleeves of silvery gauze, and with it she wore a diamond-and-emerald dog collar in the style set by Queen Alexandra, and a diamond aigrette with pale green osprey feathers in her hair.

Her dancing lessons at Longwarden had shown her to be quick to learn the steps of the valse and the lancers, and it was only her fear that Caspar would feel the bones of her corset that made her nervous of dancing with him. However, to her relief he seemed not to notice the stiffness of her waist, and soon she dismissed her misgivings and gave herself up to the lilting rhythm of the valse played by the Viennese orchestra.

It was during that first dance with Caspar that she felt someone staring at her and caught the eye of a man who was standing by himself. His distinguishing features were his height—he was as tall as Caspar—and his curly fair hair. As they passed him there was no mistaking the admiration in his gaze, and when they reached the other end of the ballroom she saw that his eyes were still following her.

She wondered if Caspar had noticed, but when she glanced up at him he was looking over her head with an expression that suggested his thoughts were elsewhere.

The next time she saw her admirer, he was coming toward her with Lady Conroy, who introduced him as Captain Cromer of the Blues.

"What are the Blues?" inquired Flora when he had asked her to dance and she'd assented.

"It's the nickname of my regiment—the Royal Horse Guards."

"I see. You must forgive my ignorance. I have only very recently come to England."

"I would forgive you anything, Lady Carlyon, and so would every man here. The whole of London is talking about you. It's not every year that a beauty illumines the season. We have heard rumors, of course, but rumor sometimes exaggerates. However, since your presentation last night the word has been spreading that this time rumor underrated the truth."

Mrs. St. Leger had instructed Flora in everything but the correct way to parry the onset of an experienced philanderer. She had to rely on her instinct, which was to smile and say lightly, "I feel sure there has always been a beauty—if not several—to illumine the season since you made your first appearance, Captain Cromer."

His hazel eyes twinkled. "You think I am flattering you? I assure you I am not. We military men are not adept at making pretty speeches. We leave that to the diplomats."

"While you concentrate on tactics," she murmured, remembering Corporal White. "Do you know my husband, captain?"

"We have met, but we are not well acquainted. Lord Carlyon is some years my senior. He and my elder brother, Rufus, knew each other at Cambridge."

The following morning, describing the ball to Mrs. St. Leger, who was leaving London later that day to return to her own home, Flora mentioned the attractive young Guards officer.

"Ah, yes, Harry Cromer, Louisa's grandson. An engaging young scamp, so she tells me, but something of a worry to her. Don't allow him to flirt with you, Flora."

This advice was not easy to follow. Wherever she went—whether to a ball in Berkeley Square, a performance of *Faust* at the Lyceum Theatre, an exhibition of fine art at the Prince's Skating Club in Knightsbridge, or to one of the many other events that crowded her engagement diary—Captain Cromer seemed always to be present. Even at a tournament and fete at the London Hippodrome, in aid of Charing Cross Hospital and attended by the Queen and her daughter Princess Louise, Duchess of Argyll, he was there, taking part in a cavalry display by his regiment. And whenever they met he paid court to her; not boldly, giving her an opportunity to rebuff him, but with great subtlety and charm, so that she could not honestly profess to dislike his attentions.

If only it were Caspar who seized every chance to talk to her, she often thought wistfully. But since their walk in the park on the morning of her presentation, there had been no more *tête-à-têtes*.

Life in London during the season was a continuous round of entertainments, with no time for the luncheons à deux or quiet evenings at home with which she would have liked to counterbalance their public engagements.

Even though Mrs. St. Leger was no longer an ever present third, Flora and Caspar were seldom alone together. His left hand was now free of bandages, but his right hand—the one he used most—still needed the protection of dressings. Because of the unsightly scars on his left hand, he continued to wear gloves in the house as well as outside it.

The first time he took them off was when they were traveling by train to spend Friday to Monday at Crowthorne Castle, the seat of the Duke and Duchess of Runcorn.

They were accompanied on the journey by Durrell and Burton, but the valet and maid were traveling in a second-class coach. Shortly after the train had steamed out of London, Caspar removed his gloves and showed her his hands, the right one now free of bandages.

As she gave an exclamation of dismay, he said, "Yes, they're not a pleasant sight, I'm afraid. I shall continue to keep them hidden as much as possible."

She had always admired his hands, which were shapely as well as strong. Her exclamation had been caused not by the sight of the patches of shiny pink tissue but by the realization that the burns, and the pain they must have caused him, had been even worse than she suspected.

Controlling an impulse to seize his right hand and press her lips to it, she said, "The only thing that matters is that you can still use them fully."

He flexed his long fingers. "Their function has not been impaired, only their appearance. Given time, so I'm told, the scars will become much less noticeable."

He retired behind *The Times*, and Flora took up a copy of *The Lady*. Reading the social notes, she found descriptions of several dinner parties at which she had been present. Most dinners took place in the great private houses of Mayfair and Belgravia, but it was becoming the fashion to entertain at certain hotels. *The Lady*'s social columnist reported:

Lady Ancaster's dinner at Claridge's the other night was a very magnificent affair, the table being decorated with quantities of the loveliest roses conceivable. Among her guests were Princess Hatzfeldt, Madame de Brienan and Mrs. Arthur Somerset. The Duchess of Marlborough looked very graceful in a white embroidered lisse gown, wearing her wonderful necklace and collarette of diamonds and turquoises, and chains of lovely pearls. Lady Carlyon wore black velvet, a perfect foil for her exquisite complexion, with a diamond stomacher and matching shoulder knots. She is gaining the reputation of always being perfectly dressed.

She was tempted to show the reference to herself to Caspar but decided against it, in case he should think her in danger of becoming conceited.

Before their arrival at the castle she had wondered if they would be given one room or two. On arrival she found that not only were they accommodated in separate bedrooms, but that these were at opposite ends of a long corridor.

Caspar, she thought, looked put out when they were conducted in different directions. She wondered if, now that both his hands were out of bandages, he had intended the castle to be the setting of their long-delayed wedding night.

Perhaps she had only imagined a flash of displeasure in his eyes when a maid led her to her bedroom and a footman conducted him the other way.

After Burton had helped her to change from her traveling clothes into a *vieux rose* bridge frock, she found her way down to the drawing room. Her hostess greeted her warmly but performed no introductions, it being taken for granted that everyone present knew each other.

Since Flora knew very few faces and Caspar had not yet come down, the sight of Captain Cromer approaching was a relief. She responded to his greeting with a warmth that later she regretted.

For the rest of that day and the next she saw little of her husband. After dinner on the first night he was monopolized by their host, who kept him engaged in some conversation of a grave nature in a part of the room removed from the groups of guests discussing more frivolous matters. Caspar and the duke were still talking when the rest of the party retired.

The next day she scarcely laid eyes on him. Re-

membering Lady Conroy's warning, she concluded
he must be in conclave with the duke's gardeners. For
her part she would have been happy to spend the
hours between meals in her host's splendid library
and picture gallery. But everywhere she went she was
soon followed by Captain Cromer, now more persistent in his attentions.

On Saturday afternoon, when she thought she had
found a safe refuge from him in the arbor at the heart
of the maze that was one of the features of the castle
gardens, he not only pursued her there but took advantage of their seclusion to kiss her.

At first she was too surprised to resist. Like being
kissed by Corporal Jim White, it was not an unpleasant experience. Indeed this time, because of the captain's height and build, it was reminiscent of being
held in her husband's strong arms.

"I've been wanting to do that since the first time
I saw you," he said, smiling down at her startled
face.

But when he would have repeated the kiss she
pushed him away, protesting, "No, please, Captain
Cromer—you must not!"

"Why not?" he asked, clasping her waist.

"Because I am married," she said simply, trying to
disengage herself.

He gave a shout of laughter. "Do you think your
husband would object? I've no doubt he's busy in-
dulging in similar pleasures."

She felt a sharp thrust of pain. "Do you? With
whom?" she asked unguardedly.

The captain shrugged. "No idea. He was always
uncommonly discreet. I remember someone once
saying that what made him so deuced fascinatin' was

that offhand manner in public and the superheated stuff in private.''

. She flinched and sprang to her feet. With all the dignity she could muster she said, "You shouldn't listen to gossip, Captain Cromer. I never do. I'm going back to the house now. Please don't follow me again.''

He leaped up and caught her in his arms. ''Oh, I say, don't be cross with a fellow because he finds you adorable. Don't you like me? Not even a little bit?'' he asked her teasingly.

She tried to fend him off. ''I should like you. . . if you behaved properly. Please—''

Her protest was stifled by another kiss.

HALF AN HOUR LATER, lying down in the sanctuary of her bedroom before it was time to change for tea, Flora realized that if it had been her impetuous admirer's intention to arouse warmer feelings toward him, his unprincipled behavior had been a lamentable failure. What he had succeeded in doing was to make her ache with longing to feel her husband's arms around her and her husband's kisses on her mouth.

Although before escaping from the maze she had treated Captain Cromer to probably the most indignant dressing down he had ever received from a woman, she had not succeeded in quashing him. At tea and again after dinner he was as attentive as ever; and she could not snub him in public.

There was one place where he could not flirt with her, and that was in her husband's company. Eventually, after he had murmured something particularly outrageous to her, she was driven to cross the room to Caspar. He was talking to an elderly politician and looked somewhat surprised by her advent, but he introduced the other man to her, and if privately it irked them to change their conversation to include her, both men were far too courteous to give any sign that her presence was less than welcome.

Presently, when the older man had left them, Caspar said, "Is anything the matter, Flora? I notice young Cromer seems to be somewhat *épris*. He's not being a nuisance, I hope? If so, I can very easily squash him."

"Oh, no, that isn't necessary. It's merely that I'm not yet accustomed to such continuous social intercourse. I—I can't help wishing we were at Longwarden...alone," she added in a low voice.

Perhaps he did not catch the afterthought, for just then they were joined by another person.

When she retired to her room that night she found a sealed note on her dressing table. There was nothing written on the envelope. Puzzled, she slit it open and drew out a single sheet of vellum die-stamped with "Crowthorne Castle" and a ducal coronet. On it was written: "May I come to you later?"

All her weariness instantly dissipated, she flew to the pretty inlaid *bonheur du jour* and after some thought wrote three words: "Need you ask?"

Then she rang the bell for Burton, to whom presently she said, "This is a reply to the note I found on my dressing table. Would you deliver it for me, please?"

"Certainly, m'lady."

The maid, she thought, looked disapproving. No doubt Burton considered it foolish for a married couple to exchange *billets-doux*.

By eleven Flora was in bed, her hair released from its fashionable coiffure to slide smoothly over her shoulders. She had chosen to wear the most daring of all the nightgowns Caspar had chosen for her. It was made of carnation-red gauze, as sheer as a dragonfly's wing, and it had a matching dressing cape made of row upon row of narrow ruffles.

At first she left her bedside lamp alight, but after a time she decided to extinguish it and sat in the dark, listening to the ticking of the clock and the beating of her heart and waiting for the bedroom door to open.

By this time the fire was reduced to a few smoldering embers, giving little or no light. The maid who should have replenished the coal scuttle had forgotten to do so, and since Burton hadn't noticed the oversight Flora had not drawn her attention to it for fear of getting the maid into trouble. With such a large house party staying at the castle, the underservants must be run off their feet. She had no wish to cause the girl to be reprimanded.

However, she had not realized how quickly the last lumps of coal would be consumed by the flames, or how soon the huge room would grow chilly.

Never mind: she would be warm enough with Caspar's arms around her. What was delaying him, she wondered.

CHAPTER TWO

IT SEEMED A LONG TIME before the door opened and she saw a tall figure slip into the room from the dimly lit corridor. She heard the key turn in the lock.

Glad of the darkness that concealed her palpitating shyness, but fearing that he might have some difficulty in finding his way to her, she said in an unsteady voice, "I thought you weren't coming."

The sound of her voice brought him to her in a few swift strides. The mattress gave under his weight.

"Foolish darling," he whispered, reaching for her.

As their lips met her shyness fled. It was if the long interval while his hands healed had never been; as if it were still the same night he had held her in his arms by the fire in her bedroom at Longwarden.

The only difference was that this time, feeling how willingly—eagerly—she surrendered to his embrace, he didn't hold his own feelings in check. While he smothered her face with passionate kisses, his hands fumbled impatiently with the dressing cape, hurriedly seeking its fastenings.

Not yet so carried away as not to care if it were torn, she murmured, "Wait...wait. I'll take it off."

He released her. A few seconds later the cape had been tossed into the darkness, and the lacy straps of the nightgown were no longer over her shoulders but at her waist, with the rest of the top part of the nightgown.

"Now!" she whispered, trembling with excitement.

They embraced again, exchanging sweet feverish kisses. When his hands found her naked breasts it inflamed his desire to such a pitch that he pushed her roughly back against the pillows and, catching her wrists and pinning them on either side of her, began to press hot hungry lips to the curves of her bosom.

For a few moments the combination of being held down and the ravenous pressure of his mouth rekindled the dormant fear of enforced submission. Then his lips found the peak of her breast, and as before, a long wave of pleasure engulfed her, drowning the instinct to resist in a tide of rapturous response.

This time there was no alarm bell to cut short her delight. They had the whole night to enjoy each other; for she found that, lovely as it was to be kissed and caressed, she also wanted to touch him, to stroke his hard shoulders and chest and to feel his bare skin under her hands.

"Why don't you take your clothes off?" she whispered, modesty forgotten.

At once he let go of her wrists, and she heard him stripping off his clothing.

"You'll be cold. Come under the bedclothes," she urged him softly.

He needed no second bidding. The next moment he was in the bed with her. As his arms closed around her she felt a hard rodlike pressure against the top of her thigh. With an involuntary recoil she recognized it as the thing that had injured her so cruelly at the mission.

Almost at the same instant her hands came into contact with his chest. But instead of the smooth

bronzed skin she had both seen and felt at Longwarden, there was now an expanse of coarse hair
curling around her fingers.

For some seconds she couldn't understand it.
Then, instantly paralyzed with horror, she remembered Sylvia Conroy's tale of the rose left in the
wrong keyhole. The man in her arms was not Caspar!
He was someone else; someone who had mistaken
her room for that of another of the guests.

"Ah, mon Dieu! Quel malheur!"

Her appalling predicament caused her momentarily to relapse into the tongue that was still the
language of her dreams and often of her thoughts.

She began to struggle frantically to free herself.
"Let me go...please...let me go. You're in the
wrong room. You've made a terrible mistake."

It was several agonizing moments before her agi-
tated protests seemed to register. When he grasped
what she was saying, he did let her go, and she scrambled out of bed in as great a panic as if she had found
herself between the sheets with a poisonous snake.

Forgetting she had pushed her nightgown down to
her waist and that as soon as she stood up it would
slip to her feet, she ran blindly away from the bed
only to trip and fall.

Her cry of pain as she crashed to the floor was
followed by several smothered oaths from the bed.
Before she could pick herself up, the lamp by the bed
was switched on and she saw who it was she had mistaken for Caspar.

"Captain Cromer! What are you doing here?"

Blushing from head to toe in an agony of embarrassment, not only at his seeing her naked but at her
abandoned behavior with him in the darkness, she

tried desperately to untangle the nightgown and cover herself.

"Why the surprise? Who else were you expecting?" he asked.

"M-my husband, of course. *Oh!*" she exclaimed as a thrust of pain lanced the elbow that had taken the brunt of her fall.

"Let me help you." He sprang off the bed and moved to assist her to rise.

At the same moment, having succeeded in pulling on her nightgown, which although transparent was some covering, she raised her eyes and saw him coming.

He was as naked as she had been, his skin pale, his legs as hairy as his chest. As he stooped toward her she shrank back, her dark eyes dilating.

"No!"

The cry was a strangled whisper of remembered terror as she stared, transfixed, at his groin.

As he reached down to grasp her, she sprang to her feet, striking his hands away. Too distraught to consider her scanty clothing or whom she might meet in the corridor, she fled across the room and saw with a sob of relief that he had not pocketed the key but had left it in the lock.

A few seconds later she was flying pell-mell along the passage in the direction of Caspar's room. She was not sure which one it was, but mercifully every door had the occupant's name written on it by means of a card slipped inside a small polished brass frame.

When she came to the door marked Lord Carlyon, without knocking she burst into the room. She didn't know what she meant to say; she knew only that in this predicament Caspar was her one sure sanctuary.

But her husband was not in his bedroom. Nor was his valet there waiting for him. The lamps were alight and the fire was still burning behind its guard. But the bed was as immaculate as when the maid had turned it down.

As she stared at the plump white pillows and smoothly folded sheet, Flora had a sinking feeling that Captain Cromer had not been alone in arranging a midnight tryst; and although his plan had misfired, evidently Caspar's had not.

IT TOOK HER SOME TIME to recover from the shock of finding the room empty. Her first reaction was to hasten back to her own room, but she changed her mind when it struck her that Captain Cromer might still be there. The following morning she realized he was most unlikely to have lingered after she had run away from him, but at the time it did not seem improbable.

To remain in Caspar's bedroom was equally unthinkable. She had no idea how long a man usually spent with his paramour, but perhaps it was not very long, and she must not be there when he returned.

She could think of only one refuge, and that was behind the heavy cut-velvet curtains drawn across the tall windows that lit the corridor by day. The windows had deep embrasures with cushioned seats, and although in winter such a hiding place would have been bitterly cold, on a warm spring night it was not uncomfortable.

Closeted there, she lapsed after a time into a doze from which she was startled into wakefulness by the click of a latch somewhere along the corridor. The small noise sounded quite loud in the stillness of the early-morning hours. It was followed by a soft swishing sound. Holding her breath and peering through the narrow gap between the curtains, she saw her husband striding toward her, the hem of his green velvet dressing gown brushing the thick pile of the carpet that muffled his footsteps.

After he had entered his room, she waited for several minutes before she emerged from her retreat and sped toward her own room. Facing the head of the staircase was an ornate boulle commode surmounted by a gilded clock. The hands showed ten minutes past two.

Once in bed, with her door locked, Flora buried her face in the pillow and burst into tears. She was not in the habit of crying, but the strains of the past twelve hours had been too much for her self-control, and she wept long and bitterly.

In the morning when Burton woke her she felt unrefreshed and heavy eyed. She was thankful that the ladies were not expected to go down to breakfast if they preferred to have it in their rooms.

While her maid was dressing her hair she said, "Burton, there is something I wish to make clear to you. The note I gave you last night was intended for his Lordship. The note I received was in a handwriting very like his, and I thought it had been written by him. I did not—and do not—expect to receive notes from anyone else; that is to say, from any other gentleman. If you should ever be asked to bring another one to me, you have my authority to refuse. Do you understand?"

"Yes, m'lady. I'm sure I'm very sorry, m'lady."

"There's no need for you to apologize. You were not in any way to blame for the misunderstanding."

Fortunately one of the hats that Burton had packed was a small flowered toque with a veil, and this Flora wore to church, the spotted meshes of the veil helping to hide the traces of a disturbed night.

She spent the sermon trying to guess which of her fellow guests was Caspar's inamorata.

None of them seemed a likely candidate. Yet what other explanation was there for her husband's absence from his bedroom? Sylvia Conroy had made it clear that Fridays to Mondays, and the house parties of longer duration that took place after the London season, were planned to facilitate the liaisons that were the inevitable outcome of the many loveless marriages.

"Planning the table for a dinner party is child's play compared with the difficulty of disposing one's guests in convenient bedrooms," she had told Flora when they had luncheon together. "People will refuse invitations to houses where they know they may be put next door to their husbands and in different wings from their lovers."

"But if everyone is so discreet, how does one know which people *are* lovers?"

"Oh, you will soon discover that. Meanwhile Caspar will know," Sylvia had answered airily.

As she sat beside her husband in church and faced the probability that, of all the duke's and duchess's guests, she was the only one who did not know where and with whom he spent the small hours, she felt profoundly humiliated.

When he spoke to her before luncheon, Captain Cromer behaved as if nothing untoward had happened. But during the afternoon he contrived to be at her elbow when no one else was close enough to hear him say quietly, "I'm sincerely sorry if I alarmed you. But I think you owe me an explanation. May I see you in the library after tea? You have my word I shall not distress you further."

When Flora hesitated he murmured, "*Please*, Lady Carlyon," in such a contrite and anxious tone that she felt obliged to agree.

He was at their meeting place before her. As she entered he rose from a chair but remained where he stood. "Thank you for coming," he said gravely.

Flora had rehearsed what she would say to him. Without delay she began, "I'm sorry you were misled, Captain Cromer, but you see I had no idea that the note I received was from you. I read it quickly and noticed the Greek *e*'s, which are also a feature of my husband's handwriting, and naturally I assumed it was from him."

"Is Lord Carlyon in the habit of writing for permission to visit you?"

She blushed. "He...that is, we are not usually so far away from each other. I thought he was being... amusing."

"Did you go to him when you ran away from me?"

She had foreseen this question and had her answer ready. "No, I meant to, but I changed my mind. I—I hid behind a curtain for some time, and then I returned to my room."

"I see. That explains the absence of any alteration in your husband's manner toward me today. Do you propose to tell him what occurred last night?"

She shook her head. "There's nothing to be gained by embarrassing you and annoying him. I think it was wrong of you to write such a note to another

man's wife, but I realize that such things are not uncommon in English society. Perhaps I should have
explained to you that I was brought up very differently.''

"I think I knew that from the outset, but I chose to
ignore it," he said slowly. "You are unlike any
woman I have known. I believe I have fallen in love
with you."

"Oh, I do hope not!" she exclaimed.

He smiled at that. "Most women delight in making
conquests.''

"They must be extraordinarily heartless. I'm sorry
for anyone who suffers the pain of loving someone
who doesn't return his affection."

"You speak with great feeling, but not from experience, I feel sure. No man whom you loved could
possibly remain indifferent to you."

He was making love to her, she realized. She said,
"I must go now, Captain Cromer," and gave him no
chance to detain her.

That night after dinner it was not Harry Cromer
but Caspar who contrived to draw her away from the
rest of the party.

To her consternation he murmured, "I thought
later on we might repeat the champagne supper that
last time was interrupted. Dismiss your maid early
tonight. I will brush your hair for you if necessary.''

Flora drew in her breath in mingled surprise and
dismay.

She said, "Oh...may we postpone it? I—I had
such a bad night last night, and tonight I can scarcely
keep awake."

His eyes searched her face for some moments.

"Yes, you look a little tired," he agreed. "Why did you sleep badly last night?"

"The wainscoting creaks, and I think there are mice running behind it."

"I shouldn't have thought mice would alarm you."

"Oh, no—not at all. I shall sleep perfectly soundly tonight."

"I don't know why the duchess put us so far from each other."

"Isn't it the custom in England?" she replied with a lightness she was far from feeling.

"In cases where there is known to be an estrangement—yes," he agreed with a shrug. "I can only surmise that our convenience had to be sacrificed to someone else's. It wouldn't occur to the duchess that, rather than being so widely separated, we might have preferred to share a bedroom."

"Do people ever share a room?" Both he and Mrs. St. Leger had given her the impression that this was never the case among the aristocracy and gentry.

"The lower classes have no choice but to do so. In the slums of our cities I believe the sleeping arrangements are even more crowded and insanitary than those in poor Chinese households. It isn't usual in this milieu—" he made a gesture that encompassed all the beautifully gowned, jeweled women and dress-coated men grouped about the vast drawing room "—but there are some eccentric couples who can tolerate each other's company at night as well as by day. You and I slept side by side on more than one occasion in China. Should you find it less tolerable here?"

It seemed to Flora, as she searched in vain for a

reply, that a deep flush suffused her face and spread downward to her décolletage. Even her ears felt hot.

Caspar added to her confusion. "I shall have to make you blush more often...my apricot rose," he said caressingly.

Had he spoken thus the night before, she would have trembled with pleasure. Now his power to stir her disgusted her. She could not forget that last night he had shared another woman's bed.

She said stiffly, "In China one had no choice. I think the greatest hardship of poverty must be the lack of privacy. It would make me very unhappy to have to give up my seclusion."

She opened her fan and used it to cool her warm cheeks, avoiding her husband's eyes until, when some seconds had passed, she stole a swift upward glance at him.

He was watching her with an expression she could not fathom. She wondered if he believed her excuse for postponing his visit to her. It was not untrue; she *was* tired. But in spite of her fatigue she had little expectation of sleeping well.

At times during that third interminable night at the castle, she wondered if, now that Caspar seemed bent on exerting his conjugal rights, she had no choice but to submit to him. She was haunted by the memory of Helen Layard saying desperately, "But where there is no such affection, you cannot imagine how abhorrent one's obligations are."

In Helen's case the lack of love was mutual. Flora wondered if it made any difference if one partner felt warmly toward the other. Her own deep feelings for Caspar were founded as much on her respect for his character as on the disturbing effect of his physical presence; but now her respect for him was shaken.

His relations with women during his bachelorhood had never disturbed her peace of mind. However, although neither of them at heart was a member of the Church of England, they had solemnized their marriage with promises that had seemed to her then, and still did, to express all that was finest and best in the relationship between a man and woman.

She remembered the clergyman asking Caspar, "Wilt thou love her, comfort her, honor and keep her in sickness and in health and, forsaking all other, keep thee only unto her, so long as ye both shall live?"

And Caspar saying firmly, "I will," and later taking her hand and looking into her eyes as he repeated the promise, "I, Caspar, take thee, Flora, to my wedded wife, to have and to hold from his day forward, for better for worse, for richer for poorer, in sickness and in health, to love and to cherish, till death us do part...."

Perhaps few people achieved the perfection of love and harmony defined by the author of the marriage service, and perhaps in society in England even fewer believed it to be attainable. But she had always believed in it, knowing that her father had found it with Most Rare Flower; as had, long ago, the former French marquis known in China as Père d'Espinay.

Caspar's reference to the nights they had spent side by side had reminded her of their journey from western China to the coast. Although often severely uncomfortable and at first overshadowed by her grief at the loss of her teacher, the journey now seemed in retrospect to have been a time of great happiness.

Compared with her present surroundings, the inns

in the backwoods of China had been crude and comfortless shelters. But after tramping across country in which it might take ten hours to cover forty *li*—less than fifteen English miles—she had not minded the dirt or even the stench of the livestock that shared the accommodation.

Once or twice, when it had been cold and there was no inn in the area, they had shared the *kang* of a peasant family.

The *kang* was a form of divan built of sun-dried clay bricks and intersected by flues through which smoke from the primitive cooking range was intended to circulate. This, with variable efficiency, it did. On the *kang*, wrapped in their bed quilts, whole families would swelter or shiver.

Sometimes part of a *kang* would crumble suddenly, and Flora could remember a spring day during her childhood when she had watched a *kang* being dismantled and pulverized into manure for the household crops. As clearly as if it were yesterday, she could see the profusion of bedbugs and other vermin that had been evicted by this process.

Yet in spite of the fact that a *kang* was invariably infested, she looked back on those nights beside Caspar not with a shudder but with regret for the camaraderie that had existed between them. He had treated her with the fraternal kindness he might have shown to a younger sister, and secretly she had longed to make him see her as a woman. Now that her wish had been granted, she pined for their former relationship.

THE DAY AFTER THEIR RETURN TO LONDON they were on the point of setting out to watch an interregimental polo match at Ranelagh when a basket of Malmaisons was delivered with a note addressed to Lady Carlyon.

Thinking the carnations must have been ordered by her husband and wondering why, since the house was always full of flowers sent up from Longwarden, she opened the note. The florist's card inside bore four lines of poetry.

> Beauty sat with me all the summer day
> Awaiting the sure triumph of her eye;
> Nor mark'd I till we parted, how, hard by,
> Love in her train stood ready for his prey.

Before her visit to Crowthorne Castle she might have mistaken the handwriting. However, to ensure that she did not fall into the same error a second time, the sender had written "H.C." in the lower left-hand corner.

She made no attempt to conceal what was written from Caspar, and he did not scruple to glance at it over her shoulder.

"Who is the poet among your admirers?" he asked her—as if there were nothing unusual in a married woman's receiving bouquets from other men.

"He isn't a poet. The verse is borrowed," she answered, handing him the card.

"Robert Bridges, I believe," said Caspar when he had read it.

"Yes, and no doubt I am not the first to be blandished by that particular quotation."

"I imagine not," he said casually.

To Flora, his cool indifference to Captain Cromer's gallantry was further proof that he saw their marriage as one of convenience and felt not the slightest twinge of jealousy. Not that jealousy was an emotion she thought desirable in a husband, but it was galling to feel that he didn't care who paid court to her.

That night he came to her room.

She was reading in bed with Jacopo curled in his basket by the window, already asleep.

When she heard the light tap on the door, there was no time to turn out the lamp. She could only sink back on her pillows and let her book fall onto the sheet, pretending to be sleeping as soundly as the little black dog, if somewhat less stertorously.

The minutes that followed seemed endless. She heard Caspar come across the room and guessed he was standing at her bedside. It took all her self-control to appear to be relaxed and peaceful and not let her eyelids flicker. In a way she detested the deception; it was not in her nature to use guile. But her reaction had been as instinctive as that of a small wild creature whose only defense when a predator threatens is to freeze.

She did not expect Caspar to wake her, but it was a surprise when the weight of the book was removed, the sheet lifted and her hands placed gently beneath it. Then he put out the light and for some time stood in the darkness while she wondered what he was thinking, and how much longer she could stand the suspense of his nearness.

At last she heard him move away and, a little later, the click of the latch as the door closed.

Her forehead was damp and her heart was thumping when she changed the position his coming had forced her to hold. She knew it was a respite merely. She could not always feign sleep or plead fatigue or a headache. Sooner or later, like Helen, she would

have to fulfill her obligations. The only alternative
was to leave him. But where could she go?

EVERY NIGHT for the rest of that week she retired to
bed with the fear that the tap on her door would be
repeated. Not daring to read, she would lie tense with
apprehension until at last sleep overcame her.

Fatigued by the pace of their social life and her
restless nights, and with the unaccustomed physical
discomfort of being constricted by a corset for hours
at a time, as well as her agony of mind at Caspar's
latest infidelity, she sank into very low spirits.

Her only comfort was Jacopo. On him she could
lavish the affection that had no other release; to him
she could show the woebegone face that reflected her
innermost feelings.

With everyone else, including Sylvia and Helen,
she was forced to wear a mask of lightheartedness.

On Friday they went to Longwarden, there to entertain a dozen guests. That night, while Burton was
still with her, Caspar entered his wife's bedroom and
seated himself in the chair by the fire.

Flora signaled to her maid to leave them. Rising
from her place at the dressing table, she crossed the
room to the sofa.

During the week she had purchased some nightgowns and peignoirs that were lighter and more comfortable than those selected by Mrs. St. Leger, but
less diaphanous and seductive than the garments
chosen by Caspar. Tonight she had on a nightgown
of white washing silk under a loose flowing wrapper
of white-spotted blue zephyr lawn. The fullness of
the wrapper over the silk was no more revealing than
a tea gown.

For some minutes they discussed their guests. Then he stretched out his hand and crooked his forefinger.

"Come here, Flora."

Part of her longed to obey. However, it happened that night she had a valid excuse for avoiding his embraces. With some awkwardness—she was not sure how much men knew about female physiology—she explained.

"I see," he said without surprise. "I thought you looked a little wan at dinner. How long do you expect to be incapacitated?"

"Four or five days. I...I'm sorry."

"There's no need to apologize. No doubt you'll be glad to go to bed. I won't keep you up any longer. Good night."

Rising, he gave her a rather formal bow and left the room. He had not sounded annoyed with her, but perhaps he was inwardly. Although she had been glad to be spared the necessity of explaining her condition in greater detail, she couldn't help feeling that his quick understanding was yet another indication that his relations with women had long been of a dissolute nature

The following morning she discovered that during their absence in London a change had taken place among the staff.

She was woken by the dawn chorus and could not resist the temptation to walk in the garden at sunrise. As she was going quietly downstairs with Jacopo under her arm she startled a housemaid who had been polishing the banisters and who, perhaps because she was half-asleep, had not heard Flora's approach.

The girl gave a nervous squeak and gaped at Flora as if she were a ghost.

"Good morning. I'm sorry I startled you. I'm Lady Carlyon. Who are you?" Flora asked with a smile.

"I'm Millie, ma'am...your Ladyship," the girl answered timidly.

"I don't think I've seen you before. How long have you been here?"

"Three weeks, your—m'lady. I was took on in Kate Catchpole's place."

"Kate has left us? I didn't know that," Flora said in surprise.

The garden at that early hour was wonderfully soothing and refreshing. It made her feel like a wild plant restored to its natural habitat after being potted and put in the artificial heat of a greenhouse. By the time she returned to her room her boots and the hem of her skirt were soaked through with dew, but she felt much less tired and strained.

That morning she had a talk with the housekeeper, at the end of which she remarked, "I hear Kate Catchpole has left us. Why was that, Mrs. Foster?"

"I had to dismiss her, m'lady."

"Dear me, I'm sorry to hear it. What did she do to deserve dismissal?"

"She had a follower, m'lady," the housekeeper replied with some reluctance.

"A follower? Do you mean a young man? But surely there is nothing wrong in that?"

"We don't allow followers, m'lady. It's one of our rules, as it is everywhere in good service. The maids have plenty of time for respectable walking out when they go home on their half day. The girls here are all from local families, and their parents rely on us to keep as strict a watch on them as they would themselves."

"Yes, I understand that, but it seems a trifle severe to give the girl her notice. Perhaps a reprimand from his Lordship—"

"I don't think his Lordship would wish to be troubled with such a matter, m'lady. You may be sure the girl's father will make her see the error of her ways, if anyone can. It was Mr. Warner who wished me to give her a place, on account of her mother being friendly with the late Mrs. Warner. I should never have allowed him to persuade me against my better judgment. I thought she was flighty from the first."

"I don't think you need blame yourself on that account, Mrs. Foster, and possibly you are right in thinking his Lordship has enough to concern him without being consulted over the maids' misdemeanors. But I wish you had spoken to me before you gave her notice. I don't like to think of anyone being dismissed from our service without our knowledge. Will Kate be able to find another place?"

Although Flora had expressed her displeasure as tactfully as possible, it was plain that Mrs. Foster resented so mild a reproof.

She said sourly, "Not in her present condition. It was my intention to spare your Ladyship the more unsavory details of the case, but seeing as your Ladyship is not satisfied with my way of dealing with it, I'd best put the facts more plainly. Kate Catchpole was in the family way."

"Oh, poor girl! No wonder she looked so unlike herself," said Flora, recalling the day she had noticed the housemaid's unusual pallor. "When is the baby expected, and who is the father?"

"She was three months gone when she left. As for the father, I couldn't say. Some good-for-nothing fellow, I've no doubt. She was the type of girl to make mock of a quiet, sober, God-fearing man who might have made an honest woman of her."

Flora let the subject drop. Later in the morning she sent for the butler.

"Mrs. Foster has been telling me about Kate Catchpole, Warner. I should like to talk to Kate. Is her parents' home within walking distance?"

"It is, m'lady, but if you'll permit me to say so, I wouldn't advise you to call there. Mrs. Catchpole is a decent woman, but Catchpole is a queer-tempered man. Not being one of his Lordship's tenants, he might not be as respectful toward you as he should."

"What does he do for a living?"

"He's a watchmaker, like his father and grandfather before him. They say he's an excellent craftsman, but he's an unsociable fellow, not liked in the village."

"In the circumstances I shouldn't expect him to receive me with great cordiality," she said. "I shall call on his wife this afternoon, when my absence will not be much noticed."

"Shall I order the carriage for you, m'lady? It's not a great distance in cooler weather, but I think you may find the walk tiring in the present heat wave."

"Perhaps, but I prefer to go on foot. My visit will attract less attention without the carriage waiting at the gate."

Thus it was that while some of the house party were resting and others promenading in the gardens, she slipped away to the village. She was wearing a summer dress of white muslin with lace insertions, and had she been idly sauntering in the dappled shade of the Broad Walk she would not have minded the high temperature. But as she hastened by the quickest way to the village, her tightly laced waist and the weight of her hat, trimmed with pale blue birds' wings and a cloud of tender green tulle, caused drops of moisture to trickle down her spine and bead her temples. By the time she reached her destination she felt tired and thirsty and not at all sure that she was right to intrude on Kate and her parents.

The doorbell was answered by a small wispy woman who looked taken aback by the sight of the white-clad stranger on her doorstep.

"Mrs. Catchpole? Good afternoon. I'm Lady Carlyon. I've come to see Kate."

"Good afternoon, ma'am."

The woman bobbed respectfully, then glanced quickly over her shoulder as if there were someone behind her, although in fact the hall was empty.

"Will you step in, please," she murmured. She opened an inner door and ushered her visitor into a parlor where the dim light was the result of the green Holland blinds that were drawn down almost to the stills of the two sash windows.

The room was furnished in the stiff cumbrous style of an earlier decade. It had the appearance of being regularly cleaned but rarely used. Having closed the door, Mrs. Catchpole made no move to raise the blinds. Nor did she invite Flora to seat herself.

"Is Kate in? May I see her?" asked Flora, instinctively lowering her voice to suit her surroundings and the almost furtive care with which Mrs. Catchpole had shut the door to the hall.

The other woman shook her head. "She's gone, ma'am. She's not here no more." Her eyes filled with tears and she pressed a hand to her mouth to still the trembling of her lips.

As Flora took a step toward her, the door opened to admit a man wearing a celluloid collar, with his shirt sleeves held back from his wrists by expanding metal armlets. His gray hair was parted in the center and slicked into place with pomade. A heavy mustache drooped on either side of his thin mouth. He had a stern humorless face.

"Who is it, Maud?" he asked gruffly.

"It's her Ladyship, Samuel." Mrs. Catchpole shrank back in a way that reminded Flora of a child accustomed to being cuffed.

She said, "Good day, Mr. Catchpole. I called to speak to your daughter, but I understand she isn't here."

"I have no daughter," he answered. "Maud, show her Ladyship out."

"I will leave if I am so unwelcome, but I hope you will not refuse me a drink of water first. It's a long way to walk on such a hot afternoon," said Flora quietly.

The woman looked uncertainly at her husband, who after some hesitation nodded his head in grudging consent to the request.

Left alone with him, Flora opened the silver mesh purse that hung on two chains from a clip attached to her waistband, which usually contained a lacy handkerchief and a tear-form glass bottle of smelling salts given to her by Mrs. St. Leger. Today, in place of the bottle she had brought her dearest possession.

"I'm told you are an exceptionally clever watchmaker, Mr. Catchpole. I should be interested in your opinion of this watch," she said, extending her palm to show him the musical watch that had once belonged to Père d'Espinay's mother.

It was an exquisite object with an engine-turned gold dial with enamel hour plaques, signed, "A. Chambery Avenier Fecit An 1814." The back of the case was dark blue translucent enamel over guilloche, decorated with a cipher of split pearls. The front of the case opened to reveal a classical scene in polychrome enamel.

The gleam in the man's eye when he saw it showed that, as she had anticipated, he felt a strong desire to examine it.

"Take it. I'm sure there is no danger of your dropping it. The key was lost many years ago. Could you make one to fit it?" she asked.

"I could—but why not take it to his Lordship's jeweler in London?"

"I will if you are too busy or don't wish to do it. It's very natural that you feel some animosity toward me, but I do assure you that Kate was not dismissed on my instructions. We have been in London of late, and I thought she was one of the staff who had stayed to keep Longwarden in order. It was only this morning that I learned the truth of the matter and came at once to offer my help to her."

As she spoke, Mrs. Catchpole returned with the water. Flora thanked her and drank a long draft. She was draining the glass when the watchmaker said, "You may do as you please, but you won't find her under my roof. I sent her packing the same day she lost her place. I'll have no whore in my house."

Flora swallowed the wrong way and choked. "Mr. Catchpole! You can't mean that!" she exclaimed, gazing at him in horror.

He did not trouble to reply. She saw in his face an implacable coldness that made her pity his wife.

"Where has Kate gone?" she asked them.

"To the devil is all I can tell you," he said with a shrug.

Flora plucked the watch from his hand. "Then I certainly shan't leave this here. It belonged to a man who would never have turned away anyone in trouble, least of all his own daughter. Good day, Mrs. Catchpole. Believe me, I'm sorry to have added to your distress. If only Kate had come to me...."

Boiling with impotent fury at the watchmaker's loathsome self-righteousness, she marched back to Longwarden at twice the speed she had come, arriving in no fit state to mingle with her guests.

Fortunately she was able to reach her room without meeting anyone. Had she been able to unfasten her dress without assistance she would have taken a bath before ringing for her maid. As it was she had no choice but to wait for Burton's arrival before she could begin to disrobe.

"Whatever is the matter, m'lady?" the maid asked when she entered and found Flora pacing the room with an angry sparkle in her eye, her dress sticking damply to her back, its freshness lamentably wilted.

For a moment Flora was tempted to pour out her indignation. Then she remembered Mrs. St. Leger's advice that it was never advisable to make a confidante of one's maid.

She said only, "I have been walking too fast for this hot weather, Burton, and must have a cool bath to make myself presentable again. Why can't gowns be designed to close at the side, I wonder? It really is dreadfully irritating not to be able to reach the fastenings oneself."

Later, after her bath, she said, "Do you know why Kate Catchpole was dismissed, Burton?"

"I have very little to do with the underservants, m'lady."

What a prig she is, Flora thought. Not for the first time she wished she could have a French maid to whom she could chat in the language she had spoken throughout her years at the mission.

Indeed it was still an effort to stop thinking in French, and to try to adopt the fashionable jargon used by Sylvia Conroy and her friends. To them everything pleasant was "deevie," everything unpleasant "diskie," and tea gowns and nightgowns were known as "teagies" and "nighties."

She said, "No, I realize that, but I should have thought you would have heard something of the matter."

"It came as no surprise to me, m'lady. Girls like that—always saucing their superiors—usually do end in trouble, in my experience."

"Don't you feel at all sorry for her?"

"Why should I, m'lady? She's made her bed and she must lie on it, as the saying goes."

"There are worse crimes than having a baby out of wedlock. Did you know her father had disowned her?"

"You couldn't expect him to do otherwise," was Burton's sanctimonious answer. "There'll be plenty of talk as it is, but if he'd allowed her to stay he'd have lost half his trade. He has his living to consider, and respectable people won't go to a house with a girl of bad character in the background. I'm sorry for her mother, I will say. She lost all her other children, and he's not an easy man to live with, by all accounts. But they say Mrs. Catchpole was always too lenient with Kate. Spare the rod and spoil the child. That's the cause of it, I daresay.''

Privately Flora felt sure that any leniency on Mrs. Catchpole's part had been more than balanced by the severity and even brutality of the watchmaker's treatment of his daughter, but she kept this opinion to herself.

Later she consulted the butler.

"I'm very worried about Kate, Warner. What will become of the girl? Surely there must be some way to find out where she has gone?''

His attitude was less censorious than that of the housekeeper and Burton, but clearly he felt there was little to be done. When Flora suggested consulting Caspar, Warner took the view that his Lordship would not wish to be bothered with such a matter and would disapprove of Flora's involvement. She received the impression that if she insisted on telling Caspar she would bring down a great deal of censure on the heads of the senior staff without in any way benefiting the errant housemaid.

Flora had no wish to antagonize Warner and Mrs. Foster, but she could not dismiss her anxiety. She ate her dinner with the consciousness that Kate, wherever she was, might have nothing to eat; and when she climbed into bed that night it troubled her deeply to think that, for all anyone knew, the girl's only shelter might be a hedge or a haystack.

On Monday morning, after their guests had departed but before it was time to return to London, Flora was walking alone in the garden when one of the gardener's boys approached her.

He was one of a number of lads who eventually would be promoted to undergardener. Although the boys were not often seen in the pleasure gardens during the hours when the Carlyons and their guests frequented them, whenever Flora did glimpse one of them she was reminded of her father, who had started his working life on the grounds of a house not unlike Longwarden.

"Good morning. Do you wish to speak to me?" she asked with an encouraging smile, seeing that the boy was nervous of addressing her.

"If you please, m'lady, I were told to give you this, m'lady."

Having thrust an envelope into her hand, he would have run off, but Flora stopped him by saying, "Wait a moment. What is your name?"

"Billy Blake, m'lady."

"Who told you to bring this to me, Billy?" she inquired as she opened the envelope.

"My gran, ma'am."

The envelope contained a single sheet of cheap ruled writing paper covered with the painstaking pothooks of someone unused to handling a pen. The letter was addressed "Dear Ma" and signed "Kate," and the news it contained made Flora sigh with relief.

She said, "Go to the kitchen, Billy. Give Cook my compliments and tell her you have done me a service and I should like you to have something nice to eat. If anyone asks what you did, you may say it was confidential."

When he had left her she read Kate's letter a second time. It was written from an address in London where Kate was lodging with someone called Gertie. She had not yet found work but hoped to do so very shortly. There was no need for her mother to worry about her, for she was finding London much more to her liking than Longwarden.

The letter was still in her hand, and Flora was wondering how and when she could contrive an opportunity to visit Kate's address and make sure the girl was not merely seeking to allay her mother's anxiety, when Caspar came into view.

She thrust the letter into her waistband—but not before he had seen it, of that she felt sure. However, if he was curious to know what it was she had hoped to conceal from him, he did not ask but said only, "I'm ready to leave whenever you are."

More than once on the train to London Flora turned from her contemplation of the scenery to find Caspar eyeing her over the top of *The Times*.

Each time she was tempted to confide in him, and each time she was held back by the fear that, in spite of his own peccadilloes, her husband might not be tolerant of a lapse on the part of one of his servants.

As soon as they reached Park Lane she went to her boudoir to study the leather-bound book that lay on her writing table, in which she kept a note of their social engagements and her fittings at Lucile's salon. She found it would be at least a week before she could cancel one of them and take a hansom cab to Clerkenwell, the district where Kate had taken refuge. It irked her that her life should be so full of frivolous occupations that something important must be delayed.

"Where is Clerkenwell, Helen?" she asked while she and Mrs. Layard were conversing at a reception that night.

"It's one of the horrid slum districts on the outskirts of London," said Helen. "Why do you ask?"

"I heard someone mention the name and I wondered where it was." For an instant she was tempted to tell Helen the truth and to ask her to go with her.

However, a few seconds' reflection convinced her that Helen was an unsuitable companion for such an expedition. Sylvia was a more likely ally, but even Sylvia could not be relied on for support. She was a woman of whims, and her moods were as changeable and unpredictable as mountain weather. In one of her bored restless moods she might regard a visit to Clerkenwell as an amusing escapade. But Flora knew her to be extremely nervous of infections, and therefore it was equally possible she might regard the expedition as a foolish risk to their health.

Toward the end of the week Caspar took her to see Adeline Genée dance at the Empire Theatre.

She had first heard about the Empire from Mr. Sutton, a man on board ship. A bachelor like Mr. Eliot, he had spent his life in remote parts of the British Empire. Whenever he went home on leave, his first night in London was always spent in the Promenade bar behind the Circle at the famous music hall in Leicester Square.

"You can always be sure of meeting someone you know there," he had told her. "You should coax your husband to take you, Mrs. Lomax. You'd enjoy it. There's nowhere better than the dear old Empire for a rousing good show. Mind you, there are a few straitlaced old busybodies, like Mrs. Ormiston Chant, who would like to see it closed down. But what do they know of enjoying life?"

Caspar had needed no coaxing. He had seemed amused by her wish to go to the Empire and had made the arrangements some time earlier.

They had dinner at home before setting out for the theater. Remembering Mr. Sutton's reference to Mrs. Ormiston Chant, Flora asked Caspar if he had heard of her.

"Yes, I remember her leading a campaign to close the Promenade. I was up at Cambridge at the time, and boat-race night was always celebrated at the Empire. It was the only night of the year when the theater did become rather disorderly. Nevertheless it isn't a place where people take their daughters, and some men wouldn't wish their wives to see or be seen there."

"Why not?"

"It's frequented by the demimonde. If you notice anyone you know accompanied by someone you don't know, the wisest course is to pretend not to see them," he told her in a tone of cynical amusement.

Chilled by this fresh evidence of his casual acceptance of infidelity as a commonplace, she said, "I wonder if my father ever went to the Empire."

"Not if his last visit to England was some years before you were born. The place wasn't built in his time."

Presently, as they were driving down Park Lane in the brougham, with the park at its best in the soft golden light of a perfect early-summer evening and the windows open to the breeze, he took off his gloves and laid them aside with his silver-mounted ebony cane. From an inner pocket of his dress coat he drew out a slim leather case.

"I intended to give you this earlier. You needn't wear it tonight if it isn't in keeping with your gown."

He opened the case and took from its white velvet bed a delicate bracelet of enameled gold flowers and

leaves, the flowers having centers of diamonds,
pearls and green peridots.

"It's a piece by Lalique in the style the French call
art nouveau, but if you decide you don't care for it I
can very easily exchange it for something more conventional."

"It's beautiful."

"May I put it on for you?"

She gave him her wrist; she was wearing long ivory
gloves. The deftness with which he fastened the clasp
made her wonder how many times he had performed
the same service for other women, and whether the
bracelet was a sop to his conscience because he had
visited the jeweler to buy a present not for his wife
but for the unknown person with whom he had spent
the small hours at Crowthorne Castle.

With such a thought in her mind it was difficult to
thank him with any sincerity. But if he found her
manner tepid, he chose to ignore it.

It was a relief to arrive at the theater, which
more than fulfilled her expectations of the blue-and-
gold opulence described by her shipboard acquaintance.

The foyer, with its great vaulted ceiling supported
by pairs of columns, was as grand as the entrance to a
palace. From the foot of the immense staircase
leading up to the notorious Promenade she could
glimpse the gilded proscenium arch glistening in the
glow of the houselights and hear the orchestra playing a Waldteufel waltz.

Caspar had taken a box with a view not only of the
stage but of the whole auditorium. There were times
during the variety bill that preceded the ballet when
Flora found the audience sitting in the luxurious blue

plush stalls as interesting as the performers behind the footlights.

The people who composed it were of a very different order from those she was accustomed to seeing at the theater and the opera. Here were no pleasure-weary aristocrats dutifully attending an opening night or a gala performance. Here every face was alight with the enjoyment of a special occasion, and the women laughed and applauded as heartily as the men.

At the beginning of the season Caspar had given her a pair of opera glasses veneered with slips of mother-of-pearl. From time to time Flora could not resist turning them in the direction of a young couple who had caught her attention by the way in which between each turn they exchanged loving looks. Sometimes they glanced at each other during the acts. She could not help envying their happiness and wishing she and Caspar shared that kind of intimacy.

Sometimes when he was intent on the performance she stole a glance at her husband and saw his eyes gleaming with amusement, his cheeks seamed by two deep creases. He was not a man who laughed aloud often, but she had never doubted that he had a strong sense of humor—at least she hadn't before they left China. In England he seemed to find less to amuse him.

When the interval came she said, "May we walk through the Promenade?" And when it seemed he meant to refuse she persisted, "Please, Caspar. There can be no harm in it, surely? Not if I am with you."

"Very well, but I think you will find the depravity greatly exaggerated," he answered, rising and offering his arm to her.

At first she could see little difference between the company in the Promenade and the guests at a society function. The principal difference seemed to be that the air was pungent with the smoke from many cigars.

Then she noticed a tall handsome negress in a gown of rich crimson velvet, and nearby a girl who might be Italian or Spanish, both of them chatting coquettishly to men old enough to be their grandfathers.

Indeed there were women of every size, shape and complexion, including a Chinese beauty at whom she could not help gazing, for it seemed so odd to see a Chinese face framed by the sweeping brim of a hat of *couleur de rose* straw trimmed with yards of rose moiré ribbon and tufts of paler pink osprey feathers. But when the girl matched her look with a stare of equal curiosity, Flora realized that she herself must seem even more bizarre in the ballrooms and drawing rooms of Mayfair and Belgravia.

She was prevented from dwelling on this uncomfortable reflection when behind them a voice cried, "Good God! If it isn't Caspar. This *is* a surprise, my dear fellow. I heard you were botanizing in India or somewhere out East."

The speaker was a man of medium height with the sun-browned complexion of someone recently returned from a hot climate. With him was a girl with flaming red hair and merry blue eyes that scanned Caspar and Flora with undisguised curiosity.

"Richard! When did you get back?"

The two men shook hands with a vigor that would have crushed a woman's hand.

"Docked at Tilbury this mornin'. Paid a short call

on m'grandmother on m'way to Rutland Gate and came straight here to enjoy the feminine society I've been missin' for too long," said the other man with a smiling glance at the pretty girl on his arm.

But he did not introduce her.

"Yes, I heard you were serving in East Africa. Third battalion King's African Rifles—is that correct?" said Caspar. "Guarding that deuced expensive railway from Mombasa to Lake Victoria from the depradations of the natives, so I was told."

"Among other things. It's wonderful territory, Caspar. You should come out and see it. I'm interested in shootin' the game, but there's plenty of plant life to keep a botanist happy. Near my present station there are flowers everywhere: gladiolus, belladonna lilies, forget-me-nots, red-hot pokers, not to mention dozens I can't name. Mind you, you might need some of my *askaris* to keep an eye on you. The natives can be troublesome at times, and one or two settlers have been murdered in a devilishly unpleasant manner."

He leaned closer and lowered his voice to regale Caspar with an anecdote unsuitable for feminine ears.

His companion withdrew her hand from the crook of his arm and moved closer to Flora.

"D'you speak English, dear?" she inquired.

"I am English," Flora replied.

"I thought per'aps 'e'd brought you back from the East with 'im." The red-haired girl's voice was uneducated but not unpleasant to the ear.

"He did. I was living in China."

"Oh, I see—you're 'alf and 'alf, eh?"

"Yes," Flora agreed, smiling slightly at the girl's

blunt statement of a fact that everyone else, even Sylvia and Helen, ignored.

"I wish I 'ad your looks," the girl went on. "My 'air's not my choice, I can tell you. My face wouldn't never catch *'is* eye," she added ruefully, appraising Caspar's tall figure and comparing him with her own escort. She leaned closer, engulfing Flora in a powerful wave of patchouli. "Is 'e generous?"

"Extremely."

"I don't know about my chap yet. As you 'eard, we've only just met. But they usually make a splash when they're on leave. I could do with some extra at present. I'm 'elpin' a friend 'oo's in trouble, poor little wretch. Not one of us. A good girl." This last she said with a wink and a laugh that, although not so vulgarly loud as to draw the attention of everyone, was enough to make Caspar glance at her.

Briskly declining the other man's invitation to drink with them, he brought the encounter to an end and took Flora back to their box, where a bottle of champagne was waiting on ice for them.

"An unfortunate meeting, which you must put out of your mind when next you see Richard," he said dryly as he poured out the wine. "Although when he learns who you are he may be sufficiently embarrassed to avoid being presented to you unless it becomes unavoidable."

"Why should he be embarrassed?"

Caspar raised a sardonic eyebrow. "The girl he had with him was not the type a man would wish to make known to his mother or his sisters. What was she saying to you?"

Flora saw an opportunity to sound his opinion of girls in Kate Catchpole's situation.

"She said she hoped your friend was a generous man because she is helping another girl—not a demi-mondaine—who is expecting a child soon. It must be terrible to be seduced and then disowned by one's family."

To her disappointment, Caspar ignored this feeler and said only, "Perhaps in a year or two I might take up Richard's suggestion and spend a winter in East Africa. Have you given any thought to where you would like to go when the season is over? Does Biarritz appeal to you?"

"Must we go away? Mightn't we stay at Long—" she began.

But already the houselights had dimmed, and her suggestion was lost in a burst of music from the orchestra.

To Flora, who as a child had been excited by the fairground hubbub surrounding Chinese theatricals, but who had never greatly enjoyed the play itself—always interminably long, performed in shrill falsetto voices and punctuated by blasts of excruciating music—the European ballet was magical.

When it was over and the curtain fell for the last time, she turned an enraptured face to Caspar.

"Wasn't it beautiful? Oh, to be able to dance like that! Thank you for bringing me. Did you enjoy it as much as I did?"

Her enthusiasm seemed to amuse him. Although he agreed that he had, she was left with a feeling that he might have been a trifle bored.

By the time they were seated in the brougham her delight in the ballet was ebbing and her earlier worries reviving. She wondered if he had noticed the Chinese cocotte and if it had also crossed his mind that his wife's appearance was only slightly less incongruous.

They were nearing Park Lane when an insect flew through the open window and blundered against her face. Instinctively she recoiled, although the next instant she knew it was merely a large but harmless moth.

Caspar, however, seemed to think she was alarmed. With the swift reactions that had more than once saved them from very real hazards in China, he drew her protectively against him, caught the moth in the crown of his opera hat and ejected it into the night.

"Oh, poor thing...thank you," she murmured, attempting to straighten.

By putting his arm around her shoulders he had pulled her off balance. Afterward he did not immediately release her but seemed to grasp her more firmly. At that moment they passed a streetlamp. As the brief flare of light illumined the interior of the brougham more clearly than the pale moonlight, she saw on his face an expression that made her heart pound with mingled excitement and dread.

Had he said one small word of affection she would have yielded to the pressure of his arm around her and the gleam of desire in his eyes. Without that word she could not. It repelled her to have to surrender to an embrace that she knew meant no more on his part than if she were one of the pretty demimondaines from the Empire.

What followed happened so swiftly that she had no chance to change her mind. As soon as he felt her resistance—her averted face, her gloved hand pressed defensively against his shirtfront—he let her go and stopped the carriage.

As it halted, he sprang onto the road.

"I'm going to my club for an hour. Take her Lady-ship home," he instructed the coachman. Then he closed the door and bowed to Flora. "Good night," he said with icy courtesy.

As the brougham began to roll forward, she put her head out of the window and watched him striding away, his tall figure silhouetted against the lights of a house where a dinner party was taking place.

He was not going in the direction of his club. Where was he going, she wondered miserably. To seek the society of someone more complaisant than his wife?

With an abrupt revulsion of the feelings that had prompted her resistance, she was tempted to halt the carriage and run after him.

But what could she say? And wouldn't such undig-nified conduct merely exacerbate his anger?

As she hesitated, her husband turned a corner and disappeared from view. Flora sank back against the squabs, closing her eyes against an uprush of tears that she dared not shed for fear of giving the servants food for gossip.

CHAPTER THREE

SHE SLEPT FITFULLY and woke at first light, her dilemma still unresolved in spite of the mental debate that had kept her awake long past midnight.

Presently she slipped out of bed and went to the chair by the window near Jacopo's basket. The little dog opened his eyes, but in spite of his mistress's being up he seemed to know it was not yet time to bestir himself.

At this hour the park was deserted. After a while she heard footsteps and saw three poorly clad women passing. She had seen them before and on inquiry had discovered they made their living by cleaning front doorsteps.

"They're a very rough class of person," Warner had told her.

Not long after seeing the cleaners, she heard the clop clop of hooves and saw a hansom approaching. It drew up outside the house. With startled eyes she saw her husband step down and toss a coin to the driver perched at the back.

When the cabbie had driven away, Caspar stood at the edge of the pavement, gazing up and down Park Lane. He was wearing his top hat at a more rakish angle than usual, and his opera cloak was tossed back from his shoulders. One hand was tucked in the pocket of his trousers; the other held his cane and was tapping it lightly against the side of his leg. He looked alert and untroubled, like a man who had slept long and soundly and now was anticipating his breakfast.

It was his air of carefree well-being as he turned to enter the house that crystallized Flora's decision. As he disappeared from her view, she went to her writing table and, taking a pen from the inkstand and opening the blotter, she began to write a letter.

When she had finished, she read over what she had written to him.

My dear Caspar,

After long and serious consideration I have reached the conclusion that it is not possible for me to continue to live as your wife. It was wrong of me to accept your offer of marriage. At the time I did not realize we belonged to such very different worlds. I have tried to conform but have found it impossible. Therefore I must beg you most earnestly to agree to our separation.

I know such a step may give rise to unpleasant gossip. But I feel you regret our marriage as deeply as I do, and it is better for us to part now. To continue the sham can only cause greater unhappiness. I believe the best plan is for me to live in France, where I feel sure I can find work if you will be so kind as to lend me fifty pounds. I will repay it as soon as I have established myself. Believe me, I am deeply grateful for your many kindnesses to me.

Flora

She went out for the greater part of the day, having arranged to accompany Sylvia to a luncheon in aid of a charity. Before she left the house she gave the letter to Edward to put on the desk in Caspar's study.

"You're very pale today, Flora," her friend remarked after the luncheon. "And you ate almost nothing, I noticed. You are not expecting a baby, are you?"

When Flora shook her head she went on, "Since you don't ride, it wouldn't be too disappointing if you were in that condition during the hunting season. There is no *very* convenient time for being enceinte. I'm heartily thankful my duties in that sphere are over."

By accepting Sylvia's invitation to have tea with her in her boudoir, Flora delayed going home as long as she could. But with the arrival of her friend's hairdresser she felt she could linger no longer. She walked slowly back across Berkeley Square and up Mount Street.

No sooner had she entered the house than the butler appeared. "His Lordship would like a word with you when you have time, m'lady."

"I have time now, Warner. Where is he?"

"In the study, m'lady."

With considerable apprehension Flora composed herself to face her husband.

Caspar had been writing when she knocked, but he rose to his feet as soon as he saw her hovering nervously on the threshold.

"Ah, Flora. . . come in. Please be seated," he said, gesturing to the chair on the other side of his desk.

There was nothing in his manner to indicate his reaction to her proposal. However, it was not his way to approach any subject circuitously, and without preamble he said, "I have read your letter—several times. Perhaps you wouldn't mind clarifying certain points that are not clear to me."

She cleared her throat. "Certainly. Wh-what are they?"

He unlocked a drawer and took from it a sheet of paper that she recognized as her letter. Placing it on the blotter in front of him, he said, "You refer to finding work in France. What form of work had you in mind?"

"I—I thought I might become a governess."

"Without references? Without the ability to play any musical instrument or to ply a needle? I think it unlikely."

"I have other accomplishments. Greek and Latin...botany."

"You would find few parents who consider Greek and Latin suitable for their daughters to study, and certainly no French family whose ménage included sons of an impressionable age would engage a young foreign governess with your face and figure. Even in the absence of young men, you might be considered distracting to the head of the household."

"But I shouldn't be dressed as I am now," Flora protested. "I should dress very plainly...in black."

He regarded her thoughtfully for a moment. "You were dressed in black when we met, but it didn't succeed in making you look like a novice. I remember thinking that if you were a novice you had very little vocation for it."

"That was a long time ago. I was still in the schoolroom as it were."

"But eager to become a woman, and piqued when you were treated like a child," he reminded her sardonically.

Flora said nothing. In her mind's eye, as clearly as if it were a photograph fixed in an album, she remembered the scene at the supper table on the night of his arrival at the mission. Most of his conversation had been with Père d'Espinay, but sometimes he had addressed a remark to the French nun or smiled at the small Chinese nun, whom most of their visitors ignored when they learned she was unable to speak. It was only herself he had ignored, as if she were a child whose place was to be seen and not heard.

"Now, I fancy, the position is reversed and you want to prolong your girlhood and put off becoming a woman," he went on.

She summoned the courage to meet his eyes. "I should have been born a boy. I wasn't brought up like a girl or taught the things girls are taught. I was reared to be a traveler or a scholar, not a suitable wife for a member of the English peerage. You must have known that at Shanghai, even if I didn't then."

He picked up an ebony rule and turned it between his strong fingers.

"My peerage is not the sum of my existence, Flora," he said dryly. "I'm also a naturalist and traveler. At Shanghai I knew you would make an admirable wife for any man with those propensities. Your ability to fit the role of a peeress remained to be seen, although your manners and your general deportment left little to be desired. Since then, all things considered, you've acquitted yourself admirably."

He rose and strolled around the desk, saying as he did so, "You suggest in your letter that I regret our marriage. You are wrong. I'm sorry to hear it has made you regret your sex. But since both your sex and our marriage are unalterable, it would be wiser to make the best of it, rather than seeking ways to escape the inescapable. Let me make myself clear. I will not release you from the bond made between us in Shanghai."

She would have argued with him, but at that moment Warner entered.

"A telegram for you, m'lord. The messenger is waiting, should you wish to send a reply."

"Thank you. Excuse me, Flora."

Caspar slit the edge of the envelope with the blade of an Oriental dagger. Having scanned the message, he said, "My old nurse is gravely ill. I must leave for Brighton immediately. I'm afraid you must convey our apologies to Lady Dysart. We shall have to forgo her ball tonight."

Remembering his deep affection for the old woman who had looked after him as a little boy, Flora forgot her own concerns. "Shall I come with you?"

He shook his head. "Not at present. If she rallies—unlikely at her age—I will send for you."

She was in her boudoir writing the note to Lady Dysart when, less than half an hour later, he looked in to bid her farewell.

"It may be necessary for me to remain in Brighton for a few days," he told her. "If Nurse dies I shall stay for her funeral."

"Yes, naturally."

"It's unfortunate that I have to leave you in your present unsettled state of mind, but it can't be helped. Don't brood on it, *ya-t'ou*. Rely on me to know what is best for us."

Unexpectedly, he drew her to her feet and took her

in his arms. His mouth came down firmly on hers in a long possessive kiss. Against her will she found her body yielding, her lips responding.

But later, when he had gone, she remembered their conversation in the study and felt a fresh spurt of rebellion at being overruled.

"Let me make myself clear. I will not release you from the bond made between us in Shanghai."

He had stated his views, and that was the end of the matter. As far as he was concerned, no further discussion was necessary. But what right had <u>he</u> to annul, in that arbitrary fashion, a choice she had made only after a great deal of heart searching?

"Rely on me to know what is best for us." Why? Because he was older and wiser, or merely because he was a man and therefore a superior being?

After further reflection it struck her that she would be in a stronger position to argue if she could first confound all *his* arguments by proving herself to be employable.

To obtain the address of a reputable employment agency would not be a problem, she thought. Only that afternoon Sylvia had been bemoaning the difficulty of finding a governess who did not either terrorize the children or allow them to terrorize her.

"They are either gorgons or dormice. There seems to be no happy medium," she complained to Flora.

It would be easy to raise the subject again and find out the name of the agency Sylvia had mentioned. What was not so easy was to dress as befitted a governess; and on this score she had also to consider her visit to Clerkenwell. Accustomed as she had been to living among very poor people, she knew that to visit the slums dressed for paying calls in Mayfair would never do.

She must dress as plainly as could be. It was therefore vexing to discover that all her least obtrusive garments had been left at Longwarden.

"I didn't think you would need that costume in London in this weather, m'lady," said Burton the following morning when she found her mistress searching for the navy serge skirt she had worn on the night of the fire.

"I don't. I—I was going to lend it to some children who are getting up a play."

"I can have it sent up by the train if you wish."

"No, no; it isn't important. No doubt someone else can provide a skirt for the part of the governess."

"I'm surprised the young persons' own governess is not able to do so," replied Burton.

"Perhaps she is not the right size."

Flora made her escape, despising herself for a fabrication that had probably sounded as unconvincing to Burton as it had to her own ears.

Had she liked and trusted her maid, she would have asked Burton to lend her one of the plain skirts she wore on duty. But since she did not like or trust her, and knew her to be unsympathetic to Kate Catchpole's plight, she felt the maid might conceive it her duty to report the matter to Caspar; or if not directly to him, then to Warner or the housekeeper.

In the circumstances her only recourse was to buy a plain blouse and skirt and the plainest possible hat. Also, a lockable hatbox in which to conceal them from Burton's prying eyes.

The purchase of these was not a problem, since on

their arrival in London Caspar had opened accounts
at various emporiums for her. However, the expense
of engaging a hansom to take her to Clerkenwell, and
her wish to help Kate with a present of money and
baby clothes, were hurdles that could be surmounted,
she decided, only by selling the watch bequeathed to
her by Père d'Espinay.

Loath as she was to part with it, she could see no
alternative. Although Caspar had been extremely
generous in the matter of her dress allowance, the
only ready money she ever handled was the sovereign
he gave her to put in the collection box on Sunday.

Otherwise money was unnecessary. She had the
brougham to convey her wherever she wished to go,
and if she wanted to buy something at a shop where
she had no account she had only to show her card
and ask for the bill to be sent to her husband.
Whether Caspar studied such bills, and the items
listed on the accounts, she had no idea. But in case he
did, it seemed advisable to pay for the baby clothes
with cash.

Her visit to a jeweler to sell the watch was not as
fraught with embarrassment as she feared. Not wishing to be observed by anyone who might know her,
she called at the shop she had chosen at an hour when
most people were having luncheon.

She had been there before with Sylvia, who had
bought a silver rattle with a coral teething ring for a
godchild. On that occasion Sylvia had been attended
to by the proprietor of the establishment, but fortunately he was not present when Flora paid her second visit. She was ushered to a chair at one of the
velvet-topped tables by a much younger man, perhaps his son.

She had thought he would show astonishment at a lady wishing to sell something. But he seemed unsurprised at her somewhat hesitant explanation. Having examined the watch, he asked her to excuse him while he went behind the scenes to discuss the work of putting it in order.

While he was gone Flora realized that deep in her heart she had hoped he would tell her he could not resell such an object. Much as she wished to help Kate, the prospect of parting with her treasure made her deeply depressed.

Unaware that from an inner room she was being observed by the proprietor, she rose from the chair and began to pace restlessly about, looking without interest at the silver and jewels displayed in the showcases. Before long the young man returned and offered her twenty guineas, more than she had hoped to receive.

Her sacrifice was rewarded a little while later when she had the enjoyment of choosing a selection of clothes for Kate's baby. The assistant, concluding that she was buying the layette for her own child, was inclined to display tiny garments designed for an upper-class infant tended by a nurse and two nursemaids. Temptingly pretty though they were, Flora had too much common sense to think them a practical present for someone in Kate's shoes. In addition to the things for the baby, she brought a light warm cape for Kate, since it would be winter, and chilly, before the young mother was confined. Having completed her purchases, she asked for the parcel to be kept at the shop until she called for it.

She returned to Park Lane to find a long telegram from Brighton awaiting her. The old lady's life was still in the balance, and Caspar was remaining at her bedside in case she recovered consciousness.

The following afternoon, as soon as Burton had left to visit a friend who was also a lady's maid, Flora forsook the chaise longue on which she was supposed to be resting. Hurriedly she dressed for her role as a well-bred but penniless young woman in search of a place as a governess.

She had taken care to buy a blouse that she could fasten unaided, and it was not too difficult to braid her hair and wind the braid into a bun, on top of which she perched a plain straw hat.

The proprietress of the employment agency was a severe-looking woman whose expression became more disapproving as Flora entered her office and obeyed her instruction to be seated.

Having taken down Flora's particulars, she said, "I will endeavor to place you, Miss Jackson, but it will *not* be easy, I fear. Such few qualifications as you have are more suitable for a tutor than a governess. You have character references, of course?"

"No—but I'm sure I could get some," Flora assured her.

"In view of your, er, foreign blood, I feel it would also be advisable to show your certificate of birth. You have it with you, no doubt?"

Flora was forced to shake her head. "I was born in China. I don't think they have such things there."

Miss Marchant raised her thin eyebrows. "You were baptized, I presume?"

"I don't know," Flora admitted.

Two patches of irritable color appeared on Miss Marchant's gaunt cheeks.

"I hope you don't mean to tell me that your

parents were unmarried, Miss Jackson. *That* would unquestionably preclude any possibility of your being considered a suitable person to have charge of innocent children.''

It was lowering to find that Caspar had been right. Clearly, unless she could furnish some official proofs of respectability, her prospects were poor if not hopeless. She could not even be certain that Helen or Sylvia would give her character references. Although they professed to be her friends, they might not wish to be a party to her defiance of her husband.

THE NEXT DAY she collected the parcel and went to see Kate. She had been prepared to find the girl living in a slum; however, when at last the cab horse came to a standstill at the pavement's edge, it was on the corner of a street that, although poor and drab by Park Lane standards, was by no means the squalid alley she had expected.

Indeed at that moment the street presented a spectacle that made her eyes brighten with surprise and pleasure. Halfway along it a man was winding the handle of a barrel organ, and all around him children were dancing to the music.

"Now there's a sight I likes to see. Cheers you up, does the old hurdy-gurdy," said the cabbie as Flora paid him.

As he touched his hat and drove off, she felt a pang of misgiving. They seemed to have come a long way from the part of London she knew. However, as she approached the source of the music her spirits revived.

The dancers were nearly all girls between the ages of four and twelve, their shabby dark dresses pro-

tected by voluminous white pinafores, some clean
and crisply starched and some bedraggled and
stained. They all wore black stockings and boots, and
most wore straw hats. They danced in groups or
pairs, their pasty faces alight with enjoyment; and
from doorways and upstairs windows they were
watched by tired-looking women, the children too
young to dance and the old people whose dancing
days were long over.

She stopped to watch for a few minutes. Suddenly,
instead of feeling adrift in unfamiliar surroundings,
as she had at first, she began to feel oddly at home.
Although there was no physical resemblance, the
street had something of the atmosphere of a Chinese
village; the cooking smells, the shouted remarks, the
sense of a small community in which everyone knew
everyone else—all combined to remind her strongly
of the village near the mission.

The only difference was that Wang Chia Miao was
so remote from the rest of the world that the coming
of a stranger, particularly a foreign-looking person,
would have attracted much attention. Whereas in
Sebastopol Street, Clerkenwell, her arrival seemed to
pass almost unnoticed.

Not entirely unnoticed, however. Before she
turned away from the dancing to look for the house
numbered 39, a touch on her arm made her swivel to
find Kate standing by her.

"Kate...Kate, how are you?" she exclaimed,
clasping the maid's hands in hers.

"I thought I was seeing things, m'lady. Whatever
brings you down here?"

"I've come to see you. I've been worried about
you. Are you well? How are you living?"

"I'm better now," the girl said. "At first I felt sick all the time, but that seems to have stopped, I'm pleased to say. How did you know where to find me, m'lady?"

"When I found out what had happened I went to see your mother. That was before she had heard from you. As soon as she knew where you were, she let me have your address. May we go there and talk more privately?"

"Yes. . .yes, of course, m'lady. It's this way."

As they walked down the street, Flora said in a low tone that wouldn't be overheard, "We aren't mistress and maid any longer, so there's no need to call me 'm'lady' every time you speak. I was very distressed by your dismissal, the more so when I found your father was not prepared to stand by you. I'm surprised you should welcome me here, considering how harshly you were treated."

"I don't blame you for that, m'lady. It was old Mrs. Foster who turned me off, and I can't really blame her, can I? It's my own fault I'm in the family way. I shouldn't have done what I did. I knew it was wrong when I gave in to him."

"Did you tell him there was a baby coming?"

"What for?" said Kate with a shrug. "He'd gone by the time I was sure; I reckon he had a wife somewhere. But it's lucky I had Gertie to help me. I don't know what I'd have done if it hadn't been for her. Thrown myself in the river, I reckon."

"Who is Gertie?"

"She's my cousin—my mother's sister's girl. She was in service at first, but she didn't like it so she came up to London and found a place as a barmaid in a theater up West. She has to work ever so late, but she don't mind that so long as the wages is good. I expect you'll meet her. She's out at the moment, seeing her dressmaker, but I shouldn't think she'll be gone long.''

By this time they had reached number 39, which, like all the others in the row and those opposite, was a narrow-fronted house with two windows one above the other. Flora stepped through the door from the pavement into the parlor.

The room within was concealed from the eyes of curious neighbors by thick lace curtains at the window and a large green baize four-fold screen arranged to form a kind of vestibule. The screen, unadorned on the outer side, was decorated on the inside with a profusion of picture postcards.

''They're theatrical people Gertie knows,'' Kate explained, seeing Flora's interested glance. ''Would you like a cup of tea, m'lady? I was going to make one for myself when I heard the organ starting and went out to see the fun.''

''Yes, please, Kate. What an interesting room! I've never seen anyplace like it.''

''Gertie doesn't believe in keeping the front room for best. You should see her bedroom, m'lady. It's lovely—all pink and gold. She keeps all her hats on hooks all over the walls, so she can enjoy looking at them when she's in bed.'' Kate laughed. ''She's a character, is Gertie.''

She disappeared into the inner room, leaving Flora to gaze her fill at a parlor bright with color and so crowded with curious objects that the sight of it was an almost physical shock. Clearly Cousin Gertie was a person whose taste in furnishings was influenced not by current fashions but by her own fads and fancies, the most immediately noticeable being an enthusiasm for the glitter of gilt.

All the furniture was either gilded, enriched with ormolu mounts or inlaid with patterns of brass. Indeed the chairs by the fireplace, which had arms and legs in the form of lions' heads and paws, were out of a style that Flora associated with the staterooms of very grand houses. How a barmaid had come by such things she couldn't imagine.

The walls of the parlor were papered in vivid emerald green, which would have been overpowering had not most of it been hidden by paintings, elaborate gilt mirrors and colorful china ornaments standing on gilded brackets.

When Kate returned Flora said, "In your note to your mother, you mentioned looking for work. Have you found any?"

The maid shook her head. "Gertie says she'll keep me till the baby's born. I can clean the house and wash and cook for her, and I'm earning a little sewing on trimmings for her dressmaker. Gertie says when I've got my figure back she'll find me a job with her up West."

"But who will look after the baby?"

"I will, during the day. When I'm out in the evening I'll have to pay someone to mind it. Gertie thinks I'm silly to have it. She wanted me to go to a woman she knows who gets rid of babies for girls in trouble. But I've heard you can die from what they do to you, so I didn't fancy it. This sounds like her coming home now," she finished as the sound of brisk feminine footsteps could be heard approaching the front door.

Flora's first glimpse of Gertie was a swirl of pale

blue ostrich feathers fanned by the breeze from the opening and closing of the door.

"We've a visitor, Gertie," Kate announced.

"Oh, 'ave we—'oo?" The hat passed behind the screen and its owner stepped into view.

"This is Lady Carlyon, who I told you about."

Gertie stood with her hands on her hips and looked Flora up and down.

"Lady Carlyon, eh? Well, I never!"

Masking her surprise, Flora rose and held out her hand. "How do you do, Miss. . . . I'm sorry, I don't know your surname."

"Forget the 'Miss.' Call me Gertie." The gleam of amusement in her eyes mingled with a certain wariness. "And what brings you 'ere, your Ladyship?" she inquired.

"I've brought some things for Kate's baby."

"Very kind, I'm sure; although it might 'ave been more 'elp to 'er if you'd kept 'er on until 'er time came."

"Gertie, you know it had nothing to do with Lady Carlyon," Kate protested, looking embarrassed.

"So you say, but she was your mistress, weren't she? If I was rich and 'ad servants, I wouldn't send a girl packin' and refuse to give 'er a character just because of what you did."

"Nor would I," Flora intervened. "It was my housekeeper who dismissed Kate. As soon as I found out what had happened, I gave her instructions never to do so again. The fact is, I'm afraid, that I'm a very inexperienced mistress. As Kate may have told you, I've been in England only a short time, and the way of life here is strange to me. Believe me, I know what it's like to be alone in the world, without relations or friends or anywhere to take refuge. I should always do everything I could to help any girl in similar difficulties.''

Gertie said nothing for some moments. She appeared to be weighing Flora's sincerity, while Kate looked anxiously from one to the other.

At last the red-haired girl said, ''I suppose you must 'ave a good 'eart, else you wouldn't 'ave come all this way. You'd be lyin' down in your boodwar, not giving a thought to 'ow the likes of us lives.''

Flora could not resist saying, ''*You* seem to live very comfortably.''

''Oh, yes—I'm not complainin'. Though I earn my comforts, by Gawd I do!'' Gertie retorted.

She unpinned and took off her hat and, using the brim as a screen, gave Flora a warning wink not to let slip their previous encounter. But Flora had already grasped that Kate was as yet unaware of the true nature of her cousin's livelihood. Did Gertie see Kate as a likely recruit for the Promenade, she wondered uneasily.

''It's not every day we have a lady of title to tea, so let's 'ave somethin' better than sugar in it, shall we?'' Gertie suggested.

She opened a cupboard and produced a bottle of whiskey.

Flora did not demur when a liberal dash of the spirit was added to her cup of tea. She had first drunk tea made in the European way on board the ship from Shanghai and had yet to acquire a taste for it. Sometimes she felt a great yearning to drink fragrant jasmine tea, unadulterated with milk, from a porcelain bowl.

The whiskey gave the tea a pleasant aroma, which

she sniffed appreciatively before saying, "While Kate was making this, I was admiring your furnishings. They are very unusual and interesting."

"Yes, that's what I think," said Gertie. "I bought these two chairs and the sofa off a rag-an'-bone man I know. 'E 'as 'em off an old girl what'd died, but whether she was a nob come down in the world, or 'ad been in service and 'ad 'em given to 'er, 'e couldn't say. Some of my china I bought in the Caledonian Market up the Camden Road of a Friday. Course this 'ouse is too small to show off posh furniture. It'll look better when I gets a bigger place. It ain't rented, you know," she added ingenuously. "It was goin' cheap and I bought it out of me savings. I don't mean to end in the gutter like some girls do."

"I'm sure you won't."

Flora was forming the opinion that Gertie had a shrewd ambitious nature that would have been wasted in domestic service. Had it not been for the way she made her living, she would have felt nothing but liking for her. Indeed in this little East End house, drinking laced tea with a demirep and a disgraced housemaid, she felt more at home than she had for months.

The consciousness of it depressed her. It seemed to prove that in spite of Père d'Espinay's insistence on a classical education and cultivated manners, he had failed to change a buzzard into a sparrow hawk; or as the English would put it, to make a silk purse from a sow's ear.

When it was time for Flora to leave, Gertie said that since cabs were not often to be found in that neighborhood, she would see her safely onto a tram.

Kate would have come with them, but her cousin prevented her by saying, "No, you look tired, dearie. You 'ave a nice rest for 'alf an hour."

"These are a few things for the baby," said Flora, giving Kate the parcel. "If I may, I'll come to see you again."

"Oh, thank you, m'lady. You are kind. You'll always be welcome, anytime."

In the street Flora said, "Kate tells me that after the baby is born she is going to work with you. Do you think she can stand the late hours?"

"I don't see as 'ow stayin' up late is no worse for the 'ealth than draggin' out of bed at half-past six on a cold winter morning to clean the grates and light fires and take up cans of 'ot water," Gertie said dryly. "What you mean, I reckon, is you don't approve of my sort."

Before Flora could answer she went on, "Well, I don't like my life, either, but it's better than workin' for a sweater. You don't know about sweaters, I daresay. They run the workshops—mostly down Whitechapel way, and St. George's-in-the-East— where women work twelve hours a day for no more than five bob a week."

"Oh, how frightful!" Flora exclaimed.

"Yes, and dirty, filthy conditions with as many as a dozen workers crowded into a space no bigger than my front room. All you ladies and duchesses and suchlike, when you put on your pretty evenin' shoes you never think that the poor wretch 'oo stitched the beads on was only paid ninepence. Not for just the one pair, mind. Ninepence for twelve pairs!"

"But how can they live on such wages?"

"They don't live long," said Gertie sardonically.

"And while they are alive they never 'ave a full belly. Which work would you chose, m'lady? Slavin' all day for a sweater, or smilin' all night at the Empire?"

"When you put it like that there's no choice. But surely your work must have some unpleasant aspects? You yourself implied as much earlier."

"Oh, yes, it's no bed of roses," Gertie agreed. "It's not so bad while you're young and pretty and can take your pick of the customers. But it's not so good later on when you 'ave to be nice to anyone who takes a fancy to you. There's drawbacks, I won't deny—and keepin' late hours ain't the only risk to your 'ealth," she added with a sour grimace. "But at least my gums won't turn blue like they would if I worked in some factories, and I don't get tipsy on benzine like the girls 'oo French-clean your gloves."

"I had no idea of these things," Flora said, deeply shocked. "In China, where I grew up, there's always a great deal of hardship and sometimes terrible famines. But I thought it was different in England. It struck me when I arrived in this part of London that the children dancing in the street did look very pale and spindly legged, but—"

"Clerkenwell ain't a poor part, not compared with Poplar and 'Ackney. You'll see plenty of children down there with no boots on, winter or summer. A tuppenny eel-and-meat pie is their day's food often as not."

Flora was silent, her own problems swept from her mind by this glimpse of how many people lived in a city where those like herself enjoyed every form of self-indulgence.

Did Sylvia know this? Did Helen, she wondered.

And came to the conclusion they must be as ignorant as she; for how could any wealthy person sleep soundly knowing that elsewhere in London children had gone to bed hungry?

"That chap you was with the other night—was that 'is Lordship?" asked Gertie.

"What? Oh, yes—yes, that was my husband."

"I could do with an 'usband like 'im," Gertie said with a chuckle. "Rich, titled *and* tall and 'andsome. What's the fly in the ointment?"

"I—I don't understand you?"

"'Aven't you 'eard that expression? It means what's the snag? Where's the catch?"

"The snag is that I love him but he doesn't love me," Flora answered.

No sooner were the words spoken than she was amazed at herself. To confide in Gertie, of all people! What had possessed her?

"More fool 'im," said Gertie tersely. "'Ow d'you know 'e don't love you? Got a fancy woman somewhere, 'as 'e?"

Flora said nothing, which the other girl took for assent.

"Which of 'em ain't?" she said cynically. "You don't want to let it get you down, dear."

Flora searched for a way to change the subject, but before she could think of one Gertie went on, "I wouldn't 'ave took 'im for a ladies' man. 'E didn't give me the glad eye, and a chap with a weakness for the fair sex will usually look at 'em all, the same as a racin' gent admires every nice piece of 'orseflesh 'e 'appens to see."

"How did you get on with the officer on leave from Africa?"

"'E was ever so nice. A real gentleman—which I can't say for all as calls theirselves gents," answered Gertie. "After the show 'e took me to supper at Romano's, in one of their private rooms, y'know. Laugh—well, 'e made me shriek at some of the tales 'e told."

"But even when someone is pleasant and amusing, as he was, don't you find it very disagreeable to have to...that is...." Flora felt her face turning red. "I have a friend who can't bear it even with her husband."

They were turning a corner as she spoke. Instead of replying, Gertie let out a screech and began to make urgent signals to the conductor of a horse bus that seemed to be on the point of departure from its stop some way down the road.

"That'll do you better than the tram. Come on, dearie—run!" she urged Flora.

They each grabbed a handful of skirt and began to run as fast as their heels, their corsets and the weight of their petticoats would allow.

"Look sharp now, ladies. Can't 'ang about 'ere all day, y'know," said the beaming bowler-hatted conductor when they were within a few yards of him.

He helped Flora mount the step.

"I'm not coming—only 'er. See she gets off where she can get a cab easy, will you, duck?" panted Gertie.

Breathless, Flora subsided onto the seat nearest the platform and waved goodbye to her new friend. By the time the conductor had collected the fares from the passengers on the upper deck, she had recovered her breath and decided it would be more fun to experience this unaccustomed form of transport from the vantage point of an open-air seat on the top.

"Are all the seats upstairs taken?" she asked him.

"I expect we can find one for you, miss." He ushered her onto the winding staircase. "'Old tight to the rail. We don't want you slippin' and sprainin' one o' them pretty ankles."

Although she could see that the upper deck would be uncomfortably exposed in winter weather, on a hot summer afternoon she enjoyed the ride more than the journey in the hansom.

It was a relief to have Kate in comfortable circumstances, if only until the birth of her child. However, although she accepted the logic of Gertie's plans for her cousin's future, Flora felt there must be some way for Kate to support herself without suffering the miseries of the sweatshop or joining the half-world. The most obvious remedy was to reinstate her at Longwarden; but she had little confidence that the other staff would treat her kindly. Though the underservants might do so, Mrs. Foster and Burton certainly would not.

She thought how pleasant it would be to have a modest income of her own—perhaps a hundred and fifty or two hundred pounds a year—on which she and Kate and the baby could live in a cozy cottage somewhere in the country. Kate could keep house while she immersed herself in the riches of English literature, for which the library at Longwarden had whetted her appetite.

Her daydream of peaceful seclusion, surrounded by books, was interrupted by the conductor. He had come to tell her they would soon reach a part of the city where she would have no trouble hiring a cab.

"Where are you going, miss?" he asked as she followed him down the staircase.

Without thinking she answered, "Park Lane."

"Park Lane, eh?" He looked impressed. "What sort o' place are you after? 'Ousemaid? Lady's maid?"

It seemed simplest to say, "Lady's maid."

"I thought so," he said with a nod. He was a dapper young man with a stiff mustache and a spick-and-span collar and tie.

"Oh, did you? Why?" she asked, amused.

"You've the style of a lady's maid some'ow. A bit more class than an 'ousemaid. Are you walking out?"

For a moment the question puzzled her. Then she realized that, thinking she might be single and wishing for a follower, the conductor was interested in her.

"I'm married," she answered with a smile.

He looked disappointed. "Is your 'usband a soldier?"

"No. He...he's a gardener."

"My brother's a soldier," he told her. "'E's married, but 'e ain't on the married roll for 'is corps, so 'is wife 'as to keep 'er situation as an 'ousemaid. If you ain't on the roll they won't give you a room in the married quarters, or the coal allowance, and you can't keep a wife on five and threepence a week."

"Is that all a soldier is paid?" Flora asked in astonishment.

"'E could get nine bob in the Foot Guards, but then they deduct for 'is groceries and greens, and 'is washin'."

When she had stepped down from the bus and the

conductor had tipped his hat to her and wished her good luck with her interview, Flora walked along Oxford Street pondering all she had learned. She felt rather as she thought her father must have felt when an arduous trek was rewarded by finding a new or rare species.

Today there was no telegram from Brighton awaiting her. She told the butler that instead of dining downstairs she would prefer a light supper to be brought to her bedroom.

"You may have the evening off, Burton. I shan't need you again," she told her maid when she had changed into a tea gown and Burton had unpinned her hair for her and given it one hundred brush strokes.

Had her mind been free from worry, she would have enjoyed her solitary supper of veal cutlets with sea kale, followed by rice flummery with stewed peaches. But she knew that Caspar's absence was only a brief hiatus, and soon she would have to resume the whirligig of balls and receptions.

After supper she lay on the chaise longue reading *The Ordeal of Richard Feverel* by George Meredith, a novelist and poet now in his seventies who, so someone had told her, had done more than any other contemporary writer to reveal women to women, and women to men.

Suddenly, without warning, her husband walked into the room.

"Caspar! When did you get back?" she exclaimed, greatly startled by his unexpected appearance.

He must have been in the house for some time. He was wearing his dressing gown, and his hair was still damp from a shower bath.

"About half an hour ago." He came toward the chaise longue, where he held out his hand. When she gave him hers he bent to touch his lips to her knuckles. "Nurse died early this morning but will not be buried until Friday. I shall go back to Brighton for the funeral. Come in," he called then in response to a knock at the door.

Durrell, his valet, entered with a tray.

"You have already eaten, I believe, but perhaps you will join me in a glass of wine," Caspar said to her. "I understand nothing of moment has happened during my absence."

"No, nothing," she agreed as he seated himself on the end of the chaise longue and reached down to pat Jacopo. The dog had left his basket and trotted across the room to sit at Caspar's feet.

"I'm sorry the old lady has died," she added. "Was she conscious when you arrived? Did she know you?"

"Yes, and died without pain, I'm glad to say. She was eighty-four—I was the last of her charges—and a devout believer in an afterlife. There is no cause for grief," he replied, his tone matter-of-fact.

"No, but there is always some sadness when a person one has loved is no longer there."

As Jacopo leaped up beside her, Flora made room for him to curl himself close to her thigh.

Having filled two glasses with chilled hock, Durrell bade them good-night and withdrew. Caspar handed her one of the glasses before helping himself to a cold roast beef sandwich. While he ate he made conversation; as if they were strangers who found themselves sitting side by side at a dinner party rather than a husband and his wife in the intimacy of her bedroom.

She sipped the fine dry Rheingau wine and stroked the pug's thick glossy fur. If this was how Caspar chatted to the women who did sit beside him at dinner parties, no wonder they enjoyed his company. He exerted himself to be agreeable to far greater effect than most of her table companions, whose interminable prosing on the dullest of subjects made it hard to listen attentively.

"That's a very fetching garment you're wearing," he said presently.

She glanced down at the filmy folds of accordion-pleated gold chiffon falling from an ecru guipure yoke.

"Thank you. It's one of Lady Duff Gordon's designs. It's called 'Golden Spring Moon over the Nile.' All her designs have very fanciful names."

"I think I shall call you that in future—when we're alone." He paused to refill their glasses. "From now on, instead of *ya-t'ou*, you will be Golden Spring Moon."

Flora felt her breath catch in her throat. He was speaking in the very same tone Captain Cromer had used when flirting with her. The difference was that the caressing flatteries the captain had murmured in her ear had left her unmoved, even vexed; but when Caspar exerted his charm he was irresistible.

He rose and set down his glass before snapping his fingers to the dog, who lifted his head and after a moment's hesitation uncurled and jumped to the floor.

Caspar crossed the room to Jacopo's basket, picked it up and, with the dog at his heels, disappeared into the adjoining bedroom, where she heard him telling her pet to stay.

"Wh-why have you put him in your room?" she asked when her husband returned.

He sat down where the dog had been lying, removing the glass from her fingers and expertly slipping an arm around her.

"Tonight *I* am going to guard you."

"But I—"

Her protest was stifled as he kissed her, instantly breaking down her will to resist him.

A long time later, having lifted her onto his lap and removed the tea gown and also her velvet slippers with the satin rosettes on the toes, leaving her barefoot and clad in nothing but a gossamer petticoat, he stood up with her in his arms and carried her to the bed.

SHE WAS WOKEN by the sound of the wooden rings sliding along the polished mahogany pole as Burton opened the curtains.

Flora liked to brush her teeth before breakfast. Usually she had done this and was sitting up in bed, reading, by the time her maid came to wake her, followed five minutes later by another maid bearing her breakfast tray.

This morning she came awake slowly. It wasn't until she saw Burton picking up and shaking out the crumpled tea gown that she remembered what had happened last night and realized that under the bedclothes she was naked.

Without sitting up she said, "Good morning, Burton. I—I should like a . . . a Bath bun for breakfast. Would you go down and have someone sent out to buy one for me, please."

"A Bath bun, m'lady?" Burton looked astonished.

As well she might, thought Flora, suppressing a strong desire to laugh.

"Yes, a Bath bun. There must be a bakery nearby. If they can't supply one, I'm sure Harrods will be able to."

She had discovered that when the household was in London, everything used in the kitchen was either sent up from Longwarden or purchased from Harrods, the city's largest department store. This emporium was distinguished not only by being even larger than William Whiteley's and by its telegraphic address "Everything London," but also, for the past five years, by its amazing moving staircase. When it was introduced there had been an attendant at the top to administer brandy or sal volatile to customers unnerved by their first ascent on it.

"Yes, m'lady."

Clearly much taken aback by her mistress's whim for one of the candied-peel buns that were usually eaten at teatime—and more often in the schoolroom than the drawing room—Burton hurried from the room.

Normally Flora's nightgown and peignoir were laid out on the bed during the evening, either by Burton or by the housemaid who turned down the bed. Last night, however, Burton had been off duty and Caspar must have told Durrell that they were not to be disturbed.

Since the fire at Longwarden Flora had made a point of being able to find her belongings. It did not take long to slip out of bed and put on a nightgown and dressing cape.

Then, as usual, she brushed her teeth and washed her face before returning to bed.

As she sat up awaiting her breakfast, she was able to let her mind dwell on the change that had come upon her since yesterday. No longer—to borrow a phrase from Keats's "Ode on a Grecian Urn"—a "still unravished bride," she was at last fully a woman.

As she thought of the incredible difference between the Frenchman's brutality and Caspar's gentleness, she was filled with gratitude toward him. No man, she felt sure, could have been more patient, more tender.

If only his physical tenderness had found some expression in words. If only his slow skillful lovemaking had not been confined to caresses but had included whispered endearments, and the words that had hovered on her own lips: *I love you*.

She had fallen asleep in his arms. During the night he had woken her with kisses before making love to her again. After that she had slept too deeply to have any recollection of his leaving her to return to his bedroom.

Now, examining her reactions, she was conscious first of a strong sense of bodily well-being and second of a great deal of mental relief, because the mystery was a mystery no longer.

But in her heart there was even greater desolation. For she knew that taking possession of her had meant no more to him than bedding any willing woman. He had pleasured dozens and no doubt would continue to do so. Why should he not? In his world, where so much was "not done," to enjoy a discreet liaison was one of the things that *was* done—as often as possible.

She was dipping a spoon into a lightly boiled egg

when Caspar opened the door connecting their bed-rooms.

"Good morning, Flora." He glanced over his shoulder. "You may bring the basket in, Durrell."

Dressed to go out, and followed by Jacopo and his valet, he came into her room and approached the bed.

"Good morning. Good morning, Durrell."

Her cheeks flushed with sudden confusion, Flora laid down her spoon and strove to retain some self-possession in the face of her husband's quizzical smile as he strolled toward her.

"Don't let me interrupt your breakfast," he said, seating himself on the edge of the bed. "How did you sleep?"

"Very well, thank you. No, Jacopo, you know you are not allowed to jump up here," she warned as the black pug looked hopefully up at her.

"He will have to be trained not to snore," said Caspar. "I object to sharing my bedroom with a dog that sounds like an old man sleeping off a heavy lunch and too much claret."

By this time Durrell had withdrawn, allowing him to add with a teasing look, "Or, if that is impossible, you will have to surrender your privacy and allow me to stay with you all night."

"I didn't ask you to leave me. I thought you would stay...now," she answered, her gaze fixed on the pot of honey beside the silver toast rack.

"No, you didn't—but I know how much you value your solitude." He put his hand under her chin. "Look at me, Spring Moon."

With reluctant obedience she raised her long lashes and met his amused gray eyes.

"Do you find yourself more resigned now? To your sex and to our marriage?" he inquired.

She swallowed a tightness in her throat. "I shall not be afraid anymore," she said in a low voice.

"I hope you will never be afraid of me." He leaned across the breakfast tray to kiss her lightly on the lips.

As he straightened, Burton came in carrying a silver cake basket.

"Oh, I beg pardon, m'lady. I didn't know his Lordship was with you, or I should have knocked."

Flora said, "It doesn't matter. Is that the Bath bun? Thank you, Burton."

When the maid had gone she explained, "I don't usually have Bath buns for breakfast, but I couldn't think of any other way to get rid of her."

"Why was it necessary to get rid of her?"

"Because she is rather a prim person. I think she would have been shocked had she seen that I had nothing on. She looked very disapproving that my tea gown was on the floor."

"I suspect that her mistress was somewhat shocked, too," he said mockingly. "Were it not for the servants' conjectures if your door were found locked at this hour, I should be tempted to rejoin you. But I have appointments this morning, so that is a pleasure that must be deferred until later. We are dining with the Goughs, I believe, before going on to Lady Kerr's ball. I suggest we leave the ball early, having better things to do with ourselves."

With a pat on her cheek he stood up and left her to finish her breakfast by herself.

THAT NIGHT he made love to her again, and Flora lay in his arms aching with longing to pour out her innermost feelings, but knowing they would only embarrass him.

Other nights followed when he would have left the lamp alight had she not begged him to extinguish it. It was not, as he seemed to think, that she was still shy of exposing her body to his gaze. What she wanted to hide were her emotions. In the light, even if she kept her eyes closed, she was afraid her face would give her away.

For the same reason, although she could not prevent herself from responding to his caresses, she never allowed herself to touch him lovingly or to press her lips to his shoulder when she lay beneath him, their bodies still fused but the storm spent. There were many nights when afterward she felt like sobbing her heart out. But the tears remained pent up inside her. She never shed them.

Very soon it was painfully apparent that Caspar's initial appetite for her was waning. He continued to share her bed, but more and more often without touching her. Sometimes after beginning to make love to her he would suddenly stop and turn away.

She longed to know why but dared not ask. The only reason she could think of was that he was bored with her body—being accustomed to more opulent female flesh—and with her passive submission.

But although when he moved away she felt not relief but rather a perverse longing to snuggle against him and try to rekindle his desire, she never succumbed to the impulse. As she had already discovered, without giving her heart and soul she could not surrender her body without a sense of guilt—and Caspar did not want her heart.

She was his wife and might soon be the bearer of his child. But once the first of his heirs was *fait accompli*, she had a depressing conviction that he

would return to his own room; and from then on
would only come to her bed when further propaga-
tion was necessary.

During this unhappy time she took a cab to Clerkenwell as often as her other engagements allowed.
Usually she was accompanied by the black pug.
When she had been several times, the street children
began to greet her and to chaff her about her ugly
pet.

One day she found Kate minding two children.
Their father was dead and their mother had been
taken to hospital. One was three years old. The other
was a lively infant whom Flora held on her lap so that
Kate could get on with some sewing.

Gertie was not there. She was on a Thames steamer
excursion with some other barmaids, said Kate, still
unaware of her cousin's true occupation.

Flora was late home that day. She had lingered
longer than usual because Kate seemed in low spirits.
As a result she missed the bus and had to walk much
of the way. By the time she arrived in Park Lane she
was beginning to fear that she might have to account
for her lateness. It was past the hour when she should
have been in her bath before dressing for the evening's dinner party.

To her relief she was able to slip into the house and
to scurry upstairs without being seen.

Her maid was not in the bedroom. Thinking she
must be in the adjoining bathroom, she called,
"Burton...Burton, I'm here! I've been delayed. I
haven't time for a bath. Quickly, come and unfasten
me, will you? My hair needs dressing more than
anything."

As she spoke she flung up her skirt and rested one

foot on her dressing stool, the better to unlace her boot.

"Burton is not here at present, but I can unfasten you."

Flora gasped.

She looked around to see Caspar rising from the comfortable chair in the corner of the room beyond her bed. He was already dressed in evening clothes. As she saw his eyes on her upraised leg, her involuntary reaction was to put her foot to the ground and shake down her skirt.

"You're too modest," he said, smiling at her. "After all, this is your bedroom and I am your husband."

Although greatly taken aback, she was still impelled by the need to be ready for their guests, and her hands went up to her hat and felt for the two long pins that held it in place.

As she cast it aside, Caspar said, "Yes, your hair does seem rather disheveled. How did that come about?"

Without waiting for her reply, he took her lightly by the shoulders, spun her around and began to undo the buttons that fastened her blouse.

It was only then, with her back to him, that she recognized the tigerish quality of his smile.

"Wh-where is Burton?" she stammered.

"I sent her away. I wish to talk to you."

"Couldn't it wait until later? Our guests will be here in an hour, and it takes half an hour to dress my hair."

He did not reply but continued to deal with the buttons until he undid the last one and opened the back of the blouse.

"You may take it off now," he told her. She felt his hands at her waist and knew he was undoing her skirt.

Her camisole was one he had bought her, with shoulder straps that were little more than wisps of lace threaded with pale green baby ribbon. As she drew the sleeves of the blouse down her arms, she waited for him to explode at the sight of her tightly laced waist. To her surprise, he seemed not to notice the corset.

"Where have you been this afternoon?"

"I—I've been leaving cards and paying calls."

"On foot?"

"I like to walk sometimes, and it's good for Jacopo." She freed her wrists from the sleeves but kept the blouse clutched to her chest.

"I was under the impression that calling ended at half-past five."

"It does, but my last call was to a friend who had no other visitors. We were chatting and didn't notice how late it was."

"Indeed? And which friend was this?"

"I don't believe you are acquainted with her."

"I'm quite sure I'm not."

With heavier hands than before, he swung her to face him. He had undone not only her waistband but also the tapes of her petticoats. The sudden twisting of her body made them start to slide down her hips.

"Are you sure it was *her* and not *him*?"

"Of course it was *her*. One doesn't pay calls on men."

Caspar swept the blouse from her grasp and flung it away. With a face like thunder he said, "You play the shrinking violet with great conviction, Flora, but

I am no longer convinced by your timidity. You've been in society long enough to know as well as I do that assignations frequently take place during the at-home hours. Who is this mysterious person whom you know but I do not? And why do you hurry home late, with your bodice not properly fastened and your hair in disorder? Can it be that you are a cheat and I am a fool? That while I've been restraining myself, some other damned blackguard has been making love to you?''

PART FIVE

POND COTTAGE

CHAPTER ONE

"YOU MUST BE MAD!" she exclaimed. "How can you think such a thing? The reason my hair is untidy is that I've been playing with two small children. One of them rumpled my hair, and I suppose the other must have been playing with my buttons while I was talking to Kate."

"An undisciplined brood, by the sound of it," he said with sharp sarcasm. "Most small children spend the afternoon in the park with their nurse. When they are allowed in the drawing room they are certainly never permitted to tousle the guests. Come, come—think of something more plausible."

She saw that from his point of view it was not a convincing explanation. In his world it was usual for children to stay in the country during the season; or if they were brought to London, they took little part in their parents' lives. Sylvia saw her children for only half an hour a day. Sometimes, dressed for a ball, she would go up to bid them good-night.

"Nevertheless it's the truth," Flora answered. She was mustering her courage to add, "There are no drawing rooms in Clerkenwell, and the children *are* very unruly," when Caspar interrupted her.

"What have you to say about this?" he challenged, unfolding and thrusting at her a paper he'd taken from his pocket.

It was, she soon saw, a letter to him from a firm of jewelers—the jewelers to whom she had sold Père d'Espinay's watch. They wrote that although the watch might have seemed an unimportant trinket to her Ladyship, investigation had revealed that it was of considerable antiquity and, if sold to a French connoisseur, would fetch a sum of money considerably in excess of that paid to her Ladyship. Before disposing of it, therefore, they felt it proper to inquire if, in view of the rarity and historical interest of the watch, her Ladyship might prefer to retain it.

"I recovered it for you this morning," said Caspar when he saw she had finished reading. "Now perhaps you would care to explain the purpose that drove you to sell it."

"I—I wanted some money of my own."

"Having such a skinflint for a husband that you dared not ask him for even that trifling sum?" he said caustically.

"You don't understand," she protested. "Do you think I'm not constantly conscious of how generous you are to me? I don't forget it for a moment. I wasn't born into luxury, and it isn't likely that I'll ever take it for granted. But even a woman needs to feel a little independent."

"By that I suppose you mean you scrupled to ask me for money to pay your cab fares—the fares to your place of assignation. Don't trouble to deny it: I happened to see you stepping into a cab this afternoon, and no doubt other people have seen you on other occasions and drawn the same conclusion as I did. For all I know, half of London may be privy to these secret trysts of yours."

Her sense of injustice began to kindle her temper. "And that, I suppose, is what annoys you? The dreadful danger of scandal? The horrifying prospect of gossip? I could have any number of lovers as long as nobody suspected."

He had been angry before, but now his face took on a look that made her feel a thrust of panic. There was a devil in his eyes as he said to her softly, "So you admit it? You are embroiled in a liaison?"

A woman bred in England would have shrunk from him or tried to placate him. But Flora's upbringing had taught her to put a brave face on fear and to meet threats with cool disdain.

"You are being absurd," she said calmly. "Please go and allow me to dress." Forgetting her unfastened petticoats, she turned to walk to the bellpull, tripped on a trailing flounce and would have fallen headlong had not Caspar caught her as she lost her balance.

Perhaps he meant only to save her from hurting herself; but when, resenting his touch, she attempted to push him away, his gray eyes narrowed and gleamed with unpleasant mockery.

He drew her more firmly against him. "First you must *un*dress, my girl. Allow me to assist you." He pushed down one strap of her chemise and applied her lips to her bare shoulder.

She started to struggle, only to find herself clamped by one muscular arm while his free hand took an ungentle hold of her chin. He tilted her head back and kissed her.

He had kissed her before, many times, but never like this. His lips pressed savagely against hers, forcing them apart, his tongue invading her mouth and twining like a serpent around her tongue.

She sensed that the kiss was meant to be a punishment; that because he thought she had betrayed him, he was treating her like a harlot—and this was only the beginning of what he intended to do to her.

She began to struggle again, wrenching and straining to free herself. But her efforts were futile; she was as helpless against his strength as she had been with the Frenchman. Except that this was not a dirty drunken stranger with greasy hands and rotten yellow teeth. This was her husband, fastidiously clean, whose skin had a faint natural scent she would now recognize blindfold, and which was as pleasant to her nostrils as mown grass or leather or beeswax.

So why was she fighting him? Whatever he did to her could never be as terrible as what she had suffered at the mission.

But it was. In a different way, it was.

As her resistance slackened into submission, he tossed her facedown onto the bed with her knees at the edge. With a single violent wrench he removed her skirt and her petticoats. Her knickers, fastened at the waist by two small buttons, were the next thing to go.

For a moment she thought he had stripped her in order to spank her, and she gritted her teeth and waited for the first blow, her anger reviving at the humiliation of being chastised like a child for a sin she had not committed.

Instead, locking her legs between his hard powerful thighs, making it impossible for her to right herself, he began to unlace her corset.

Flora lay with her face twisted sideways, listening to his rapid angry breathing as his fingers ripped the silk laces out of their eyelets, releasing her waist from its tight cage of coutil and whalebone.

His touch deliberately lascivious, he stroked her

soft hips and buttocks, kneading her flesh with his fingers, trailing them down her bare thighs to the tops of her stockings. For a few seconds her legs were released while he rolled her onto her back, deftly unclipping her suspenders in order to free the corset and throw it aside. As she lay sprawled on the bed, vainly trying to pull down the hem of her camisole, he stood over her, cruelly appraising all she was trying to hide from him.

That he remained fully dressed while she was now virtually naked—for the gossamer texture of the camisole did not conceal her heaving bosom—was an indignity that made her struggle onto her elbows and then into a sitting position.

He did not, as she half expected, force her down again. Instead he grasped the camisole and pulled it over her head, leaving her totally nude. And then he went down on one knee and clipped her wrists firmly behind her while his free hand and his warm mouth made her tremble with unwilling pleasure as, slowly and with consummate sensuality, he caressed and kissed her small breasts until she was out of control, her head flung back, her eyes closed, breathing in short frenzied gasps as his tongue lapped the tip of her right breast and his fingers played with the other.

It seemed to go on forever, that exquisite humiliating torment against which she had no defense; to which she could only surrender with smothered whimpers of ecstasy as her insides melted like honey in the heat raging through her body.

From then on she was too bemused to be more than vaguely aware that her wrists were no longer imprisoned. She was allowed to sink backward while his mouth burned a path to her navel and his hand moved ahead, sliding over the plain of her belly to the thicket of short silky curls at the confluence of her closed thighs.

The first time he had touched her there it had brought back horrible memories of the Russian woman's brothel in Shanghai, and her public debasement. Now, in bed, in the dark, she no longer cringed and recoiled from his searching fingers. He could make her forget that vile nightmare, make her think only of him and the throbbing, pulsating delight induced by those unseen caresses.

To submit to them in daylight was different. She reached down to snatch at his hand, pressing her legs tightly together.

"Lie still!"

The low hoarse command was enforced by his arm across her ribs, and he went on with what he was doing until of their own volition her slender thighs slackened and parted, and soon her whole body was writhing in helpless response.

She thought that would be the end of it; that when he had proved his mastery of her treacherous senses he would leave her lying spent and ashamed, his own angry feelings appeased by the rape of her pride.

But no, it was far from the end of it. As she lay, all her energy sapped by those wild surging waves of pleasure, he began again.

At first, while his hand was gently stroking her thighs, she thought he might be regretting losing his temper. Hardly daring to breathe for fear of reviving his fury, she felt him rake his long fingers along the inside of her leg, from her knee to the tender place where her pulse beat quickened each time his fingers returned to it.

Soon her own hands were clenching the white lace on which she was lying as the feelings she had thought were exhausted began to revive.

When she felt the moist warmth of his mouth replace the light touch of his fingers, her heart gave a startled lurch. She peeped through the fringe of her lashes, her eyes widening in dismay as she saw his dark head moving slowly upward from her knee.

Surely he couldn't intend. . . ?

Her mind shied away from a thought that made her cry, "No. . . Caspar. . . *please*!" while her limbs thrashed and twisted frantically.

There was no escape. Even as she struggled, she knew it would be her own fault if tomorrow there were bruises where he had held her. She had only to lie still again and he would do nothing to injure her body. There were other, more subtle punishments for a wife who—so he imagined—had dared to pay him in his own coin.

With a broken cry of despair she gave up her futile resistance. At once his strong hands relaxed and no longer hurt her.

When what he did then was over, she knew that in a different way it had changed her as much as that terrible night at the mission. That experience had taught her to fear the beast that lurked in some men. This time she was forced to recognize the erotic depths in her own nature; the wanton creature within her who felt neither shame nor revulsion but only a wild storm of pleasure more intense than any before.

Again and again he drove her half-mad with excitement until her whole skin was dewed with a fine film of moisture, and she could hear herself panting as if she were fighting for breath.

When he took her, she thought she might die. The swift fierce thrusts of his body fulfilled a primitive need. She clung to him, burning and trembling.

Afterward she couldn't believe he could still be bitterly angry with her. But he was. As he rose from the bed and quickly adjusted his clothing, she was appalled to see that his face showed no sign of relenting. The taut skin over his cheekbones was unusually flushed, but otherwise he was completely in command of himself. As her eyes filled with tears, his expression became even colder.

"You haven't much time to make yourself presentable," he reminded her curtly. Then he strode from the room by the door leading to his own bedroom.

She allowed herself five minutes to pull herself together before she rang the bell for Burton. The maid already knew which gown and which jewels were to be worn, and she seemed to sense that her mistress was extremely distrait.

In a daze of confused, bruised emotions, Flora submitted to having her hair put to rights and her waist relaced. Soon she was elegantly dressed in a gown of *eau de Nile* satin, the bodice and sleeves and train overlaid with exquisite old family lace embellished with iridescent beads.

A spray of artificial roses, made from silk of the same pale green, had been attached to a comb to be worn at the back of her head; and that morning she had selected some of the Carlyon emeralds—earrings, a collar and two matching bracelets. When the flowers and jewels were in place it was hard to believe that only a short time before she had been sprawled on the bed in an attitude of total abandonment.

She entered the drawing room with only minutes to

spare before the guests were expected. Caspar was standing at the windows overlooking the park. At the sound of the door being opened he swung to face her. With profound dismay she saw that he was no calmer than when he had left her. As he crossed the long room to her side, he looked as dangerous as a leopard.

"Spare me that injured look, Flora," he said with a snap.

"I'm angry, not injured," she answered, lifting her chin. "That you, of all people, should think—"

The sound of voices on the staircase made him grip her wrist and say curtly, "You may be as angry as you please. I have been patient long enough. From now on—"

But at that moment, as they glowered at each other, her tall slender figure made small by his much greater height, the double doors opened and Warner announced the Comte and Comtesse de Muraille.

The dinner party was a nightmare. Instead of being seated between two elderly bores who, given the smallest encouragement, would have subjected her to tedious monologues to which she need only have given part of her attention, Flora found herself next to a witty French aristocrat and an English diplomat, both of whom were more than ordinarily amusing and attentive to her. To respond to their conversation with the interest and gaiety it deserved, while inwardly raging at Caspar's groundless and hypocritical jealousy, was not an easy task.

She could still feel his brutal kisses, and she had no doubt that his urbane manner as he sat at the other end of the table would last only while their guests were present. Once the last guests had left the house his temper would take command again. Regardless of what the servants might think, she would find herself hustled upstairs, the bedroom door slammed, the key turned, and all her frail hopes and daydreams finally shattered forever.

There was only one way to avoid such a horrible debacle, and only one chance to do it. Somehow, in the interval between the ladies' leaving the dining room and being joined by the gentlemen, she had to escape the house—and in a way that would not cause ripples of scandalized speculation to begin spreading through society, at least not by the medium of their guests. To prevent the servants' hall knowing that something untoward had happened was clearly impossible. She could only hope that Warner had the power to stop his underlings from spreading the news to the staff of other households.

Usually she and Caspar exchanged a glance when she passed him on her way out of the dining room. Tonight she avoided his eyes. Foolishly, she felt that if she looked at him he might somehow divine her plan.

In the drawing room Warner and the two footmen were preparing to serve coffee. Flora caught the under footman's eye and beckoned him to her. She said in a low tone, "Never mind the liqueurs, Edward. I want you to do something for me."

Although her instructions must have astonished him, he was far too well trained to question them. When he had left the room Flora forced herself to join a group of her guests and to make appropriate conversation. It took all her self-control to conceal her nervous impatience for the footman's return. If he should be delayed, and if the gentlemen came upstairs sooner than usual. . . .

Suddenly the strain of the past several hours overcame her tight self-control. She began to shiver as if the night air were not mild but bitterly cold. In a way it was a relief to abandon a life that she knew would never seem natural to her. But the ending of the travesty of her marriage was as sharp a grief as the death of her parents, and of her tutor. Sharper indeed, for although she had loved them it had been a filial affection, not the aching unquenchable love she would always feel for Caspar.

She reached up to rap on the roof. When the cabbie slid back the hatch she gave him her real destination. "And please go as fast as you can."

CHAPTER TWO

THE JOURNEY TO CLERKENWELL seemed endless. No sooner had her fear of pursuit abated than it was replaced by a new worry: that when she arrived at her refuge Kate might be too soundly asleep in the small back room för Flora's knocking to rouse her.

What am I to do if I can't wake her, she wondered anxiously. *I can't stand on the doorstep until Gertie gets home. She may not return until three or four in the morning.*

However, greatly to her relief, when at last the cab reached Sebastopol Street the glow of lamplight showed through the parlor curtain at number 39.

"Is that you, Gertie?" asked Kate's voice in response to Flora's urgent tattoo on the door.

"No, it's Flora. I know it's a strange time to call, Kate, but please let me in. I need your help."

There was a pause before a key scraped in the lock. The door, secured by a chain, was opened a cautious two inches.

"It *is* you m'lady," Kate exclaimed, peering through the narrow gap. "I thought someone must be playing a trick on me."

"Thank heaven you aren't in bed, Kate. I was so afraid I shouldn't be able to make you hear me," she said as she entered the house.

"Why, you're all of a tremble, m'lady. Whatever's the matter?"

There seemed no point in prevaricating. "I've left

my husband," Flora told her. "I've been unhappy
for a long time, and tonight I could bear it no longer.
Will you let me stay here? It will only be for one
night."

"Oh, Lor', you poor thing," Kate said kindly.
"No wonder you look so upset. Of course you can
stay here, m'lady. You're welcome to my bed any
day. It won't take long to change the sheets. I'll go in
with Gertie; she won't mind."

"No, no, I shouldn't dream of turning you out of
your bed. You must stay where you are. If you have a
light blanket to spare I shall be quite comfortable on
the sofa. You have no idea how many strange places I
slept in before I came to England," Flora said with a
laugh that threatened to turn into a sob.

Once the cabbie was dismissed and the door
locked, Kate suggested making a cup of tea.

"Most nights I am in bed early, but tonight I've
been reading and I didn't notice how late it was," she
explained. "You like reading, don't you, m'lady. I
remember them talking about it in the servants' hall
soon after his Lordship first brought you to Longwarden."

"They must have thought he had chosen a very
strange and unsuitable wife, didn't they?"

"Oh, no! We all thought you was beautiful," Kate
said with patent sincerity. "I remember the night you
and his Lordship gave a dinner party, and you came
down the stairs in a lovely gown of pink silk. Well,
no, it weren't a true pink but more the color of a nec-
tarine. You had butterflies made of diamonds in your
lovely black hair, and you smiled at us and said good
evening as sweetly as if we weren't servants but ladies
and gentlemen. Why, even old Mr. Warner said it

made his heart fair melt to see you, and Edward said that if you was anything to go by it surprised him more gentlemen didn't go to China for their wives. Everyone liked you, m'lady, even that old cat Miss Burton. I remember hearing her say she'd never had another lady as easy to manage as you was, what with never losing your temper nor changing your mind half a dozen times the way most ladies do.''

By the end of this unexpected encomium Flora was almost in tears. She had never dreamed that the staff liked her.

''Nevertheless, I am not a fit wife for his Lordship,'' she said sadly.

''Does he know you've run away? Did you leave a note?''

''No, only a message with Edward. But tomorrow I shall write a letter.''

''Perhaps his Lordship won't allow you to leave him. Perhaps he'll make you go back.''

''He won't know where I am,'' Flora answered. ''Tomorrow I'm going to leave London and go to my father's relations.'' *If they exist and if I can find them,* she added mentally.

''I thought his Lordship seemed a very nice gentleman,'' Kate said, eyeing her uncertainly. ''Not that I ever saw much of him, but the menservants always spoke well of him, and so they did in the village— especially after that fire when he burned his poor hands so bad to save old Mrs. Crane's treasures.''

''He *is* a fine man,'' Flora answered. ''It's not his fault this has happened. It's mine. I wasn't brought up to become an English peer's wife, and I find it impossibly tedious. You may not believe me, Kate, for I daresay you have never had enough leisure, but nevertheless it is a fact that a life of nothing but leisure quickly becomes very wearisome.''

"I always thought you must be ever so happy, with with all your lovely gowns and jewels, and being waited on, and able to buy anything what took your fancy," the other girl said in a tone of mingled wistfulness and puzzlement.

"No, I should have been happy to live quite quietly at Longwarden with only an occasional visit to London," Flora answered with a sigh.

"That sounds like the kettle on the boil."

Kate went away to fill the teapot. When she returned with a tray she asked, "Are you hungry, m'lady? Shall I cut some bread and butter?"

"No, thank you. I'm not at all hungry—and please don't call me that, Kate. I'm not Lady Carlyon anymore. From now on I'm plain Flora Jackson."

Kate filled two cups with strong tea. "I'll call you 'Miss Flora,' then," she said after thinking it over. "Just 'Flora' wouldn't seem right. It wouldn't never come natural to me."

Suddenly Flora felt exhausted. As soon as they had drunk the tea she prevailed on Kate to go to bed and to leave her to sleep on the sofa.

"Shall I help you undress, Miss Flora?"

"Yes, please, if you wouldn't mind."

When Kate had unhooked her bodice, Flora took it off and draped it over a chair, where its iridescent beading caught the lamplight.

She noticed Kate eyeing it longingly.

"Would you like to have it?" she asked. "I don't know when you would wear it, but if it would give you pleasure you are more than welcome to it. We're much the same size, except now because of the baby."

"Oh, Miss Flora—do you mean it?" Kate exclaimed.

She held the bodice against her and peered at herself in a mirror that reflected her head and bosom but not her distended waist.

Her excited expression clouded. "But you could sell it. If you don't want it no more, one of Gertie's pals would buy if off you. They often buy gowns made for ladies from a place what buys them from ladies' maids."

"I would rather you had it, Kate. But we'll talk about it tomorrow."

While Kate unlaced her corset for her, Flora unpinned her thick hair and shook it down over her shoulders.

However, although it was not uncomfortable lying on the sofa in her chemise, with a blanket wrapped around her, the oblivion she craved did not come. Instead her overtired mind began to torment her with doubts about the past and the future.

Had she been right to run away? Had Caspar truly believed her capable of infidelity? What had his reaction been when Edward gave her message to him? And would he, as Kate suggested, try to force her to go back to him?

Jacopo.

With a muffled groan of dismay she realized that in all the turmoil following her late return to Park Lane she had not once thought of her pet. He had not been in her bedroom when she came back to find Caspar there, of that she felt sure. He must have been in the garden, where he often stayed when she went out without him.

But would the servants have kept him with them in

the basement after Edward had told them what had happened? Or would Jacopo have been taken upstairs to his basket in her room? And what would he think when he opened his eyes in the morning and found his mistress not there? Would he whimper and whine, and scratch at the door of Caspar's room?

I should have brought him with me, she told herself, overcome with self-reproach. But presently, thinking about him and missing the comforting sound of his heavy breathing, she decided that perhaps after all it was better for Jacopo that she had forgotten him. Soon, if she could not find work or a temporary refuge with relations, she might not be able to feed herself, let alone a hungry little pug dog.

She was still awake when Gertie came home in the small hours. When Flora heard the cab approaching, she lit a lamp so that when Gertie unlocked the door she would not be startled by finding a fugitive in her parlor.

"You should be in bed, silly girl. You'll ruin your eyes with all your readin'," said Gertie as she entered the house.

"It isn't Kate. It's me—Flora."

Gertie walked around the end of the screen. "Well, I'm blowed! What the 'ell are you doin' 'ere?"

"There was nowhere else for me to go. It's only for tonight. Kate thought you wouldn't mind my staying here just for one night."

Gertie eyed her in silence for some moments. "Run away from 'im, 'ave you?" she asked.

Flora nodded. "I—I had to."

Gertie yawned and rubbed the back of her neck.

"We'll talk about it in the mornin'. Make me a nice cup of tea while I'm gettin' undressed, will you, dearie? You'll never get to sleep on that," she added, jerking her head at the sofa. "You'd better come up and share my bed. There's plenty of room in it for two."

So Flora spent the rest of the night on the soft feather mattress upstairs, with a bolster between them in case Gertie kicked in her sleep. Shortly before she fell asleep she thought she heard Gertie chuckling softly.

SHE WAS WOKEN by someone gently shaking her shoulder and opened her eyes to find the room lit by daylight. Gertie was sitting up in bed with a pile of pillows behind her. On the far side of the bed Kate was pouring out tea.

"What time is it?" Flora asked as she struggled into a sitting position.

"'Alf-past eleven," Gertie told her. She began to chuckle, just as she had the night before.

"Share the joke, Gertie," said Kate. "Good morning, Miss Flora. Did you sleep well?"

"Good morning. Yes, thank you, Kate."

Flora looked questioningly at Gertie, who, clad in an unexpectedly prim nightgown, was reclining against her pillows, shaking with suppressed laughter.

"I was thinkin' that no one'd ever credit this if they 'adn't seen it," Gertie explained. "The likes of me and the likes of you sharin' a bed. Whatever would all your posh friends say? And my pals at the theater? They wouldn't believe it, and that's a fact."

"Give over, Gertie. It's no laughing matter. Have a cup of tea, Miss Flora."

" 'Ow about makin' some toast, Kate?" Gertie suggested. "I feel peckish this morning, and I daresay 'er Ladyship wouldn't say no to a nice slice of toast, would you, dearie?"

"If it's not too much trouble. . . ." To her own surprise, Flora was hungry.

After Kate had left the room, Gertie finished her tea and lit a cigarette.

"You don't mind me smokin' in bed, I 'ope? Why don't you try one yourself?"

Flora shook her head. "I don't think I will, if you don't mind."

"So. . . you've run away from 'is Lordship. I can't say it comes as a surprise. You made it plain you wasn't 'appy the first time you came 'ere. What 'appened to drive you to this step?"

"He—we had a terrible quarrel."

"Hmm." Exhaling billows of smoke, Gertie eyed her in silence for some time. At length she said, "That friend you was tellin' me about, the one what—'ow shall I put it—the one what couldn't abide 'er marital duties. You wasn't talkin' about yourself, by any chance?"

"Oh, no," Flora said unhesitatingly. Then a faint flush colored her face, because she could not help recalling that although she had been referring to Helen Layard, she had hoped Gertie's reply might illuminate her own darkness.

Gertie saw the flush and said kindly, "You needn't be shy of tellin' your troubles to me, love. I've no doubt I've 'eard 'em before—and not once but 'alf a dozen times. You couldn't say nothin' to shock me, and you know the old sayin': a trouble shared is a trouble 'alved.''

But Flora, although grateful for Gertie's sympathy, found it impossible to confide the circumstances that had prompted her flight to Clerkenwell. Much as she valued Gertie's experienced counsel, she felt it would be disloyal to discuss Caspar with her.

"You ain't got no bruises that I can see, so it ain't because 'e knocks you about that you've left 'im," Gertie remarked after a pause.

"Oh, no—no, never," said Flora. "Caspar would never strike a woman."

The older girl shrugged. "There are gents as do, love. I've met one or two in my time. 'Owever, this ain't the moment to tell you the tale of my life. Your troubles is what we're discussin'. What was this quarrel about, eh?"

Faced with a direct question, Flora said reluctantly, "My husband saw me stepping into the cab on my way to see Kate yesterday. He concluded I was going to meet a lover. When I gave him a partial explanation, he didn't believe me."

"'Ow like a man," was Gertie's comment. "Keeps a mistress 'imself but flies off the 'andle if 'is wife looks elsewhere for 'er pleasure. 'E'll 'ave calmed down by now, I should think. Them what flares up quick, cools down quick. It's the ones 'oo sulk which is worst. If you want my advice you'll go back to 'im."

"No, I can't go back—ever," said Flora.

"Now look 'ere, my girl," Gertie began. "You ain't seen the world like I 'ave. It's a cruel 'ard place for us females, and you ain't a tough 'un like me.

Your 'usband may not be perfect, but you say you love 'im, and whether or not 'e loves you, you're a lot better off as 'is wife than you will be strugglin' on your own. If I'd ever 'ad an 'usband I'd 'ave stuck to 'im like a leech, I would. *And* I'd 'ave made 'im a good wife. It don't take much to keep a chap 'appy, y'know. A decent meal in 'is belly, a smile and a joke instead of a long face and naggin', and—to put it refined—some affection whenever 'e wants it, and you'll 'ave 'im eatin' out of your 'and. In your case, you don't even 'ave to cook for 'im. You only 'ave to look pretty.''

''I don't think he thinks I am pretty. However English my style of dress, I can never disguise my Chinese blood,'' Flora said sadly.

''And would be a fool if you tried,'' Gertie retorted. ''D'you know what that fellow said to me—that pal of 'is Lordship's? 'E said 'Trust old Caspar to find 'imself an Oriental beauty. I wonder where 'e discovered that little darlin'?' Them's 'is exact words, honest.''

''But he thought I was Caspar's mistress. He never dreamed I was his wife.''

Kate returned with the toast and Flora changed the subject by asking if there was somewhere nearby where they could procure some cheap clothes for her.

Later Gertie reiterated her advice, but Flora was not to be dissuaded from her plan to visit the village near the south coast where her father had been born and had started his working life.

By three o'clock that afternoon, having written a brief note to Caspar to assure him of her safety, she was on her way to the station to catch the train out of London.

The journey to the nearest station—some five miles from her destination—took less than an hour. She was fortunate in being the only passenger to alight, for the station boasted only one hackney. By five she had been set down on the green of her father's native village and was making her way toward the churchyard.

It did not take long to find the headstone marking the grave of her grandparents. The sight of their names incised in the lichen-stained York stone gave her a reassuring sense of not being wholly a stranger there.

Next she sought out the verger and found him sweeping the chancel inside the church. She judged him to be about sixty; too old to have been a boyhood crony of her father's, and perhaps too young to remember her grandfather.

"Good afternoon. I wonder if you can help me? I'm anxious to trace the descendants of Thomas and Ellen Jackson, who are buried in your churchyard and who both used to work at the hall," she said.

The verger put aside his broom and scratched the back of his head. It was plain that he found her a puzzle, and reading his mind she could tell that he was pondering the incongruity of her foreign face, her educated English voice and her working girl's clothes.

Eventually, when it seemed she would have to repeat her inquiry, he answered, "Well, now, miss, that's a problem, that is. I well recall old Keeper Jackson *and* his good wife. But you won't find none of their descendants hereabouts. They only had the one son and he died without issue, as the saying is. If you want to hear tell about him, you'd best call on Mrs. Merry at Pond Cottage yonder."

"Thank you; I will."

"'Tis the other side of the green. You can't miss it."

Pond Cottage was precisely the kind of cottage that Flora had visualized when daydreaming of a peaceful retreat in the country. Clean curtains fluttered at the open windows, and a well-swept brick path bordered by miniature hedges of box led from the gate to the porch, where a tortoiseshell cat was drowsing on the sunny doorstep.

Her knock was answered by a stout elderly woman with a black alpaca sewing apron tied around her ample middle.

"Good afternoon. Are you Mrs. Merry?"

Like the verger, the woman took her time about answering. Finally after inspecting her caller from head to foot she said, "I am—and you must be Tom Jackson's girl."

Flora blinked at her. "H—how did you know?"

"It's plain to see where you come from, my dear, and I should be surprised if any other young person from China were to call on me. You'd best come in and sit down, and I'll make you some tea. By the look of you, you've had a tiring journey."

"I don't understand how you knew I existed," said Flora when a few minutes later she was ensconced in a chair in a corner of Mrs. Merry's kitchen, with another fat cat arranging itself on her lap and the scent of hot scones in her nostrils.

"I've known since Tom wrote about you," replied Mrs. Merry. "The letter was meant for my daughter, but as she was dead I opened it. It was a long time ago—sixteen or seventeen years maybe. He wrote that he hoped she had found happiness, as he had.

He said he had a Chinese wife and a baby daughter, and he didn't think he'd ever come back to England.''

"I see. He and your daughter had been sweethearts when they were young, I gather?''

Busily cutting and buttering half a dozen of the fragrant scones, Mrs. Merry nodded.

"But when he asked her to marry him, she wouldn't. She was afraid of the places he wanted to take her to, and he wanted to travel as much as he wanted to marry her. I'd have gone with him if I'd been her. But Beth was never adventurous. She took after my husband in that way, and he never set foot outside this village from the day he was born until he died.''

"Did your daughter marry someone else?''

"She did. She married a coachman, and a very good husband he was. But I don't think she loved him like Tom, and she died when their first child was born. The baby died, too, more's the pity, for I'd have dearly loved a grandchild.''

"You had no other children, Mrs. Merry?''

"No, only my Beth, poor girl.''

"I'm sorry,'' Flora said gently. "It's lonely, having no family.''

While she was talking, the old lady had spread a cloth over one end of the kitchen table, set a place and fetched a pound pot of jam from a well-stocked pantry.

"Now come and make a good tea, for you look half-starved,'' she said kindly. "Have you lost your mother as well as your father, my dear? I heard of Tom's death from the rector, who read about it in his newspaper. Tom was killed by a terrible avalanche, as I recall?''

"Yes, when I was ten. My mother died long before. I can scarcely remember her."

"And you've been on your own ever since? Dear me, what a dreadful experience for you."

"No, because I lived at a mission where I was quite safe and very happy," Flora explained. "And then I married an Englishman, and he brought me back to my father's country. This jam is delicious, and so are your scones, Mrs. Merry."

Her hostess smiled and nodded. "It was my calling, my dear. I went into service as a kitchen maid up at the hall, where your old grandmother was cook. After I was left a widow, I cooked for Sir John at the friary for twenty-five years. Now tell me about your husband. Where do you live, and what does he do for his living?"

Flora hesitated before replying.

"He's a plant hunter, too, but not quite the same as my father. My husband has private means, and much of his time is spent in England. Unfortunately our marriage has not turned out well. He married me only to save me from being left unprotected in China after the priest at the mission had died. It was a foolish thing to do. I'm not at all a suitable wife for him. So I've left him," she ended abruptly.

"Left your husband!" exclaimed Mrs. Merry, her lined face puckered with disapproval. "Oh, my dear, you must go back at once. If he doesn't know where you are he will be very worried. What makes you think you aren't suited? A few cross words and black looks? There never was a young couple who didn't have tiffs at the start. I quarreled with Joe more than once. I had a temper in my young days."

Afterward Flora supposed that what overcame her

normal reserve was the likeness between Mrs. Merry and her mental picture of her grandmother. As much to her own surprise as that of her listener, she found herself confiding in the old lady as freely as if they were closely and lovingly related.

Mrs. Merry listened in silence, at times her faded blue eyes growing round with astonishment.

"Well, I never! Tom's girl a countess...and presented at court...with a house in Park Lane and a country seat. Who would believe it?" she murmured.

"I'm a little surprised that you should," Flora said dryly. "I don't look much like a countess." She glanced down ruefully at her drab skirt and cheap poplin blouse.

"Ah, but that's where you're wrong," said Mrs. Merry. "It's never clothes that make a lady. It's manners—quiet, gracious manners. And you have those, my dear, whatever you may say of yourself."

She heaved herself up from her chair and took off the starched white apron with which she had covered her black one before she began buttering scones.

"We'll go up and make the bed in my little spare bedroom, and then you can wash and tidy yourself while I'm preparing our supper. A good night's rest is what you need. Nothing ever looks so black in the morning after you've slept well."

"You mean I may stay here?" asked Flora.

"You've nowhere else to go, have you?"

Flora shook her head.

"Well, then..." said Mrs. Merry comfortably. "To stay here will suit us both, won't it? You'll have a nicely cooked supper and a clean bed, and I'll have company for a change."

Several hours later, enveloped in one of Mrs. Merry's voluminous nightgowns, Flora leaned out of the dormer window in the spare bedroom and watched the small dark shapes of bats flitting through the quiet summer dusk.

She could hardly believe her good fortune in finding this haven; and it was only now that she was safe that she realized how deeply she had dreaded being homeless and friendless.

THE NEXT MORNING she was woken by one of Mrs. Merry's three cats, which must have come in by the window. When Flora opened her eyes the cat was kneading the patchwork quilt with its forepaws and purring.

After breakfast she went to the village post office to send a telegram to Clerkenwell, and later she posted a letter explaining her message in detail.

Once Mrs. Merry was convinced that Flora's husband was in no doubt about her safety, she did not press her to return to him.

"Far be it from me to come between a man and his wife, but perhaps it will do you both good to be separated, just for a short time," she said.

Physically, Flora found life at Pond Cottage ideal. Rising and retiring early and living on plain wholesome fare suited her constitution much better than the late nights and long rich menus of the London season.

Mentally, it was another matter.

With plenty to occupy her hands—feeding the six white leghorns, picking beans, weeding the borders—but nothing to distract her thoughts, she could not help brooding. The more she thought about it, the more she regretted the failure of courage and fortitude that had caused her flight from Park Lane.

It was Mrs. Merry's habit each night to read a chapter of the Bible. While Flora was staying with her she read it aloud. Although Flora pretended to listen, usually her attention would wander. But on her fourth night at the cottage, Mrs. Merry read a phrase that lingered in her mind.

"It is more blessed to give than to receive."

That night in bed she saw that if she truly loved Caspar she should have bent to his will like a flower to the wind. Perhaps now it was too late. If she went back would he accept her? No doubt he believed she had fled from him to a lover, and although given the opportunity she could convince him otherwise, he might not even be willing to allow her a hearing.

Nor could she be certain that her sudden departure from the dinner party had not burgeoned into a scandal of such proportions that even Caspar's rank and wealth could not save her from being ostracized.

The next morning she was sitting in the arbor, writing another letter to Kate and Gertie, when she heard the squeak of the gate and looked up to find, with astonishment, that her task was unnecessary.

"Gertie? What brings you here?" she exclaimed, jumping up and crossing the grass with outstretched hands.

"'Allo, love. 'Ow are you? Not too chirpy by the look of you." Gertie's sharp eyes scanned Flora's face and saw the shadows under her eyes and the pinched look about her soft mouth.

"I'm very well," Flora assured her. "How are you? Come inside and meet dear Mrs. Merry."

"Yes, I will...in a tick," said Gertie. "First I've somethin' to tell you—somethin' important."

Flora's smile of welcome faded into wariness. "About my husband?"

Gertie sat down at the shady end of the arbor seat. She was dressed in two shades of green: a leaf-green skirt with a paler green blouse and hat. Without any paint on her face, and dressed less flamboyantly than usual, she looked a different person.

"Yes...'e paid a call on us," she answered.

"C-called on you?" Flora stammered. "How did he know where you lived, or anything about you?"

"It seems 'e looked in your boodwar and found a letter from Kate what she wrote to thank you after you gave 'er them baby clothes."

"You didn't tell him where I was?"

"I couldn't, dearie. I didn't know. The first time 'e came, you 'adn't been gone more than an hour. All I told 'im was that we expected to 'ear from you shortly and I'd let 'im know you was safe and sound."

"Was he fearfully angry?" asked Flora. "What did he say?"

"I wouldn't describe 'im as angry. More like distraught with worry, I'd 'ave said. I reckon the night you ran away 'e was nearly beside 'imself, poor devil. You may think 'e don't care about you, but I think 'e cares somethin' desperate. 'E'd lay down and die for you, dearie. That's my opinion."

Flora gazed at her, dumbfounded. "Oh, Gertie, you must be mistaken," she said at last in a shaken voice. "If he cared for me he would have told me."

" 'Ave you ever told 'im you're fond of 'im?'' Gertie asked dryly.

"No—no, but that's different. It's always the man who takes the lead in these matters."

"Well, I don't know *why* 'e ain't told you, but no doubt 'e's got some good reason. 'E's daffy about you, poor blighter."

"Has he been to see you again?" Flora asked in a low voice.

"No, I went to 'im, as a matter of fact. 'E'd been very civil when 'e called on us, but I wanted to see 'ow 'e'd act if I called on 'im in Park Lane."

"And how did he act?"

"No different," Gertie said approvingly. "The butler looked down 'is nose, but 'is Lordship was as polite as could be. 'Please be seated, Miss Jones. Would you care for tea?' 'e says to me. If anyone 'ad 'eard 'im they'd 'ave took me for a duke's daughter," she added with a giggle.

"What did you tell him?"

"That you was stayin' with an old lady what 'ad known your father."

"Did he press you to say where I as?"

"No. 'E asked me to bring you a letter and some money, and some clothes 'e thought you'd be needin'. The letter's 'ere in my purse, and the trunk and the 'atbox are in a cab down the lane. I didn't drive up to the gate 'cause I thought you might think it was 'im and take fright and make a run for it."

As she spoke, Gertie unclasped her purse and produced the letter.

With fingers no longer steady, Flora opened the envelope. She saw at a glance that the note it contained was very brief.

"Flora," her husband had written, without any prefix, "if you still wish to end our marriage I will not oppose you. However, I hope you will consent to see me once more before we part."

CHAPTER THREE

"Will you see 'im?" asked Gertie. As Flora looked up she added, "'E told me what 'e'd written to you and said I could bring 'im your answer."

"How can I refuse him?" Flora responded.

"Right-oh. In that case I'll fetch 'im," Gertie said briskly. 'E'll be 'ere in about 'alf an 'our. Now don't fly up at me, dearie. I 'aven't let on where you are, but I felt sure you would want to see 'im, so I left 'im kickin' 'is 'eels in a public 'ouse a few miles back."

To Flora's amazement, she rose and went to the gate, where she took off her glove and, putting two fingers in her mouth, emitted a piercing whistle. A few minutes later a four-wheeled cab came into view.

The sound also caused Mrs. Merry to emerge from the cottage. Thrown into great consternation by the thought of seeing Caspar so soon, Flora uttered a confused introduction.

Fortunately the cabbie was a burly fellow who had no difficulty in unloading the cumbersome trunk and carrying it into the cottage. As soon as he had dealt with the baggage, Gertie bade him take her back to The Plough.

"If I was you I'd prink myself up a bit, dearie," was her parting advice accompanied by a wink, to Flora.

"How did you come to be acquainted with a young

person of that class?" asked Mrs. Merry as the cab drew away from the gate. "A flighty young piece, by the manner of her."

"A very kind friend," returned Flora. Although at that moment she was not sure whether to be grateful to or angry with Gertie for intervening in her affairs.

She explained to Mrs. Merry that her husband was coming to see her.

"Coming here? Oh, my word! Why didn't you say so before, child? I must go and wash the best china."

"But he may not be here very long," Flora protested.

The caution was wasted: Mrs. Merry had already bustled away.

After hovering by the gate for some moments, Flora returned to the arbor to try to compose herself. Could there really be any foundation for Gertie's extraordinary conviction that Caspar was not as indifferent as she had thought?

It seemed far more than half an hour before she heard the sound of the carriage returning. Her mouth grew dry with apprehension. She clasped her hands tightly together to control their trembling.

From her seat in the creeper-clad arbor she had a good view of the gate without immediately being noticed by anyone entering the garden. Thus when Caspar sprang down from the carriage and opened the gate in the hedge, she had several moments' grace before he spotted her.

The sight of his tall erect figure made her heart seem to cease to beat. For a breathless moment she watched him start up the path, only to check his stride several yards short of the porch. As if he felt someone watching him, he looked about him and saw her.

When he took off his hat and came toward her, her hands clenched even more tightly than before. She licked her dry lips and wondered if she would be able to speak, or if her voice had deserted her.

At a little distance he stopped. That he, too, was under a strain was shown by the set of his chin and the line of his mouth.

"It's good of you to see me," he said formally.

"Not at all," she murmured. "Won't you sit down?" She gestured at the other end of the bench.

Caspar seated himself and put down his hat and cane. He began to strip off his gloves. Stealing a glance at his profile, Flora saw the hard knot of muscle bunched at the angle of his jaw and quailed at the thought of another furious altercation.

When he spoke his voice held no hint of repressed anger. He said quietly, "I owe you an apology, Flora. I know now that my accusations a few hours before you ran away had no vestige of truth in them. I should have known—I did know—that you were incapable of betraying any trust placed in you. But that night my judgment was distorted by an emotion that I have since recognized as jealous rage. Although our relationship had been regularized, it was still far from satisfactory—to either of us. I am not excusing myself, merely trying to explain my behavior...and to ask your forgiveness."

When after a long pause she failed to reply, he turned his head to look at her.

"Are you still determined to leave me? Your friend Gertie has led me to believe that I blundered in my handling of matters between us, not only that night but from the first. She seems to think that neither of us has been sufficiently frank, not only in regard to our personal feelings but by drawing conclusions about each other without making sure they were correct. For example, she tells me that you are convinced I have a mistress.''

''H—haven't you?'' Flora asked huskily.

His mouth twisted in a grimace. ''No, I have not,'' he said flatly. ''If I had I should not have lost control of myself and frightened you into running away. I won't deny that there have been women in my life, but not for some considerable time... not since our arrival at Longwarden.''

''But if that is true, why were you not in your bedroom on our second night at Crowthorne Castle? And where did you go on the night we went to the Empire Theatre? You said you were going to your club for an hour, but you were out all night. I know that is so, for I saw you come home the next morning.''

''Did you indeed? I never saw you. When I looked up at your window I supposed you to be sound asleep and quite unaware of the miserable night I had spent.''

''I thought only I was miserable. Why was it miserable for you?''

''Because having held you in my arms, I wanted very much to keep you there. But it seemed to me that you had felt only revulsion.''

''Oh, no—it wasn't revulsion that made me repulse you. In fact I... I wanted you to kiss me. Only not because it was your right, or without saying something fond first. Without any word of affection, I felt like one of the girls who work at the Empire.''

"I see. Clearly I had as little insight into your feelings as you had into mine," he said thoughtfully. "As it happens, you were right in suspecting that I didn't spend all night at my club, although I might well have done so. That is the purpose of clubs—to provide a home away from home, you know. However, not being in a convivial mood on that occasion, after an hour or two at White's I went to a Turkish bath, where I steamed myself into a more tractable frame of mind. As for the other time at Crowthorne, may I ask you how you knew I was not in my room all that night?"

"If you promise not to lose your temper?"

"You have my word on it."

She explained the circumstances that had caused her to hide in the window embrasure near his bedroom. When she came to Captain Cromer's part in the episode, her husband's eyes flashed with anger, but his voice remained level as he said, "And who, among our fellow guests, did you suspect of being my mistress?"

"I don't know," she admitted. "None of them seemed very likely, but what else was I to think? Particularly as everyone had told me that country-house Saturday-to-Mondays are designed for precisely that purpose."

"Yes, in general they are," he agreed. "But had you confronted me with your suspicions instead of keeping them to yourself, I should have explained that it was our host who kept me talking until the small hours. The duke—and I tell you this in the strictest possible confidence, Flora—is in charge of a small and extremely private department of the government. Its function is to keep an eye on the activities of countries whose leaders may have it in mind to disrupt the peace and prosperity of our country. Once or twice in the past I have gleaned various pieces of information of interest to his department. The reason we were asked to Crowthorne recently was so that the duke could try to persuade me to undertake a special mission. Being a roving botanist provides an excellent screen for other activities.''

''Yes, I suppose it does,'' she agreed. ''But isn't it dangerous? I mean, if the foreign powers were to suspect—''

''I didn't accept,'' he intervened. ''But the duke was extremely persistent. It must have been two in the morning before he saw nothing would budge me.''

''It was ten minutes past two,'' she told him. ''I had been asleep for a time, and then I heard a door click and peeped through the curtains and saw you.''

''It's a pity you didn't jump out and insist on being told where I'd been. Tell me: how did you phrase your reply to the note you thought I had written?''

She flushed and avoided his eyes. ''The note said, 'May I come to you later?' and I replied, 'Need you ask?' ''

''And was that reply inspired by a sense of duty merely or by something warmer?'' he inquired.

She said in a low voice, ''I think more than anything I wanted to end the uncertainty. I hated the falseness of my position. I felt such a burden upon you, and yet I—I shrank from fulfilling the obligations that Helen said were so hateful when no affection was present. There *was* affection on my side, but not on yours . . . or so it seemed.''

Caspar captured one of her hands and held it firmly between his. "There was more than affection, Flora. I had come to love you very dearly. I admit it was not so at first. When I asked you to marry me, I did it for selfish reasons."

"I don't understand," she said, puzzled.

It had always seemed to her that their marriage had been an act of extreme self-abnegation on his part.

"I thought you would suit my needs much better than any girl brought up in England. You were accustomed to travel and equally accustomed to solitude. I felt I could take you with me or later, when you were enceinte, leave you behind without any word of complaint from you. I'm afraid it didn't occur to me then to consider your wishes. It was not until later, after we arrived in England, that I realized I was in love with you and that I wanted to give you everything women enjoy. . . jewels, pretty clothes, the pleasure of being greatly admired. Unfortunately, by then you had changed. You'd learned how to mask your feelings. Instead of reflecting every thought that passed through your head, as they used to when I first knew you, your beautiful eyes had a curiously shuttered expression."

"Do you really think my eyes are beautiful? In China they never used to trouble me, but after we came to England I never looked in my mirror without wishing I could change this—"

She raised her free hand to her face and touched the little fold of skin at the inner corner of her eyelid, which, even more than her blue black hair and dark brown irises, showed clearly her Chinese ancestry.

"Change it!" Caspar exclaimed. "My dear girl, it's half your charm. Oh, Flora...Flora...."

He pulled her into his arms and began to kiss her.

It was at least five minutes before either of them recollected that the arbor was not altogether a suitable setting for so ardent a rapprochement.

"We seem to have an audience. There is someone peering at us from the window on the far side of the front door," murmured Caspar, looking over Flora's head but not releasing his hold on her.

"It's Mrs. Merry. She knew my father."

Briefly and somewhat confusedly Flora explained the circumstances leading to her sojourn at Pond Cottage.

"I think I should introduce you. She knows about our...estrangement."

"By all means. I must thank her for taking you under her wing."

Caspar drew her to her feet and kissed first her left and then her right hand before reluctantly letting her go.

A short time later—the cabdriver having been told to refresh himself at the inn and to come back at half-past two—an oddly assorted but nonetheless festive luncheon party took place in Mrs. Merry's front parlor.

Flora was too excited and happy to feel hungry, but fortunately both Gertie and Caspar were able to do justice to the hearty fare that their hostess had produced from her well-stocked cupboards.

Toward the end of the meal Caspar said, "Mrs. Merry, I wonder if you would allow my wife to remain here for a few days—and let me stay with her?"

"I should be honored, m'lord, but would you be

comfortable? It's only a very small room where her Ladyship's been sleeping. I think you'd find it too cramped, sir.''

"Dear Mrs. Merry, *please* don't call me that,'' Flora intervened swiftly. "You made me welcome because I was 'Tom's girl.' Why mayn't I always be that to you?''

"Well. . .if his Lordship has no objection,'' the old lady answered uncertainly.

"On the contrary, I am delighted Flora has found a link with her forebears. As for your fears for our comfort, my only concern is that in soliciting your hospitality I may be asking too much of you.''

"Oh, no, sir—no, not at all. I should be pleased to put you up,'' Mrs. Merry assured him.

The matter was settled, and later Gertie returned to London on her own. Before she departed she contrived to draw Flora aside and murmured some words of advice.

"If there's one thing you learn in my profession, it's that most of the troubles between 'usbands and wives start on the weddin' night, dearie. What 'appens between the sheets don't come as no 'orrible shock to the poorer classes cos they don't 'ave the privacy that toffs do. I reckon most you ladies don't even know 'ow a man's made until you get married. If your mothers 'ave told you anythin', it's that what 'appens won't be very nice, but you'll 'ave to let 'im get on with it and try and think of somethin' else. Maybe, not 'avin' a mother, you 'aven't been told all that nonsense. But if you 'ave, you forget it. If there was more ladies what knew the tricks of my trade, the likes of us girls at the Empire would be out of business in no time. Some ladies—a few of 'em—do know. They may be ever so refined and 'aughty in public, and even with their 'usbands—but not with their lovers. Not likely! In their boodwars they don't care what they do. I daresay they could give lessons to some of us tarts. I've been told as 'ow there's one duchess what—"

She leaned closer to whisper in Flora's ear, then gave vent to a shriek of laughter. "'Ow about that, eh?"

"Do you believe it?" Flora asked incredulously, blushing.

"'Course I do. Whyever not? Where's the sin if it's 'ow she enjoys it? So if 'is Lordship wants you to stick a ruby in your belly button or lie in a bath of champagne, or sit on 'is knee in a pair of black boots and your birthday suit, you do it, duckie, and no argument. In your bedroom, forget you're 'is wife. Make believe you're 'is mistress and 'e's your lover. Then 'e won't never need no other women, and you won't need no other men. Now I must be off. Bye-bye, dearie."

Flora kissed her goodbye and stood at the garden gate waving until the cab was out of sight.

When she returned to the cottage, Caspar suggested a walk.

"Perhaps I should change my clothes first," she said, comparing their appearances and feeling a strong desire to replace her drab clothes with something more becoming.

"Later perhaps, but not yet," he said firmly. "If I allow you to open your trunk now I shall not see you again for an hour at least. You may have five minutes to put on your hat, but no longer."

She ran upstairs to fetch the small hat of stiff straw

that she had worn since leaving London. One of the
cats was asleep in the center of the bed, and she wondered if Caspar would object to the sound of purring
during the night, and possibly a whiskered face in-
vestigating his features. She smiled to herself at the
thought of his smothered expletive should Bella or
Blackie spring onto him while he was sleeping. And
then, at the realization that tonight would at last be
her wedding night in the truest sense, she drew an
unsteady breath.

"Were you fearfully angry with me when Edward
gave you my message the night I ran away?" she
asked her husband as they set out.

"Not with you—with myself!" he replied. "I
thought you had fled to your lover and that I had lost
you forever."

"You truly believed I had a lover?"

"My dear, you have been the most admired beauty
this season. In general young married women are considered to be out of bounds, at least until they have
provided their husbands with an heir. But there are
always a few blackguards—Cromer among them—
who will disregard the code."

"But, Caspar, how could you think that I would
disregard *my* code?"

"I felt your promises to me had been made under
duress. I had bound you to me unfairly, before you
had realized your power to command other men or
had your rightful choice of suitors. You were forced
to marry me, Flora, and a vow made under pressure
of circumstances is not like a vow made freely. I
couldn't have blamed you for giving your heart to
someone else. To be faithful to a man you don't love
only because to leave him is to lose your place in
society is not true fidelity."

"What I don't understand is how you could fail to guess that I *did* love you."

"At the time of our return to Longwarden I did think you had some affection for me. Had it not been for that confounded fire, our union would have been consummated long ago. But a man with badly burned hands is in no position to introduce his bride to the pleasures of the marriage bed. By the time my hands had healed you appeared to have undergone a change of feeling. Indeed, when once I reminded you of sharing a *kang* with me in China, you made it abundantly clear that the prospect of sharing my bed in England was extremely repugnant to you."

"Yes, but that was at Crowthorne and within a few hours of your seeming to have a mistress. And when we returned to London and you came to my room and I pretended to be asleep, the fact that you left without disturbing me seemed to confirm your indifference to me—except for the purpose of begetting your heirs."

"My indifference! If only you knew how long I spent pacing my own room, knowing that you had *not* been asleep," he admitted with a twisted smile. "I was torn between my longing to make love to you and the fear that to override your reluctance could be a fatal mistake. No man worthy of the name wants to force himself on an unwilling bride. However, once that step had been taken, I hoped matters would improve between us. But every time I held you in my arms I was conscious of your lack of response. It wasn't until the night when I lost my temper and caused you to take the desperate step of running away that—"

"Perhaps it was a good thing you did lose your

temper," she intervened, her cheeks growing hot at the memory. "If you hadn't we might still be at an impasse. Did people believe my excuse, or is there a great deal of gossip?"

"I think not, but such as there is will quickly be scotched when we go back to London and are seen to be on terms of the greatest felicity."

"I'm glad we're not going back immediately. I shouldn't want to begin my honeymoon in a house where I have been so very unhappy, surrounded by servants all agog with curiosity," said Flora. "Which reminds me: I have a confession to make to you, Caspar."

"What is it?" he asked, raising an eyebrow.

"I—I think that night you were too enraged with me for other reasons to notice I had disobeyed you in wearing a corset."

"I had known that for a long time," he answered, an unmistakable gleam of amusement in his eyes.

"You had known? But you expressly forbade it. How had you known?"

"I should have been singularly unobservant not to notice that after your first visit to London with Sylvia you became a different, more modish shape."

"And you weren't angry with me?"

"I think it's a foolish practice. It can't be comfortable, and from a masculine point of view a stiffly corseted waist is far less seductive than one that feels soft and pliant when a man puts his arm around it. But if it pleases you to conform to the vagaries of fashion, I have no strong objection at present. I shall be less tolerant if you persist in tightly lacing yourself when you are enceinte. That, I'm told, can be very injurious both to mother and child."

"Oh, yes, I'm sure it must be. I should never do that," she assured him. "But I wish I had known you did not disapprove in the ordinary way. I thought you did, and it's been very much on my conscience. Every time we danced I was afraid you would find me out."

They had come to a secluded stretch of lane. Caspar put his arm around her.

"How is it that you're not flouting my edict today?"

"I have no one to help me to dress here. I have to manage by myself, and in any case my present clothes don't fit me properly. Do you realize that if we should meet anyone I will be taken for a servant being led astray by her master? Speaking of being led astray, will you help me to help poor little Kate? Perhaps Mrs. Merry would be willing to give her a home. She shouldn't be forced into working at the Empire. Kate is not as stouthearted as Gertie. Nor, whatever her father may think, is she a bad girl; merely a foolish one. Please, Caspar, say you will help her."

"By all means, but not today. Today, and for several days more, it's my intention to live 'the world forgetting, by the world forgot,'" he said, coming to a halt and putting his other arm around her.

As she stood in the circle of his arms, with crickets chirping in the grass, butterflies fluttering along the hedgerows and the muffled cry of a dove coming from deep in the beechwoods, for a moment the sounds and scents of the English country lane were erased by a memory of China. She remembered the day he had come to the mission and how with one careless smile he had made her long to be a woman.

She returned to the present and asked him, "When did you begin to love me?"

He pressed her more closely against him. "I'm not sure. Perhaps while we were at sea, or possibly even before that. I only know that on the night of our first dinner party, when you came into the drawing room looking so amazingly beautiful, I wished all our guests in Hades and you in my arms, as you are now."

CHAPTER FOUR

AT THE FINAL BALL OF THE SEASON, which took place at Holland House in Kensington, it was noticed by all the chaperones that although Lord Ilchester's beautiful gardens were known to be the scene of many proposals, it was not an excited debutante whose eyes shone most radiantly that night, nor any of the eligible bachelors who most clearly showed himself captivated.

The couple who danced together repeatedly, with eyes only for each other, were the Earl and Countess of Carlyon.

It was by no means the first time that onlookers had seen Lord Carlyon direct a burning glance at his lovely wife while dutifully dancing with someone else, or she gaze meltingly at him from the arms of her partner. That theirs was a passionate love match had long been obvious to everyone; and now, as the season ended, their absorption far from diminishing, seemed to have grown more exclusive.

Watching them circle the ballroom, Sylvia Conroy envied their transparent happiness and felt a spasm of guilt that in spite of her liking for Carlyon's bride she had once succumbed to an urge to make mischief between them. It had been an unworthy impulse of which now she felt ashamed; but at the time it had amused her to see that Carlyon, once impervious to the tender passion, had become capable of fierce jealousy.

She had told him nothing but the truth: that his wife exhibited all the signs of being deeply in love. She had merely refrained from adding that the object of Flora's adoration was himself. One would have expected him to know it; he had always been supremely confident of his power to hold his mistresses in thrall until he chose to discard them. But love makes fools of the wisest men, and Carlyon, it seemed, was no exception.

In another part of the ballroom Lady Chiltern said to her husband, "Flora Carlyon has always been a beauty, but tonight she has a special radiance about her. It wouldn't surprise me. . . ." She dropped her voice to a murmur for his ears alone.

"I daresay you're right," Lord Chiltern responded. "It will be interesting to see if their progeny are as handsome as they are. Pity Caspar's grandfather isn't alive. I've no doubt he would have doted on her—as indeed must everyone who knows her."

"Yes, she is the sweetest creature, and even though it may be true that her father must have been a ne'er-do-well to have married a Chinese, I don't believe for a moment that he wasn't a man of breeding," replied his wife, still keeping her voice discreetly low.

"Is that what the gossips are implying! What absolute poppycock!" Lord Chiltern said contemptuously. "As a matter of fact it's very probable that her father was a cadet of a very old French family. The Comte de Muraille is convinced of it. He says she speaks French to perfection, and her manners are very much those of the *ancien régime*."

Not far from the Chilterns, someone else had his eyes on Flora's delicate profile.

"No use your covetin' *that* neighbor's wife,

m'dear Harry," chaffed the man beside Captain Cromer. "Even if the lady were willin', Carlyon wouldn't stand for it. Couldn't plead not guilty to a spot of poachin' himself in the past. But I hear he's a reformed character now."

"Which of us wouldn't be in his place?" Captain Cromer answered moodily.

He had not been exaggerating when he told Flora he had fallen in love with her. Now, knowing himself to be a fool, instead of putting her out of his mind he could not stop himself watching her.

Unaware of anyone but her partner, Flora danced in a glow of happiness exceeding her wildest daydreams. An hour before, while discussing their plans for the future, she had made the delightful discovery that, far from wishing to spend every summer in London, Caspar had endured the season only because he had felt sure she would enjoy it.

"Shall we stroll in the garden?" he suggested as the waltz ended.

As they made their way from the ballroom Flora caught sight of Helen Layard. She felt a pang of compassion for someone doomed never to know the bliss revealed to her by Caspar. By the time they had come back to London he had made all her fears seem absurd. She had returned to Park Lane too exalted to care what the servants thought of her absence, or to mind facing Burton again. Nothing and no one could daunt her now that she knew Caspar loved her.

"This time tomorrow, Spring Moon, we shall be in Paris," he remarked as they strolled in the leafy coolness of the starlit, fairy-lit garden. "Are you looking forward to it?"

"I look forward to everything—now," she answered. "Where shall we go after Paris?"

"I thought we might find the château where Père d'Espinay spent his boyhood. You would like to see the places he described to you, wouldn't you?"

"Oh, yes—very much. I've never asked you... did Père d'Espinay make you feel obliged to marry me?"

"On the contrary, he never mentioned the matter. The only charge he did put on me, knowing he was dying, was to see you safely embarked on a ship to Europe."

He led her under some trees, where the shadows veiled them from view, and took her in his arms. "Père d'Espinay did once remark that when you were a little older there would be in you a rare combination of Chinese fortitude, English spirit and the style and sparkle of a Frenchwoman. I've no doubt he would have thought you deserved a husband far worthier than I."

"But he had no idea you were a peer, and very rich."

"That would not have impressed him," said Caspar, tilting her face up.

"No, not at all," she agreed. "But he said that any man who offered me marriage would be a good man, and you are. I'm sure I should be just as happy if you were a gardener and I were a housemaid."

Caspar laughed and lightly kissed her upturned lips. "I daresay you're right, my darling, and certainly you would look very beguiling in a starched cap and streamers. But I think I prefer you in a tiara. Perhaps while we are in Paris I shall have you painted by Boldini so that our grandchildren will know—"

his voice dropped a tone and grew husky "—how lovely you were in your bloom."

WHEN LATER THAT NIGHT Burton had helped her mistress to disrobe and had brushed her hair and replaced her jewels in the miniature chest of velvet-lined drawers that at night was locked in a safe, the countess surprised her by saying, "Leave the jewel case here, if you please. Good night, Burton."

Since during her absence from Park Lane, Lady Carlyon had acquired a new firmness of manner, her maid made no comment upon this curious instruction but said merely, "Good night, m'lady."

For a few minutes after she had gone Flora remained at her dressing table. Then, after locking the door, she shed both her wrapper and nightgown. Naked, she hurried to a drawer containing a diaphanous scarf of cherry-colored silk gauze. Wrapping it around her slender hips, she fixed it in place with an amethyst brooch. Around her bare ivory waist she fastened the diamond rivière that Caspar had given her on the day of her debut. Not until her throat, arms and wrists were alight with the flash of precious stones did she step back to see the effect as reflected in her looking glass.

If only Burton could see her now, she thought with a stifled gurgle of laughter.

Covering herself with a new evening cloak of white velvet trimmed with ermine, she bade Jacopo good night and went to join her husband in his room. Because her preparations for the night took longer than his, it was usually she who joined him, and his valet no longer entered his master's bedroom in the morning until Caspar rang for him.

Her husband was seated in a chair, drinking champagne and glancing at a copy of *Country Life*, which he tossed aside with flattering alacrity the moment she entered.

"Is that Lucile's latest creation? It's very becoming. But a trifle warm for the time of year, I should have thought," he remarked, rising to his feet.

"That depends on what one wears beneath it," Flora said demurely.

She let the cloak fall to the ground.

His dark eyebrows arched in surprise at the sight of her half-naked body glittering with jewels. As his keen gaze swept over her figure she saw laughter tugging at his mouth. But there was a gleam of desire as well as amusement in his eyes as they lingered on her uncovered breasts and the thinly veiled junction of her thighs.

"Not an ensemble that would meet with everyone's approval, but it certainly has mine. I have never seen the family jewels displayed to greater advantage. Who devised this unusual deshabille? Not Lady Duff Gordon, I feel sure."

"It was an idea of my own. Well, no...that isn't quite true. It was Gertie who suggested it to me. At least what she said was that...that if there were more ladies who knew the tricks of her trade, there would be fewer unfaithful husbands. I'm not really sure what she meant, but I do remember that the girls in that place in Shanghai were dressed like this, except that their jewels were not real ones. And I thought that if the Englishmen who went there liked seeing them dressed up as houris, you might like it, too," she explained.

"Undressed like a houri would be a more accurate

description.'' He beckoned her to him, his gray eyes narrowed and brilliant.

Flora stepped from the pool of white velvet, the diamond bracelets around her ankles and the rings on her toes drawing his glance to her slender bare feet.

When she was within arm's length she stopped. ''Do you like it?'' she asked in a whisper.

For a long tense moment they stood gazing into each other's eyes. Even though he had not touched her yet, she felt her breasts swelling and her insides melting and throbbing.

Then he swept her into an embrace that answered her question far better than words ever could.

EPILOGUE

By the end of the 1970s only one of the mansions on the east side of the park, between Marble Arch and Hyde Park Corner, remained as a monument to the elegance of Park Lane in Edwardian days. The others had been converted into offices, or replaced by blocks of apartments and two of London's largest hotels, the Dorchester and Grosvenor House.

The last surviving private house belonged to the Dowager Countess of Carlyon, now in her ninety-fourth year but still interested—if no longer actively—in the social reforms that had occupied much of her long happy life.

Unlike some famous beauties of her generation, she had grown old without regret for her vanished youth and without trying to hold age at bay with face-lifts or a thick mask of makeup. Yet even now, with her black hair turned white and her ivory skin netted with wrinkles, it was still a pleasure to look at her.

In full possession of her faculties, and free from the distortions of rheumatism, she had not lost her straight-backed posture or the expressive grace of her gestures.

Although, unlike the Chinese, the English did not always respect their aged relations, they did revere public figures who outlived three score and ten. Like Lady Violet Bonham Carter, Dame Edith Evans and Dame Sybil Thorndike before her, in her seventies and eighties old Lady Carlyon had become a television star. She had appeared on numerous panels and chat shows, her common sense and lively humor endearing her even to viewers who would have liked to see the aristocracy and the monarchy swept away.

In spite of her wealth and position, the countess had not been exempt from life's miseries. During the First World War she had turned her husband's country seat into a hospital for soldiers who had been shell-shocked and gassed, and had herself helped to nurse some of the most pitiful cases.

In the Second World War Caspar's heir—their only son—had been killed in action in Italy.

Few outside her own circle knew of that deep private grief. In public she had continued her lifelong battle against injustice, especially in relation to her own sex. Although in earlier years she had been a determined supporter of women's right to vote, to be educated and to limit the size of their families, she was also stoutly in favor of their right to choose to be homemakers rather than careerists.

In May 1979 the Chinese tree *Paulownia tomentosa*, which Caspar had planted in his London garden at the beginning of the century, put out its finest show of fragrant foxglove-shaped blossoms.

Familiarly known as the empress tree, the *Paulownia* had the curious habit of forming its flower buds in autumn, so that in Europe they often succumbed to winter frosts. This time the buds had survived and word of the tree's beauty spread, causing a number of distinguished botanists to ask Lady Carlyon's permission to admire its spectacular display.

The color of the flowers was the pale shade of

heliotrope that had been in fashion during Flora's first London season. One particularly warm afternoon, when she was expecting a visit from one of the few people in London to remember that season, she sat under the tree's spreading branches, enjoying the warmth of the sun and the exquisite scent of the flowers overhead.

On her lap was a bundle of letters. Written from remote villages in the Sierra Nevada mountains of southern Spain, they were Caspar's first and last love letters to her.

Although by the end of the Second World War her husband had celebrated his seventieth birthday, he had still been a fit active man and impatient to resume the travels that the years at war had interrupted.

She, too, had looked forward to traveling again, but had been prevented from accompanying him to Spain by the illness of her widowed daughter-in-law, of whom she had been particularly fond. Knowing Caspar's need for adventure, she had urged him to go on his own—their first separation, except for an occasional night apart, since the time she had run away from him.

She had missed him every day of his absence. But had he not gone without her, she would not have possessed the bundle of twenty-one letters to sustain her through the years of her widowhood. He had died in 1957. For more than two decades of loneliness the letters had given her courage to go on without him.

Now, although she knew them by heart, it gave her comfort to reread his clear, well-formed handwriting.

My darling girl,

Last night I slept under the stars and longed for your head on my shoulder, and the softness and scent of your hair close to my cheek.

You would have enjoyed today; and I should have enjoyed it more had you been beside me. I was climbing at an altitude of above five thousand feet and saw patches of brilliant pink that turned out to be *Viola cazorlensis*, a superb violet of great rarity, growing on limestone scree. I had thought it confined to the Sierra de Cazorla farther north, but....

My dearest love,

Today I walked through a meadow of *Narcissus triandrus*, a miniature species popularly known as angels' tears. How they would have delighted you—and how the sight of your pleasure would have delighted me. I miss you almost intolerably—particularly when I think of the expeditions we made together. Do you remember when we followed the route of Stevenson's *Travels with a Donkey*? It's hard to believe it is now more than twenty years since that happy summer in France. How right Stevenson was when he wrote, "For there is a fellowship more quiet even than solitude, and which, rightly understood, is solitude made perfect. And to live out of doors with the woman a man loves is of all lives the most complete and free."

I find, it strange that the author of those words, which I know to be true, should also have written, "Times are changed with him who marries; there are no more bypath meadows where you may innocently linger, but the road lies long and straight and dusty to the grave.''

For myself, I can think of no greater happiness than to be able to return to the beginning of our road together, my lovely one. It isn't given to many men to spend their lives with a woman as good and as clever as she is beautiful. Are you missing me as much as I miss you, *ya-t'ou*?

Remembering their tender reunion when, in spite of the abundance of flowers to be found in that untamed terrain, Caspar had cut short his trip because three weeks were as long as he could bear to be without her, Flora felt a tear slide down her cheek.

She brushed it away, telling herself not to be foolish. The terrible thing about age was that it was only the flesh that decayed. The heart remained young forever and could still ache with love and longing no matter how frail and withered the body became.

In her husband's case there had been little physical deterioration. To her he had never seemed old. All his life he had remained upright and active, his thick steel-gray hair and bronzed skin—he had liked to winter in the sun—causing much younger women to eye him with interested speculation.

Flora, guessing their thoughts, had often smiled to herself. She alone knew the answer to the question in their minds. Sometimes she thought it was Caspar's continued virility that had helped to preserve her own looks, so that when she was seventy people took her for sixty. To the end they had been lovers as well as friends.

The warmth of the afternoon sun must have made her doze for a few moments. When she roused she was no longer alone. A light wheelchair had been positioned not far from her cane chair.

As she blinked at him, her back automatically straightening into the upright posture that distinguished her generation from its successors, the occupant of the other chair raised his Panama hat.

"Good afternoon, Flora."

"Harry! How long have you been here? Why didn't you wake me?"

Major-General Sir Harry Cromer, M.C., stretched out a thin knobby hand to the only woman he had ever wished to marry.

"I saw no reason to disturb you. How are you, m'dear?"

Gently she pressed his cold fingers. "I'm very well. How are you?"

"Oh, I'm always pretty fit, y'know."

He came to tea twice a week, and this was his invariable answer to any inquiry about his well-being. In fact his health was not good, and she wondered what kept him going when all his contemporaries were dead and now, as an economy measure, his beloved club in Pall Mall was no longer open to its members during what, in the idiom of the young, was known as the weekend.

True, he took a close interest in the doings of the two young people dearest to her—her great-grandson and his sister—but it wasn't the same as having descendants of his own.

"Any news from North or Allegra?" he asked with a glance at the letters lying on her lap.

Flora put them away in what had long been her workbag. It contained an unfinished piece of needlepoint, for her fragile hands were still capable of working a simple design in *gros point*. But nowadays after a few stitches she was apt to succumb to reminiscence. She continued to keep the bag by her mainly as a container for the love letters and certain favorite photographs.

"Yes, Allegra telephoned last night. The dear child is having great fun in Scotland and comes back to London next week. Where North is just now I don't know, nor does his mother. But whereas Penelope fusses when he vanishes for a few weeks, I understand his need to disappear from time to time. Had he been born a year later I should have been almost convinced that there is something in reincarnation. He is extraordinarily like Caspar, both in looks and temperament."

"You're too lenient with the young scalawag. He has no business worrying his mother by not letting her know where he is," was the general's gruff reply. "How old is he now? Twenty-three? High time he stopped fooling about and settled down to something useful."

"I'm sure he will. Give him time. Caspar was much older than North before he settled down," she said, smiling. "Ah, here comes our tea," she added, catching sight of Garnett, her butler, crossing the lawn with the tea tray.

Her memory, of late unreliable in recalling recent events yet still capable of conjuring the most vivid recollections of the distant past, called to mind a picture of Warner supervising the service of tea in the shade of the cedars at Longwarden.

Thinking of Warner reminded her of his grandson, the freckle-faced scamp who had at that time been the hall boy. He had never succeeded his grandfather in the dignified office of butler. Poor Alfred had grown up to become one of the sixty thousand casualties on the first day of the Battle of the Somme in 1916.

She remembered unveiling the memorial inscribed with his name and that of eighteen other young men who had left the estate to fight for king and country. Of the volunteers and conscripts from Longwarden in the 1939-45 war, only one had not returned: her own darling son, Rollo.

It was strange to realize that had he survived he would now be in his mid-seventies, probably a retired general like Harry, not the dashing, much decorated colonel who had kissed her goodbye on his last leave.

Rollo's eldest son, Edward, had been a disappointment to them. Dedicated to the pursuit of field sports and lacking any sense of humor, he had married a girl whose thick ankles and lack of charm had not met with Caspar's approval.

Caspar had not lived to be pleasantly surprised by their offspring; and indeed it had been some time before Flora had realized that North and his sister, Allegra, were to be the light of her old age.

After her husband's death she had spent several years in America, where their daughter had lived since her marriage to an American banker. Returning to England, Flora had found her infant great-grandson grown into a dark-haired small boy with a marked resemblance to photographs of Caspar at the same age.

The likeness had increased as North grew older, so that when, in his twentieth year, he had succeeded to the title, he had been almost the living image of the seventh earl. The difference between them was that

North's eyes were blue, not gray, and his aquiline Lomax nose had been broken in the fight that had led to his expulsion from Eton.

Far from detracting from his good looks, the injury gave him a raffish air that seemed to enhance his appeal to the opposite sex. Flora could perfectly understand why so many young women succumbed to him. He had all the qualities that had won her own heart long ago. But as yet he had not met a girl with the power to hold his interest for more than a few weeks or months.

"But there must be one somewhere who will. I do hope I meet her," she murmured, unaware of speaking her thought aloud.

"Meet who?" inquired General Cromer.

Made aware that her mind had been wandering, she gave herself a little shake. Nowadays, instead of merely lighting the spirit burner under the copper kettle and leaving it to her to fill the teapot, Garnett completed the ritual. He was afraid she might have an accident and scald herself. As Harry's question roused her from her reverie, the butler was in the act of filling their teacups.

At one time she would have waited until they were alone before confiding what had been in her mind. But like Warner before him, Garnett had been part of her life for too many years for the Edwardian caveat, *"pas devant les domestiques"* to apply to him.

She said, "The girl with whom North falls in love."

General Cromer, more of a stickler for the manners and customs of his younger days, did wait until Garnett had departed before he answered, "Seems to

me there have been too many young women who
have caught your great-grandson's eye, Flora. Including a number whom you would *not* have wished
to be the mother of your great-great-grandchildren.
Singers...television actresses...even shopgirls, so
I've been told."

"My dear Harry, can you really have forgotten
what a shocking philanderer you yourself were at
North's age? As for shopgirls, they are no longer
beyond the pale, you know. Some delightful girls are
to be found behind shop counters—and not only in
Harrods. Allegra has worked as a waitress in a café.
She and North and their generation are not hedged
round by all the restrictions that governed our lives. I
applaud and envy their freedom."

"Far too much freedom, if you ask me. Discipline!
That's what they need. Most of 'em—including your
two young people—don't know the meaning of the
word."

Unaware of the affectionate twinkle in his companion's dark eyes, the general warmed to a favorite
theme.

It was a diatribe to which Flora had listened many
times. Sipping the Indian tea with milk that she
drank because Harry preferred it to smoky-flavored
lapsang souchong, she plied him with watercress
sandwiches, freshly made scones and seed cake. In
spite of his sedentary existence, there was nothing
wrong with his digestion.

SOME TIME LATER on the other side of the house,
where now to walk across the road to Hyde Park was
made virtually impossible by two wide streams of
heavy traffic, a taxi pulled in to the curb.

It had only one passenger, a long-limbed young
man with a sun-browned, devil-may-care face who,
having stepped onto the pavement, turned to heave
out a large canvas holdall before paying the driver.

Disdaining the ubiquitous jeans in which most of
his contemporaries traveled—he was by nature a set-
ter of trends, not a follower—he had returned from
abroad in clothes bespoke fifty years earlier and for
long put away in a trunk in the attic at Longwarden.

It had been his sister, Lady Allegra Lomax, who,
searching for something to wear at a fancy-dress
party, had unearthed a forgotten hoard of men's
clothes, among them some unworn jodhpurs that she
thought might fit her tall brother.

Impressed by the quality of the cloth—far superior
to any his London tailor could offer—and finding
them a perfect fit, North had looked for other useful
garments and had found a considerable number,
some originally worn by his grandfather and some of
an earlier date.

At the moment he was comfortably clad in a pale
khaki drill Norfolk jacket with buttoned-down
pockets, matching breeches tucked inside stockings
and light boots, laced up the front, of soft tan
leather, ideal for walking in rough country. His
Brooks Brothers oxford-cloth shirt he had bought
while staying in Boston with his American cousins.
He wore the collar unbuttoned, with a colorful scarf
loosely knotted at the base of his long powerful neck.

Having tugged the old-fashioned bellpull, he
turned his back to the door and stood idly surveying
the traffic, disliking the smell of exhaust fumes,
which after five weeks of the pure air in the foothills
of the Himalayas seemed unpleasantly concentrated.

Hearing footsteps crossing the hall, he turned again to the door.

"Hello, Garnett. How are you?" With a smile he offered his hand to the man who had known him all his life.

"Very glad to see you back in London, m'lord."

North tilted a dark eyebrow. "Is anything wrong?"

"No, m'lord. Not at present. But both Mrs. Howard and myself have noticed a change in her Ladyship. She has not been herself for some time now. Her great age is beginning to tell."

"Where is she? In the drawing room?"

"Her Ladyship and General Cromer are having tea in the garden today. The empress tree is in flower, m'lord."

As the butler would have taken the holdall, North said, "No, this is too heavy for you, Garnett. I'll run it up to my room and have a quick wash. Don't tell her Ladyship I'm here. I'll surprise her."

"Very good, m'lord. Would you like tea?"

"No, some cold lager, if you have it."

"Certainly, m'lord."

Even encumbered by the holdall, North took the stairs three at a time. On the half landing he stopped, gazing up at the portrait of his great-grandmother that hung at the head of the second flight.

Her husband had commissioned a number of paintings of her. There was one by László and others by Boldini and Helleu. But the finest—at which he was looking—had been painted by John Singer Sargent, whose brilliant brush had captured the youth and beauty of many Edwardian society women.

The full-length portrait showed the countess standing beside a gilded mirror that reflected her lovely bare shoulders exposed by a décolleté ball gown. She was wearing the Carlyon emeralds and holding an ostrich-feather fan; but it was the radiance of her eyes and the satiny texture of her skin that made people catch their breath when they saw the portrait for the first time.

North had known many gorgeous girls, but never one to compare with his great-grandmother in her heyday. Each time he returned to Park Lane after one of his journeys, he was struck by her transcendent beauty and wished he had known her as a girl. Even now she had not lost her charm, and he never found himself bored when he spent an evening in her company.

IN THE GARDEN Flora's head was nodding and the general was brushing cake crumbs from the rug that covered his knees. At half-past five his manservant would come to wheel him home. Although the twice-weekly outing made a break in his monotonous life, it saddened him to see how the streets of Mayfair had gone down since the gracious days that he and Flora remembered.

Looking up, he was surprised to see North emerging from the house. He tapped her arm.

"A pleasant surprise for you, m'dear."

She woke up with a startled expression.

"Look who's here," he said with a smile.

She had been dreaming of China. Confused, dazzled by the sunlight, she looked in the direction Harry indicated and saw the tall silhouette of her husband striding toward her.

"*Caspar!*" She sprang to her feet, her small face alight, arms outstretched.

As she hastened toward him the ground tilted sharply beneath her. She would have stumbled and fallen but instead was swept off her feet by the familiar strong arms.

For a moment, with her cheek against his shoulder, she saw the unclouded spring sky through a tracery of flowering branches, and she couldn't think where they could be.

Then, from long, long ago, she remembered the hidden plateau that Père d'Espinay had called the Garden of Eden.

She breathed a long sigh of contentment. "You said we should come back here one day."

"Has she fainted?" the old man asked.

After a pause the young man slowly shook his head, "She has... gone, sir," he said in a low voice. "I wanted to surprise her, but I should have let Garnett warn her. She... she always seemed so much younger than she actually was."

General Cromer took off his hat. "You musn't blame yourself, m'boy. She mistook you for Carlyon... her Carlyon. She always missed him, y'know. There was no one like him in her eyes. You had better take her inside. I shall stay here and wait for my man."

Speaking half to himself, he added, "Shan't hang on—not now she's gone. Only kept going to be company for her. Shouldn't have liked her to have no one who remembered the old days... remembered him. Thought about asking her to marry me after he died. Never did pluck up the courage. Just as well, I daresay. She wouldn't have liked turning me down."

"She was always very fond of you, sir. She might have said yes," North said quietly.

"No...I think not...I think not, m'boy. There was only one man for Flora, and he was your great-grandfather. But I knew her and loved her for over seventy years, and I'm glad that after she lost him I was able to be of some service to her."

Beneath the white walrus mustache his purple lips worked for a moment before he said huskily, "She was an exceptional woman. If you can ever find her equal, you'll be more than fortunate...more than fortunate."

A breeze stirred the flowers on the tree, wafting their sweet heady scent. Wondering where his great-grandmother had been in the final moment of her life, North carried his light burden to the house.

For a truly SUPER read, don't miss...

SUPERROMANCE

EVERYTHING YOU'VE ALWAYS WANTED A LOVE STORY TO BE!

Contemporary!
A modern romance for the modern woman – set in the world of today.

Sensual!
A warmly passionate love story that reveals the beautiful feelings between a man and a woman in love.

Dramatic!
An exciting and dramatic plot that will keep you enthralled till the last page is turned.

Exotic!
The thrill of armchair travel – anywhere from the majestic plains of Spain to the towering peaks of the Andes.

Satisfying!
Almost 400 pages of romance reading – a long satisfying journey you'll wish would never end.

SUPERROMANCE

Get this book FREE!

Mail to:
Harlequin Reader Service

In the U.S.	In Canada
1440 South Priest Drive	649 Ontario Street
Tempe, AZ 85281	Stratford, Ontario N5A 6W2

YES! I want to be one of the first to discover the new **Harlequin American Romances**. Send me FREE and without obligation *Twice in a Lifetime*. If you do not hear from me after I have examined my FREE book, please send me the 4 new **Harlequin American Romances** each month as soon as they come off the presses. I understand that I will be billed only $2.25 for each book (total $9.00). There are no shipping or handling charges. There is no minimum number of books that I have to purchase. In fact, I may cancel this arrangement at any time. *Twice in a Lifetime* is mine to keep as a FREE gift, even if I do not buy any additional books.

Name _____ (please print)

Address _____ Apt. no. _____

City _____ State/Prov. _____ Zip/Postal Code _____

Signature (If under 18, parent or guardian must sign.)